THE KILL LIST

THE KILL LIST

NADINE MATHESON

HANOVER
SQUARE
PRESS

HANOVER
SQUARE
PRESS™

ISBN-13: 978-1-335-45505-5

The Kill List

First published in 2024 in Great Britain by HQ, an imprint of HarperCollins*Publishers* Ltd.
This edition published in 2024.

Hanover Square Press
22 Adelaide St. West, 41st Floor
Toronto, Ontario M5H 4E3, Canada
HanoverSqPress.com

Printed in U.S.A.

To my brothers, Gavin & Jason. Because you're cool.

Also by Nadine Matheson

The Binding Room

The Jigsaw Man

I

16 October 1996
Central Criminal Court
Old Bailey, London

"Do you know that you're sitting about seventy meters from Dead Man's Walk?" asked Detective Sergeant Rhimes. He pushed his hands deep into the pockets of his freshly dry-cleaned suit trousers as he walked into the cell and looked down at Andrew Streeter. "Seventy short meters," Rhimes repeated.

Streeter dragged himself along the aged wooden bench, which had been engraved with the initials and incomprehensible doodles left by defendants who had come before him. A bluish hue had spread across the white, tightened skin of Streeter's knuckles. He clasped his hands tightly and kept his head bent forward as though he was in prayer.

"Can you imagine leaving this cell, walking along Dead Man's Walk, begging and pleading to God to grant you leniency? Literally pleading for your life and then the next thing you know, you're in court watching the judge as he reaches for a black cap and places it on top of his wig."

"I didn't do it," Streeter said quietly.

Rhimes slammed his hand hard against the tiled wall above Streeter's head, ignoring his plea. "And that's when you knew"—he paused—"you knew that you were going to have to walk back down those stairs, along the stone path, back down Dead Man's Walk, step into a cold square where the hangman would be waiting with your noose."

"You know it wasn't me."

Rhimes grabbed a fistful of Streeter's hair, pulling his head back. "That's what you deserve. The noose. A rope breaking every bone in your pathetic neck."

"Let go of me," Streeter said, his voice strained as the tendons and muscles in his neck grew taut. His eyes began to water.

"You're not getting what you deserve."

Rhimes let go and took a step back. He could feel his heart beating angrily against his chest. He tried to control his breathing as he inhaled the sickening odor of Streeter's fear-infused sweat and the lingering smell of excrement left from the previous occupant of the cell.

"I didn't do anything," Streeter said. He scurried further along the bench and pushed himself into a corner of the cell.

"Just admit it," Rhimes said. He pulled Streeter up from the bench. "That's all I want. That's all you need to do. Admit it." Rhimes put his hands around Streeter's neck and squeezed. Streeter's eyes bulged, the pressuring increasing on his carotid arteries. The tiny blood vessels in his eyes began to burst as he clawed at Rhimes's hands.

"Admit it," Rhimes repeated, releasing the pressure a little.

The pained singular word was barely audible, but Rhimes heard it.

"No."

Rhimes released his grip and watched Streeter fall to his

knees, violently coughing as he tried to refill his lungs with stale air.

"Even now," Rhimes said, disgusted, "you're still insisting that—"

"No. You know that it wasn't me. That I didn't do it. This is all on you," Streeter said defiantly, leaning back on his heels and looking up at Rhimes. The color slowly returned to his face, a face that was now fixed with a steely determination. "You left the real killer on the street. This is all on you."

2

R.
v. Andrew Streeter
Sentencing remarks of
His Honor Judge Diarmuid Joseph QC
Central Criminal Court
16 October 1996

Sentencing Remarks: The offenses of murder for which I must sentence you, Andrew Streeter, were committed over the course of six months from August 1995 to January 1996.

1. *You took the lives of five innocent people. Melissa Gyimah aged 15, Stephanie Chalmers aged 17, Fallon O'Toole aged 23, Penelope Callaghan aged 17, and Tiago Alves aged 19. Four young women and a young man who had yet to fully make their mark on the world because their lives were cruelly taken from them in the most horrific of ways.*

2. *The facts of this case were disputed by you from the minute you*

were first arrested by police on 18 November 1995 and again on 6 January 1996. You continued to dispute the facts of this case over the duration of the trial, which included the three days that you spent giving evidence in the witness box. The jury quite rightly returned unanimous verdicts of guilty. Verdicts which I understand you still do not accept. You had the opportunity to put the families of these innocent victims out of their misery by admitting what you had done but instead you chose to put them through the horrific ordeal of a four-week trial.

3. I do not wish to subject the families of Melissa, Stephanie, Fallon, Penelope, and Tiago to hearing the full details of the murders of their daughters, son, sisters and brother. I will also remind you that you robbed Penelope Callaghan of the gift of raising her own child, Sofia, who lost her mother at the tender age of 18 months. I seek only to summarize the facts in a very broad outline.

4. Your modus operandi for each of the five victims was the same. You had a method that you did not deviate from. Each victim was taken off the street and into a white Renault Trafic van which had been stolen by you two months before the first victim Melissa Gyimah was reported missing. You created, for want of a better phrase, a "Kill List" with the names of the victims who you had chosen, leaving no doubt in my mind that your decision to take the victims was premeditated. You chose each victim carefully and monitored their movements for several weeks before you kidnapped them. You abducted each victim and took them to your garden flat in Bellingham, southeast London. With the exception of Tiago Alves, you sexually assaulted your victims and then removed them from the property and took them to another location. At the second location, you removed the clothing of your victims, tied their hands and feet and buried them alive. Your victims suffocated and died. You then removed your victims from their graves, cleaned their bodies, dressed them, placed a coin in their mouths, sewed their eyes and mouths shut, and dumped their bodies.

5. *There can be no doubt in my mind that you, Andrew Streeter, were responsible for the unimaginable mental and physical suffering that these five young people were subjected to before they died. You have irretrievably damaged the lives of the family and friends who loved them. The sentence that I will impose will do little to take away the pain of loss, but it will hopefully give them the small satisfaction that justice has been served.*

6. *Will the defendant please stand.*

7. *Andrew Streeter. You kidnapped, and murdered five innocent people, raping four of them. In addition, you destroyed the lives of their family and friends and held the residents of southeast London hostage as you carried out your reign of terror. Your own family have expressed their deep shame and remorse for the pain and destruction that you have caused but you chose to express no remorse or accept any responsibility for your evil actions. Your counsel, Ms. Johnson, sensibly chose not to make any submissions in regard to mitigating circumstances. The only mitigating submission that I would have chosen to have accept would have been a plea of guilty. Despite the evidence against you, you chose to maintain your innocence. Your counsel did submit that you were a man of previously good character and I do not take any issue with counsel for submitting that fact. However, the fact that you had not committed any previous offenses will have no effect on the sentence that I will impose.*

8. *As Ms. Johnson has correctly submitted, the sentence which I must impose upon you is prescribed by law. However, in my opinion each of the victims needs to be recognized and I will not pass a sentence that does not recognize the lives that were cruelly taken by you.*

9. *Count 1. For the murder of Melissa Gyimah, I pass a sentence of life imprisonment. For the murder of Stephanie Chalmers, I pass a sentence of life imprisonment. For the murder of Fallon O'Toole, I pass a sentence of life imprisonment. For the murder of Penelope*

Callaghan, I pass a sentence of life imprisonment. For the murder of Tiago Alves, I pass a sentence of life imprisonment.

10. *It is my duty as a trial judge to submit a report to the Home Secretary, which includes a recommendation as to the appropriate length of the penal element in each of the life sentences; in other words, how long I think you should spend in prison. As a matter of course, this is not usually disclosed in a public forum; however, I am not of the opinion that you deserve the luxury of privacy at any stage of your sentencing. My recommendation is that you will spend the remainder of your days in prison. Life will mean life. Take him down.*

3

Present Day—2 May

"Are you sure I look OK?" Michelle asked, peering into a compact mirror and patting her forehead with the powder puff. "I want to make sure I look OK."

"You look absolutely fine," Salim Ramouter said. He turned his head and saw his five-year-old son, Ethan, marching ahead along the pavement, with a clear idea of his destination.

"Fine. I only look *fine*?"

"I didn't mean... You're beautiful."

"But you didn't say beautiful," said Michelle, brushing away a stray eyelash. "There's a big difference between *fine* and *beautiful*."

"What I meant was..." Ramouter paused and ran his hand across his beard. "I meant that you don't have to worry about impressing Henley."

"I know I don't have to impress Henley. She's not like that," Michelle replied, placing her mirror back into her bag. "I'm worried that I look ill... I don't want anyone looking at me and the first thing that pops into their head is, *Oh, poor Michelle. She's got early-onset dementia. How many times am I going to have to tell her where the toilet is?*"

"Michelle," Ramouter said firmly as they stopped outside Henley's front gate. He took hold of his wife's hand and kissed it. "No one is going to be thinking any of those things."

"I don't want people feeling sorry for me," Michelle said quietly. Ethan ran up Henley's driveway and started banging the letter box.

"There is nothing wrong with empathy. At least you know they care. Also, you know where the toilet is."

"You're right," Michelle said, laughing as the front door opened and Henley's husband, Rob, appeared. "I do know where the toilet is."

"I'm starting to think I should give Ethan his own key," said Henley. She started spooning rice and peas out of the rice cooker and into a white bowl.

Ramouter settled down on the chair in front of the kitchen island and pried the cap off his beer with a bottle opener. "I think you might have to. He loves coming here," he replied. "Aren't you breaking some old Grenadian rule by cooking rice'n'peas in a rice cooker? My mum would kick me out of the house if I even suggested that she bought one."

"Oh absolutely," Henley said with a grin. "I'm breaking so many rules. But you know what? It's either this or arguing with Rob about who has to clean the pressure cooker with the burnt bits of rice on the bottom. I did enough of that when I was living at home with my parents and brother, and between me and you, I keep burning the rice."

"That brings back memories. Trying to get away with leaving the pot to soak in the hope that you would never have to wash it."

"Exactly." Henley pushed the bowl to one side, opened the

oven and pulled out a dish of macaroni and cheese and placed it the stovetop. "So…how are things at home? How long have Michelle and Ethan been with you now? Four weeks?"

Ramouter looked past Henley and through the open French doors where Michelle was sitting at the garden table drinking wine with Rob and Glen, the husband of DC Paul Stanford, who was an original member of the Serial Crime Unit and one of Henley's closest friends. Stanford was at the other end of the garden, playing football and debating the legitimacy of a goal with Ethan and Emma, Henley's three-year-old daughter.

"Three weeks," Ramouter replied softly. "But it feels like longer."

Henley took off her oven gloves and watched Ramouter for a second, making sure she could see on his face what she'd heard in his voice. Doubt.

"It's going to take a bit of time," she said, picking up her glass of wine. She sat down next to Ramouter. "You have to adjust. All of you have to adjust."

"Ethan doesn't," Ramouter replied.

"He's a kid. Kids are resilient. Well, that's what we tell our-selves: that they can handle it. To be honest with you, Ethan seems fine. And Michelle—"

"Michelle." Ramouter released a deep, heavy sigh, turning the beer bottle around in his hands. "I've had three weeks off. It was the three of us together for two weeks and then Ethan went to school, and it was me and her in that flat. I feel like such a shit for even thinking this."

"Go on, get it out. It's better that you say it instead of sitting here brooding about it."

"Aye, I know. I know."

"So, what is it? You better hurry up and tell me before I call everybody to the table. You know what Stanford is like if he doesn't get fed." Henley nudged Ramouter gently with her shoulder.

"The flat used to feel too big and now it feels too small."
Ramouter sighed. "I shouldn't be pleased about coming back
to work tomorrow, but I am. I can't wait. I wouldn't even be
bothered if I spent the next month with the Community Support Unit chasing shoplifters or drunk and disorderlies."

Henley took a swallow of wine and turned her head toward
the excitable screams coming from the garden.

"That's terrible, isn't it?" sighed Ramouter.

"Not really," said Henley. "It makes sense to me. You've had
your own space for nearly a year. Living your life, the way you
want to, and now you have to get used to sharing it again. You're
not only responsible for yourself. Shit, that sounds a bit—"

"No. I know what you meant. But it's not the sharing and
being responsible for other people that's the problem. Michelle
has been good these last few weeks—with her memory, I mean.
You wouldn't think there was anything wrong, but I'm worried about what's going to happen when Ethan's at school and
I'm at work."

Henley was about to reply when she caught sight of Stanford
making his way toward the kitchen with the children by his side.

"Looks like the mob need feeding," said Ramouter briskly,
pushing his chair back and standing up.

"Ramouter," Henley said softly, making sure that Rob and
Michelle were still out of earshot. "You wouldn't have moved
your family down to London if you weren't sure that you could
cope and manage her condition. You're going to have to take it
day by day. And this might sound strange, but you need to trust
Michelle. And yourself."

"You make it sound easy."

Henley shook her head. "It won't be easy. Our jobs, trying
to make family work with what we do… None of it is easy. But
for the right person, it's worth the effort."

"Oi. Was the plan to invite me to Sunday dinner and then
starve me?" Stanford asked as he strode into the kitchen.

"Stop moaning," said Henley. She picked up a tea towel and playfully hit him on the shoulder. "How are the kids so much better behaved than you?"

"Mummy, I'm hungry," said Emma, right on cue. She wrapped her arms around Stanford's leg.

"See. You're starving the children now." Stanford gave Henley a pointed look while ruffling Emma's hair.

"Give me a couple of minutes," Henley replied as she swallowed the rest of her wine and eased herself out of her chair. "Ethan, why don't you take Emma and tell your mum and Uncle Rob that dinner is ready?"

"I'll help you bring the food out," said Ramouter. He picked up the macaroni cheese and walked out of the kitchen, following behind the children as they raced back into the garden.

"Everything all right?" Stanford asked as Henley handed him bowls of steaming vegetables.

"Yeah. It's…he's adjusting," she said, breaking off as her phone buzzed, announcing the arrival of an email.

"Maybe he should take another week off work. It's not as if we're swamped with cases at the moment," Stanford said.

"True. But the SCU might be the best place for him right now." Henley picked up her phone and opened her emails. The SCU, officially known as the Serial Crime Unit of the Metropolitan Police, was experiencing a lull in cases that were defined as a serial crime. The lull had given the team the rare luxury of enjoying a bank holiday weekend without interruption.

Henley read the heading in the subject box and felt her throat constrict immediately. Her breath caught and her forehead prickled with sweat. She read the email and then made the mistake of opening the attachment.

"Hey, you OK?" Stanford placed the bowls down on the counter and looked at Henley with concern. "You look…you don't look right."

Henley took a breath, and placed her phone, screen down,

onto the counter. "I'm not sure," she said eventually. She looked at the phone apprehensively.

"You're not sure? What's happened? Has someone died?" Stanford asked, watching as Henley busied herself with plating up the resting chicken onto a platter.

"No one's died. It's... I don't know what it is yet," Henley said, forcing a smile.

Stanford studied her for a beat, and then said, "Probably something, most likely nothing?"

"Exactly that," Henley replied with the knowledge that it most definitely was not nothing.

4

Elias.Piper@RedemptionFoundation.Org
To: AnjelicaIHenley@mail.uk
Subject: R v Andrew Streeter—Wrongful Conviction
Investigation

Dear Anjelica,

My name is Elias Piper and I'm a senior lawyer who leads the UK litigation team at the Redemption Foundation. The Redemption Foundation is a nonprofit legal organization committed to investigating wrongful convictions and miscarriages of justice. I have been instructed by Andrew Streeter to review his murder convictions. I have attempted to contact you multiple times and have had no response to my emails. It's possible that my email may have been directed to your junk folder.

You may recall that Mr. Streeter was convicted of five counts of murder at the Central Criminal Court in 1996 and that his subsequent applications to the Court of Appeal to dismiss his sentence were refused. We are in the process of finalizing Mr. Streeter's application for his case to be reviewed by the Criminal Cases Review Commission on the grounds that there were serious irregularities in the original murder investigation which include a serious violation of the Police and Criminal Evidence Act 1984 and Codes of Practice by the investigating officers. The original case papers confirmed that you were a prosecution witness and gave live evidence during the course of the trial. I would like the opportunity to discuss your involvement in the original investigation, ideally in person. I understand that you are extremely busy, but your attendance, either at our office or a location of your choosing, would be greatly appreciated. I've attached a copy of your original witness statements dated 18 November 1994 and 18 August 1995. I look forward to your response.

Kind regards
Elias Piper

Solicitor-Advocate
UK Litigation Team
Attachment: PDF

RESTRICTED (when complete)
WITNESS STATEMENT
CJ ACT 1967, s.9 MC ACT 1980, ss.5A(3)(a) and 5B

Statement of: *Anjelica Ione Henley.*
URN: *01 BG 1864 14*
Age if Under 18: *15 (if over 18, insert over 18)*
Occupation: *Student*

This statement (consisting of 2 pages each signed by me) is true to the best of my knowledge and belief and I make it knowing that, if it is tendered in evidence, I shall be liable to prosecution if I have willfully stated anything in it which I know to be false, or do not believe to be true.

Signature: Anjelica Henley
Date: 18-11-1994

I am the above-named person and I live at an address known to police. This statement refers to the disappearance of Melissa Gyimah on Thursday, 17 November 1994.

I have known Melissa since I was six years old when she moved to Gilbert House in Deptford and joined Friedmann Fields Primary School in Deptford. Melissa and I are in the same class and we both went to St. Carmen's Secondary School in Greenwich. Melissa and I were best friends but were in different form classes at school. Melissa and I would always go to school together. I would meet Melissa in Charlotte Turner Gardens, a small park which we called "The Green" between Gilbert House and my house, and we would walk to school together. We would always walk home together except on Tuesdays when I had netball practice after school, and on Wednesday when Melissa had drama class. On Thursday morning at 8:45 a.m. I waited for Melissa on the park bench next to the swings in The Green. I was listening to my Discman. Five minutes after I arrived, I saw Melissa on the other side of the green. There was a man with her. The man was white and taller than her. Melissa is tall. I think that she is 5'8" tall. I got up and started walking toward them. It was freezing and I recognized Melissa because she was wearing her pink woolly hat. I don't think that Melissa saw me as she turned her back and was standing in front of the man. I then shouted out Melissa's name. Melissa turned around and the man walked off in the direction of the primary school on the left. Melissa ran up to me and I asked her who the man was. She said that he was just a friend. I turned around and could see the man getting into a blue car. I cannot tell you what the man looked like because I was too far away. Melissa didn't tell me his name.

I finished school at 3:45 p.m. My last class was History. Melissa's last class was Geography. I would usually meet her outside the school gates but, when I arrived, she wasn't there. I thought that maybe she was at the sweet shop around the corner from our school. On my way to the shop, I saw Melissa on the other side of the road. There was a man with her. I don't know if it was the same man who I saw on the green earlier that day. I then saw Melissa and the man walk past the bus stop. I crossed the road and tried to catch up with her. I called Melissa's name, but I don't think she heard me because of the traffic. I thought I saw the blue car that I saw earlier that morning on Greenwich High Road, I don't know the make and model of the car, but it was a small car, similar to a Ford Fiesta.

I would describe the white male that I saw in the morning as slim build, maybe about 5'10" tall, possibly in his early twenties. Brown hair, wearing a black hat, a black T-shirt, a light blue jacket, and blue jeans and white sneakers.

I don't know if the man that I saw with Melissa in the morning and the afternoon was the same or a different person.

Signature: *Anjelica Henley*
Signature Witnessed: L.F. Kelly PC 973L

RESTRICTED (when complete)
WITNESS STATEMENT
CJ ACT 1967, s.9 MC ACT 1980, ss.5A(3)(a) and 5B

Statement of: *Anjelica Ione Henley.*
URN: *01 BG 1864 14*
Age if Under 18: *15 (if over 18, insert over 18)*
Occupation: *Student*

This statement (consisting of 2 pages each signed by me) is true to the best of my knowledge and belief and I make it knowing that, if it is tendered in evidence, I shall be liable to prosecution if I have willfully stated anything in it which I know to be false, or do not believe to be true.

Signature: *Anjelica Henley*
Date: *18 August 1995*

This statement refers to my discovery of a body.

On 17 August 1995 I was making my way home after I'd been to Catford cinema to watch Batman Forever with my cousin Tatum and my older brother Simon. We left the cinema at 6:15 p.m.

and took the 47 bus home. We got off the bus at Deptford Church Street and decided to go and hang out by the River Thames on Borthwick Street, which is not far from our house. Everyone can easily access the River Thames from Borthwick Street. It's a place where a lot of kids in the area hang out and people sometimes fish and walk along the riverbank when it's low tide. Simon and Tatum decided that they wanted to get some drinks, chips, and sweets from the corner shop. I told my brother and cousin to go without me and that I would meet them at the river. I crossed the road at Creek Road and walked along Deptford Green as this was the quickest route to the river. As I was walking, I saw Melissa's mum and dad walking into St. Nicholas Church. I didn't speak to them as they had their backs to me and had already entered the gates of the church. I have known Melissa's parents since I was six years old. I knew that they had told my parents about arranging another community meeting at the church.

I think I arrived at the entrance to the river at about 7:00 p.m. There was a group of boys playing football on the grass next to Friedman House. I also walked past a group of five men who were walking in the direction of the church. They were all wearing the uniform of A&J Hauliers, which was navy trousers and navy T-shirts with the A&J logo in white on the front. I've seen these men before and said hello to one of the men called Louis who is my next-door neighbor. There was also a man sitting on the low wall that borders the grass where the boys were playing football. I can't remember what he was doing. I crossed the road and walked toward the river. You actually have to walk up what I would describe as a ramp but is actually part of the riverbank and is filled with pebbles, and then there is a flat piece of the riverbank when you're at the top. On the left is the electricity substation and on the right is a scrapyard. When it's high tide, the water will reach the top of the flat piece of ground but when it's low tide you can walk down to another level and to the water's edge. On the left is a small brick platform which is where we usually hang out. When

I arrived, there was no one there and the river was at low tide. I walked down the riverbank and could see that an old shopping trolley and a tire had washed up. There was no one else there. As I walked further down, I noticed something lying against the river wall. It was covered in a dark green material. As I got closer, I could see that the object was long, and I could see what looked like an arm on top. I pulled back the material and I saw her face. I think I screamed because I then heard my brother and cousin call out my name. I turned around but couldn't see them, which meant that they were still on the roadside. I shouted out, "I'm here." I walked back up and saw my brother and cousin. I told them that Melissa was down by the river. They followed me down and my brother went to check. We could hear the water lapping the shore more quickly which meant that the tide was coming in. My brother told me to run home and to tell our mum to call the police. It was quicker to run home as the nearest phone box was on Creek Road and our house was around the corner. When I got to the roadside the man who had been sitting on the wall was still there, but he was standing on the pavement, and he was watching me. I would describe this man as white, skinny, wearing a baseball cap, black T-shirt and a black parka, jeans, and white sneakers. I don't know his exact height, but he was quite tall. I couldn't see his face clearly. I ran home and told my mum, and she was the one who called the police. My mum came back to the river with me. My brother and cousin were still at the river with Melissa's body. We stayed until the police arrived about twenty minutes later.

Signature: *Anjelica Henley*
Signature Witnessed: G.O. Portland DC 5375

5

Present Day

"I hope the coffee is OK," said Elias Piper, placing the jet-black mug with the Redemption Foundation's silver logo in front of Henley. "I'm not the best with beverages, especially with this new fancy machine we've got. Normally one of the assistants would do it, but as you can see, it's just us in the office."

"Thank you," Henley picked up her cup and took a sip. "It's fine."

"Good, I don't have to worry about poisoning you," Elias said with a smile, sipping his own coffee.

"So, is it your intention to speak to Anjelica Henley, who discovered your client's murder victim twenty-six years ago, or to Detective Inspector Henley who used to work for the late DCSI Rhimes, who was one of the investigating officers on the original murder investigation?" Henley asked, looking directly into Elias's eyes. He was the image of a man who had been preparing himself for something bigger in life, with his dark blond hair, slightly graying at the temples, gray eyes behind the black-rimmed designer glasses and an assured smile. Henley was sitting at the opposite end of a glass table in a meeting room on the first floor of a glass-fronted, four-story building on Upper Street in north London. The early-morning sun streamed through the windows, casting a glare across the glass conference table.

"I can see you like to get straight to the point," Elias replied. He pushed aside his coffee and opened the large lever-arch file in front of him. "I'm a bit of a traditionalist. I've tried to work on a digital version of a case, but it just doesn't feel right. I don't feel as though I can get a proper understanding of a case unless I can run my hands across the pages. Does that make sense?"

Henley had no intention of admitting that she agreed with him, especially as Elias was responsible for making her relive the events of the summer of 1995, ever since she had read the email from him four days ago. She was working hard to make sure her resentment wasn't written all over her face.

"So, which is it?" Henley asked, watching Elias turn the pages in his folder. It was a small trick, one she recognized from watching lawyers cross-examine a witness in a courtroom. A small device to take back control by not giving the witness any attention, to make them uncomfortable. Henley waited for the games to stop.

"I would have emailed you at work if I'd wanted to talk to you in your professional capacity," Elias eventually replied, looking up at Henley with a smile. "But that's not why I invited you here. Ah, here it is. Your original witness statements."

He released the lever in the file, removed several pages and placed them in front of him. "You were fifteen years old when Melissa Gyimah went missing. It must have been quite traumatic for you when you found her body?"

"Have you ever found a dead body?" Henley asked.

"No."

"The body of a dead friend?"

"I'm sorry."

"There were a lot of things that I should have been doing at the age of fifteen, but finding my friend's body, murdered by your client, should not have been one of them," said Henley determinedly. She pushed her cup to the side and folded her arms, a clear sign to anyone who knew her that she was pissed off. "Can you imagine being buried alive? Did you discuss that with your client? How he kidnapped and kept Melissa captive for nine months. How he raped and tortured her, and like the others, buried her alive?"

Elias didn't flinch. "I understand how much pain you must feel," he said with what sounded like genuine sincerity.

"I'm not in pain," Henley replied.

"How could you not be in pain?" Elias asked, curious. "What else could you feel, other than pain?" He waited as the air around them grew frigid. "I suppose there is anger," he concluded eventually.

Henley silently simmered with the emotion Elias had correctly identified. "Melissa's family and the families of the other victims are in pain, and they will always be in pain," she said.

"Of course. I would never attempt to diminish the pain of the families. But Andrew Streeter didn't murder those four girls and young man."

Henley took a deep breath. It felt different to hear those words spoken out loud. She hadn't been in court when Andrew Streeter had given evidence. Her parents had insisted that she go to school, but they'd agreed to act as her proxy and to support Melissa's parents. They'd relayed back to her how Streeter had denied his crimes and had cried out more than once that he'd been framed.

"A jury unanimously decided otherwise," said Henley.

"They did and we're not criticizing the decision they made but—"

"And the Court of Appeal dismissed his application to appeal against his sentence twice. Once in 1997 and again in 2001."

"And we don't take issue with the decision that was made by the court more than twenty years ago, but things have changed. We are asking the Criminal Cases Review Commission to examine the evidence that was presented to them. Evidence which I have submitted was unreliable and—"

"Is that why you've got me here? To tell me why my evidence was unreliable?"

"And a police investigation that was rife with corruption."

"Corruption?"

Elias held up his hands in surrender and shook his head with a well-practiced look that said, *Don't shoot the messenger. I'm only doing my job.*

"You didn't identify Andrew Streeter at the crime scene, did you?" Elias asked, picking up a silver fountain pen and holding it above a yellow legal pad.

"Not at the crime scene," Henley replied as the word *corruption* whirled around her brain. "I gave a description of the person I saw at the river and the man who was with Melissa when I saw her for the last time."

"And even though you were unable to give a full description at the time, you were able to identify Andrew Streeter at an identification parade, six weeks later?"

"It feels like you're cross-examining me."

"I assure you, that's not what I'm doing."

"You can check the court transcript when I was questioned about this in 1996."

"Detective Sergeant Harry Rhimes, as was his position at that time, was with you when you made the identification."

"You already know that."

"Did he prompt you?"

Henley remained silent.

"It's part of our case that DS Rhimes and others planted evidence that incriminated Andrew Streeter in all five murders, and DS Rhimes specifically falsified the results of the identification procedure. You have to remember this was way before Video Identification Parade Electronic Recording, known as VIPER."

"I know what VIPER is," Henley snapped.

"Of course. I didn't mean to offend you."

"I'm offended by this entire line of questioning."

"I would be too if I was in your position," Elias conceded. "But these are the grounds of our application and I need to ask you if—"

"No, he didn't."

"I haven't finished my question."

"You don't have to. You were going to ask me if Rhimes pointed out or insinuated somehow that Streeter was the man I saw. That didn't happen. He did nothing untoward."

"But it was just you and him in that ID parade? No one else, let's say, *supervising*?"

Henley tried to think back to that day, but the truth was that she could barely remember the ID parade. She did know that for some reason the ID parade had taken place in Rotherhithe police station and not Deptford police station, which was a ten-minute walk from her house, or Ladywell police station which was where Rhimes and the murder squad were based. It had been a hot day and she could recall that the room they had been in had had no windows. She remembered Rhimes telling her to take her time. To not be scared.

"You called him Rhimes. A bit overfamiliar," Elias said, breaking Henley's efforts to recollect.

"Don't act as if you don't know that he used to be my boss."

"Coincidence?"

"Life has a funny way of working out."

"Did he ever talk to you about the case? I mean, that's quite a connection the pair of you had. It would be surprising if you hadn't talked about it over the years you worked together."

"It was never discussed," Henley lied.

"Not once?"

Henley didn't reply. Instead, she reached down and picked her bag up from the floor.

"There was something else," Elias said hurriedly as Henley rose to her feet. "In addition to allegations of corruption by a senior investigating officer, I also have the evidence to prove it—and it won't be long before that evidence is released publicly."

"Only if the CCRC think you have a case."

Henley could hear the stern authority in her voice, but her chest was fluttering with the familiar sense of fear-infused panic.

"I don't bring cases that I can't win," Elias said matter-of-factly as the gray in his eyes took on the appearance of granite.

Henley stared at Elias for a moment, before making her way toward the door.

"Andrew Streeter wants to see you."

Elias's words stopped Henley in her tracks. She turned to look at him. "He wants to what?"

Elias closed the space between them, a white envelope in his hand. He was so close that Henley could smell the spicy sea salt scent of his aftershave.

"He's instructed that he would like to see you. He's been diagnosed with cancer."

"Is he dying?" Henley asked bluntly.

Elias smiled. "Streeter is resilient. There was a time when I thought he wouldn't live long enough to hear the result of his application, but he keeps making a comeback. Like he's got something to live for."

"What does he want to talk to me about?" Henley asked. She looked at the envelope in Elias's hand. Her name was on the front, written in capital letters.

"He wouldn't say."

Henley raised an eyebrow.

"I've no reason to withhold anything from you. Obviously, it's entirely up to you, but you don't strike me as the sort of woman who has any issues revisiting the past," Elias said, making no attempt to hide the fact that he was impressed. "A lot of people I've approached about this case have either ignored my requests or have told me to get lost. But less politely than that."

"Don't make any assumptions about me just because I'm here."

"I wouldn't dream of it."

"So, does he want to see me as a detective or civilian?" Henley reluctantly took the envelope from Elias and put it in her bag.

"Both," Elias replied with a confident smile.

6

Present Day—Friday,
28 May

"You've got another one," Joanna, the office manager, said, dumping a pile of post onto Henley's desk. "I never thought you would be the type to receive prison fan mail."

"I don't have prison fan mail." Henley reached for the envelopes in front of her.

"Oh really?" Joanna grinned as she walked back to her desk. "That's the third letter this month. As I said: prison fan mail."

Henley had received two further letters with a prison postmark since Elias Piper had handed her Streeter's letter, which was still burning a hole in her bag. Henley examined the new envelope closely. It was made from cheap, thin paper—standard prison-issue stationery. The handwriting closely matched the handwriting on the envelope Elias Piper had handed her. Medway Mail Centre was printed in faint ink next to the first-class stamp. Henley knew there were four prisons in the Medway area—HMP Swaleside, Elmley, Cornwell Hill and Ruxley—but there was nothing on the envelope that indicated which prison was holding Andrew Streeter.

"Jo, can you do me a favor please?" Henley asked, standing up and stretching.

"Are you off to make tea?" Jo asked, her tone making it clear that today was not the day she would be obliging anyone with favors.

"How about I go across the road to the posh bakery and get you a Chelsea bun?"

"And a cheese scone too."

"Fine. Whatever you want."

"Good. What's the favor?"

"Can you please contact the Prisoner Location Service and find out where Andrew Streeter is? And please don't give me that look."

"Would you prefer that I give you a look, or have me ask questions about your prison fan mail? Is Andrew Streeter the one writing to you?"

Henley's reply was drowned out by the sound of drilling.

"For God's sake! How much longer are they going to be?" Ramouter exclaimed, exasperated.

A man wearing a navy polo shirt bearing an alarm company's logo walked into the room. He stopped and stared at a white-board covered with crime scene photos.

"Keep moving," Henley said loudly, seeing the man's face pale as he took in the unfolding timeline of arsons, which included magnified photographs of a man who had been carbonized in the fiery mayhem. The question for the Serial Crime Unit was whether the recent spate of arson attacks was the work of one person. Henley watched the workman hurry across the office floor and disappear into the hallway.

"You wouldn't think that it would take more than three weeks to install a new alarm system," said Henley.

"Maybe they like it here," said Ramouter. "I don't know why anyone authorized upgrading anything around here, though. Stanford said someone has made an offer on the building."

"I won't believe anything until I see a sold sign on the wall, the locks have been changed, and they're escorting us out the door," Henley replied. She scanned the office. Stanford and DS Roxanne Eastwood were both out, and their boss and head of the SCU, DSI Stephen Pellacia, was currently on day four of a ten-day holiday with his girlfriend, Laura Halifax. Henley ignored the feelings of jealousy and disappointment bubbling in her chest and reached for her purse. "Do you want anything from the bakery, Ramouter?"

"A sausage roll or maybe a...do you know what, I'll come with you, but before we go..."

"What is it?" Henley asked, turning away from Pellacia's office and giving Ramouter her full attention. She felt a pang of sadness as she scanned his face and saw the look of a man who seemed almost ecstatic about leaving his complicated home life behind for eight hours, even if it meant contaminating himself with death on a daily basis.

"It could be one to add to the list," Ramouter said as he scooted his chair to make way for Henley. "It's a commercial premises in Sydenham, but it doesn't have the same traits as two of the fires."

"So what do you want to do?" Henley asked. Part of her job involved mentoring Ramouter and turning him into an even better detective, so she pushed thoughts of her "prison fan mail" to one side.

Ramouter leaned back in his chair and tapped his pen against his lips. "I want to wait for the fire investigator's report—but you should have asked me what sort of premises were set on fire."

Henley smiled. "Well? What sort was it?"

"The constituency office for the Member of Parliament for Lewisham West and Penge, Oliver Elson. The good thing is that he wasn't in the office at the time, but it changes things if Elson was the target."

"It does," Henley agreed. "OK, let's see what the fire investigator's report says first and wait for Lewisham CID to take statements from Elson and his staff, then we can make a final assessment."

"Fine with me," Ramouter said, jumping when Joanna suddenly appeared at his desk. "Bloody hell, Jo. Has anyone told you that you move like a ninja?"

"What can I say? I'm gifted," Jo replied. "So, about Streeter."

"Don't tell me you found him already?" Henley asked with bemusement as the phone on her desk began to ring. She walked back to her desk and saw a phone number with the area code 01634 flashing on the caller display screen. She hit *send to voicemail*. "Probably another call center trying to tell me that I had an accident," said Henley. "So, Streeter?"

"God only knows how he managed it, but he's in HMP Ruxley," Jo said.

"Are you sure?" Henley exclaimed. "Ruxley is an open prison."

"Of course I'm sure," Jo replied as Henley's phone rang for a second time. "You have to wonder how someone like him got himself into an open prison."

"It must be a mistake," Henley said, sending the call through to her voicemail for a second time. "It makes no sense for Streeter to be in an open prison."

"It makes no sense for him to be writing you letters either," Jo replied.

"Who's Andrew Streeter?" asked Ramouter.

Jo and Henley exchanged a look.

"And why he is writing you letters?"

"Go on then," Jo prompted, nudging Henley's shoulder. "There's not much that's secret in this place."

Conceding defeat, Henley perched on the edge of her desk.

"Andrew Streeter was the man who was convicted of the murder of my friend when I was fifteen years old."

"Oh," Ramouter said softly. "You found her by the river."

"Yes."

"Shit. And her murderer, this Streeter, is writing to you?"

"Yes."

"What on earth for? What does he want from you after all these years?"

Henley blew out a breath as she shook her head, knowing that the answer was in the unopened letters.

"Three letters in the past month," Jo said. "Sounds like a man who wants to get something off his chest. Pellacia won't like this one bit."

"Don't you dare, Jo," Henley said firmly.

"Excuse me. You've got a—"

"I mean it, Jo. I don't need you mouthing off about my private business."

"Private? You've asked me to use our resources to—"

"Jo. I said to leave it," Henley said, her tone low but hard.

Ramouter looked away, uncomfortable at the glacial silence while Henley waited for Jo's response.

"Fine," Jo snapped. "But don't be surprised if this all comes back to bite you on the ass."

"Oh, for God's sake," Henley exclaimed when her mobile phone began to ring as she and Ramouter walked across a pedestrian crossing. She glanced at the screen. "It's the same bloody number."

"Someone is determined to get hold of you," Ramouter said, taking a bite out of his sausage roll. "Must be important."

Henley hit the green accept button. "Hello? Who is this?" she asked over the sound of passing traffic and the enthusiastic shouts escaping from the nearby betting shop.

There was no answer, but Henley could make out the sound

of soft beeps, similar to the warning sounds of a vehicle revers-
ing. Then she heard someone coughing and the sound of a door
closing.

"Can you hear me?" asked a voice.

"Barely," Henley replied. She handed Ramouter the box of
Chelsea buns and scones and indicated that she would catch up
with him.

"Is that Anjelica? Anjelica Henley?" There was an echo, as
though the person on the other end of the line was standing in
a fully tiled bathroom.

Henley felt a knot in her stomach as the caller repeated her
name. She remembered the first time she had heard his voice.
It was the second time that she'd felt pure fear.

"Who is this?" she asked, desperately hoping he would give
a name that was unknown to her.

"This is you, isn't it, Anjelica?"

"It's Detective Inspector Henley."

"Well, Detective Inspective Henley, you haven't replied to
my letters."

Henley paused and then made her way to a small piece of
grassland opposite Greenwich police station. She sat down on a
bench and looked across at the station, home to the SCU.

"I wrote you letters."

"You're breaking prison law by calling me on a mobile phone,"
Henley said in an effort to regain control of the situation.

"You know I'm dying, right? My lawyer, Elias Piper, told
you that."

"Firstly, no one said that you were dying, just that you were
sick, and secondly, you're calling the wrong person if you're
looking for sympathy."

Streeter sniffed and, if Henley didn't know better, she would
have sworn he was crying.

"I want to see you," Streeter said. "You haven't replied to my
letters, and I've sent you a visiting order."

"I don't need a visiting order. What is it that you want to say that you can't tell me over the phone?" Henley asked.

"Everything."

"What does that mean?"

"No. You need to see me. I'm begging you. Please."

Henley inhaled deeply, pulled the phone away from her ear and looked at the screen. She had already spent five minutes longer on the phone with Melissa's murderer than she wanted to. She returned the phone to her ear and heard Streeter's pleading voice again.

"Please," he was saying. "I won't stop calling or writing. I need to talk to you. Face-to-face."

The teenage Anjelica, who had grown into a woman with a family of her own, who was still on some subconscious level grieving the brutal loss of her best friend, had no desire to breathe the same air as Andrew Streeter. Anjelica wanted Streeter to admit to his crimes and to die a slow and painful death. Anjelica's dreams were haunted by Melissa's face, her mouth and eyes sewn shut. Teenage Anjelica had stood under a steaming hot shower, scrubbing herself with carbolic soap as she tried to get rid of the smell of the river and decomposing flesh that had seeped into her pores and coated every strand of hair on her head. But Detective Inspector Anjelica Henley of the Serial Crime Unit had a different story. DI Henley was emotionally detached. DI Henley was curious. DI Henley wanted to know what would motivate a convicted murderer to seek out the witness and friend of one of his victims. DI Henley wanted to look in the eyes of a murderer and see the demons that tortured his soul.

"Fine," Henley said.

There was a pause, the silence filled by the sound of Streeter struggling to breathe.

"Thank you."

Henley picked up the pain in Streeter's voice. "Don't call me again," she said.

7

23 September 1995

It was early: 5:48 a.m. The only people awake were the office cleaners making their way home from their overnight shifts in the city, early joggers, empowered by watching Michael Johnson winning gold in the 200 and 400 meters at the World Athletic Championships, and Terry, the owner of a scrapyard on Thurston Road in Lewisham. Terry had agreed to be at the yard early to receive a couple of cars that had been used in a robbery in Manchester, despite his raging hangover after drinking his weight in whisky at his uncle's wake the night before. The toilet in his office was blocked again and he'd gone to the back of the Portakabin to relieve himself.

It had taken 3.8 seconds for his brain to register the smell. His fingers were still gripping the buttons of his jeans when 2.8 seconds later he saw the cause of the smell and warm urine began to travel down the inside of his left leg. He'd run blindly out of the yard and into Thurston Road, ignoring the loud screeches of

a 47 bus and a cussing driver who'd hit the brakes to avoid hitting him. Terry had completely forgotten about the two stolen
cars in his yard when he ran toward the row of red telephone
boxes. He made the 999 call and a police car had arrived seventeen minutes later. PC Clarens immediately picked up the
smell of piss on Terry and had his hand on his radio ready to
call it in as the rantings of a drunk who'd pissed his pants until
his colleague, WPC Sabato, ran past him, abruptly stopped, and
vomited the fried egg and bacon sandwich that she'd had for
breakfast, inches from his feet.

The tall gates of the scrapyard were closed and guarded by a
couple of police officers, who watched the passing traffic, not
sure if the passengers on the top deck of the passing bus could see
the body in the scrapyard; later, articles in the *South London Press*
would reveal that they could. DS Rhimes had arrived twenty-
eight minutes after WPC Sabato had been sick and he was in a
mood. He was usually a stickler for not breaking his morning
routine. Glass of warm water. A cup of instant coffee, a bowl of
Frosties and a slice of toast with Marmite. He was grateful that
the early-morning call had meant that he was unable to even
think about food. He pulled out the monogrammed handkerchief that his niece had bought him for Christmas, and pushed
it hard against his mouth and nose, but it didn't help. The smell
of decomposing flesh that had festered in the dry heat of an un-
expected heatwave was enveloping him. The soured scent penetrated the cotton fibers of his shirt and coated the skin on his
back. Beads of sweat traveled from his forehead and tickled the
upper eyelashes of his left eye. He blinked and instantly regretted removing the handkerchief from his mouth to rub it across
his forehead. He stepped back and looked at the crowd of crime
scene officers, reluctant to start their jobs, standing far away from
the perimeter of the crime scene.

"Have you ever—" DS Ian Turner didn't finish his sentence

as he began to dry heave, his eyes turning red and beginning to water.

"No, I haven't," Rhimes replied. He placed the handkerchief back against his mouth and nose and walked toward the body. It was obviously a woman, but he wasn't sure about the age. The body had been wrapped in a clear plastic sheet but that didn't stop the gases from the decomposing flesh and organs from rising like steam into the air. Rhimes crouched, careful that his knees didn't touch the ground.

"Can you see it?" Rhimes asked Turner. "Her face."

"Hard to miss," Turner replied, coughing. "Do you think that it's her? Chalmers. It looks like her, I think."

"Has to be," said Rhimes, leaning in and taking in the details of the woman's face. He gently pushed the tip of his right index finger against her auburn hair. The hair was rigid as though it had been styled with gel. Rhimes ran his gloved finger along the track lines that had been left behind by a comb. There were dark red patches on her face where the skin had blistered and burst. Rhimes coughed deeply, the force rattling his rib bones as the hot repugnant air of death caught in the back of his throat. He quickly stood up, turned and walked toward the gaggle of officers who still hadn't moved from their spot. Whether they liked it or not, it was time to get to work. Rhimes shook his head but there was nothing he could do to get rid of the image in his head. An image that would keep him up at night and pierce his dreams for the next five years. The image of the woman's eyes and mouth sewn shut with thick black thread.

Two Weeks Later…

He squeezed. Placed his hands around her neck and squeezed. She was too weak to fight back. Too weak to raise her hands and claw at his face, but he squeezed anyway. He didn't want to kill her. Not yet, but he needed her to know that she had no power. That he was the one in control. He could feel the jugular vein in her neck thicken as her pulse became erratic, her blood frantically struggling to find a clear route to her brain. There was no gasping for air but more of a strangulated, violent choking as the muscles around her voice box pulsated against his fingers. He didn't want her dead, but he could see that she was close, edging toward the dark void. There was power in that moment as he watched her. He squeezed tighter and waited for something to stir inside of him. He should have felt something: fear, ecstasy, or empathy. But there was nothing.

Her bloodshot eyes had squinted at first, trying to adjust to the poor light, but then they had widened as she tried to force her lips to push aside the dirty rag wrapped tightly around her mouth. He enjoyed seeing the fear in her eyes, and how the feeling of power increased the adrenalin and the dopamine in his body. The silent pleading, the initial fight when he removed their clothing and then the inevitable acceptance as he felt their muscles slacken in defeat...it was enough. He thought that being inside their bodies would be what he wanted but it wasn't. This wasn't about sexual satisfaction; it was about control, and right now he was the one in control.

There was another one in the room. He'd turned his head to check that she was still curled in the fetal position. He'd been careful with the amount of GHB he had given her. Just the right amount to make her docile, but not too much to risk killing her.

He turned his attention back to the woman in front of him. There was beauty in that moment. The spiraling of the thin threads of blood breaking through the dull whiteness of her eyes. That he could appreciate. The brief respite of tenderness in the savagery. Two more seconds and that would be it. The heart would give up. But that wasn't the plan.

He let go.

He watched as she fell to the ground like a spineless doll; too weak to even let instinct take over and force her hands to meet the ground to break her fall. He stepped back and listened to the sounds of her throat muscles releasing and violently swallowing the stale oxygen in the air. It looked even more painful than when the life was being squeezed out of her. He took a step forward, reached down and grabbed the crown of her hair. The long brown and blond strands which had glowed like a halo in the setting summer sun now felt like straw in his hand. He dragged her toward the back of the room, not realizing that the gag had slipped from around her mouth.

"Please...please," she begged weakly.

"Don't do that. Don't beg," he said softly, as though soothing a baby back to sleep. He looked across at her neighbor, asleep in the corner. He looked up at the light bulb and thought about changing it to something brighter. There was safety in the darkness but imagine the torture of being in a room that was brightly lit. What was that phrase that his dad would always say?

It's the hope that kills you.

"Come on. Stand up."

He didn't hide his face. He wanted them to see him. To be their last memory.

"We're...go...you're letting me go?" she asked, her words slurred.

He smiled. He could see it. The hope in her eyes.

He made her walk to her shallow grave. In the darkness he could sense the anticipation in her muscles as she walked slowly across disturbed ground, her wrists tied with rope, barefooted. There was always a moment of hesitation when they suddenly smelled the salt in the air, heard the waves breaking against the beach and the aggressive cry of seagulls. The woman's screams joined the seagulls' cries as he pushed her into the three-foot-deep hole. He jumped into the grave, grabbed her fighting feet and quickly wrapped silver duct tape around her ankles. She continued to scream when he pulled himself out of the grave and picked up a shovel.

"Deep breath," he said, breathing in the sea air himself. He could see dawn beginning to break in the distance. The pale blue light a faded bruise against the black sky.

"Deep breath," he said again, urgently shoveling dirt into the shallow gravel, ignoring the coughing and frantic shaking of the woman's head. The earth continued to fall, burying her alive.

If he'd been paying attention, then he would have realized that the girl he'd left behind in the room wasn't really asleep. If he hadn't become so lost in his task, he would have known that the girl had been determinedly loosening the ropes around her wrists after he'd left the house with the other woman. If he hadn't become lost in the rhythmic sounds of the crashing waves and the hypnotic task of the burial, he would have realized that the girl in the room had escaped the house and was running barefoot across the sharp gravel, away from the sea, and away from him.

8

Present Day—1 June

Henley turned on the television in the living room and the radio in the kitchen to bring some life to her empty house. For the first time in months, she had left work early only to find her dog, Luna, asleep in a sunspot in the living room and a note that Rob had pinned to the fridge letting her know he'd taken Emma to the cinema and that he hadn't had time to cook. Henley winced as her once broken ankle started to throb as she limped across the kitchen toward the fridge. She had a firm plan. To pour herself a large glass of Chenin Blanc, order a Chinese takeaway and to finally read the letters that Andrew Streeter had sent her. She'd thought about telling Rob or Linh about the letters, but she knew what would have happened. Linh would have told her to burn the letters and Rob would have dragged her to therapy and repeated his cries that Henley was unwilling to draw a line between her personal and professional life.

"Everything will be fine," Henley said aloud, picking up her glass of wine. She shoved the letters under her armpit, opened the French doors and walked into the garden with a now-awake Luna trailing behind her. She couldn't remember the last time she'd been able to sit alone in her garden with the warm air tickling the small hairs on the back of her neck while she listened to the rhythm of the streets in her part of Brockley. Police sirens, car horns and snatched pieces of conversations of a city that grew louder as the days grew longer.

"I suppose I should be grateful that you didn't write to me at home," Henley muttered, reaching for the first letter.

23 April
HMP Ruxley

Dear Detective Inspector Henley,
You're probably surprised to be hearing from me. I've started and rewritten this letter four times. I know that writing this letter is the right thing to do but understandably I would be a fool to believe that you would want to hear from me. You've got two options when you're in prison for life. You can humble yourself and try to change in order to live with yourself, or spend the next however long you've got being angry. I am angry. My life has been stolen from me.

I need to see you. There are things I need to say to you that need to be said in person. I have no right to privacy, which means that at least five people read this letter before it made its way out of the prison post. I know you can book a social visit to see me online, but I've also enclosed a visiting order. I know that these are for social visits and that you could visit me in your professional capacity as a detective, but I wanted to give you options, especially when I don't have any.

Sincerely,
Andrew Streeter
Prison No: 90865YL

15 May
HMP Ruxley

Dear Anjelica,
I've been thinking a lot about what my last words might be. "I am an innocent man." I'm not going to waste time by asking why you haven't replied to my letter or come to see me.

Could you please visit me urgently? By now, my lawyer would have told you of my application to the CCRC for my case to be reviewed and, God willing, overturned by the Court of Appeal. I would like to be given the opportunity to have a life outside. I was only 23 when I was sent to prison. Can you remember what you were doing when you were 23, when you thought you had all the time in the world? I'll be 48 years old in a couple of months. I would like you to take my age into consideration when you weigh up the pros and cons of visiting me. We both have nothing to lose and everything to gain by this visit taking place. There are no cons. This is not even transactional. I just want to talk to you, face-to-face. This could be career making, if you're the type of person who cares about their professional reputation, but even if you're not, then think about me. An innocent man serving life for another man's crime.

Regards,
Andrew
Prison No: 90865YL

Henley read the letter again and wondered if someone in the prison had written the letter for him. It was difficult to reconcile Andrew Streeter the murderer with the beautiful penmanship displayed on the rough sheet of prison paper. Henley picked up the third letter that Joanna had handed to her. She felt her heart gathering pace as she read Streeter's words. The third letter was shorter. Urgent. To the point. He needed to see her.

Henley picked up her glass of wine and swallowed the rest of the now warm wine in one gulp. In that moment all she wanted was to run away. To finally give in to Rob's demands to jack in the job. She tried to imagine an easier life, one that revolved around a normal nine-to-five. But she couldn't see it. And she knew that stepping one foot into that kind of life would kill her.

Henley picked up her phone and opened up her contacts. There hadn't been many times where she'd been able to predict her life was about to be turned upside down, but as she listened to the dial tone of HMP Ruxley, she knew deep in her gut that everything she had believed in was about to change.

9

"It's nice here, isn't it? Like being at the seaside," Streeter said, easing himself carefully onto the wooden bench. "I was too ill to appreciate it when I first arrived. I was busy concentrating on not dying, but now that I'm in remission. I have a second chance."

If Henley hadn't seen the large blue-and-white sign confirming her arrival at Ruxley Prison for herself, she would have been inclined to believe him. A cluster of small boats was bobbing away in the harbor, and the sound of seagulls screeching buzzed over her head. The only things missing were an ice cream in her hand, Emma building sandcastles and Luna playing in the crashing waves. It wasn't lost on Henley that every fantasy of a different life didn't include Rob.

"How did you of all people end up in an open prison?" Henley asked, sitting down on the opposite side of the picnic table.

"Let's just say it was a series of fortunate events." Streeter winced as the plastic tube connected to his cannula and to the drip hooked on a stand behind him grew taut when it became tangled around his wrist. Henley saw the plaster on Streeter's left hand wrinkle as the cannula pulled at the skin. "I keep doing that," he said, gently untangling the tube.

"You didn't answer my question," said Henley.

"I'd been at HMP Cornwell Hill for the past fourteen years. Ten years at Belmarsh and then they transferred me out to the middle of nowhere. Not that it matters. A cell is a cell. Anyway, about eighteen months ago, the cancer kicked in. I fought it once, thought that I was in the clear but then it came back and I got really sick, so sick that they had to send me to Medway Maritime Hospital for treatment. When they thought I was going to kick the bucket, they sent me to Ruxley because they have rooms here, not cells—but rooms on the hospital wing for end-of-life and respite care. They thought I was dying. I thought I was on my way out too, but then... I don't know, call it a miracle or the sea air."

Streeter slowly smiled at her. Henley took in his face. There was very little sign of the boy-band good looks that the newspapers had written about in 1996, when his custody picture had graced their front pages after his arrest. His lips were thin, almost nonexistent, disappearing into a long line on his face. The sallow skin on his swollen face was filled with deep lines. His curly gray hair was thinning, and his hands were covered with small black, purple, and yellow bruises.

"Do you know that my hair turned gray practically overnight," Streeter said. "I was twenty-three years old and I looked in the mirror and nearly had a heart attack. I reckon the shock of realizing the judge meant it when he said I would die in prison finally caught up with me."

"Some people might call that karma, that you deserve it," Henley said coldly.

Streeter scratched the side of his nose. "I'm not going to disagree with you, and I wouldn't blame them. I don't blame you."

"You don't blame me?" Henley made no attempt to hide her disbelief. "You're acting as though I'm responsible for putting you in here. I was a fifteen-year-old kid who found the body of her friend. My friend. That you killed."

Streeter closed his eyes and slowly shook his head. "I don't blame you," he repeated. "You only told them your truth."

"'*Your truth,*'" Henley repeated. "That sounds patronizing."

"I didn't mean it to be. What I meant is that you told them truthfully what you saw, and the jury, the public and the families of the"—Streeter took a breath—"of the victims. Everyone made a decision because of what the police and the media told them; they called me 'The Burier' for God's sake. Do you have any idea what it's like to be anointed with a name like that by the press? They might as well have tattooed *Serial Killer: Guilty* on my forehead. They thought they had the facts, but they didn't."

"They had the list that you wrote. Your kill list. With all of the victims' names. So Serial Killer: Guilty. They weren't wrong."

"I remember you being fiery in the witness box. Very mature. Sure of yourself. Smart. You were impressive. You didn't let my barrister get to you when she was cross-examining you."

"Cross-examining? Is that what you call it?" Henley said, trying not to fidget as the lower muscles in her back seized up.

"You didn't break," Streeter observed. "It's probably why you've gotten as far as you have—with your career, I mean. Relentless. Determined. You want things to be done the right way."

"I didn't come here to get a bloody personality assessment or for you to waste my time."

"Fairly," Streeter continued, ignoring Henley's outburst. "You want things to be fair. I don't think you would sleep well at night if you thought things hadn't been fair."

Streeter watched Henley intently, his pupils dilated as a cocktail of antibiotics and painkillers made its way through his system. Henley could see it clearly, his determination to get things in place.

"I didn't kill them," Streeter said sadly. "I said it when I was arrested."

"But you didn't say it when you were interviewed by the police."

"Because my solicitor, she wasn't a solicitor, she was a…a rep, a police station accredited rep, she advised me to go no comment. So, I did, and she wasn't wrong. The police didn't have anything when they first arrested me. It was a fishing expedition, even I could see that, but I told the truth in court. Under oath. I told them I didn't do it."

"You're not—"

"I was set up."

Henley rolled her eyes. "Is that it? Is that all you've got?"

"I heard that DS Rhimes is dead now. I might call *that* karma. Considering he was the one who did it."

It was a strange experience, feeling as though the walls were closing in, even though you were outside. Henley's breathing became labored. She wondered if this was how agoraphobics felt—as though the world was suffocating them. But this wasn't a panic attack. This was the rumblings of anger.

"What do you mean?" Henley asked evenly.

"You know exactly what I mean," Streeter said matter-of-factly but with no trace of bitterness. "He set me up. Planted evidence—"

"He would never do that."

"That supposed kill list they found in my flat. Ask yourself why no one ever got the handwriting analyzed or why the exhibit had mysteriously disappeared when my solicitors asked for their own expert to examine it."

"Rhimes did things by the book. You're just looking for—"

Streeter laughed. "Do you really think I would have asked to see you if he'd done things by the book? He planted evidence and he paid off my alibi witness. He knew it wasn't me."

"I saw you. You were by the river when I found Melissa."

"I never lied about being there, but that doesn't mean that I killed her. That I killed any of them."

A lump rose in Henley's throat. She tried in vain to swallow down her emotions.

"He came into my cell one night. He attacked me and pushed a piece of material in my mouth," Streeter said, his voice soft. "Part of the Crown's case was that my DNA was on the fragments of cloth that had been found in the victim's mouth. No one thought it was odd that my DNA was only found after I was arrested and bailed, for the second time, from Ladywell police station."

Henley tried to recall the sequence of events that led to Streeter's arrest. She remembered that Streeter was first arrested in October 1995 after the body of the third victim, Fallon O'Toole, had been found. She remembered being told that Streeter was out on bail. She couldn't remember if anyone had told her that Streeter's DNA was a match for the DNA that was found on the bodies of the first four victims.

"Did you see his face, that night in your cell?" Henley asked.

"It was dark, but I—"

"No," Henley stood up abruptly. "I'm not listening to any more of this. You've wasted enough of my time."

"Her name is Kerry Searle. My alibi witness. She won't talk to Mr. Piper, my brief. I asked but she doesn't want...she's scared."

"Scared of what?"

"Scared of him. The person who did it. The person who killed them all."

Henley studied Streeter and recognized the look of a man who was genuinely afraid. Her body jerked involuntarily, and her mouth grew dry. A groundswell of shock and anger hit her as it dawned on her that this man, this convicted murderer, was saying that he had kept hidden the identity of the person responsible for the murder of five people.

"Give me a name," she demanded.

Streeter shook his head. "No," he whispered.

"*No* you're not telling me? Or *No* you don't know and everything you're telling me is a steaming pile of bullshit?"

"No, I do…or I think it's—" Streeter stuttered. "It wouldn't even matter now. He's… I'm sure I heard that he died. Naming him wouldn't matter."

Henley stared fiercely at Streeter. "Who is it?" she demanded. "If it's not you. If you want me to believe that it wasn't you and that Rhimes, my Rhimes…that he set you up, then tell me who did it."

"I can't. Please, just accept—"

"You have absolutely no right to ask me to accept anything," Henley said icily. "Who. Is. It. Give me a name."

Streeter raised his head. Tears began to fall down his cheeks. "I'm not dead yet, and if I'm wrong then—"

"You're a lying piece of—"

"No," Streeter said, his voice thick with tears. "Speak to Kerry. Please. Speak to her."

10

_____

Four months earlier—February
Dr. Isabelle Collins's office—Shad Thames,
London

"If we're not going to talk about what bonds you and DC Ramouter, and we're not going to talk about your husband, what
would you like to talk about?" asked Dr. Isabelle Collins.

Henley leaned back as a second wave of nausea took hold
and her forehead prickled with sweat. "Someone close to me,"
she said.

"Your mum?"

"No. Not my mum. I want to talk to you about my old boss.
I need to talk about Rhimes."

Dr. Collins paused as she turned back the pages of her notebook. "Detective Chief Superintendent Rhimes. How long did
you know him—"

"His name was Harry," Henley replied. She pulled a packet

of painkillers from her bag. She stretched out her broken ankle, trying to ignore the temptation to take off the air boot.

"What have they given you?" Dr. Collins asked.

"Fifteen milligrams of co-codamol and ibuprofen." Henley turned the silver packet over with her fingers before she pushed a single caplet out. "Anything stronger and I'll be curled up on the sofa. And I'm not taking them all the time, only when the broken bone in my ankle starts to protest."

"Are you still not taking the sleeping tablets I prescribed?"

"I take them when I have to."

"Fine. So DCSI Rhimes. Harry. You worked together, on and off, for over ten years? That's a long time."

"We first started working together when I transferred to Lewisham CID about twelve years ago. I transferred to Rhimes's CID team first and Stanford followed about three months later."

"And Pellacia?"

"He was already there."

"So, you followed Pellacia?"

"No, I did not follow him," Henley said sternly. "It's insulting to suggest I followed a man."

"It wasn't a suggestion but a question, but we'll move on. How would you describe your working relationship with Rhimes?"

"It was good. We were, still are, a close team. He trusted us and we trusted him. That's the main reason we all agreed to join him when he was asked to set up the Serial Crime Unit after the Abigail Burnley case."

"Abigail Burnley? Why does that name ring a bell?"

"Burnley was a district nurse who killed fifteen people under her care. It was a big case. Our biggest case."

Dr. Collins sipped her coffee. Henley recognized the look in her eyes. She was pondering how best to structure her next question.

"You never answered my question," Dr. Collins said.

"Yes, I did. I told you when we started working together."

"But the first question I asked was *how* long you had known him for. That's a completely different question."

There was no way around answering the question without explaining the events that led up to their first meeting. "I've known him since I was fifteen," she finally said.

"Fifteen years old. Was he a family friend?"

"No. It was nothing like that. I wish that was my story. My best friend was murdered. He was one of the detectives. I found her body and he interviewed me a couple of times," Henley explained matter-of-factly.

"You say it so…as if you were explaining an old case."

"Well, it is an old case."

"It wasn't just a case. It was your best friend's murder. Were you close?"

Henley's mind flashed back to sitting on Melissa's bedroom floor as they planned their outfits for the club night that they were sneaking out to. "We were fifteen," said Henley. "You're always close when you're that age, but who's to know if things would have stayed that way."

Dr. Collins wrote something in her notebook, then looked up again. "Did you remain in contact with Rhimes once the case concluded?" she asked.

Henley shook her head. "The last time I saw him was about a year after the trial. He popped in to check up on me. My parents were there and I spoke to him for a couple of minutes and I left to go to the library. I didn't see him again until I walked into Lewisham CID twelve years ago. I recognized him straight away."

"But he would have known you were joining his team before your first day. You didn't take your husband's surname when you got married."

"That's not correct. In my personal life I'm Anjelica Campbell but I didn't see the point in changing it for work."

"So you remained Anjelica Henley. Rhimes knew who you

were—why did he agree to your transfer, considering your history?"

"I don't know. He never really gave me a clear answer."

"You asked?"

"Of course I asked. We had a history and I needed to know that he didn't take me on out of some misguided obligation or... I don't know, guilt."

"And what was his answer?"

"He said that if I wasn't up to the job then he would get rid of me. Not once did he give me special treatment."

"No special treatment, but you became close?"

"We were. He was at my wedding."

"Knew all of your secrets?"

"Most of them."

"What about your team. Did they know about your association with Rhimes?"

Henley shook her head. "Not in the beginning. Talking about what happened to Melissa and the trial was hard. Too hard. Up until last year, I was telling Pellacia, Jo and Stanford that Melissa's murderer has never been caught. It was as if I'd forgotten about that part of my life."

"Dissociative amnesia," said Dr. Collins as she watched Henley closely. "You had to relive the event of finding your friend's body when you gave evidence. It's not uncommon to block out certain events in your life because they're associated with trauma. Can you continue?"

"Yes," Henley said softly.

"So why now? What's happened that you want to talk about him?"

"I can't get my head around the fact that he killed himself."

"Two close deaths in a short space of time."

"I'm not talking about my mum, remember."

"Of course."

"Can you imagine getting the call that your boss, your friend, has killed himself and now, well over a year later, the talk of him being corrupt has started up again."

"Again?"

"I received a request yesterday from a journalist who was asking questions about corruption."

"And this isn't the first time?"

"No. The first time was a few years ago. An ex-police informant decided to make a name for himself, and he recorded a podcast about police corruption."

"And he named Rhimes?"

Henley nodded, "Among others, but he made noise about it and a journalist picked it up. The story died but I think it's going to come up again."

"You think or you know?"

Henley felt her phone vibrating in her coat pocket. She sighed deeply. "I know and it seems there's more traction this time. There's a reporter, Callum O'Brien, who's been asking questions. They're the same questions as a few years ago but he's surer of himself."

"And how does this make you feel?"

Henley leaned back as the muscles around her broken ankle began to pulse. "Uncomfortable and nervous, and I'm not the sort of person who usually gets nervous."

"Can you pinpoint what is making you nervous?"

"I feel that something is going to come out that I won't be able to disprove, and if I can't disprove it then that means it's true."

"And if it's true then that means you have to question everything about a man you cared about, who was there for you from when you were a child."

"But what does it say about me and my judgment if I couldn't see the truth, and allowed a man who was corrupt to be such a big part of my professional and personal life?"

11

Henley looked at the address Streeter had scribbled down on a scrap of yellow paper to double-check she was at the right place. She knew better than to make assumptions about people, but for some reason she was finding it very hard to reconcile the landscaped front garden, containers filled with bright blue hydrangeas, and a two-year-old electric BMW charging on the driveway with a woman who was an associate of a convicted killer.

"Can I help you?"

Henley turned around and found herself facing Kerry Searle. She was dressed head to toe in expensive activewear. Henley had checked Kerry Searle's personal details with the Driver & Vehicle Licensing Agency which gave her age as forty-five, but she looked older. Her face had the telltale signs of too much filler, her forehead had not wrinkled in surprise, and her nose was far too perfect.

"I'm not interested in anything that you're selling," Kerry said.

"I'm not selling anything." Henley hesitated. She wasn't on

official police business, but she pulled out her warrant card anyway. "You're Kerry Searle?"

"I go by Huggins." Kerry's eyes narrowed. "Searle is my maiden name. Who are you?"

"Detective Inspector Anjelica Henley, attached to the Serial Crime Unit." She held out her ID.

"Serial Crime? Why on earth… I don't understand."

"Maybe it would be best if we went inside and talked," said Henley.

"Is it my kids? They're staying with my ex-husband at the—"

"No, it's nothing to do with your kids. Please, Kerry. I just want to have a word with you, and I'd rather do it inside."

"Am I in trouble?" Kerry asked.

"Why would you be in trouble?" Henley watched Kerry's demeanor switch from confused to fearful.

Kerry turned around as a neighbor's door opened, and a woman walked out holding an empty cardboard box. The neighbor made a show of struggling to put the large box into the wheelie bin, clearly trying to work out who the woman confronting her neighbor was, in the middle of this exclusive cul-de-sac around the corner from the famed Wimbledon tennis courts.

"Look, I won't take up much of your time," said Henley. "Can we go inside?"

"You want to come inside my house?" Kerry asked, looking across at her neighbor.

"Fine," Henley said with annoyance. "Let's sit on your doorstep and talk about Andrew Streeter."

"I told him I didn't want to get involved," said Kerry, dropping tea bags into two brightly colored mugs.

Henley made a mental note of the small CCTV camera that was attached to the large kitchen window and the empty box for a new home alarm system on the kitchen table. There was also a window and door brochure, despite the windows and the front door looking relatively new.

"I told him, but he didn't listen," Kerry said, placing the cup in front of Henley and returning to her position at the kitchen counter.

"How did he get in touch with you?" asked Henley.

"Through his lawyer. I don't know how they found me. I'm ex-directory. I'm not on social media except for WhatsApp, if that counts, but I suppose they have their ways. They wrote to me and then called me at work."

"What do you do?"

"I own a spa in the town center. I told his lawyer, and I wrote to Andrew and told him to leave me out of it. I've got my family to think about. I don't want them getting caught up in this."

"Can you tell me how you know Andrew Streeter?" asked Henley.

"It was a long time ago," Kerry finally said, turning to face Henley. "I don't think I'd even turned twenty yet when I first met him."

"What were you? Boyfriend and girlfriend?"

"Something like that."

Henley didn't push it. "Streeter was insistent that I speak to you."

"Why?" Kerry said warily.

"You did say that Streeter's lawyer tried to talk to you."

"But I didn't actually speak to him. I told him not to call me and that I wanted nothing to do with Streeter and I put the phone down," Kerry avoided Henley's gaze and ran a hand through her hair. Henley saw her wince slightly as one of her rings caught a hair extension.

"I saw Andrew a couple of days ago," said Henley. "Did you know he and his legal team referred his case to the CCRC?"

"No, I didn't," Kerry said quickly—too quickly for Henley's liking. She had been expecting Kerry to ask what the CCRC was.

"Well, they are."

"And what has that got to do with me?"

"Because Streeter made a point of telling me about you and something that happened when he was first arrested."

There it was, the silence again. Kerry's hand began to tremble, and some tea spilled over the edge of the cup. She finally placed it down on the counter. Henley wouldn't have been surprised if Kerry's legs had given way as she made her way to the kitchen table and finally sat down.

"I'm just going to ask you a few questions," Henley said gently. "Did you tell the police that you were Andrew Streeter's alibi twenty-five years ago?"

Kerry nodded.

"Who did you tell?" Henley asked as her heart began to beat faster.

"They arrested Andrew at my grandmother's flat in Stepney. He's the only one who knew that I sometimes stayed there," Kerry said, her eyes taking on the haunted look of someone who was reliving the past. "He wasn't hiding there at my nan's but that's how they made it sound in the papers; that he was on the run."

"Was he on the run?"

"He mentioned going to Amsterdam, but you've got to understand that he was scared."

"So, what happened when the police arrived at your grandmother's house?" asked Henley.

"It was bloody chaos. My nan was away at the time, she was visiting her sister in Southampton, but the police just barged in. Loads of them. They dragged Andrew out and they threatened to arrest me, but they didn't."

"What happened next?"

"They arrested Andrew and I tried to tell them he didn't do anything. The police turned up again the next day and I told him that Andrew didn't kill those people and that he'd been staying with me when Tiago went missing."

"Who exactly did you tell?" asked Henley. "Who was the officer?"

"The officer who took my statement?" There was a tremor in Kerry's voice. "Sergeant Rhimes."

Henley felt sick and pushed her cup of tea away. "Are you sure?"

"He said that his name was Detective Sergeant Rhimes."

"And he took your statement?" asked Henley. "An alibi statement? A written one?"

"Yes."

"Signed by you and taken by a police officer?"

"I can't remember signing it, but he wrote it all down. But then…" Kerry paused and stared back at Henley. "He said no one would believe me. He said if I gave evidence in court, they would bring up my history."

"What history?"

"Drugs," Kerry whispered. "I used to run drugs for some local dealers, selling cocaine and ecstasy in nightclubs. I never kept drugs at my nan's house, but he said that they found drugs in my room at my nan's when they arrested Streeter. Only—"

"You never kept drugs at your nan's house," Henley said with resignation.

"There was nothing there, but the officer, Rhimes, he had pictures of packets of pills and cocaine in my drawer, which was shit because I never—"

"Are you suggesting that Rhimes planted it there?"

"I can't see how else it got there," Kerry replied.

"So, what happened next, after you gave your statement?" Henley asked, struggling to come to terms with Kerry's revelations. In all the years that she'd worked with Rhimes she'd never seen him act in a way that would suggest he would bribe a witness or step outside the code of conduct to get a result. Rhimes wasn't perfect but he followed a moral compass. Henley's gut told her that Kerry might be telling the truth, but her head was working through a different scenario. Streeter was a manipulative murderer. Kerry was an associate of Streeter and a drug dealer. Kerry was a criminal. Kerry couldn't be trusted.

"I had a lot going on in my life. I'd been through a lot. My nan had been ill and then there was the stuff with Andrew. It was all too much, and he offered me money."

The words of disbelief were already forming on Henley's tongue as she tried to make sense of what she was hearing. "Who offered you money?" Henley finally asked, instead of saying what was really on her mind—that Kerry was a liar.

"Two grand. All cash, in an envelope."

"Rhi—DS Rhimes offered you two thousand pounds?" Henley asked, aware that her voice had grown quieter.

"He didn't offer it to me. He *gave* it to me. In cash. In a white envelope. In my hands."

"And you took it?"

"I was scared."

"Scared of what exactly?"

"Don't talk to me as though I've done anything wrong. He… that man threatened me. He scared me."

Henley took a breath and tried to push down the confusion. "What did he want you to do for the money?"

"I was young and I was scared. You have no idea about what I'd been through," Kerry said angrily.

"OK, OK. Calm down," Henley said. "What did he want you to do?" she asked again, aware that her voice was shaking with anger.

"Withdraw my statement," said Kerry. "And to say that Andrew was never with me."

"And you withdrew it."

"No one had ever heard about it anyway. And no one ever asked me about it again. Until today, when you turned up."

"What are you doing here?" Henley asked. Pellacia was standing in the doorway of the SCU when he should have been strolling along Las Ramblas in Barcelona with his girlfriend, local MP Laura Halifax. "I thought you weren't back from holiday until Monday?"

"Change of plans," Pellacia answered.

"Did you finally see the light and dump her?" came Joanna's disembodied voice from somewhere within the office.

"Why don't you...do you know what, Jo, never mind," Pellacia said. He placed his hand across the door frame, effectively blocking Henley.

"Are you not going to let me through?" Henley asked, trying to ignore how much she wanted Pellacia to answer Jo's question.

"No, I'm not," Pellacia said softly. "I need to talk to you."

Henley sensed the telltale signs of a tension headache forming. She knew the tension was a by-product of the guilt she was feeling and the pressure of keeping secrets from her team. She thought about telling Pellacia about Streeter's letters, Kerry Huggins, and the prison visit. But what would be the point? Streeter had been convicted of five murders, had appealed his conviction twice and lost. Henley's brief visit to the past was over.

"Can we do this later?" Henley asked, looking up at Pellacia. "Can you excuse me, please? I've got work to do."

"Work. I didn't think you were interested in work. You've got Ramouter working on this arson case by himself while Eastwood is coming up with piss-poor excuses for you not being here. It's almost..." Pellacia raised his left arm and checked his watch. "It's 12:54 p.m., Henley."

"I know what time it is, and I'm sorry."

Pellacia paused and stared at Henley, biting the inside of his cheek. The silence stretched.

"Look, it was personal," said Henley finally, breaking the tension. "Something came up and this morning was the only time I could deal with it."

Pellacia released a frustrated sigh. "Fine. Fine."

"So, can I get back to work now?"

"No."

"What do you mean, no?" Henley folded her arms in agitation.

"As I said, I need to talk to you. Do you want to take a walk?"

Henley flinched as she picked up the switch in Pellacia's tone. It was warm and empathetic. She realized that she had made a mistake by interpreting Pellacia's words as hostile.

"What's going on?"

"Let's walk. I'll get you a cup of tea or something."

"I've had enough tea," said Henley. She looked over Pellacia's shoulder and caught Eastwood's gaze. Henley cocked her head to one side, and Eastwood shrugged her shoulders and mouthed, *No idea.*

"What's so important that you had to take me out of the station?" Henley asked. They had walked from Starbucks toward the Greenwich foot tunnel, and were now sitting on a bench facing the river. Students from the nearby university and the early influx of summer tourists milled around them.

"You can almost pretend you're somewhere else," Pellacia said. "Forget all about the chaos that's going on out there."

"You can never really forget." Henley watched a conga line of primary school children, all wearing bright yellow high-visibility vests, follow their teacher.

"How's Emma doing?" Pellacia took a sip of his coffee and shifted closer to Henley.

"She's fine. Causing chaos in nursery. Can't believe she's going to be four years old next year, which means I'll be sending her off to primary school soon. Time flies."

"Yeah, it does," Pellacia replied sadly. He moved again so that their knees were touching.

"What's going on?" Henley asked, turning to face him. She knew him well enough to know when Pellacia was trying to find a way to deliver bad news softly.

"I didn't want you to hear it back at the station. I wanted to be—"

"You wanted to be what? What is it, Stephen? You're not sick, are you?" Henley felt a panic rise in her chest as her mind started to flick through an infinite number of scenarios that ended with Pellacia being buried six feet under.

"No. No. I'm not sick. It's nothing like that." Pellacia sighed. "It's about Andrew Streeter." Pellacia took Henley's coffee from her and placed it next to his, to the side. Henley didn't say a word as Pellacia took hold of her hand.

"Andrew Streeter?" Henley asked, silently praying that her voice had followed the right inflections that came when someone was surprised. "Why are you bringing him up?"

Pellacia squeezed Henley's hand even tighter. "Fuck, I don't want to put this on you. I know how much Melissa meant to you and this is... I didn't want you to hear this from anyone else but me."

"Are you going to tell me what's going on because this is... this is a lot."

"It looks like Streeter may be released."

A rush of heat swept through Henley's body as Pellacia continued to speak. She could see his lips moving but she had no idea what he was saying. Even though she'd sat with Streeter two days ago and knew what his lawyers were planning, the prospect of Streeter walking around London wasn't one that she'd fully considered.

"As I understand it," Pellacia was saying, "his case was referred to the Criminal Cases Review Commission last month and they agreed with his application and—"

"What do you mean, they agreed? That would—" Henley forced herself to stop talking, in case she revealed that she knew more than she was letting on.

"You need to let me finish," said Pellacia. "The CCRC agreed with his application and referred his case to the Court of Appeal." Henley felt exposed as Pellacia stared at her so intently. "Yesterday afternoon the Court of Appeal granted Streeter leave to appeal," he said solemnly.

"How do you know all this?" Henley asked, stunned.

"A court clerk informed the Director of Public Prosecutions this morning and advised him to inform the families of the five victims before they issued a press release tomorrow morning. The information trickled down and I got a call from the borough commander about an hour ago. She thought you should know. I've got a copy of the CCRC decision, here."

Henley waited as Pellacia took out his phone and tapped in his passcode. "Just because the Court of Appeal have granted Streeter leave to appeal doesn't necessarily mean that he's going to be released." Henley could hear the denial and desperation in her voice. In that moment she knew she sounded like a mother insisting that their child was an angel even though a witness had seen them stab someone in the neck. Henley had looked into the eyes of a murderer, but the CCRC had flicked through the paperwork with a stone-cold detachment. She felt sick. "Do you know how many murder convictions are referred to the Court of Appeal every year? Look at how many of our cases have gone to the Court of Appeal and those cases have been laughed out of court. This will fail," she said.

"I would usually agree with you, but look at the speed at which this happening. Listen to what the CCRC said in their decision: *After careful consideration, the CCRC has found compelling evidence that calls into question the credibility of the investigating police officers who questioned him at the time of his arrest and presided over the murder investigation of Gyimah et al. Having considered the Court's findings in that case, the CCRC considers that the credibility of these police officers, one of whom was earlier criticized in the Court of Appeal's decision in R v Duff, Branton and Sage [2002] 1 EWCA 90 as 'a witness of truth in criminal proceedings,' is substantially weakened. On that basis there is a real possibility that the Court of Appeal would conclude that Mr. Streeter's convictions are unsafe.* They're basically saying that—"

"I know exactly what they're saying," Henley replied, burying her head in her hands. "You know who one of the officers who questioned him was, don't you?"

Pellacia didn't reply as he put his phone away.

"It's not just the fact that they're saying Streeter's conviction is unsafe," said Henley. "It's the fact they're saying—"

"Rhimes was corrupt," said Pellacia, disbelief coating every single one of his words.

"All those rumors, all those years of denial. He sat in front of us and denied it. He came to my house, sat in my living room, and said it was all lies."

"You're not saying you believe this, are you? You can't be saying that?"

Henley turned her gaze away from Pellacia. In the past month she'd embarked on a journey where she'd stood up and blindly defended a dead man. Her loyalty to Rhimes had overridden her ability to listen to Elias Piper and Streeter and objectively analyze and assess what they had told her. As far as she was concerned, everyone was lying and looking to absolve themselves of any responsibility by placing the blame at the feet of a dead man. What if *she* was the one who'd been wrong? Henley couldn't hide from the truth anymore.

"What did that decision say? *The CCRC has found compelling evidence that calls into question the credibility of the investigating police officers.* Compelling evidence. They haven't reached this decision on a whim. They have something."

Pellacia rose from his seat, placed his hands on his head, and walked toward the railings. After a few seconds he turned and faced Henley with a look of disbelief and betrayal on his face.

"What are you saying?" Pellacia finally asked. "That you believe Rhimes—our Rhimes—was corrupt?"

"It doesn't matter what I believe, does it?" Henley replied.

"What I believe, think, or feel isn't going to make a blind bit of difference."

Henley stood up and joined Pellacia. She turned her attention toward the growing City of London skyline in the west, and watched the waves lapping against the river wall below. Should she tell Pellacia about Streeter's letters and her visit to see him?

"There's more," said Pellacia, stepping away from Henley.

"What more could there possibly be?" asked Henley, taking a deep breath to calm herself down.

"The Court of Appeal are going to fast-track the appeal against conviction," said Pellacia. "It could be as early as next Monday."

"Well, that's it then," said Henley. "Those three judges have already made up their minds if they're fast-tracking this."

"Are you OK?" Pellacia asked, his voice softening as he finally faced Henley.

"It's just a lot, Stephen." Henley looked out across the river. Melissa's body had been found less than a mile away. "Twenty-six years is a long time, but I never forgot what happened and what I saw. I had nightmares for months and I would sleep in the top bunk in Simon's room because I didn't want to be alone. I don't think he wanted to be alone either."

"I'm so sorry, Anj," Pellacia said, pulling her to his chest.

"As long as he was locked up, I didn't have to give Andrew Streeter another thought. Now, I have to consider the possibility that in a few weeks he could be walking around without a care in the world. He killed five people. *Five.*"

"Maybe it won't actually come to that," Pellacia replied unconvincingly. "It doesn't mean that Streeter will go free if there's a retrial. He'll still be in jail."

"And pigs might fly," said Henley, pulling away from Pellacia. "We'd better get back to the station. Thanks for...well, I'm not sure if the news is something that I should be thanking you for."

"Don't worry. I know what you meant. I just didn't want you

finding out from anyone else, or by a breaking news notification on your phone."

"Melissa was my friend and not a day goes by when I don't think about what kind of life she would be living if she was here, but it's the victims' families I'm worried about," Henley said as she and Pellacia walked away from the river. "What are they supposed to do now, when twenty-five years later, the court rocks up and says, *Sorry but there's been a mistake*? How is anyone supposed to live with that?"

12

Monday, 14 June
Royal Courts of Justice
Court of Appeal—Criminal Division

The Burier adjusted his nonprescription glasses and looked around the exquisite halls and the imposing Gothic architecture of the Royal Courts of Justice. Photographs and news footage didn't do the building any justice and were unable to portray the rich sense of judicial history. He'd been surprised at how easy it was to get access to the court building once he'd pushed his way through the protestors standing outside in the sun on Fleet Street. There had been no online applications to make or arguments to be had with the security guards at the entrance. He'd simply explained that he wanted to sit in the public gallery to watch one of the proceedings and had been directed to court 13 once he'd completed the security checks. No one had glanced in his direction as he walked past wigged barristers in their black robes and solicitors sitting with their clients on red-cushioned benches. They were all too involved in their own lives to give him any attention.

"You've got to wait until the court usher comes out and opens the doors," said a man in his early sixties, wearing a tight-fitting blue polo shirt, after he tried to push the door to court 13 open. "And we've got our own entrance, if you're sitting in the public gallery. That's the door for the barristers and solicitors. That is where you're going?" he added cautiously.

"I am," said The Burier, stepping back from the door.

"First time?" the man asked brightly.

"Yeah. I've got a couple of hours to kill, and someone recommended that I should come here."

"My name is Godwin, by the way. And I promise, you won't regret it. It's the best show in town."

The Burier was so close to the barrister in front of him that he could see the tightly coiled white horsehairs on his wig and could, if he wanted, run a finger along the frayed edges of his black gown. Court 13 was grand, covered in dark oak paneling, but it was smaller than he'd expected. He was sitting cheek by jowl with the ten other people who had joined him on the two benches reserved for the public in the back of the court, waiting for the three judges to enter and take their places in the high-backed chairs at the front of the court. His new friend Godwin was leaning forward, peppering a young, nervous-looking female barrister with questions while they waited for the judges.

He looked up as Elias Piper entered the courtroom with a young black woman who was holding a laptop and an overflowing blue lever-arch file, and another tall and elegant white woman in her midsixties wearing a silk black robe and a black bar jacket with three buttons across the sleeve. The Burier knew who she was—Ms. Johnson, the barrister who had represented Streeter twenty-five years ago, now Queen's Counsel. The court clerk banged the door loudly and everyone rose in unison as the three judges entered from the door at the back and took their seats. The Burier felt the stirrings of anger in the pit of his stomach. He was angry with all these people for disrupting his life. He'd been quiet for so long, establishing businesses, building relationships, and creating a family, but his life was now hanging in limbo and his future actions depended on Ms. Johnson QC's submissions to the court and whether the three judges would side with her.

"Your lordships, the only thing that I will add in conclusion is that Mr. Streeter has always maintained his innocence." Ms. Johnson's voice rang out from the speakers. "He has and has always been prepared to assist the police and has provided those who instruct me with in-depth instructions and further details of potential witnesses, including details of the alibi witness who was disregarded by the original investigating officers. I risk simply repeating my detailed submissions in my written application if I were to remain on my feet any longer, unless I can assist you any further, m'lord?"

"No, you've been most helpful," replied Lord Justice Kherson, although his face said otherwise. "We will rise to consider our decision."

The Burier pushed his glasses up and wiped away the sweat from the side of his nose. He'd developed a cramp in his right leg during the hour of legal submissions from Streeter's barrister and the prosecutor, and the slow, legal and confusing questions from the judges who gave no clue as to their final decision. It was less than ten minutes later when there was a loud knock from the back of the court and everyone in the courtroom hurriedly rose to their feet as the judges reentered the room. The Burier looked around in confusion. Ten minutes? It was then, as the court descended into arctic silence, that The Burier realized the judges had made their decision before today's hearing. Lord Justice Kherson nodded to his colleague, Lord Justice Soyer, who was holding only two sheets of paper in his hand.

"This is the judgment of the court to which all members have contributed," began Lord Justice Soyer. The Burier listened intently as the judgment was read. He occasionally lost his way with the references to statutes, case law and legal principles, but he clearly heard the conclusion.

Lord Justice Soyer cleared his throat and continued, "On sixteenth October 1996 in the Central Criminal Court before Diarmuid Joseph J., the appellant, now aged forty-eight, was found guilty of five counts of murder. We consider the appellant is, on his own case, a reliable narrator of events and agree that Detective Sergeant Rhimes was inconsistent in this regard. We accept that there is evidence that an investigating officer deliberately ignored the statement of a potential alibi witness and that there was no attempt to establish the whereabouts of a sixth person who, on the evidence submitted by Streeter's instructing solicitors, may have escaped from the person who was responsible for the murders of Gyimah, Chalmers, O'Toole, Callaghan, and Alves. For these reasons, we allow the appeals in relation to all five counts of murder on the indictment and the convictions on those counts are all quashed."

An audible ripple of shock swept the courtroom.

"Wow," Godwin whispered. "Can you believe that?" He elbowed The Burier excitedly.

"No. No, I can't," he replied.

There were only three questions in The Burier's mind as he watched Elias Piper and Streeter's barrister shake hands.

How did they know he'd lost one of his girls?

When did she speak to Elias Piper?

And where was she now?

13

"Seems to be a day for good news," said the nurse, entering the room with an IV bag and pulling a face mask on.

"Yeah, it is," Streeter replied, trying to push himself up on the bed.

"Here, let me help you," said the nurse, picking up the remote control and pressing a couple of buttons to adjust the bed.

"Ah, thank you. I keep pressing the buttons, but I can't get it right." Streeter sighed as the mattress rose at his back and gently bent his knees. "I can't believe it's finally happened."

"That's an understatement. We were all convinced that you wouldn't last the summer. Right, I'm going to give you your blood thinner now and then change your IV."

"I spoke to my solicitor last night and he said he'd bet his house that the CPS wouldn't retry me," Streeter said excitedly.

"I can't imagine how you must feel." The nurse raised Streeter's hospital gown, revealing his pale white thigh, and said, "Here we go," as the needle went into the muscle.

"Ow," said Streeter. He put a hand to his thigh and rubbed

vigorously at the flesh. "The blood thinners always sting. It hurts less when you take blood."

"Sorry about that."

"Don't worry—I don't even care. I feel as though I've won the lottery. Do you know how hard it is to get the Criminal Case Review Commission to accept a case? They make it sound easy: fill in an application, show new evidence and you don't have to spend a penny. It's all free but it's an entire process. They have to review it and then someone else has to review it and then it goes before a committee and then a commissioner. It's a lot, and nothing is guaranteed, and it doesn't happen overnight."

"You've obviously got a good lawyer though. The Criminal... Reviews Case or whatever they're called, agreed with him and the Court of Appeal."

Streeter's face brightened. "They believe me. I feel blessed. I told them I didn't do it. I told everyone I didn't do it."

"Do you know who did?"

Streeter absent-mindedly scratched at a scab on his wrist. "I didn't in the beginning, when the first girl disappeared. After I was charged, I had time to think and look at the people around me and there was only one person that fit. Then, being inside for twenty-five years, well the more I thought about it, the more it made sense to me."

"Twenty-five years knowing the real killer was walking around living the life of Riley and you were in prison. I would have gone mad. Did you tell anyone?"

"I told my lawyer who I thought it was." Streeter grimaced as the scab on his wrist fragmented and fresh blood began to weep. "If I'm right, then the real killer is six feet under right now."

"He's dead?" The nurse picked up an antibacterial wipe and cleaned Streeter's reopened wound. "Won't that be a problem for you?"

"Nah, my lawyer thinks we can use that tactically and financially. I've got to start thinking about my future now." Streeter smiled, revealing yellowing and uneven teeth. "My future," he said in wonder.

"Most definitely. I'm made up for you. You can start making plans now. Short-term and long-term." The nurse replaced Streeter's IV bag and released the valve on the drip. "I'm going to give it a couple of minutes to make sure there's no issues with the drip and then I'll leave you to rest."

Streeter settled back against the pillows and a bloodstained tear trickled down his cheek. "Twenty-five years in here. But I'm not going to die here."

"Are you sure about that, Andy?"

A ripple of goose bumps spread across Streeter's skin. He felt moisture gathering in his nostrils, and in the groove between his mouth and his nose. He ran his tongue along his top lip and tasted blood. Panic rose in his chest.

"I'm not dead."

Streeter stared back at the nurse, first with confusion and then with knowing.

There was a moment when it felt as though the world had stopped moving and that gravity, just for a second, was suspended. Streeter caught the changes in the nurse's voice—it became deeper and the accent, which he had thought sounded like it came from the northeast of England, changed. It became softer, the vowels elongated. His cockney accent was less pronounced than it had been twenty-five years ago, but it was there. The lisp too, evident when he had said the word "sure." The lisp used to scare Streeter. It scared him again, now.

"No," said Streeter hoarsely. Blood ran from his nose. He tried to speak again and to reach the alarm button, but the hot pain tearing through his gastrointestinal tract was too much to bear. His body folded into itself like a broken accordion.

"We're fine as we are, Andy," said the nurse. He picked up the alarm button and let it drop to the floor.

Blood had pooled in the back of Streeter's throat. His organs were failing. He felt the thin cotton sheet underneath him grow warm and wet as his urine and bloody diarrhea settled in a pool. There was a brief moment when he was able to open his eyes. He tried to see beyond the surgical gloves and face mask, and he saw how the light picked up on the synthetic fibers in the nurse's hair. He looked closer at those eyes, eyes hidden behind a pair of thick black-rimmed glasses. Dark green eyes that should have been gray.

"It can't...be...can't," Streeter stuttered, the pain now intense.

The nurse watched as Streeter released a strangulated and high-pitched wheezing. The bronchial tubes in his lungs were narrowing and slowly filling with blood. The nurse wasn't concerned when the cannula tore away from Streeter's hand as he rolled off the bed and fell to the floor. There was the sound of bone cracking as Streeter's hip and skull hit the tiled floor. His body was overcome with a violent seizure, and he began to convulse. It would be another ten minutes before Streeter's heart would finally stop beating.

He walked down the short and empty corridor, making a fuss of fiddling with the strings of his mask and lowering his head so that the CCTV cameras wouldn't pick up his face. Caroline, the ward nurse, came out of the staff room with a coffee cup in her hand.

"Morning, Caroline. Have you had your hair done? It looks nice." He finally removed his mask, revealing a full but neatly maintained beard. After listening to her daily rantings about her cheating ex-husband, he knew that Caroline liked the attention he gave her.

"Oh, thank you, Filip." Caroline blushed as she touched the side of her hair. "I fancied a change. It's a bit short but I'm getting used to it."

"It suits you. Reminds me of Demi Moore in *Indecent Proposal*. Have you ever seen that film?"

"No, I haven't."

"Great film."

"I'll try to download it." Caroline sat down and logged into the computer, unable to meet Filip's eye. "Have you checked on Streeter and Marston?"

"All done. Marston was moaning as per usual, but he cheered up when the ambulance finally arrived to pick him up and I gave Streeter his meds, so he'll probably be out of it for a while."

"Thank God. The man creeps me out. I overhead him talking to his lawyer last night, saying how close he was to the real killer. He was going on about writing a book or selling his story to the papers." Caroline shivered dramatically. "I thought to myself, I could get in there first, speak to the papers, for a fee."

"You heard everything he said?" Filip walked over to Caroline's desk and perched on the edge.

"The walls are thin and there wasn't much going on." Caroline looked up at him. "I can't believe it's your last day. It's such a shame. It was really nice working with you, even if it was for a short while."

"It was only temporary until something permanent came along," said Filip, placing his hand on Caroline's shoulder. "I really enjoyed working with you. Why don't you give me your number and I'll give you a call? We could organize a film night."

"That would be fantastic." Caroline almost knocked her coffee over as she scrambled for a Post-it note and a pen.

A few minutes later, still wearing his surgical gloves, he pushed open the side door and walked into the staff parking lot. There weren't any cameras in the parking lot, just warning signs that users of the lot did so at their own risk. Anyone watching the CCTV footage from the prison hospital ward would eventually notice that the nurse always kept his head down or had his back to the camera. He wasn't worried about the cameras recording him getting into a black Hyundai. It was stolen and had fake number plates. He got into the car, turned on the engine and wondered how long it would be before Caroline would finally get off her ass and check on Streeter. It wasn't his concern—he had other things to focus on.

It was time to start a new list.

"Aren't you worried?" asked Jemima, senior paralegal and Elias Piper's lover for the past seventeen months. She blindly searched for her panties, which she knew were somewhere under the leather sofa. "You hear all sorts of stories."

"What are you talking about?" Elias asked with a grin, zipping his trousers.

"I'm talking about the Streeter case," said Jemima. The light from the streetlamp cut through the blinds and placed a spotlight on the photograph of Elias's wife and children. "We've never had a case like this. We've had wins before, but not anything as high profile as this."

"You sound as though you can't believe that *I* actually achieved this."

The adrenalin rush of what she'd just done, sex once again on the sofa with Elias, drifted away. Jemima blinked rapidly as she caught the hardness in his voice. She sat on the floor, temporarily giving up the search for her underwear.

"No. No. That's not what I'm saying at all," she said. "Of course I knew that you could do this and it's a silly thing to get—"

"Silly?"

"That's the wrong word. I didn't mean silly. I…" Jemima paused, searching for the right word that wouldn't kick-start Elias's fiery temper. The last thing she wanted was to lose him. Not after he'd promised her that his relationship with his wife was truly over. This time he was going to leave her.

"I meant that it was a silly thing for *me* to get concerned about, but this case is different."

"Streeter is an innocent man. You saw the evidence," said

Elias. "And even if he wasn't innocent, the prosecution evidence against him couldn't be relied upon. The forensics—"

"I know, I know," Jemima interrupted the well-rehearsed legal submissions that she'd been listening to for months. "I worked on this case just as hard as you did."

"I doubt that," Elias mocked. "And you're forgetting that we have to wait for the CPS to make their decision about whether Streeter will have a retrial or not."

"I can't imagine what the families must be going through," Jemima said. She spotted her panties in the soil of the monstera plant and got up to retrieve them. "They've got to deal with the fact that Streeter may be out on the street and the real killer of their kids is out there somewhere."

"This is about justice not feelings," Elias said, putting on his shoes. "If what Streeter told me is correct, then it's highly probable that the real murderer died years ago."

"You know who did it?" Jemima exclaimed. The lights in the corridor turned on, then quickly turned off again.

"Shit, that's probably the cleaners," said Elias. "The last thing we need is for one of them to come in and put two and two together."

"Who would they tell?" Jemima replied as she sat back down on the sofa. "And how long have you known about the identity of the real—"

"Jemima," Elias said sternly. "Just because we're fucking doesn't entitle you to question me about how I'm conducting my business. Is that understood?"

"Elias, all I was saying—"

"Is that understood? Jesus Christ. It's as if you're determined to ruin what was a good night."

"I'm sorry." Jemima got up and kissed Elias on his cheek. "All I was trying to say is that I'm worried someone out there won't be as happy as we are about the result. And I don't mean the families. You've accused the police of being corrupt, and complicit in putting an innocent man in prison while they left the real killer on the streets."

Elias remained quiet as Jemima kissed his neck.

"Some people may not take too kindly to that, and God knows what they'll say when you reveal you know the name of the person who was responsible. You hear about lawyers being attacked all the time," she said.

"No, you don't. Politicians yes, but not lawyers. People don't come after us. The chances of some loon barging in here with a sawn-off shotgun and blowing us all away is slim to none."

"That's a bit much. I'm only saying that we may have to be more cautious."

"How about I hire a couple of bodyguards? Will that make you happy?"

"Don't mock me, Elias. I may be younger than you but I'm not— What was that?" A series of beeps rang out through the building. "What was that?" she repeated.

Elias stood stock-still when he heard a door opening and closing. "Fuck," he said. "Someone has deactivated the alarm. I told you the cleaners would be coming in."

"You really are overreacting about the cleaners."

"It's my reputation. Not yours," Elias said coldly. "We'll go out the back door. I don't want to bump into them."

"Fine," said Jemima. She walked past Elias in a huff, opened the door and stepped into the hallway. "Give me a minute. I left my bag in my—"

Jemima knew she should scream, but she couldn't. Fear had frozen the muscles in her throat. She was staring at a man wearing a balaclava, and he was holding a large kitchen knife. His presence hadn't activated the motion-sensor lights and the hallway remained encased in darkness. He pushed the point of the knife against Jemima's neck.

"Don't scream," he said softly, as though he was reading a bedtime story to a child. "Get back in there."

"Please," Jemima whispered. The point of the knife lightly pierced her skin, and she felt the warm trickle of blood running down her neck. She stepped unsteadily back into the office.

"Jem…what the—" Elias stopped as his brain attempted to process what he was seeing.

Elias pushed Jemima out of the way and she screamed as she tripped, hitting her head against the sharp edge of the cabinet. There was a dull thud as she fell to the floor, bringing the display of awards and heavy books down on top of her. Elias didn't look back as his university rugby training kicked in. He barged, shoulder first, into the man, causing him to fall heavily against the wall. Elias sprinted down the corridor toward the stairwell. He took the stairs two at a time, determined to make it to the front door.

"No. No!" Elias had reached the door but couldn't open the locks. His next option was the back door, but when he spun around in a fear-filled panic, his exit was blocked.

"What do you want? Money? I'll give you money," Elias pleaded, pushing his hands into his pockets and coming up empty. "Or is it drugs? I can get you drugs if that's what you need?"

"Shut up," the man snarled. He punched Elias hard in the face.

Elias's head slammed against the metal lock on the door. He tried to fight back but was too slow to stop the second and third blows raining down on his face. It was the third blow that rendered him unconscious and, had he known what was waiting for him, he would have wished that he'd died in that moment.

14

"Do you need to talk?" Rob asked as he picked up the last of Emma's toys and placed them in the toy box. "I swear that these things multiply by themselves."

"She's spoiled," said Henley. She was sitting on the sofa, feet curled underneath her. She took a long sip of her vodka and tonic. "Everyone is always buying her stuff."

"It's to be expected when she's an only child," Rob replied as he disappeared into the kitchen and returned a few seconds later with a bottle of beer. He sat next to Henley. "And before you say anything, that wasn't a dig about having another kid. I was just saying, she's the only one."

"It's fine. Don't worry about it."

"We need to start doing something else with our evenings," Rob said as he looked quizzically at his bottle of beer before he popped the top. "Give it a couple of months and we'll be sneaking our empties into number twenty-four's recycling bins to cover our tracks."

"Don't even joke about it," said Henley, stretching her legs out onto Rob's lap. "We need a holiday. Two weeks away where we don't have to worry about hiding the wine bottles in next-door's wheelie bin."

"We could do it. Your dad or my parents could take Ems for a couple of weeks, and we can get away."

"Leave Emma? Our Emma for two entire weeks? And what about the dog?"

"Simon can look after her. The kids love her. Or your dad could take both Emma and Luna. I can have a chat with him about it when he gets back from Grenada."

"If he gets back," Henley replied. "Uncle Patrick has convinced him to extend his ticket for another six weeks."

"Lucky him," said Rob. "To be fair, he does deserve it."

"Yeah, he does." Henley thought of all her dad been through in the past eighteen months, with the loss of his wife and the struggles with his mental health. "I suppose we could join him out there. All three of us. It's not as if Uncle Patrick doesn't have the room."

"That's not a bad idea," Rob said brightly. It was impossible for Henley to miss the spark in his eyes. "I'll look at some flights later. I'm sure you've got loads of leave to take."

"That's an understatement."

"Cool. That's something to look forward to. Anyway, stop avoiding my question." Rob placed his free hand on Henley's leg. "Do you need to talk? The idea that Streeter might be released has been all over the news since yesterday and you've hardly said a word about it."

"He won't be released, that would be madness," Henley replied with a huff. She downed the rest of her drink. "The Court of Appeal have given the CPS fourteen days to make a decision about what they're going to do next, and I can't believe they wouldn't find a way to keep him in jail."

"You need to prepare yourself for the possibility that they

might decide to let him go, or grant him bail while they make their decision."

"No way. Absolutely not." Henley pulled herself up. "Can you imagine how it would look if they granted Streeter bail and he goes off on a killing spree while the CPS are making up their mind?"

"So, you're not even going to consider the possibility of Streeter being out?"

"It's a nonissue. It's not going to happen, and you don't have to worry about me disappearing to my bed because I can't cope."

"But what about the stuff about Rhimes? The Court of Appeal judgment mentioned him specifically," Rob pressed. "It's all over the news, Anj. Bloody hell, it was the lead topic on *Newsnight* yesterday. Give it a week and I promise you there will be a podcast about it. Police corruption. Another murder case from the nineties where corrupt police officers allowed a murderer to walk free while an innocent man rotted in prison."

"Rob, I don't want to talk about Rhimes. I can't talk about him and what he…what he might have done. Rhimes wasn't corrupt. You can't be sitting here and telling me you believe that."

Rob leaned his head back and took a long drink of his beer. "It doesn't matter what I think. What do you think?"

"I told you I don't want to talk about it." Henley swung her legs off his lap and sat on the edge of the sofa. "It's complicated."

"How on earth is it complicated?" asked Rob. "Every day you assess evidence and conclude if the person sitting in front of you is a thief, liar or murderer. How can—"

"Rhimes wasn't any of those things. He was a friend."

"He was *your* friend really."

Henley shifted away from her husband. "So, what does that make Stanford? Is he only *my* friend?"

"Don't be ridiculous." Rob finished his beer and placed the empty bottle in the crook of the sofa. "Stanford is different.

He's one of Emma's godfathers, for Christ sakes, but I know you, Anj. I know you better than you think I do. I know when you're hurting, when you're happy, when you're keeping secrets and when you have doubts, and you have doubts about Rhimes. Big doubts."

"You're reading too much into this."

"Am I? I sleep with you, and I wake up with you. I've seen you laugh, and I've seen you cry. So, I can't believe that none of this is affecting you."

"Rhimes was not corrupt. It's that simple," Henley said determinedly.

"Is it though?" asked Rob. "I haven't read the entire court judgment, but I have heard the bit they keep repeating, it's all over Twitter—the compelling evidence that calls into question the credibility of the investigating police officer. They didn't pull that out of thin air."

Henley swallowed back the guilt of knowing she was keeping another secret from Rob. She could tell him about her visit to see Streeter, and Kerry Huggins' revelations about Rhimes bribing her. But if she spoke it out loud, gave it oxygen, then it could only mean one thing. That she had doubts.

"I've told you that I don't want to talk about it. You don't listen and then you wonder why we have problems."

"*We* don't have problems, Anjelica. *You* have a problem. You're acting as though I've done something wrong. I'm not the enemy. I'm your husband."

Henley froze as the iron tone in Rob's voice hit hard. He only ever used her full name when he felt backed into a corner. The use of her full name was a warning. She stood up and tried to think of something to fill the deadly silence, but there was nothing.

"You're not the enemy," she finally said. "But put yourself in my shoes. I can't believe that Rhimes would have done anything to jeopardize a case—"

"Maybe he'd changed when you were working with him. We're talking about the nineties here. I'm not saying that the police are any bet—" Rob broke off and held his hands up apologetically as Henley shot him the dirtiest of looks.

"I am the police," she said coldly. "I can put up with the scrutiny and the questions out on the streets but not in my own house, Rob."

"All I'm saying is, they were making their own rules and breaking all the ones they should have been following back then. Even you must see that."

"All I see is that someone out there is using an innocent dead cop as a scapegoat. That's my objective view."

"No, that's your stubborn view. You're only saying this because you're upset. No one wants to think the worst of someone they care about."

Henley's phone began to ring, breaking the tense silence.

"I'm coming straight back. We're not done." Henley stalked into the hallway and rummaged in her bag. She could have sworn her ringtone was becoming more insistent as the ringing ended and then immediately started again.

"What took you so long?" Stanford asked when she picked up. "I almost called your landline."

"I was…never mind. Are you OK?" Henley asked, registering the agitation in his voice.

"Have you seen the news?"

"No," Henley replied slowly. Her phone began to beep repetitively with the arrival of several text messages. She walked back into the living room. "Why, what's happened?"

"Go and turn on the TV. It doesn't matter which news channel you turn on. It's on all of them."

"What's on all of them?"

Henley grabbed the remote control, turned on the television and found BBC News. She grew cold as the overflow of emotions rushed through her body and her frustration with Rob was quickly replaced by cold tentacles of dread and panic.

"…*This is tragic for everyone involved. We all thought that this case was resolved twenty-five years ago but the Court of Appeal, by overturning the convictions of Andrew Streeter on Monday morning, has created a horrific domino effect that has put this case back to square one.*"

"*Do we know if Andrew Streeter was aware that the CPS had taken the decision not to retry him for the five murders before he died?*"

"*As far as we're aware, there was a meeting that took place yesterday, Tuesday the fifteenth of June, between the Director of Public Prosecutions, Katherine Gayle, the Acting Metropolitan Police Commissioner, Franklyn Tasshaw, and the Home Secretary where it was confirmed by the senior reviewing lawyer that the CPS would not be pursuing a second trial of Andrew Streeter.*"

"*To be clear, with the prosecution confirming that there was no longer a case against Andrew Streeter, shouldn't he have been released immediately?*"

"*Well, that's what should have happened, but that is where the confusion lies. A representative from the Redemption Foundation stated on social media that they hadn't received any notification from the CPS that they were dropping the case against Streeter. But according to the court records the CPS had formally served a notice of discontinuance on the digital court system yesterday afternoon at 4:52 p.m. The Redemption Foundation is adamant that they did not receive a copy of that notice of discontinuance.*"

"*If the Redemption Foundation is correct, then Andrew Streeter was technically being unlawfully held in prison from 4:52 p.m. yesterday afternoon.*"

"*That's correct, but shortly after 9:00 p.m. tonight, almost an hour ago, the Redemption Foundation was informed that Andrew Streeter was dead.*"

"Do we know how he died?"

"No, Jean. No. We know nothing about the cause of death. We do know that Andrew Streeter had been diagnosed with cancer—Hodgkin's lymphoma—but as to the actual cause of death we don't know. And we don't know when exactly Andrew Streeter died. Unnamed sources have said that Streeter may have died yesterday morning, but we have yet to receive an official confirmation from the prison. What is clear is that there are many unanswered questions. Why was the Redemption Foundation not informed that there was no longer a case against Streeter? And how and when did Andrew Streeter die?"

"Henley. Hey, are you there?" asked Stanford.

"Yeah, I'm still here," Henley said, dropping the remote control into Rob's lap and slowly sitting down. "I don't know what to say. I don't know what to even think. This is...it doesn't make any sense."

"I'll tell you what I think," said Stanford. "This is not a good thing. Not a good thing at all."

"Whatever you want. Whatever you need. Tell me. I'll give it to you."

Elias's voice was hoarse from the hours spent screaming out in the dark to no one. The last thing he remembered was that someone wearing a balaclava had punched him hard in the face. He had no idea if Jemima had called the police and told them that he'd been kidnapped or if she'd done nothing because he'd pushed her aside like rubbish to save his own life. He squeezed his eyes shut as pain pinched at the nerves around his temple and he felt his blood pulsating around the bruise on the back of his head. His fingers probed the bruised spot. Strands of hair were bonded together by blood. He ran his fingers over the thick dried blood but stopped when the terrain of his scalp changed from dry blood to blood that was warm and oozing.

"Please," he shouted. "We can talk."

His unanswered words echoed around the windowless room. He stretched out his hands, surprised that he hadn't been restrained. No gag or blindfold. He stood up, wincing as the muscles in his right calf protested. He could smell himself. Stale sex and body odor. He ran his hands blindly along the wall as he continued to cough, the force of it rattling his chest. A slim line of light appeared on the floor. He walked toward the light, hands out, searching for what he knew was a door. He ran his finger along the groove.

"What the—" He pushed his index finger into the rough hole where the door handle should have been. He winced as the splintered wood scratched the thin and sensitive skin on his finger. He angled his finger and gripped the side of the door, but there was nothing as he pulled. The door would not give an inch. His stomach rumbled. The last thing he'd eaten had been an overpriced tuna melt, but that was...

Elias quickly unbuttoned his left sleeve and rolled it up. It was there. Still on his wrist. A smartwatch. He'd bought the watch three weeks ago after he saw the updated version being advertised. He liked new things. It went back to his childhood, all those years of being the recipient of his brothers' hand-me-downs. Hiding from the bailiffs and having to watch his mother standing in the kitchen, eating the leftovers from their plates after their dad cleaned out their bank accounts and disappeared with his too-young girlfriend. He remembered charging the watch in his office around lunchtime because he'd forgotten to charge it the night before. The salesman had promised all-day charge and even longer if he placed it on battery-saving mode. He pressed his finger against the black screen and waited. There was nothing.

"Shit. Come on."

Elias pressed the screen again, hard. He pursed his mouth shut as the screen came to life. It was 03:38. Battery life 8 percent. Elias swiped the screen and zoomed in on the messages app. He wasn't sure if it would even work. He had no idea if he was in a basement or in an attic. A garage or a store cupboard in a multistory parking facility. Elias sat down with his back against the door. The thin slither of light remained, but he couldn't hear anything—not that it mattered. He didn't plan to make a call. He didn't have enough battery life for that, but he could send a text.

15

Dominique Piper placed her finger on the doorbell for the Redemption Foundation and held it there. This was only the third time since the foundation had opened its doors that she had visited her husband's office, choosing instead to focus on her own legal career and ambitions. Ambitions that Elias had said more than once were unrealistic.

"For God's sake, open the door!" Dominique shouted.

Finally the intercom buzzed and the irritated voice of the office manager rang out.

"How many times do I have to tell you: we are not commenting—"

"Marshall, open this bloody door. It's Dominique."

"Oh bollocks, one sec. It's open."

Dominique released an impatient breath and pushed the door open as soon as she heard the click of the locking mechanism releasing.

"I'm sorry about that, Dominique," said Marshall, hurrying to meet her. "It's been an absolute bloody nightmare ever since—"

"Where's Elias?" Dominique demanded, barging past him. She made her way up the stairs to the first floor, ignoring the stares of the staff members. "I've been trying to call him ever since you left me a voice message asking if I'd heard from him. His phone is going straight to voicemail."

"He isn't here," Marshall replied, following her into Elias's office.

"Has he been in at all this morning?" asked Dominique, looking around the office impatiently.

"He usually works from home on Thursdays and Fridays, but with all the publicity from the Streeter case…"

"Probably out ambulance chasing and booking more TV appearances," Dominique said knowingly.

"Streeter's case is the big one. I can't see him pushing it aside, especially after what's happened," Marshall said as he walked over to Elias's desk. "I thought… Dominique, when was the last time that you saw him?"

"Wednesday morning. He dropped me off at Euston station, I've been in Manchester visiting my mother—she had a fall. I came back this morning."

"I'm sure there's a good explanation. It's like you said. He's probably out seeing a client and didn't put it in the diary. You know what he's like."

"Marshall, I am so sorry. I burst in here like a bat out of—" Dominique put a hand to her mouth, her face flushed with embarrassment. "It's been a tough time with mum and it's made me… I haven't been myself. I've obviously overacted to the message that you left me."

"Don't apologize," Marshall said. He looked around the office, searching for anything that might have been out of place, but there was nothing there. "You're probably right. Elias is out there chasing opportunities."

"Exactly. Elias doesn't know how to be present and be still," said Dominique as she adjusted her bag on her arm. "He's always thinking about the next big case. I keep telling him to take a break. He's never been the best at—"

"Yeah," Marshall replied distractedly as he picked up Elias's "Lawyer of the Year 2019" award and ran his finger along a groove where the glass had chipped.

"Marshall, are you even listening to me?" Dominique said, tapping him on the shoulder.

"What? Sorry," Marshall said, placing the award back on the shelf. "You said you're going home?"

"I didn't say that, but that's what I'm going to do. I'll call you if I hear from him," Dominique said and then walked out of the office.

Marshall picked up the award again and took a closer look at the chipped glass. Elias was too much of a narcissist not to notice that one of his accolades was damaged. Marshall couldn't ignore the feeling that Dominique was not overreacting. He walked over to the built-in wardrobe where Elias kept his suit jackets. The pricklings of anxiety heightened when he saw the bespoke charcoal-gray suit jacket with the emerald green lining hanging there—the same jacket that Elias was wearing on Wednesday. When he checked the pockets and found Elias's wallet and car keys, he knew something was very wrong.

Marshall ran out of the building onto Upper Street and turned the corner onto Richmond Grove, a quiet enclave of residential apartments and off-street private parking spaces. Marshall shakily held out the keys and pressed the car fob, hoping that the blue E-Pace Jaguar SUV wasn't the same car that Elias drove. That hope was dashed when the indicator lights flashed and the alarm let out its trio of beeps to confirm that its security system had been deactivated.

11:58:17

*END OF DATA AUTOMATICALLY COPIED FROM
OPEN PROMPT*

ENTERED BY: CHS (c701654) AT: 11:59:01

Operator: 999—Do you need fire, police, or ambulance?
^INFT: I need to speak to the police.
Operator: What is your emergency?
^INFT: My boss, Elias Piper, is missing.
Operator: You will need to call 101.
^INFT: Why do I need to call 101? 101 is for nonemergencies. Can't
you put me through to the police. It's—
Operator: Sir, could you please not shout. What's your name?
^INFT: Marshall Wollerton. My boss hasn't been—
Operator: Transferring you now.

12:07:36

Operator 2: 101—How can I help you?
^INFT: I need to report a missing person. His name is Elias Piper.
He's a solicitor.
Operator 2: Are you sure that he's missing?
^INFT: Well…he didn't turn up for work.
Operator: Is this person a member of your family or a friend?
^INFT: No. I told you, he's my boss. His wife hasn't seen him since
Wednesday morning and it's now Friday.
Operator: Has his wife reported him missing?
^INFT: (inaudible)…she came to the office, but she hasn't reported
him.
Operator: Sir, it's probably nothing. You can report him missing at
your local police station if he doesn't turn up by Saturday.

^**INFT:** I haven't got a local police station. This is ridiculous. Can you put me back through to 999?
Operator: No. 999 is for emergencies, and this isn't an emergency.

***** END OF CALL

12:11:54

Concern For Safety: (LOW)
Urgency: (LOW)
Action: (NONE)

"We've got a missing person case."

"We don't do missing people," said Stanford, kicking the paper drawer of the photocopier that was refusing to cooperate with his request. "And why are we, the Serial Crime Unit, taking…" Stanford gave the photocopier a final kick and muttered a stream of obscenities under his breath as the photocopier finally complied and began to work.

"Because we've been ordered to, which is why you're here on a Sunday morning, on Father's Day, which I apologize for," said Pellacia, connecting his laptop to the smartboard.

"And which we probably won't be getting overtime for," Stanford volleyed back. He picked up his clutch of still-warm papers and made his way back to the desk.

"Are you OK?" Henley whispered, placing her hand gently on Stanford's arm.

"Do you need to ask?" Stanford replied, turning his attention toward Pellacia. "Dragging us in at ten in the morning for a missing person. It better be the bloody queen who's done a runner."

"We'll talk later." Henley gave his arm a squeeze. It had been two weeks since Stanford had received the latest setback in his adoption process with the match and then unmatch of a prospective child after the paternal great-uncle had made threats to take the council to court after he'd been informed that his great-nephew would potentially be adopted by a gay couple.

"As I stated in my email, the SCU has been allocated a missing person case, which I don't need you to remind me, is not our usual remit," said Pellacia.

"That's an understatement. It says serial crime unit on the door," Stanford snorted.

"I don't need a running commentary from you, Stanford. Keep it shut until I'm done."

Stanford mimed zipping his mouth shut.

"Our missing person is a high-profile individual and linked to the Andrew Streeter case."

The identity of the missing person had been notably absent in Pellacia's email. The tension burned and strangled the tendons in Henley's neck as she sat impassively, waiting for Pellacia to reveal his hand.

"The case of Andrew Streeter has made national headlines for two reasons," said Pellacia. "Firstly, the Court of Appeal ruling overturning Streeter's murder convictions, and then the CPS's decision not—"

"I can't believe the Court of Appeal did that," Eastwood interrupted, peeling off the cover on her container of strawberries.

"Did you wash those first?" Ramouter asked. He looked at Eastwood critically as she popped one into her mouth.

"Of course I did. What do you take me for?"

"To be honest, I'm more shocked that you're actually eating fruit."

"Excuse me," Pellacia said. "Bloody hell, would it kill you to pay attention? Streeter's conviction was overturned on Monday and then the CPS made the ludicrous decision not to have a retrial."

"I heard there were protests outside the court and the CPS offices," said Stanford. "Not that anyone could blame them. How are you feeling about it, Henley?"

Henley shrugged. "Am I happy? Not at all. Do I want this to be dragged up again after twenty-odd years? Definitely not. Am I pissed about a dead cop's name being dragged through the mud and him being used as a scapegoat? Yes. Do I give a shit that Streeter is dead?"

"Absolutely fucking not," Eastwood concluded, biting into another strawberry.

Pellacia cleared his throat. "On Friday, at 11:59 a.m., Elias Piper, the solicitor instructed by Andrew Streeter, was reported missing by the Redemption Foundation office manager, Marshall Wollerton. If you look at the screen, you will see a CAD transcript of the call to 999 that obviously went nowhere."

"They didn't try very hard," said Ramouter, reading through the transcript. "Just fobbed him off."

"No disagreement there," said Pellacia. "This is the last footage that we have of Piper. Here he is, giving a statement outside the Royal Courts of Justice after their ruling on Monday."

"Before you press play," said Henley. "I can't be the only one thinking this: Streeter is reported dead on the same day that Piper goes missing. Don't you think there's something suspicious about the timings?"

"There hasn't been anything to suggest that Streeter's death was not natural," Eastwood countered.

"Not yet," said Stanford.

"Look, I know that you're all pissed off about being here, but let's concentrate on the task in hand," said Pellacia as he pressed play.

The team fell into silence as the face of Elias Piper, full of arrogance and pomposity, filled the screen. The sun picked up the fine strands in his tie as he stroked the navy silk. The bustle of journalists and early lunchtime city traffic couldn't cover up the sounds of people screaming venomously in Piper's direction. Piper turned around as a woman holding a large blue sign emblazoned with the words "Justice for the Five" ran into the background before she was removed by police, but that wasn't what caught Henley's attention. A petite black woman stood behind Piper, holding a large lever-arch file, her gaze fixed on Elias. Henley leaned forward, to be clear about the look she was seeing in the woman's eyes. It was more than pride. It was adoration.

"For twenty-five years Andrew Streeter protested his innocence. He stood in a court of law and spoke his truth and the jury delivered a verdict that caused irreparable damage to his life. Andrew wants me, as his instructing solicitor, to make it clear that he does not blame the jury for the verdict they delivered. He understands that they made a judgment based on the evidence that was before them, evidence that we now know was handled by corrupt police officers.

"This miscarriage of justice has not yet been fully rectified. Make no mistake, lives have been ruined. Families have suffered. This ordeal has been traumatic for everyone involved and I fully understand the confusion, anger and hurt that the families of the victims are undoubtedly feeling. Andrew Streeter protested his innocence from day one. It was never his intention to drag out or add to the horrific ordeal of losing a loved one in such terrible circumstances. Andrew's fear was that he would die in prison with the unfortunate legacy of being a murderer. The fact that he was diagnosed with cancer made that fear even more unbearable, but we fought hard, and the right decision has been made. We hope that Andrew Streeter will be given the opportunity to live the rest of his life in peace and that the police will use their resources to do what should have been done twenty-five years ago and find the real murderer. Thank you. Yes. I'll take a few questions."

"Sounds like a twat," said Stanford.

"Enough," said Pellacia, pausing the video. "According to the initial report, Elias Piper was reported missing by Marshall Wollerton at 11:59 a.m. on Friday. Fifteen minutes after that call ended, at 12:26 p.m., Piper's wife, Dominique, called 999. She was told the same thing, to call 101, which she did at 12:38 p.m."

Pellacia picked up the sheet of paper that he'd placed on the desk earlier. "Dominique Piper made a second 999 call at 8:23 a.m. yesterday morning, and was again told to call 101," he said.

Ramouter turned around and opened his laptop and started typing. "So, it wasn't the young black woman standing next to him outside the court who reported him missing?" he asked. "Jemima Brisby. Paralegal at the Redemption Foundation."

"Why would you think she would be the one to call the police?" Pellacia asked. He rewound the footage to the right place, and then hit pause.

"Look at her," said Ramouter. "Look at how she's looking at him. She's close but not too close, but it's the way she's staring at him. It's… I don't know. Almost intimate."

Henley felt a swell of pride.

"You can tell all that from a couple of minutes of film?" Pellacia asked.

"I'm not an expert in body language or anything, but…"

"I agree. There's something," Henley concluded.

"You two are spending too much time together," Pellacia muttered. "Anyway, Dominique Piper also went in person to Bishopsgate police station on Friday afternoon, which we all know is under the jurisdiction of the City of London Police. She reported her husband missing at the front desk. A PC from the Community Support Unit took a statement, logged it on HOLMES but failed to either log it as a missing person investigation or to transfer it back to the Metropolitan Police."

"Shit," said Stanford. "So, they've done fuck all with this and now we're being dumped with it. They were supposed to have logged Piper's disappearance with the UK Missing Persons Unit seventy-two hours after he went missing. According to that transcript Piper has been missing since Wednesday which means that seventy-two-hour clock ran out yesterday."

"I still don't understand why we've been allocated this case," said Henley, trying to calm the growing swell of mutiny.

"Elias Piper received threats from the minute he took on Andrew Streeter as a client," explained Pellacia.

"What sort of threats? A keyboard warrior having a moan on Twitter isn't usually our thing," said Stanford.

"This was a lot more than a social media rant," said Pellacia. "Bricks through windows, complaints to the Solicitors Disciplinary Tribunal, threatening phone calls, slashed car tires and a physical assault."

"An assault by whom?" asked Eastwood.

"By a relative of victim number five, about two months ago. I haven't got the full details." Pellacia eyed the team. "I don't want to hear any moaning about caseload, because we've already handed over the arson investigation to the NCA and the moped robbery investigation has stalled, so we've got capacity. Ramouter, you're taking lead on the Elias Piper case."

"Hold on. Me?" Ramouter straightened in his chair. "Of course."

"I wouldn't get too excited," said Stanford. "This will be the equivalent of investigating a missing crate of ginger beer from the local church fair."

"Are you OK with this?" Henley asked Ramouter. She had followed him to the kitchen area and switched on the kettle.

"You don't think that I can handle it," Ramouter said with a grin, picking up two mugs from the draining board.

"You know full well that's—"

Henley stopped as the repetitive wail of an alarm pierced the air. She closed her eyes and covered her ears, waiting for the regulatory twenty-five seconds to pass before the alarm reset itself.

"Bloody hell. I thought they'd replaced it?" Ramouter asked once it was quiet again.

"God forbid anyone actually tries to break in. It probably

wouldn't even work," Henley said, fishing around the drawer
for a spoon. "And I wasn't insinuating that you couldn't handle
this Piper case. I know on the surface it looks like a straightforward missing person's case but—"

"People like Elias Piper don't just disappear."

"You need to stop doing that. Finishing off my sentences.
It's disturbing."

"Sorry." Ramouter grinned, not sorry at all.

Henley rolled her eyes. "Anyway, it's true. People like him
don't just disappear into the night."

"It must have something to do with Streeter. The death
threats. I don't mean to pry, but was there anything in his letters to you that—"

"No," Henley said, far too quickly. "Get the full crime report
and let me know what your game plan is."

She tried to ignore the heavy weight in her stomach. Even
without any concrete evidence, she would be a fool not to think
that Streeter's death and Piper's disappearance were linked.

Ramouter put his mug back in the cupboard. "I'll let you
know my game plan once I'm back."

"Back from where?"

"Back from seeing Piper's wife. See if she knows anything
about that member of staff giving Piper the doe eyes."

"On your own?" Henley couldn't help but sound skeptical.

"You're acting like I'm eight years old and I'm going to the
corner shop on my own for the first time."

"I want you to go into this with your eyes wide open, that's
all. Being the OIC, because that's what you are, the officer in
the case, that comes with—"

"Don't tell me you're going to give me the Spider-Man responsibility speech," Ramouter smirked.

"Ramouter," Henley said sternly. "I'm serious."

"Sorry, boss. I know you are."

"I could go and see Dominique Piper, while you go home and enjoy what's left of Father's Day with your son."

"Honestly, it's fine," said Ramouter. "I doubt it'll take that long. Anyway, I've already experienced the best part of Father's Day with Ethan bringing me burnt toast and weak tea in bed this morning."

"Fine. Fine," Henley said with resignation. "Keep in mind, this isn't going to be your average missing persons case. I doubt that Piper's disappearance and Streeter's death taking place within forty-eight hours is a coincidence."

"Got it. Anything else?"

"Piper's wife will ask you to promise her that you'll find her husband and bring him home." Henley looked Ramouter dead in the eye. "Don't. Do not make promises you can't keep."

16

Dominique Piper looked as though she hadn't slept for days—her face was swollen and flushed from crying.

"I'm sorry about the mess," she said as she sat down on the sofa, clutching a glass of water. "It's been...our cleaner doesn't come in until tomorrow morning and it's just been... God, I can't believe this is happening."

"You don't have to apologize," said Ramouter, looking around a room that might have been lifted from the pages of *Ideal Home* magazine. If Dominique thought this room was a mess then she needed to visit his flat, which was nothing short of a bomb site.

"It's funny how the things you thought mattered seem unimportant when you're in the midst of a crisis." Dominique pulled a used tissue out of her pocket and blew her nose.

"Are you here on your own?" Ramouter asked. He scanned the black-and-white photographs on the wall of candid family photos. "You have children?"

Dominique nodded and wiped at the tears streaming down her face. "We've got three. The twins, Madison and Autumn, they're nineteen, and our son, Asher, he's twenty-one. They're all away at uni."

"You don't look old enough," Ramouter said with a smile. "Have you told them that their dad is missing?"

"You're too kind and no, I haven't told them because I thought that Elias would be home by now. No point worrying them for no reason."

"How often do you speak to your kids?"

"I try not to bother them too much. They used to complain about me being in their business when they lived here, so now I speak to them every couple of weeks. But I text them a lot."

"So, you don't know if they've spoken to their dad recently?"

"They wouldn't have. Elias has a more 'hands off' approach to parenting. Which isn't a bad thing. He wants them to be independent."

"But what about today? It's Father's Day."

"Elias isn't into that sort of thing. He calls it commercialized nonsense."

Ramouter took another look at the photographs. Elias was absent from most of them. "I'm not sure if you were informed that the unit I'm attached to, the Serial Crime Unit, is going to be looking into your husband's disappearance."

"No one has told me anything," Dominique said bitterly. "They treated me as though I was a nuisance. How can someone going missing not be considered an emergency?"

"I'm going to ask you a few questions to clarify things," Ramouter said, opening his notebook. "As I understand it, you didn't become aware of your husband's disappearance until Friday morning?"

"That's correct." Dominique sat up straighter and clasped her hands in her lap. "I last saw Elias on Wednesday morning when he dropped me off at Euston station. My mum had a fall. She lives in Manchester, and I went straight up there. I spoke to him around lunchtime to let him know that I arrived, and that Mum wasn't as bad as we'd thought."

"How was he when you spoke to him?"

"He was still excited about the Court of Appeal verdict. We didn't talk for long because he had to get ready for a radio interview. There were a couple of texts in the early evening, but that was the last time that I heard from him. I called him on... Oh my God—"

Dominique sprang from her seat and ran out of the living room. A few seconds later, she returned with a mobile phone in her outstretched hand.

"This is Elias's phone. I completely forgot—my mind has been all over the place. The intern—Nola or Nova, apparently—she found it down the side of the sofa in Elias's office and she gave it to Marshall, who gave it to me. I thought that I would hold on to it until the police came this weekend, but...well, they never came. Could this help you find out what's happened to him?"

"Are you sure this is his?" Ramouter asked, taking hold of the phone. He turned it around and saw that the case was personalized with the Redemption Foundation's logo.

"Yes—that's his case. The battery's dead though. I tried to charge it, but I can't find the right cable."

"I'll see what we can do." He put the phone in his pocket and made a mental note to hand the phone over to Ezra, the SCU's resident forensic computer analyst, as soon as possible. "Did Elias ever express any concerns about his safety?"

"No, nothing. I know there were some complaints and protests about the Streeter case but, to be honest, I don't really get involved in the foundation's business. Criminal and human rights law isn't my area of expertise. I specialize in bankruptcy and insolvency litigation for a firm in the City."

"Is that why you reported Elias missing at Bishopsgate police station on Friday?"

"Yes, I went to the office to collect some things. I wanted to work from home in case Elias turned up." Dominique walked over to the large window. "I even slept downstairs on the sofa on Friday and Saturday night, so I wouldn't miss him if he opened the front door. I'm scared that something terrible has happened to him."

"We're going to do everything we can to find your husband," Ramouter said, and joined Dominique at the window. He counted to three before he asked the question that had been on the tip of his tongue since he'd seen the video of Piper delivering his statement outside the Court of Appeal.

"Mrs. Piper—"

"You can call me Dominique. I really don't mind," she cut in, turning to face him.

"Dominique, I don't want you to think that I'm prying, but I need to ask you about your marriage. How were things between you and Elias?"

Dominique sighed heavily. "I'm not going to lie and say that we had the perfect marriage. We've had problems in the past. I was on the verge of leaving him about two years ago." She walked back to the sofa and sat down.

He had a pretty good idea why, but asked the question anyway: "Why was that?"

"There's no point hiding it. These things always have a way of coming out." Dominique picked up a tepid glass of water from the coffee table. "I had an affair."

"Oh." Ramouter made no effort to hide his surprise.

"I was going through a lot. My son had left for uni and I knew that the twins would be following him shortly. Elias was so busy with work and I felt...neglected, a bit lost. At one point I even accused Elias of cheating on me with one of the trainees in his office, but I was transferring my own deceit onto him."

"The person you had an affair with, did—"

"Her name is Lisa, and we no longer work together. She transferred to our firm's Chicago office. It was a mistake and we've been…our marriage has been better. I'm not saying that he's perfect—my guilt has probably made me blind to some of his flaws—but things are better than they were," Dominique said unconvincingly. "So, what happens next?"

"Well," Ramouter paused. He tried not to get too distracted by the slight glimmer of optimism in Dominique's eyes and remembered Henley's advice. "We're going to do everything we can to find your husband."

"Promise me that you'll find him and—" Dominique's pleading stopped abruptly at the sound of the doorbell ringing.

"Excuse me," she said, darting out of the room.

Ramouter heard the front door opening and closing and then the sound of something being dropped on the floor. It was hard to miss the disappointment on Dominique's face when she returned to the room. "It was just Amazon."

"There was something that I wanted to ask you before I go," said Ramouter. "We have information that your husband was assaulted a few months ago by a relative of one of Streeter's victims. Do you know anything about that?"

Dominique's eyes widened with surprise. "Do you think that man had something to do with Elias's disappearance?"

Ramouter narrowed his eyes. "What do you know?"

"Only that this man was waiting for Elias outside the office. He punched him and slashed his car tires. I begged Elias to press charges, but he refused. That was months ago, though."

"Thank you. That's really helpful." Ramouter put his notebook away.

"I don't feel helpful," she replied, escorting him to the front door.

"You have been. And before I forget, here's my card. You can call anytime, if you have questions or if anything else comes to mind."

Dominique reached for his card, then gripped his hands. "Promise me that you'll find him."

"Mrs. Piper, I—"

"Promise me," she repeated. "Promise me that you'll bring him home."

"All I can promise is that we'll do our best."

Dominique nodded, clearly disappointed. As the door closed behind him, Ramouter was already wondering if it had been a mistake even to promise that he would do his best to find Elias Piper. He sighed. All he wanted to do was go home and rescue what was left of Father's Day.

"Morning, everyone." Ramouter nervously cleared his throat and took a sip from the bottle of water in his hands.

"Aw bless. He looks like he's doing show-and-tell for the first time," Eastwood jested as she swiveled from side to side in her chair.

"Honestly, it's like herding cats sometimes," Pellacia huffed. "Can you show DC Ramouter a bit of respect? This isn't a bloody joke." With that, Pellacia took his seat at the back of the room and gave a nod to Ramouter. Ezra hovered by the door with his tablet in his hand.

"Ezra, get in here and stop hanging around the door like a bad smell," Henley shouted, taking a seat at her desk.

"I'm just checking that you haven't got any disturbing images on that whiteboard of yours," Ezra said, before cautiously entering the room. When he saw that the whiteboard was devoid of images, he sat down at the spare desk. "I'm not as cold and detached as you lot. I've got feelings."

"Thanks for coming down, Ez," said Ramouter. "Right. Elias Piper has been missing since Wednesday evening. According to his wife, Dominique, who I met yesterday, she last saw her husband at 6:00 a.m. on Wednesday morning. He dropped her off at Euston so that she could catch the 6:28 to Manchester. The last sighting was at the Redemption Foundation offices in Islington by Nicholas Drayton, an associate solicitor, who left work at 7:00 p.m. and passed by Piper's office on his way out. Prior to that there had been a celebratory lunch at The Ivy Asia in St. Paul's with everyone who worked on the Andrew Streeter case. According to Drayton, everyone had returned to the office at about 3:00 p.m. It's 8:45 a.m. now, so I would say that Piper has been missing for nearly 108 hours."

"Who paid for the lunch?" Stanford shouted out.

"Why is that relevant?" Henley shot Stanford a dirty look.

"All information is relevant," Stanford said smugly. "Look at you, sticking up for your boy—it's sweet."

"He paid for it. Piper," Ramouter confirmed. He tapped the smartboard and a multicolored PowerPoint emerged. "I've drawn up a timeline."

Henley smirked at Stanford as she saw him taking in Ramouter's handiwork.

"The first attempt to report Piper missing was made at 11:59 a.m. on Friday and the second at 12:26 p.m."

"It's odd that his missus waited so long to report him missing," said Eastwood. "She doesn't hear from him for what, a day and a half, and she only starts making noises about it on Friday when he's been missing for…" Eastwood began counting on her fingers.

"Forty-four hours," Stanford chipped in. "Which places him within that golden window of being found alive. We're on day five now and he hasn't been seen by a member of the public and no one sent his family a ransom demand. The chances are he's already dead."

"Not necessarily," Ramouter said, stepping aside. "But I'll let Ezra explain."

"This is where I get to my *Mission Impossible* bit," Ezra said, bouncing out of his chair and joining Ramouter at the board. "Give me a sec to connect my tablet to the smartboard. We really need to upgrade this equipment. It's from the Dark Ages."

"As I explained in my email, Piper's mobile phone was found

down the side of the sofa in his office by an intern," Ramouter reminded the room while Ezra completed his setup. "We're waiting for CCTV from Islington council, but in the meantime I've got two theories. Either Piper went outside to meet someone, or someone came into the office and abducted him from there and used their own vehicle to transport him. On Thursday morning, Tina, the receptionist was in the office at 8:24 a.m. She said that she saw Piper's jacket hanging on the back of his chair and assumed that he'd come in early and had gone out to the bakery across the road—something he did regularly."

"But I thought the office manager found Piper's jacket in the cupboard?" asked Eastwood.

"That's correct," Ramouter replied. "When I spoke to Tina yesterday, she said she put Piper's jacket in his wardrobe because she knew he was fussy. She then got a call from her son's school at 9:00 a.m. and she left the office."

"So, he went missing after 7:00 p.m. on Wednesday night," said Henley. "What's this got to do with Ezra being up here, grinning like a Cheshire cat?"

"*Mission Impossible* stuff," Ezra repeated with a grin. "Piper's phone is the latest model, with the usual fingerprint and face recognition to gain access."

"Have you managed to get into it?" asked Pellacia.

"You know better than to ask me questions like that, boss. Of course I have. The last answered call was from his wife, last Wednesday at 12:46 p.m., but there's been activity on the phone since I woke it up. Texts, WhatsApp messages, voicemails and missed calls. The majority have been people in his contact list trying to get hold of him. Then, just over half an hour ago, a couple of text message notifications appeared on his phone."

"Text messages from who?" asked Eastwood.

"Please look at the screen. I've screenshotted images from the phone. The first is a notification of a text message to Dominique Piper."

"What's the big deal about his missus sending him a text message?" asked Stanford.

"You're so impatient," Ezra replied. "Hold on a minute, grandad."

"Smart mouth," said Stanford, but he was smiling.

"As you can see, there are two screenshots. The first is of two text messages being sent from Piper's phone to his wife's phone."

"Hold on. Did you say *from* his phone?" Stanford said, sitting up straighter. "*From* his phone, not *to* his phone?"

"Please look up at the screen," Ezra said with a grin.

To: Dominique (mobile)
Text Message: 17 June, 03:39
Help. Someone took me. don't kno whereee I

To: Dominique (mobile)
Text Message: 17 June, 03:40
Call Poli

"Poli? He must have meant 'Call police.' Did his wife get those messages?" Henley asked Ramouter.

"She did, but she only told me about them"—Ramouter checked his watched—"half an hour before I started the briefing."

"Hold on," Henley did the mental arithmetic.

"Eighty-two hours." Stanford was quicker. "An eighty-two-hour gap between Dominique Piper receiving the text messages and telling us."

"But you saw her yesterday," said Henley. "Why didn't she tell you about the text messages then?"

"I don't think that was on purpose," explained Ezra. "Mrs. Piper said Elias had a smartwatch, right? The notification didn't appear on Piper's phone until thirty-five minutes ago, after we'd charged it and turned it on, which means that transmission of the message from his smartwatch to his wife was delayed."

"What would cause the delay?" asked Pellacia.

"Most likely explanation is that the message was stuck in the cloud somewhere because there was no reception when he first sent it."

"There could be many reasons he has no reception," said Ramouter. "He could be out in the sticks somewhere."

"Or the signal was interrupted because the service provider was doing work on the cell site towers or—because this is the SCU—the signal could have been interrupted because he's actually around the corner in someone's basement," Ezra concluded with a hint of excitement.

"But how was he able to send the message without his phone?" Henley asked. "I thought you had to be close to your phone, even with a smartwatch?"

"Most people buy the cheaper watch that connects to their phone via GPS, which means you need to have your phone nearby in order to send messages or make calls," Ezra explained.

"Piper didn't seem like the cheap kind," said Henley.

"Didn't?" Pellacia raised an eyebrow.

"Sorry. *Doesn't* seem like the cheap kind," Henley corrected.

Ezra shrugged. "His watch is GPS *and* cellular, so Bob's your uncle: you can leave your phone in your side chick's house and send messages while you're watching *MasterChef* with your missus."

"If he's using GPS and cellular, are we are able to get his location?" Henley asked.

"We should be able to, and I'm working on it," Ezra said enthusiastically. "In the meantime, here's the last message that was sent from his phone." He flicked the PowerPoint to the second screenshot.

To: Jemima Brisby (mobile)
Text Message: 17 June, 03:51
T call policce aR U OK So sorry. don't tell us.

"As we know, Jemima Brisby is a paralegal at the Redemption Foundation," said Ramouter. "Those are the only messages between Piper and Brisby that Ezra has found."

"That I found *so far*," Ezra added.

"Did she reply?" asked Henley.

"Nothing. No calls from her to his phone since Piper disappeared, and no response to his text message."

"What is he asking her?" said Eastwood. "Is he telling her to call the police? Not to call the police? And why is he apologizing and what doesn't he want her to tell? Is he asking if she's OK? Or am I reading this wrong?"

"I don't think you are—" Henley stopped, suddenly remembering that this was not her investigation to lead. "Sorry, Ramouter. Carry on."

"Aye, thank you," he replied, sounding more confident than he had at the beginning of the briefing. "Eastwood, I don't think you're reading it wrong at all," he went on. "I've been asking myself why on earth he would send a message to his paralegal instead of attempting to make an emergency call. I've done some research and most smartwatches have an SOS function that allows you to call 999. I can only see one reason why Piper would text his paralegal and not call 999."

"Elias Piper and Jemima are more than colleagues," said Eastwood.

"Dominique Piper told me that she ignored some of her husband's flaws."

"Can't think of a bigger flaw than having an affair with your subordinate."

Eastwood caught Pellacia's eyes. Pellacia pursed his lips and turned his attention back to Ramouter.

Ramouter cleared his throat in the awkward silence. "As we know, the first seventy-two hours are crucial to finding a missing person alive. We're way past that. But we now know that Piper was still alive early Thursday morning, hours after anyone last heard from him. My theory is that someone is holding him captive. It's just a question of why and for how long."

"So, what next?" asked Pellacia. "Have you spoken to the CSI team?"

Ramouter flicked over to a page in his notebook where he'd recorded details of his conversation with the SCU's favored senior crime scene investigator, Anthony Thomas.

"Anthony has sent a couple of people to the Redemption Foundation offices, but I'm not sure they'll get much. The cleaners have been in three times since Piper disappeared," he explained. "The next step is for me to visit the offices myself and speak to the rest of the staff." Ramouter gave a subtle nod to Pellacia and made his way back to his desk.

"Good job," Pellacia said, giving him a congratulatory pat on the shoulder.

"I could shed a tear," said Stanford. "It's like watching your kid take his first steps."

"Stanford, did you hear me ask for smart-ass comments?" Pellacia snapped back.

"All I'm saying is that—"

"Oh, shut up," said Henley, not bothering to hide the pride in her voice. "He's doing a good job. A much better job than you did when you were given your first investigation to lead."

Stanford stood up and stretched his arms above his head. "I was given a bloody hospital pass with that drugs case. Always destined to fall flat on my ass. But this case? I never thought I'd say this but it's quite refreshing to have a nice straightforward missing person's case."

"Straightforward?" Henley queried. "When has any case we've dealt with been straightforward? Look at what we're dealing with. A high-profile lawyer who, forty-eight hours after winning the biggest case of his career, disappears without a trace and then sends three nearly incomprehensible messages to his wife and a woman who may or may not be his lover. Does that sound straightforward to you, Stanford?"

Stanford squinted at Henley and gave a snort of annoyance. "Has anyone told you that you're a pain in the ass?"

Henley couldn't help but laugh. "Can you tell me I'm wrong though?" she asked.

"No," Stanford sighed. "No, I can't."

"I'm starting to feel like your chauffeur," Henley said as she threw her logbook onto the dashboard, closed the door and joined Ramouter on the pavement.

"What are you talking about? You always do the driving and it's your car." Ramouter rummaged around in his jacket pocket as he let out a series of harsh sneezes. "Sorry," he mumbled, pulling out a used tissue and blowing his nose. "Bloody hay fever. Do you know that I never suffered with this"—he sneezed again—"until I came down to London."

"Is this your way of telling me that you want to go back to Bradford?" Henley asked. She pulled out a packet of tissues from her bag, handed it to Ramouter and went back to her car.

"God no. I'm great...sorry, we're great down...oh for God's sake!" He sneezed again.

Henley opened the passenger door and reached into the glovebox. "Here you go." She handed him a packet of tablets and a half-empty bottle of water. The cardboard box was crushed and had a visible shoe print on the side. "Antihistamines. Rob usually leaves packets all over the place, including my car, like a rubbish treasure hunt."

"Thank you," Ramouter sniffed as he swallowed the tablet. He pulled a face and took a swig of water that had become warm in the heat of the car.

"Better?"

"Aye, thanks."

"Whoever took Piper clearly isn't interested in money," Henley commented as they walked past Piper's car and turned the corner. "Otherwise, why leave a sixty-grand car behind?"

"Maybe they didn't know it was here."

"Nah. Someone like Piper? They would have been watching him, known all of his movements, and would have worked out a way to get him out of the office without raising suspicion."

"Most of these new cars have a tracking device," Ramouter reminded her. "We're not dealing with an amateur."

"Is there anything you want to run past me before we go in there?" Henley asked.

They both paused when they saw a couple of photographers chatting and drinking coffee outside the main door of the Redemption Foundation offices, cameras hanging around their necks.

"Don't worry about them," Henley muttered. "They're not interested in us. We're not the story. Keep looking forward and ignore them."

"I'm wondering how I should deal with Jemima. I don't want her to think I'm targeting her. Do you know what I mean?"

"I know exactly what you mean. Start from the ground up. You've already spoken to Tina the receptionist, so that means the office manager is next. If they're anything like our Joanna, then take it from me, they'll know everything."

"Hurry up. Hurry up. Come in." The man who opened the Redemption Foundation door ushered them in. Once they were safely inside, he pulled the door handle hard to check that it was secure, before nodding with satisfaction. "People have been trying it ever since you lot finally decided to release a statement about Elias yesterday," he explained. "Trying to come in and see the scene of the crime for themselves." He shook his head in disbelief. "*Scene of the crime.* Honestly, I blame those true crime podcasts. Anyway, nice to see that the police are taking this case seriously at last. Which one are you?"

"Detective Constable Ramouter. And you are…? I spoke to a woman, Nova, and told her that we were coming."

"Woman? She has the maturity level of a thirteen-year-old. Honestly, I don't know where HR finds these kids. Probably won't last long here. They never do."

"And you are?" Henley repeated.

"Oh yeah. Me. Marshall Wollerton. Officially, office manager. Unofficially, glorified drudge."

"This is Detective Inspector Henley," Ramouter said, taking a small step to the side.

"Detective Inspector?" Marshall said slowly. "So, you're the boss." He grinned and shook Ramouter's hand firmly. "What is this, training day?"

"Do you think it's appropriate to be making jokes at a time like this, Mr. Wollerton?" said Henley.

"No, you're right," Marshall said, suddenly serious. "Humor is my defense mechanism and it's the craziest thing trying to get my head around all of this. So, what do you want to know?"

"Is there somewhere private that we can sit down and talk?" Ramouter asked.

"Of course. I need to get Nova to cover reception and then I'll be right with you. Take a seat," Marshall said, gesturing to a sofa before disappearing up the stairs.

"Where did they find Piper's phone again?" Henley asked as she sat down. "It wasn't this sofa, was it?"

Ramouter checked his notebook. "Let me check exactly what Nova said… Aye, here it is. She says that she found the phone 'down the side of the leather sofa' in Piper's office." He sat down next to Henley. "Why do you ask?"

"Look up," Henley said, pointing at the light fixture above their heads. "Doesn't that bulb look strange to you? Look at the center."

Ramouter raised his head and squinted at the small black

dot in the center of the opaque bulb. "What is that...? Is that a camera?"

"I think so," Henley replied. "We need to ask Marshall if there are other cameras in the office."

As if on cue, Marshall arrived with Nova in tow. "Shall we?" he said, and with a grandiose flourish he invited Henley and Ramouter to follow him to the conference room.

"The foundation opened its doors about eight years ago," Marshall said, settling himself at the head of the table as though it was his rightful place. "There are five solicitors, three trainee solicitors, two paralegals and Nova, the intern. Then there's the admin assistant, Brie, Tina on reception and me. As I said, office manager and general drudge. Elias is in charge of it all. No partners. Only him."

"What's he like as a boss?" Ramouter asked.

"Put it this way: your head is bound to get big when people are constantly blowing smoke up your ass. And everyone around here likes to blow smoke up his ass, except me. So I guess you could say he's a bit of a narcissist. But credit where it's due, he knows how to manage people, which is a skill not many people have."

"And how do you get on with him?"

"We get on well," Marshall said sadly. "I've known him for years. I worked in his team way back when he was at the CPS and then he smooth-talked me out of there. I've been with him at the foundation since the beginning."

"You followed him here?"

"What can I say? He made me an offer I couldn't refuse."

Ramouter nodded. "Elias Piper has been missing for nearly five days now. When was the last time you saw him?"

"As I tried to tell that stupid woman on the phone, I last saw him on Wednesday night," Marshall replied. "I know that Nick told you that we had lunch at The Ivy Asia in St. Paul's—and very nice it was too. After that, we came back to the office. We were all here until about five thirty, when people started leaving to go home. I had to wait for a courier to deliver a box of documents, so it was getting on for six thirty when I left."

"Out of interest," asked Henley, who had been finding it difficult to sit back and be a passive observer, "who paid for the lunch?"

"Elias paid, but not out of his own pocket. He would have run it through the business accounts somehow."

"Was it something that Elias did regularly? Pay for things through the business?"

Marshall nodded. "If he could, yes. He's not the best with money. When you work with someone for years…well, you get to learn their habits."

"Are you saying that Elias had money problems?" Ramouter asked.

"Definitely. But his wife has money. He married well."

"Did Elias owe money?"

Marshall laughed. "He owed money *everywhere*." His incredulous tone suggested this was a widely known fact. "He couldn't get a credit card on his own, his wife had to add him to hers. The Jag outside? That's in her name too. And the lease on this building."

"We're aware that Elias received threats at the office," said Ramouter while Henley diligently took notes. "Were those related to money he owed?"

"No. As far as I'm aware, the phone calls and shit being pushed through the letter box were all about whatever case was considered controversial that week. No one ever came here banging the door down and asking for money."

"Did anyone come banging the door down because of the Streeter case?" Ramouter asked.

"Yeah, a few. That's the reason why we got the secret cameras in. There are a couple in the hallway."

"In the light bulbs," Henley nodded.

"Ah, so they aren't that secret then!" Marshall laughed. "Elias is so cheap that he didn't buy the ones with night vision."

"Have you checked the footage?" asked Henley.

"Yes, I did. I've got an app on my computer, but the weird thing is it was switched to privacy mode on Wednesday."

"So, you left at about six thirty," Ramouter confirmed. "What about everyone else? Not including Nick—I already know that he left at seven?"

"The three trainees didn't come back to the office after lunch. Elias said that they could have the rest of the day off."

"So, who was here when you left?"

"Nick, Elias and our paralegal, Jemima. She had a habit of hanging around after hours."

"What do you mean by that?" Henley asked innocently, as though she had no idea what the answer could possibly be.

Marshall turned his head and looked at the door, double-checking no one was eavesdropping in the corner. "Not everyone knows, but *I* know," he said conspiratorially, dropping his voice an octave. "Jemima is very good at her job. She's won a scholarship to study the Legal Practice Course at Kingsway, which is a very difficult law school to get into."

"The LPC? The postgrad qualification?" asked Ramouter.

"That's right. So, Jemima is studying at Kingsway part-time in the evening, and she's been working here as a paralegal for the past eighteen months. She used to work for the local council before she came here. Married and divorced already and she's only twenty-five. Anyway, those two, Elias and Jemima, have been at it literally since the day she joined."

"They're having an affair. Elias and Jemima?"

Marshall nodded. "I've not caught them at it, but you know how it is. Standing too close to each other in the kitchen, the way Jemima looks at him. The hotel expenses that were charged to the business account. Tagging along with him to our office in the States instead of any of the more experienced solicitors. Ten days in New Orleans. Don't know how he thought he would get away with that one."

"Does his wife know?" Henley asked.

Marshall shook his head. "Devoted and clueless."

"Where's Jemima now?" Ramouter checked his watch. "It's almost twelve. Not lunchtime yet, so I'm assuming she's in the office."

Marshall held up his right hand and wagged his index finger. "Never make assumptions. I didn't think anything of it when she texted me on Thursday morning and said she was ill. Jemima has never struck me as the type to pull a sickie. She's an idiot for getting involved with Elias, but she's diligent."

"Are you saying Jemima is off sick?" Ramouter was growing increasingly fed up with Marshall's tendency to ramble.

"I'm not sure what's wrong with her," Marshall replied. "The only reason why I know she's still alive and kicking is because she sent me a voicemail this morning."

17

Jemima looked small and fragile in oversized satin pajamas with a visible stain on the leg. She had dark shadows under her eyes, as though she had smudged it with the remnants of mascara, and the whites of her eyes were stained red. Her unwashed hair was held back from her pale face with a scarf.

"Marshall said that you called in sick, but that you didn't say what exactly was wrong with you?" asked Henley, edging forward on the sofa. She could hear the creaking of broken wood and felt the base of the sofa sink slightly underneath her.

"It's a stomach bug. Haven't been able to keep anything down," Jemima replied quietly, pulling the sleeves of her pajama top down over her hands. She leaned to her right and pushed aside the tepid cup of tea that was on the floor, as if to cover up her half lie. "I finally managed to get some toast down this morning," she added.

"You're here on your own?"

"My parents are away on a cruise with my aunt and uncle. It's just me here and the cat. I would move out but, London rents..."

"Rent is ridiculous, isn't it?" Ramouter said sympathetically. "I've not long moved down to London myself. I don't blame you for staying at home. How long have your parents been away?"

"A week. They're gone for another eight days." Jemima's eyes welled up. Henley could see every emotion, from fear to nervous anxiety, etched on her face. After a few seconds, she placed a hand to her mouth and jumped up. "Sorry, excuse me," she gulped, running out of the living room.

"Maybe she was telling the truth about having a stomach bug," Ramouter said, watching as Henley got up and walked toward the back windows. She turned the key that was in the handle and turned it back again.

"It's eighty degrees outside and she's got every single window in here closed and locked."

Henley walked to the chair where Jemima had been sitting and pulled a face as she noticed a silver object pushed between the cushion and the arm of the chair. The sound of the toilet being flushed sounded in the distance, followed by the whoosh of a flame igniting in the condenser boiler in the kitchen. Henley leaned in and pushed her hand against the side of the cushion. She knew what she had found as soon as her fingers curled around the smooth stainless steel handle. She pulled the knife out slowly and showed it to Ramouter.

Ramouter frowned. "Why does she feel the need to have a knife around?"

"To protect herself," Henley whispered, quickly pushing the knife back into its hiding place. "We need to get her to tell us what she's scared of."

By the time Jemima shuffled back into the room, Henley was back in her seat on the sofa.

"Is everything OK, Jemima?" she asked gently.

"Fine. Sorry about that," Jemima said softly, positioning herself carefully on the chair. "As I said, stomach bug."

"Should I get you some water? Or I can make you a tea if you've got any lemon and ginger in the kitchen."

"No. I'm OK. Thank you."

"You're aware of the disappearance of your boss, Elias Piper?" Henley asked softly.

Jemima nodded but kept her eyes downcast.

"We're going to ask you a few questions, but we'll take it slowly."

"Everyone's talking about it on the group chat," Jemima said, avoiding eye contact with Henley.

"But you haven't replied to the messages?"

"I told you, I was sick."

"I can see that you're ill. I'm not accusing you of anything, just trying to get things straight in my mind. Elias Piper didn't disappear into thin air. He never made it home on Wednesday night, and it seems that you may have been the last person to see him."

Jemima's eyes widened. "Why would you... No, I couldn't have been."

"We understand that you were in the office after 7:00 p.m. on the night that he disappeared."

"I don't remember the time."

"But you were in the office with Elias after everyone had gone home?"

Ramouter looked across at Henley as Jemima bent her head and her shoulders started to shudder.

"I was, but...but..."

"What time did you leave the office?" Henley repeated.

Jemima shook her head. "I can't. I can't..."

"Jemima." Henley was firmer this time—she had realized that gentle cajoling wasn't working. She got up from the sofa and approached Jemima. "Tell me what happened the last time that you saw Elias."

The woman jolted as Henley placed a hand on her shoulder. "You don't understand... I didn't see who... I can't."

Ramouter looked across at Henley and mouthed, "She was there."

"Elias has been missing for almost five days. Time is valuable in a missing person case. The longer you keep information to yourself, no matter how small, the less chance we have of finding Elias alive," said Henley. "Jemima. We're not here to judge you for anything that you may have done. Do you understand?"

"I do, but *you* don't understand." Jemima sat upright and pulled off her headscarf. A dark cut on her forehead stretched from above her temple and ran into the black hairs of her scalp. Henley looked closer and realized that what she initially thought was natural discoloration was a fading bruise around her temple.

"He... I don't know who he was," Jemima said quietly. She picked up a bottle of water from the coffee table and held onto it tightly as though it was a weapon. "It happened so quickly, and it was dark."

"Where were you?" Henley asked.

"In Elias's office on the first floor."

"Did Elias ask you to stay behind after work?"

"I didn't stay because of work. He didn't have to say anything. I knew...we knew..."

"What time was this?"

"I share an office with Nick, and he left about seven. I actually did have some work to finish, and Elias had a Zoom meeting with the US office. He finished about eight-ish and then we went to the bar across the road. I went inside and bought us drinks and nachos. Elias stayed at the table, out on the street."

"What did you drink?"

"Elias had his usual, beer, and I had lemonade."

"Lemonade?"

"I don't really drink."

"So how long were you at the bar for?"

"An hour and a bit."

"Did Elias ever go into the bar?"

Jemima shook her head. "No. I bought the drinks. It was always me."

"Did you notice anything or anyone unusual?"

"No… I mean, no one bothered us. Elias got a couple of looks and I think I heard someone say, *It's him off the telly*, but nothing to be scared of."

"So, you left about…"

"Nine thirty. We went back to the office and we…we had sex in Elias's room."

"I'm going to guess this wasn't the first time," said Henley.

Jemima shook her head. "It was…convenient. It's not as if I have my own place; we couldn't come here, and we definitely couldn't go to his. We went to hotels a couple of times, but it was mainly at the office."

"What happened next? How did you get the cut to your forehead?"

"We were getting ready to leave. It must have been about elevenish. I'd left my bag and jacket in my office," Jemima took a breath. "I heard the…when the door opens there's a…not an alarm, but an alert. We thought that it was the cleaners."

"At eleven o'clock at night?"

"The company that Elias uses, they work late, really late. It's how he arranged it. He didn't want to be disturbed if he had to work late in the office. I didn't realize anything was wrong. But the man, whoever it was, put a knife to my throat." Jemima pulled down the collar of her pajama shirt and revealed the one-inch scab on her neck.

"Would you mind if we took photographs of your injuries?" asked Ramouter gently.

Jemima nodded. "I thought he was going to kill me. I couldn't scream. I couldn't do anything." She unscrewed the cap on her bottle of water, hands shaking.

"Where was Elias?" asked Henley.

"He was there…" Jemima's voice began to waver but then grew angry. "But he did nothing. He said nothing. He was a…"

Henley was tempted to say the word "coward," but she kept the word locked in her head. "So, the man put the knife to your neck?"

"Yes." Jemima put her hand protectively to the cut on her neck. "And then he told me to get back into the room. He then… Elias…pushed me—"

"Elias pushed you?" Ramouter asked, clearly shocked.

"The fucking bastard," Jemima said bitterly. "He said that he loved me, but he pushed me and I tripped over something. I remember falling against the cabinet…or it could have been the desk, I can't really remember, and then that was it. I blacked out. When I woke up it was about 2:00 a.m. and Elias was gone."

"What did you do? Did you call him?"

"No. I wasn't allowed to call him after 10:00 p.m.," Jemima said softly.

"Because of his wife."

"He said that things between them were bad enough without his wife accusing him of having an affair."

"So, you didn't call him. What *did* you do?"

"I got an Uber and I came home. I was scared. I was so scared. I thought that whoever it was might come for me too."

"But you got a text from Elias?"

"I only saw it this morning."

"And you didn't call the police?"

"I was scared!" Jemima raised her voice in fear. "What if whoever it was came for me? What if it was a trap? You have no idea what—"

Ramouter's phone started to ring with a loud foghorn ringtone. Jemima stood quickly, as though she'd been electrocuted.

"Sorry. Sorry." Ramouter reached into his jacket pocket for his phone and checked the screen. "My son has been messing about with my phone again." He turned to Henley and said quietly, "It's Ezra. I need to step out."

"Jemima," Henley said, taking over. "I'm going to open the window and get some air in here. I want you to come here and take a deep breath."

"OK," Jemima whispered, obediently following Henley to the window.

"We're not attacking you or judging you," Henley said. "That's not why we're here."

"People *are* going to judge me though," Jemima said. She pushed the window open wider and leaned out, as though breathing in air for the first time. "They never blame the man. It's never his fault. It's going to be all me. The younger woman who led him astray and tried to break up a happy marriage. Tried to trap him."

"Trap him?" Henley repeated as Ramouter reappeared in the room. She gently rubbed Jemima's back and quickly looked at her colleague. The expression on his face was impassive but she could clearly read the message in his eyes: *wind it up.*

"How far gone are you?" Henley asked Jemima. "You can tell me I'm wrong, but I've been pregnant and that first trimester was an exhausting merry-go-round of throwing up, managing to eat a bit of toast, throwing up again and wanting to fall asleep in the middle of the day."

"I didn't trap him," Jemima put a hand to her stomach. "I haven't decided what I'm going to do... It was an accident."

"But you hadn't told Elias?"

"How could I?" Jemima lowered her head. "How could I?" she repeated, and began to cry uncontrollably. Ramouter and Henley looked at each other. There was no way they could leave Jemima alone now.

"Jemima, is there anyone you can call or at least stay with until your parents come home?" Henley asked, indicating to Ramouter to wait outside.

Jemima rubbed her eyes and wiped the snot from her nose with her sleeve. "My cousin, Sam," she managed to say. "I can go to her. She lives around the corner."

"Give me her number and I'll call her."

"Thank you," said Jemima, beginning to cry again.

"It will be OK," Henley told her, and she took hold of Jemima and held the broken girl in her arms.

"What is it?" Henley asked once they were safely away from Jemima's front door and well out of earshot.

"The phone company finally sent through the cell site data for Elias Piper's phone and smartwatch. Ezra has been through it and done his thing. He's managed to pin down a possible location of the signal that went out when Piper sent the message."

"Did he tell you where we're going?"

"That's the thing. Ezra said Little Venice," Ramouter replied as Henley got into the car and immediately started the engine. "But Piper can't be all the way in Venice, can he? His passport would have been flagged up by border control if he'd left the country."

"He's not out of the country, Ramouter," Henley said with a smile. "Little Venice is in West London." She waited for Ramouter to fasten his seat belt. "How long has he been missing now?"

Ramouter checked the clock on the dashboard. "One hundred and ten hours and thirty minutes in total. How long will it take us to get to... Little Venice?"

"Upton Park to Little Venice, from East London to West. A little under an hour, if the traffic is good," Henley replied.

"Hopefully he won't be—"

"Don't say it, Ramouter," Henley said as she completed a U-turn. "Don't say it."

18

"I can see why they call it Little Venice," said Ramouter, adjusting the straps of his stab vest as he walked up to the railings that separated the canal from the pavement. "It's nice around here. Not sure about living on a riverboat though."

Henley unwillingly breathed in the smell that emanated from the canal running through Little Venice—a mix of diesel fumes and stagnant water—as the driver of a police van slowed down in front of her and began to reverse awkwardly into a too-tight space on Blomfield Avenue.

"Can't say that I ever fancied it myself," Henley replied. "Too claustrophobic."

"Wouldn't be a bad place for a kidnapper to hide Piper though." Ramouter took hold of the railings and peered through the trees that were obscuring the views of the boats. "What is it they say? A moving target is harder to hit."

"A boat would be my first option, if I was ever in the business of kidnapping someone. As you said, makes it harder for us to do our job. Thankfully, the coordinates Ezra gave us don't place Piper—or more specifically his smartwatch—anywhere along the canal."

Ramouter turned and looked at the two houses on the opposite side of the road. There was nothing to differentiate between 134 and 135 Blomfield Avenue, two newly renovated terraced houses. A perfectly aligned bright green hedge was behind a six-foot-high white wall with a black wrought iron gate that was firmly locked. Both houses had bright yellow for sale signs in the front of the yard.

"You can smell the money on this road," Ramouter observed as a black Mercedes C class with the same estate agent logo written elegantly on the side turned slowly onto the road and parked two bays away from the police van. "Hiding him on a riverboat I could understand, but if he's in one of these houses… Look how secure they are. How would you get anyone in here without being caught on someone's personal security system? I doubt that the postman can get past the gate without secret service–level security checks."

"Let's see what the agent has to say about who's had access to these two houses," said Henley.

"How do you want to do this?" asked PS Orion, who had joined Henley and Ramouter on the pavement. He handed them each a pair of blue latex gloves.

"We'll split up. You, PCs Lucia and Gronkowski will take 135, and PC Ducasse will come with me and DC Ramouter. We'll search both houses at the same time. Keep your radio channels open and make sure your bodycams are on."

PS Orion nodded his agreement as they all made their way across the road to where the estate agent and other officers were waiting.

"Daler Chawla. Senior negotiator at Kingfisher property agents. You must be Detective Inspector Henley. We spoke on the phone," the agent said, his arms folded defiantly in front of him.

"I am," Henley replied, stepping forward and forcing him onto the pavement. She could almost see the arrogance oozing out of the agent's pores. She resisted the urge to kick him in the shins as he removed his sunglasses and flashed a smile, revealing teeth as white as his shirt.

"Before we go in, can you tell me how many people have had access to these two houses?" Henley asked.

"It's my listing," said Daler. "I'm the only one who has the keys. The owner of both properties lives in Dubai. I started viewings about two weeks ago and it's strictly by appointment. We can't have anyone walking in and out of these houses."

"So, you would have a list of everyone who's viewed the property?"

"Yeah, I do, but I can't hand that information to you. Confidentiality and all that."

"A police investigation trumps confidentiality and all that," said Henley sternly. "These houses were recently renovated, so I'm assuming you have the builders' details?"

"I will have to speak to the owner about that. He engaged our services soon after the properties were finished. So, what is this about?" Daler asked eagerly.

Henley ignored the question as she pulled on her latex gloves. "Once you let us in to 134, you're going to go next door and let the other officers in. You will then go back to your car. At no point are you to enter either property. Do you understand?"

"I don't think the owner will like you wandering about without me present. I'm his representative."

"You can represent him from outside this gate," said Henley, and then turned and walked away without another word.

Number 134 smelled of sandalwood and sea salt and the walls had been painted in a nonoffensive white paint with a hint of green. Despite the minimalism of the décor, there was a heaviness in the room as though the air had been suctioned out.

The silence was oppressive and overpowered the senses. Henley would have welcomed the sound of a clicking clock or the delicate hum of a dishwasher.

"I don't like the quiet," Ramouter muttered, as he and Henley entered the first reception room and looked around. The room was large and had been staged with a slate gray sofa and a glass coffee table featuring a collection of large art books and a vase of bright yellow tulips.

"I don't like it either," Henley replied. They left the room and with silent agreement she entered the second reception room and Ramouter walked further down the hallway.

"It's unnerving." Ramouter opened the cupboard under the stairs, switched on the light and peered inside. "Empty," he said, closing the door. "No sign of anything."

"Same in the second reception," Henley replied, and headed to the kitchen. Her police radio crackled and PC Ducasse's disembodied voice emerged.

"No signs of…well, anything upstairs, gov," Ducasse said. "Nothing looks disturbed. I'm going to head up to the next floor."

"Thanks, Ducasse. No sign of anything down here either," said Henley.

Ramouter followed her into the large kitchen. "This house is amazing," he said, turning left and opening the door to the utility room. "This room is bigger than my own bedroom. God, how the other half—"

A piercing alarm from Ramouter's radio cut him off.

"Ducasse! What, is it? Are you OK?" Henley said into her radio as they ran out of the kitchen and toward the staircase. A second later, PC Ducasse spoke.

"Yeah, I'm fine," she said breathlessly. "But you need to… Shit, I've found something. I'm on the top floor. Master bedroom. Shit."

Henley and Ramouter's radios both released a second alarm.

"Inspector, this is PC Gronkowski. We're on the ground floor of 135. In the utility room. You need to get over here. We've... found someone."

Henley's heart skipped a beat. She stopped abruptly on the landing, her breathing heavy and irregular.

"Ramouter. Can you—"

"I'm already gone." Ramouter turned on his heel and ran back down the stairs.

There was only one room on the top floor. Henley walked the short distance on the soft carpet and into a large bedroom which was filled with bright sunlight. The room had a different scent to downstairs, lavender mixed with jasmine, but a sour note cut through the perfume.

"Are you OK? You look terrible," Henley asked PC Ducasse, who was standing next to the doorless entryway to the en suite bathroom. She waved her hand as a couple of black flies buzzed above her head.

"Yeah, I'm fine," PC Ducasse replied, wiping her clammy forehead. "I'm not entirely sure what it is, but it's in the sink and it stinks."

Ducasse stepped aside from the doorway and moved further into the bedroom. Like everything else, the en suite was large. Henley walked past a shower that was big enough to fit two people, and made her way toward the sink. Henley felt the soft vibration of her police radio as it began to transmit. Ramouter's voice was in stereo, coming through both PC Ducasse and Henley's radios.

"Henley—boss. You're going to have to get over here," he said. "I'm calling CSI right now, but this is...just get over here."

"I'll be there shortly," Henley said, staring at her reflection on the mirrored tiles above the sink.

"What do you think it means?" Ducasse asked.

Henley used her phone to take a photograph of a message written on the mirror in white ink.

SLEEPING DOGS SHOULD LIE.

Henley didn't reply. She was trying to stop herself from breathing in the stench of the meat that had been left to rot in the sink. Freckles, fine brown hairs, dark hair follicles and part of a badly drawn dragonfly tattoo could be seen on the large portion of mottled, rotting, blood-streaked flesh that sat in the middle of the pristine white porcelain sink. It was slighter larger than Henley's closed fist and pieces of jagged skin stuck to the muscle had taken on a dark pink color as it dried in the warm air.

"Ducasse, get on the radio and let them know that we need a forensic team for both houses." Henley leaned in closer, already desensitized to the smell, and took in the sight of tiny black flies, spinning as though hypnotized around the sink, and a small spider crawling across the lump of flesh.

"Ducasse, I'm sorry for asking this, but did you touch the sink?" Henley turned around and removed her gloves and re-placed them with a fresh pair.

"No. Didn't touch a thing."

"I've got a pretty good idea who this belongs to," Henley said as she carefully placed her index finger underneath the flesh and lifted it up. Thin fragments of dried bloodied skin tore off and stuck to the porcelain as it peeled away. Henley delicately held on to the flesh with her left hand so that it was standing up, and with her right hand she pushed away the smartwatch that had been underneath the flesh. Her breath caught when she saw that there was something else in the sink.

"Fuck," she muttered, peeling away a strip of pale blue lami-nated paper that was one inch in width with a white plastic clip in the middle. Henley picked up the hospital band and placed it on the edge of the sink. Next to the short barcode were five lines of information:

ANDREW STREETER
DOB: 24/11/72
NHS NO: 09216570065
ADM: Medway Maritime Hospital
PN: 908654YL—HMP Ruxley

"I didn't want to say anything over the radio," Ramouter said at the front door of number 135. "It's...you need to see it for yourself, but we have to get this secured immediately."

"Did the CSI team say how long they were going to be?" Henley asked, following Ramouter down the hallway.

"Twenty minutes," he replied.

Number 135 was the mirror image of its neighbor. The scent of decomposing flesh hung in the air like smoke from an extinguished candle. Henley felt a breeze brush against her face as they entered the kitchen. The bifold doors were slightly open and PCs Gronkowski and Lucia were both sitting with their backs to the house on a low wall, while PS Orion stood next to them, facing the kitchen.

"What happened?" Henley asked as Orion stepped back into the kitchen and the other two scrambled to their feet.

"We split up," said PS Orion, heading toward the utility room. "I took the top floor, Gronkowski the first and Lucia took the ground floor. After about five minutes, Lucia shouts for me."

"I wasn't sure. It looked out of place," said Lucia. "You'll see what I mean, ma'am."

Henley turned and scanned Lucia's pale face. She had the look of someone who was trying to come to terms with what she'd seen.

"Prepare yourself," said Ramouter, and then he opened the utility room door.

The smell of decomposition was stronger but there was no body to be seen. The utility room was the same as next door, but it wasn't the luxury kitchen appliances that caught Henley's attention. It was the old fridge-freezer in the middle of the room. Lucia was right, it was out of place. It was covered with dirt, small dents and the gray remnants of stickers that had been peeled off years ago. The silver handle on the freezer door was tarnished and there were two exposed rusty screws where the handle to the fridge door should have been.

"Inside," Ramouter said. He walked around Henley and stood in front of the fridge.

"Inside the fridge?" Henley could hear the disbelief in her voice.

Ramouter nodded and carefully gripped the side of the fridge door. He grimaced and pulled it open. Henley quickly put her hand to her mouth, but it was too late to stop the fermented smell of dead flesh hitting her nostrils. Elias Piper's naked body filled every inch of space. His right arm was curled around the top of his head, which was pressed against his chest. A piece of jagged collarbone protruded from the skin on his neck. His legs were curled up tightly into his body, but the heel of his left foot was facing the wrong direction. The broken bone of the ankle had pushed into the skin and penetrated the exposed wound on his thigh. But it was Elias Piper's face that would haunt the dreams of everyone in that room. Like uneven train tracks, thick, black thread had been used to sew Piper's eyelids and mouth shut.

19

Pellacia tried to ignore the itching on his chest as he smoothed down his tie. The redness of the scars was less ferocious than a few months ago but no matter how much lotion he rubbed onto his chest, the cotton of his shirts rubbed against his scars; a constant reminder of what he'd been through and perhaps would never get over. A cruel and savage reminder of the torture that the serial killer, Peter Olivier, had inflicted on him.

They had tried to make the waiting area of New Scotland Yard feel inclusive and nonthreatening with its panoramic view of the River Thames and the South Bank, but Pellacia felt as though he was suffocating. He watched a trio of red double-decker buses make their way south along Waterloo Bridge and, not for the first time, thought about escaping the confines of the city. If Pellacia closed his eyes he could nearly convince himself that he was on holiday, eating tapas and drinking chilled Verdejo in a restaurant overlooking Port Vell in Barcelona. He'd enjoyed the escapism of a holiday with Laura Halifax, but it had taken all his willpower not to think about Henley or call out her name when a nightmare had woken him up in the middle of the night.

"Detective Superintendent Pellacia."

"Yes." Pellacia turned around and faced the young man with a far too serious face.

"Apologies for the wait. The previous meeting overran but I'll bring you through. There's tea—herbal and normal—coffee and water waiting. Feel free to help yourself. My name is Tymothy. With a *Y* and not an *I*. We're on the sixth floor."

Pellacia didn't bother with small talk as he followed the man along the carpeted corridor and toward the bank of elevators. New Scotland Yard may have been the headquarters of the Metropolitan Police, but it lacked the buzzing atmosphere of a working police station. It had the appearance of a building commissioned solely for the purpose of being an esthetically pleasing backdrop for outdoor news conferences, and for summoning police officers, senior and junior, to meetings on the top floor to make it clear where the true power lay.

If Pellacia didn't know better, he would have sworn he was being called in for a disciplinary hearing. Three high-ranking police officers, Acting Deputy Commissioner Peter Santar and Commander Nigel Monaghan from Specialist Operations were sitting to the right of Geraldine Barker, the borough commander for the southeast command unit. Only Barker stood up as Pellacia entered the room.

"Good morning, sirs and ma'am," said Pellacia as he unbuttoned his jacket and sat down.

"Sorry for keeping you waiting," Barker said, once Tymothy had closed the door behind Pellacia. "One sugar in your coffee, right?"

Barker didn't wait for an answer as she poured steaming hot coffee into two cups. She placed one in front of him and sat back in her seat, giving him a tight smile.

"Thank you, ma'am," said Pellacia, taking a sip. He caught

the look that passed between Acting Deputy Commissioner Santar and Commander Monaghan. He knew what Barker was doing by attending only to the beverage needs of Pellacia and herself. She was passively expressing her displeasure at their decision to call this meeting and whatever silent agreement had already been made.

"Tymothy," Santar said, pointing toward the coffee on the other end of table. "Thank you for coming to this meeting, DSI Pellacia," he said after Tymothy had placed his coffee in front of him. Despite the coolness of the room, there was a visible film of sweat on Santar's upper lip. He had the flushed appearance of a man who drank too much cheap whisky in the evening and whose diet included a full English breakfast every morning. Santar's graying hair was cut close to his scalp, giving him the appearance of a balding hedgehog.

"We felt, in light of recent developments, that it was important the executive branch of Specialist Operations came together with yourself and Commander Barker to discuss next steps." Santar pulled forward the blue lever-arch folder that was in front of him.

"What recent developments would you be referring to, sir?" asked Pellacia.

"You ask the question as though you're unaware why you're here," said Monaghan in clipped tones that made him sound like a housemaster at Eton or an MP unauthentically apologizing for his latest indiscretion.

"Sir," Pellacia said firmly but with a hint of reluctant deference. "Since I've overseen the Serial Crime Unit, I've never been asked to attend any meetings with Specialist Operations. As I recall, you made it clear from the beginning that the SCU doesn't come under the remit of SO. I am therefore confused as to why I'm here."

"Aren't we all," Barker said clearly, giving Santar the dirtiest of looks. "However, the recent court judgment overturning

Streeter's convictions, and the murder of Elias Piper, has led to a..." Barker folded her arms and leaned forward. "Even though these two cases should be dealt with by Specialist Operations because that's where the original Streeter investigation originated from—"

"You know full well that Specialist Operations wasn't in existence when the Streeter case was first opened," Monaghan spat out with contempt.

"After considering advice from the CPS, the SO have decided among themselves," Barker continued, "that the original murder investigations that resulted in Streeter's conviction will be reopened and—"

The sound of Pellacia noisily replacing his coffee cup in the saucer, causing coffee to spill onto the glass table, cut her off. "You must be joking," he said, looking across at the three faces in front of him.

Rhimes had always told him that there were those in New Scotland Yard who were praying for the SCU to fail. It was clear as day to Pellacia that this was more than a simple passing of the buck. Those in charge of Specialist Operations would use the Streeter case to absolve themselves of both ineptitude and corruption. They would make the SCU their political scapegoat.

"You seem to have forgotten who you're speaking to," said Monaghan.

"Oh, I'm sorry. You must be joking, *sirs*."

Barker coughed mockingly.

"And ma'am."

"Thank you," said Barker. "The decision has been made, against my advice, that the SCU will investigate the 1995 and 1996 murders of Gyimah, Chalmers, O'Toole, Callaghan and Alves."

"We don't have the resources to investigate cold cases," Pellacia said sternly.

"The recent developments in the Elias Piper investigation and the unknown circumstances of Streeter's death changes things," said Santar. "We're a couple of months into a new financial—"

"Does that mean you're going to reallocate some of the Specialist Operations budget to the SCU?" asked Barker with mock sincerity.

"You already have the financial resources," said Santar, ignoring Barker. "You're simply doing what the SCU was formed to do in the first place."

Pellacia pushed his chair back and folded his arms, a hundred thoughts racing through his mind. "You don't see a potential conflict here?" he asked icily.

"Detective Inspector Henley?" asked Monaghan.

"Not just Henley. With the exception of DC Ramouter, all of us at the SCU worked with DCSI Rhimes and—"

"We considered this and, as far as we're concerned, there isn't a problem," said Monaghan.

Pellacia could have sworn he heard Barker mutter, "Speak for yourself," under her breath.

"Not a problem? You don't consider the fact that Henley was an original prosecution witness a problem? Because I do," said Pellacia, shaking his head in disbelief.

"It's been reviewed and decided that—"

"There isn't a problem," Pellacia repeated. He loosened his tie, no longer caring about formalities of respect. "Since you're turning my SCU into an extension of the cold case unit, shouldn't the Piper case be transferred to another major investigation team?"

"No," Santar replied.

"You're sending it to the National Crime Agency then?" Pellacia asked, determined to provoke.

"Unfortunately not," said Barker. "The only thing I agree with is that the Piper case should remain with you. If Streeter's postmortem concludes that the circumstances of his death were suspicious, then that is a matter for the SCU also."

Pellacia pursed his lips and looked out the window at the

slowly rotating London Eye. "Why are you lot moving so quickly?" Pellacia asked, trying to keep his temper at a low simmer. "Tomorrow, it will be a week since Streeter's death was announced and Piper's body was only found yesterday. As far as I'm aware, Piper is still in the fridge and no one has yet suggested Streeter's death was suspicious. I may be stuck behind a desk these days, but I'm a detective and a bloody good one. I was taught by the best and I can only conclude that the decision to reopen the investigation was made before Streeter's heart stopped beating."

Pellacia studied the faces of Santar and Monaghan but there was nothing. Not a sign of admission or contrition. Pellacia shook his head with disgust and turned to Barker. "Ma'am," he said.

"You're right when you say that no one has concluded Streeter's death was suspicious," said Barker. "HMP Ruxley will need to explain the delay in confirming cause of death in the inevitable inquiry, but in the meantime Streeter's body is being transferred to Greenwich Public Mortuary so that Dr. Choi can perform the postmortem."

"This is—" Pellacia struggled to find the least offensive words to express his displeasure.

"Your demeanor suggests to me that you're questioning your ability to preside over these cases," Santar said smugly. "After all, you've only achieved the rank of superintendent and I can see from your record that there haven't been any attempts to seek further promotion."

"My ability?" Pellacia repeated angrily. He felt the scar tissue on his chest tighten. Out of nowhere, he heard Henley's voice in his head. *Don't give them what they want.* "I've been in charge of the SCU for nearly eighteen months and in that time my team have successfully solved three high-profile cases," Pellacia said calmly, but with warning. "Do I need to remind you that during the Peter Olivier and Dominic Pine cases, my team put their lives at risk? And let's not forget about my own life. I can show you the scars, if you'd like a reminder. So, with all due respect, my *ability* is not to be questioned."

Silence. Santar awkwardly shuffled the pile of papers in front of him, and Monaghan stared at Pellacia with contempt.

"Right then, if there isn't anything else you'd like to question," said Pellacia, "I suggest we move on."

Pellacia stood in front of the reflecting pool where the eternal flame burned in the center, and pulled out a packet of cigarettes, keeping his back to New Scotland Yard.

"You haven't got another one of those, have you?"

"Ma'am," Pellacia said.

"How many times have I told you? Ma'am makes me feel old," said Commander Barker, waiting for Pellacia to place a cigarette in her outstretched hand.

"Sorry, ma—gov."

"I'd cut down to three cigarettes a day," she said as Pellacia handed her his lighter. She took a deep drag and blew a plume of smoke rings into the air. "But those two in there? It's either the cigarettes or alcohol, and I don't drink. Walk with me."

Pellacia noticed that Barker had removed her name badge and was wearing a black blazer despite the warm weather; hiding all signs that she was senior police.

"I know you're not happy about this," said Barker once they had crossed Victoria Embankment and were heading in the direction of Westminster Pier.

"Not happy? That's the understatement of the year. With all due respect—and I mean that sincerely—I am bloody pissed," said Pellacia.

"Believe me, I fought against it, but powers more senior than me wanted this to happen. And I don't mean those two numbskulls up there." Barker waved her hand in the direction of New Scotland Yard.

"This wasn't down to Monaghan and Santar?" asked Pellacia.

"They had something to do with it, but they don't have the authority to allocate a case of this magnitude. I think they had words with the commissioner. They're looking to deflect and redirect the shitstorm that this case will inevitably bring. Every day the Met are fighting accusations of corruption. This case can't be written off as nothing more than malicious allegations without foundation."

"It's difficult to do that when the Court of Appeal has announced it to the world."

"Exactly. It is what it is, the decision has been made. I didn't have to be here today, but the SCU is under my command and, quite frankly, I like to see the faces of anyone who is trying to fuck me over."

Pellacia laughed as he stubbed out his cigarette on the river wall before throwing it into the dark waters.

"I don't know how I'm going to explain this to Henley," Pellacia said somberly.

"I don't envy you," Barker said. "Streeter's appeal would have brought up a lot of emotions for her, but she has the team's support, no?"

"Of course she does, but unless something has changed in the past forty-eight hours, the only people who know that Henley was a trial witness are Stanford, Joanna and myself."

"I see," Barker said slowly as they resumed their walk. "And at fifteen years old, the judge would have imposed reporting restrictions. Henley's name wouldn't have been in the public domain. She has to tell the team before you can move forward with this case."

"I agree. But what bothers me most is the feeling they're trying to set us up," said Pellacia. He absent-mindedly placed his hand to his chest and rubbed his scars. "Look, I'll be honest. We can handle Piper's case, but Streeter's death, and reopening the original murder investigations..." Pellacia paused and raised his eyes to the heavens. "We can't reopen the investigation without looking into Rhimes. If...if we uncover any evidence of corruption or breaches of the codes of practice, then it's inevitable that they'll look at every case Rhimes was involved in until the day he died. If Rhimes was dirty, then the SCU is tainted too. It's a setup."

"Of course they're trying to set the SCU up. Look, you're not the only station or unit that I'm responsible for. I've got to balance the budget and manage limited resources. I'm literally robbing Peter to pay Paul. Do you know how difficult it was to get money from them to pay for contractors to update the security systems at your station? As far as they're concerned, the building is a white elephant that needs to be knocked down." Barker stared out at the river for a moment. "The SCU is on life support and one of those sneaky fuckers is wetting themselves to be the one to pull the plug."

"It's not right. My team has been through a lot," said Pellacia.

"You've been through a lot too," Barker said sympathetically. "No one would have blamed you for walking away after what Olivier did to you. I can't tell you how much I respect you for staying. It's a sign of how committed you are to your team."

"Some people might say I'm stupid," Pellacia said. He thought back to the argument with Laura which had led to him cutting their holiday short.

"Not stupid," Barker replied. "You're committed and it's not lost on me that this investigation, which should have gone to the cold case unit, is going to test you all. This isn't only about Streeter and the original murders."

Pellacia turned to face Barker. "The long and short of it is that they're ordering us to open an investigation into our former boss. If we discover that Rhimes—"

"He's not Rhimes. He's not your boss," Barker said sternly. "You have to think of him as a suspect when you're reviewing his original investigation."

"There's no way he was corrupt," Pellacia said. "But if we uncover evidence that he was… I dread to think what that would do to us. What that would do to Henley."

"Not only you lot," Barker said, her voice wavering. "I knew that man for nearly thirty years and I'm finding it very difficult to reconcile the man I knew with the corrupt and immoral man that they're suggesting he was. All I ask is that you all do your jobs."

"But if it turns out to be true…" Pellacia paused. "I trusted him."

"So did I," Barker said sadly.

20

SLEEPING DOGS SHOULD LIE.

"Is it a warning?" Ramouter said, enlarging the image on his monitor.

"A warning or a statement?" said Henley. She pinned the photograph of Piper's body in the fridge onto the whiteboard. "If whoever killed Piper—"

"And Streeter?" Eastwood volunteered.

"We don't know that Streeter was murdered." Henley caught the look on Eastwood's face. "Don't look at me like that, Eastie."

The atmosphere in the SCU offices had changed since Sunday. This was now a murder investigation, and the transition of "lead detective" from Ramouter to Henley had been smooth and unchallenged. Henley stood in front of the whiteboard, exuding her natural authority though inside she was spiraling. She'd thought about telling the team that she'd had contact with both Streeter and Piper prior to their deaths but she knew that there would be questions.

Why did you meet a man convicted of five murders?
Did you give Elias Piper information that helped free Streeter?
How can you lead us?
How can we trust you?
Henley didn't have an answer for the last question.

"I know you're trying to be objective, but how else would you explain Streeter's hospital band being with the…" Eastwood paused and twisted her mouth as she struggled to find the right word. "Can you call it a body part when all you've got is a lump of flesh?"

"I honestly don't know," Henley admitted. "But we need to confirm whether the hospital band is legit."

"Then we're looking for someone who recently had access to Streeter and was involved in the kidnapping and murder of Piper. We need to look at the prison's visitor log," Eastwood concluded.

Henley could only nod in the affirmative, even though her name would be on HMP Ruxley's visitor's log. Pellacia's phone rang out from his empty office, snapping her back to attention.

"Sleeping dogs should lie. Warning or statement?" she asked loudly.

"If it's a warning, then the next question is who's being warned off? Us?" said Ramouter. "The estate agent confirmed that the fridge wasn't there when he had his last viewing, which was at 7:00 p.m. on Saturday."

"What's our window?" Henley asked, picking up the blue marker. "The last showing was seven on Saturday. The agent said he left the house at around seven forty-five and went back to the office. The agency is closed on a Sunday. What time did we arrive on Monday, Ramouter?"

"About three thirty."

"Weren't there any viewings before you two turned up?" asked Eastwood.

"No," Ramouter said slowly. "The agent said he had viewings booked for both houses at eleven thirty, twelve fifteen and two o'clock, but they canceled."

"All of them?" asked Eastwood.

"Two cancelations and one no-show. Too many to think it's a coincidence."

"So according to the agent, no one has been in the property since seven forty-five on Saturday evening, which gives us a window of almost forty-four hours where a piece of Piper was left in the sink in number 134 and then his body was wheeled into 135 in a fridge-freezer," said Henley. "The property was alarmed?"

Ramouter picked up his notebook and flicked through the pages. "Private alarm company based in Victoria. Garrison Security Solutions."

"Can you access the house other than via the main road?" asked Eastwood.

"No. The garden backs on to the garden of twenty-six Bridewell Avenue, and you can only access the garden through the side gate—but again it's in the middle of a terrace and you also need to have the entry code to open the gates," Ramouter explained.

"There's no way that somebody didn't see something," Henley mused. "Piper was in the Little Venice area when he sent the text from his phone on Thursday morning, but he wasn't moved to that house until the weekend."

"He could've been kept on a riverboat on the canal," said Ramouter. "There's no way that CCTV didn't capture something. What borough is Little Venice in?"

"Westminster," said Henley. "We're dealing with a murder now, not a missing person, so threaten them with court action if they start dragging their heels about providing us with CCTV footage." She turned back to the whiteboard. "If this wasn't a warning for us to stay away, then our killer was possibly making a statement about Piper's involvement in the case. Why though?" she continued. "Whether it's a warning or a statement, there is still the question of 'why?'"

"To shut him up. The killer wanted to stop Piper from talking, and he was always talking. Look how visible he was before he went missing," said Ramouter, counting on his fingers. "BBC Breakfast News, *Good Morning Britain*, Kay Burley on Sky News, CNN, plus all the radio shows: LBC, BBC Radio Five Live, Talk—"

"All right, Ramouter, I get the picture, Piper was everywhere," said Henley.

"He was everywhere, and he was talking," said Ramouter.

"And he was Streeter's voice," Eastwood mused out loud. "Acting on Streeter's instructions."

Henley replaced the cap on the marker and sat on the edge of Stanford's empty desk. "Did Streeter and Piper know something else, something they weren't talking about yet? And who wouldn't want them to say it?"

Ramouter was the one to answer: "The real killer of the 1995 victims."

Henley, Eastwood and Ramouter lapsed into silence, and a thick black cloud floated across the blue sky outside.

Eastwood was the first to break the silence. "If it was the real killer, where has he been for the past twenty-five years? Did he stop killing and disappear once Streeter went inside?"

"What if he disappeared but he didn't stop killing? If it wasn't Streeter, then are we meant to believe that the killer stopped for twenty-five years?" Ramouter contributed.

"His MO is too distinct for that," said Eastwood. "Unless he switched up how he killed people, and now he's reverted back to type because he's pissed off."

"You're missing the bigger question," said Henley. "If our killer is making sure that sleeping dogs lie, Piper and Streeter could be just the start. Who else is on his kill list?"

★ ★ ★

"Why do you have such a big grin on your face?" Henley asked Dr. Linh Choi, the pathologist and one of Henley's closest friends, who was leaning against the open window in her office. She stretched out a string of mozzarella from her pizza and placed it in her mouth.

"Because it was, for a brief moment, glorious," Linh said, taking a bite while expertly catching a slice of mushroom that had escaped from its thin base.

"The pizza?" Ramouter asked quizzically.

Linh finished her slice and closed the lid on the now-empty box. "Oh God no. That was mediocre at best," she said. "Come along, younglings."

"I think you've finally lost it," said Henley as she and Ramouter dutifully followed Linh out of her office and into the examination room.

"Don't worry, Ramouter," Linh said, washing her hands in the sink and then pulling a pair of surgical gloves from the box. "I've got no bodies on display for you this afternoon."

"Where's Piper?" Ramouter asked, looking around the room. He saw his reflection on the doors of the fridges that were keeping the dead bodies chilled. It hadn't occurred to him that he would be a regular visitor to the mortuary when he'd joined the SCU last year. He'd lost count of the number of times he'd left this very room to be sick after seeing a body with a T-incision on the chest and internal organs on display. Ramouter couldn't help but feel a little proud of himself that he wasn't in danger of bringing up his lunch today.

"I'm waiting for him to arrive. Apparently, it's not that easy to remove a human body from a fridge." Linh wheeled a trolley into the center of the room, in between two examination tables. There was a single blue cloth covering the top of the table. "Theresa is off sick, so it's just me, but I promise you I'll get to him. But first, do you know who's here?"

"Who?" Henley asked, a sinking feeling in her stomach.

"Andrew Streeter," said Linh. She pointed at locker number 12, which Ramouter was standing in front of, and then frowned. "What's wrong?"

Henley knew there was little that she could do to hide the shock and confusion on her face. She turned and read the label on the freezer. Why was Streeter's body in Greenwich mortuary when he'd died thirty miles away?

"When did he arrive?" Henley asked quietly.

Linh looked at her friend closely before answering. "Sometime last night," Linh said, all business. Henley would talk to her when she was ready. "I wasn't here, before you start having a go at me. I got an email from the pathologist at Medway Maritime Hospital telling me that a full postmortem hadn't yet been completed and my services had been personally requested. I mean, I'm flattered, but it's not as if I haven't got enough on my plate."

"Hold on, Streeter has been here since last night?" Henley asked.

"That's right. Give me a sec, let me check the paperwork." Linh picked up a pile of papers on the table behind her. "Where are we... Streeter, Streeter, Streeter. Here we go. Transfer to me. Investigating department, Serial Crime Unit. Signed last night at 11:26 p.m."

"Huh," Ramouter stepped away from Streeter's locker and turned to Henley. "Since when are we investigating Streeter's death?"

Henley caught the questioning look in Linh's eyes. She knew her well enough to preempt the obvious question.

"Don't worry. Ramouter knows about my association with Streeter," Henley clarified. "The only person who doesn't know is Eastwood, but I'm going to tell her."

"I take it you didn't know he was one of yours?" Linh asked, taking in Henley's stony face.

"No. No, I didn't," Henley replied through gritted teeth.

"That's awkward," said Linh. "OK, let's lighten the mood a bit." She turned her attention to the trolley in the middle of the room then looked up at Henley, a mischievous grin on her face. Henley felt her shoulders relax.

"Will you stop grinning?" Henley said, smiling weakly.

"Absolutely not. I live for moments like this." Linh dramatically removed the cloth from the top of the trolley. "Here we have a piece of Elias Piper in a bowl."

Ramouter moved around to the opposite side of the trolley to Henley and peered into the bowl. He screwed up his face. "It doesn't look like much, considering that it's human flesh. It wouldn't look out of a place on a butcher's shelf," he said, stepping aside as Linh reached past him and placed a set of scales on the trolley. "Was this done premortem?"

"No, postmortem," Linh said, picking up Piper's flesh and turning it around in her hand. "If you look carefully, you can see a severed artery and there is no clotting. This piece of flesh was cut from the front of the left thigh, the part of the leg where the femoral artery can be found."

"How did he die?" asked Ramouter.

"How am I supposed to know when this is all I've got of him?" Linh said sarcastically. "Didn't I say, the rest of him is still playing fridge Tetris?"

"Sorry."

"Younglings don't know they're born. Did I tell you that I'm dating a man who has never seen a Star Wars film in his entire life?" asked Linh. "Not one single film. Anyway, pay close attention. We use imperial measures for this part."

Linh carefully placed the piece of flesh on the scales' sanitized silver platform. "Ramouter, because you're only about twelve you may not remember imperial measures, but there are 16 ounces in a pound and this piece of flesh weighs exactly 8.2 ounces."

Henley looked at the digits on the scale and groaned. "Oh my God, this is why you were so happy."

"What is it?" Ramouter looked across at Linh and Henley. "I don't get it."

"This is 8.2 ounces of flesh that have been removed from a human being's body," said Linh, still grinning. "It most likely lost a tiny bit of weight due to dehydration as it was left out in the air."

"This bit of flesh is not even close to a pound," said Henley, pulling a chair toward her and sitting down. "You're such a geek."

"I don't get it," said Ramouter.

"Did you not read *The Merchant of Venice* in school?" Henley asked.

"Never heard of it."

"Bloody hell," said Linh. She placed the flesh back into the bowl and opened a small fridge door behind her. "Didn't you do Shakespeare in school?"

"Aye, of course. We did *Hamlet* and *Much Ado About Nothing*—not that I paid much attention," said Ramouter.

"Without giving you the full crib notes," said Henley, "in *The Merchant of Venice*, Shylock—"

"The moneylender," Linh interjected.

"Shylock demands a pound of flesh if a loan isn't repaid. But what I found is not a pound of flesh."

"*All that glitters is not gold*," Linh said dramatically. "That's in *The Merchant of Venice* too."

Henley rolled her eyes but was secretly grateful for the levity Linh brought to the room.

"We found Piper in Little Venice," said Ramouter. "But Piper wasn't a merchant. He was a lawyer."

"True." Henley eased herself forward in her chair. "But I think the killer was trying to make a dramatic point, not an accurate one."

"You OK?" Linh asked. All joviality had disappeared from her voice and was replaced with concern as she noticed Henley grip the chair's armrests.

"I'm fine," Henley replied. "I probably need some air."

"So, who is this guy?" asked Ramouter. "He's leaving us cryptic messages on bathroom mirrors and now he's badly referencing Shakespeare."

"And I think he's enjoying playing games with us," said Henley.

Joanna was standing at the door to the Serial Crime Unit, looking like a mother whose children were late home for dinner.

"I'm warning you now," she said as she held a manila folder close to her chest. "Something has been decided and I don't like it one bit, and if I don't like it, then you definitely won't like it."

"I think we've got a pretty good idea already," Ramouter said.

"Take my stupid advice, Ramouter," Joanna said over her shoulder. "Make sure there isn't anything next to Henley she can throw."

Henley didn't say a word as the door to Pellacia's office swung open and he stepped out. Even if she didn't already know that Streeter was now the SCU's responsibility, she would have known something was wrong. The atmosphere in the office was as heavy as death. Eastwood's shoulders were hunched around her ears, riddled with tension as she slowly paused and restarted CCTV footage, and Stanford was on the phone, tapping his pen against the side of his empty mug, a look of pained frustration on his face.

"Can you two come into my office?" Pellacia said to Henley and Ramouter. "Please."

The conciliatory tone in Pellacia's voice didn't put Henley at ease. She could feel her own anxiety creeping into the muscles in her neck, and she could sense Ramouter's demeanor becoming more cautious. Pellacia wouldn't meet her gaze.

"Before I go into the details, I want you to know I did every-thing I could to stop this," Pellacia began.

Even though Ramouter was in the room, it felt to Henley that Pellacia was talking only to her.

"But it's happening anyway," she said quietly.

A look of realization passed across Pellacia's face as it dawned on him that Henley was ten steps ahead of him.

"You already know about Streeter, don't you?" he said, sit-ting down. "Don't answer that. Of course, you know. I'm put-ting my money on either Linh or Jo."

"It doesn't matter who told us," said Henley as she remained standing next to Ramouter. "What I'm trying to work out is who in their right mind would think allocating Streeter's case to us was a good idea?"

"That's not all," said Pellacia. He reeled out the next sentence so quickly that Henley thought she'd misheard.

"We're doing what?!" she heard Ramouter say in disbelief. "Is this for real?"

"The Serial Crime Unit will be reinvestigating the five mur-ders that Streeter was originally convicted of in 1996," Pellacia repeated miserably.

"We don't do cold cases," Henley said as she attempted to rationalize what Pellacia had told them. "The Met has an en-tire unit dedicated to cold cases. We cover serial crimes that are happening now, not ones that were..."

Henley stopped the last few words from leaving her mouth. She wasn't ready to verbalize her questions and doubts about Rhimes's ethical behavior when she was struggling with her own guilt and failure to admit to her team that she'd had inter-actions with both victims before they died.

"Surely there's a conflict," asked Ramouter, looking across to Henley. "Not with me, I haven't been here long enough, and I didn't have a relationship with DCSI Rhimes. But the rest of you did. This doesn't feel right. It feels like a—"

"A stitch-up is what it feels like," said Henley. "And Ramouter is right. There is a conflict, especially with me."

"I know, and I agree. With all of it," said Pellacia. "It feels like... It's the equivalent of setting fire to Number Ten and blaming it on us even though the real arsonist is on the other side of the road holding a can of petrol."

"This is ridiculous," Henley said. "Wasn't there anything you could do?"

"Not when you've got the acting deputy commissioner sitting in front of you," said Pellacia.

"I'm assuming I'm the SIO of this entire thing—1995, Piper, Streeter, Rhimes? All of it," Henley spat.

Pellacia nodded.

"And what is the SCU supposed to do if we discover evidence that... I'm sorry, gov, I know that DCSI Rhimes meant a lot to all of you," said Ramouter carefully, "but what if we discover evidence of corruption?"

"Yes, gov," Henley said bitterly. "What exactly are we supposed to do in those circumstances? It's not as if we can arrest a dead man."

Ramouter shifted uncomfortably and looked down at his feet as Pellacia rose from his desk. For the first time in her life, Henley couldn't read Pellacia's face or body language. If she wasn't so proud, she would have apologized and showed some deference to the man who was her superior and her boss.

"Do your jobs."

"That's all you have to say?" Henley exploded. "Do you know what you're asking of us? What you're asking of me?"

"Henley, don't—"

"Don't what? Don't call this out for the shit that it is? Is there a plan to deal with the inevitable fallout of what we uncover? This won't be just about Rhimes. It will be about all of us. This isn't right. You're supposed to protect your team. You're supposed to—"

Ramouter and Henley both jumped as Pellacia slammed his hand on his desk. The air in the room grew thinner in the silence that followed. Eventually, Pellacia grabbed his cigarettes and lighter, and stalked toward the door. He turned to look at them, his hand on the handle.

"You have your orders," Pellacia said, his voice low. "Go do your job."

21

There was a time when Lillian Klein ruled the *Chronicle* news-room. The gold trim on her certificates from the Society of Journalists declaring her Journalist of the Year 1996, 1997, 2002 and 2005 had long ago lost their shine, and the sunlight that streamed into the newsroom from their position on the twenti-eth floor of 25 Churchill Place in Canary Wharf had bleached the print. Back then, in her midtwenties, award in her hand and posing for photographs with the newspaper owner's fat hand on her ass, she believed her star would always shine bright. Lillian jumped as she felt a tap on her shoulder. She pulled back her headphones and let them hang around her neck.

"Don't do that. What's wrong you?" Lillian shouted. She reached for the water bottle on her desk that contained three parts soda water and one part vodka. "No manners." She un-screwed the cap of her bottle and took a long, steadying drink.

Jake, the twenty-six-year-old trainee journalist, stood in front of her, twisting the gold signet ring on his finger. There was a small diamond in the middle of an engraved S. She had asked

him a few times what the S stood for and hadn't received a sat-
isfactory answer. The truth was that Lillian couldn't stand the
sight of him, or any of the junior reporters. Every single one of
them was another reminder of her dwindling star.

"Sorry, Lil," said Jake.

"It's Lillian. What do you want?" Lillian snapped. She scanned
the lines of desks in the large open-plan room. It was almost
7:00 p.m. and there was a frenetic buzz in the air that had put
her on edge from the minute she'd returned from her lunch
break more than five hours ago. She knew what the buzz was;
it was the energy that came from a breaking story.

"Sorry," Jake said again. All the confidence he'd once had
had drained away. "I did call you, but your headphones. They're
the noise can—"

"What is it?"

"You're needed. We're both needed by Adam in his office."

Lillian had to stand up to get a glimpse into Adam's office.
With each office renovation, her desk had been moved closer
to the fire exit.

Lillian saved the story she was working on and closed it down.
Jake jumped back as the wheels of Lillian's chair rolled onto the
rubbers of his Converses, leaving behind a scuff mark.

The night before, she'd received a text from a source with
four lines of information. She had been in the job long enough
to recognize the pieces of an explosive story. This was it—this
was her opportunity to resurrect her career.

Number Unknown
Text Message: Tuesday 22 June, 22:49

*Elias Piper's body found on Monday. Murder.
*Streeter's body transferred to Greenwich Mortuary.
*1995 murders of Gyimah, Chalmers etc—reopened.
All cases allocated to Serial Crime Unit. See attachment.
Save number. DQ

Adam had his sleeves rolled up and his shirt's top button un-done. The TV on his wall was fixed on BBC News with the volume on low. Lillian counted at least five coffee cups on his standing desk. Adam liked to give the appearance he was rushed off his feet and that it was killing him to spare you a moment of his time.

"I'll be brief," Adam said as he leaned against his desk. "Lil, about forty minutes ago Jake successfully completed his proba-tionary period, which makes him now a permanent member of the *Chronicle* staff. There will be celebratory drinks at Browns tonight for him, which we'll also use as an excuse to welcome the new intake of graduate trainees."

"Congratulations, Jake," Lillian said tersely.

"Thanks." Jake blushed in response. "That means a lot."

"You're both aware of the Court of Appeal overturning the conviction of the serial killer Andrew Streeter and the disap-pearance of his lawyer? And since the police announced a man's body has been found, we—"

"I wanted to talk to you about that," said Lillian, edging her chair forward. "I've heard from a source that the original murder investigations are being reopened and the Serial Crime Unit are investigating. There's clearly a link between Piper's and Streeter's deaths. Maybe whoever was really responsible for the murders twenty-five years ago is back."

"Are you suggesting that the original murderer, a serial killer, is back?" asked Jake, his eyes wide.

"The Burier, that's what he was called. That's the name *I* gave him," Lillian said proudly. She sat up straighter and flicked back her hair, a peacock fluffing its feathers.

"Good to see that you're thinking ahead and asking the right questions, Jake," said Adam. He turned back to Lillian. "This is a developing story, and it will be good for Jake to start a story from the ground up. Jake, you'll be covering the Elias Piper in-vestigations, and everything related to it. Your work has been impressive, and this will give you something to get your teeth into."

"His teeth into!" Lillian couldn't believe it. "But this is my— You do know that I reported on the original murders? I won awards," said Lillian, feeling her confidence deflate. "I wrote a book. It was a *Sunday Times* and *New York Times* bestseller."

"That was what, twenty-five years ago?" Adam waved his hand dismissively. "A lot has changed in twenty-five years. We're now competing with podcasts, breaking news on social media, bloggers. The public don't want an old voice from way back when. It would be good for someone to approach this from a fresh perspective. But I don't want your experience to go to waste, Lillian."

Lillian bit her lip as she tried to put a lid on her simmering anger. She knew what was coming next. The final confirmation that she was not respected and was no more than a library resource.

"As you have some knowledge of the original story, I want you to be there for Jake in an advisory capacity," said Adam. "Instead of him combing the internet for his research, he can come to you. You can assist him with any queries, routes that he should be exploring, sources that he can access, stuff like—"

"Jake, leave the room." Lillian stood up and looked down at Adam, who was at least four inches shorter than her.

"I really don't think you're in a—" Jake dared to say.

"Now, Jake," Lillian said in a tone that made it clear there was no room for debate. Jake turned on his heel and left without another word.

"This is my story," Lillian said once she and Adam were alone. "I've been at this newspaper for over twenty-seven years."

"I'm more than aware of that."

"This was my story from day one, when no one was interested in hanging around the criminal courts and standing outside police stations in the pissing rain. I own this story. I know everything about this case. It's only right that I should be on it—not Jake, who's only just worked out how to use the scanner. If anything, he should be assisting me. I'm the one who has the sources, sources which I would not be prepared to share under any circumstances. I've got my research, my original—"

"From twenty-five years ago, Lils."

"It's Lillian. We are not friends."

"We need a fresh perspective. What are you, fifty-five years old?"

"I'm fifty, and my age has got fuck all to do with it."

"Like I said. Fresh perspective," Adam replied. "I'm the editor and it's my call, so stop embarrassing yourself and see to it you're available for Jake and *his* story."

Lillian pulled her tote bag out from the bottom drawer of her desk and began to pack away her laptop, water bottle, and notebook. She tried to ignore the excitable laughter of Jake and the other graduates from the other side of the room. She couldn't remember the last time she'd been so furious. She'd seen it happen to other older journalists, gradually pushed aside, no longer considered for the big stories. She'd made the crime desk her domain and had staked her career on her ability to get to the heart of a story.

"You don't have it. You have no idea what it takes," she said to herself as she walked away from her desk and bumped straight into an intern. "Watch it," she barked. The intern was holding an A5 brown envelope in her hand. Lillian couldn't remember her name.

"I'm so sorry, Lillian," said the intern. "I've got post for you. It was put on my desk by mistake."

"Thank you," Lillian forced herself to say as she took the envelope and walked out of the office, ignoring the murmurs of, "See you tomorrow" and, "Are you coming for drinks?"

Lillian breathed a sigh of relief as she stepped into the empty elevator. She looked at the envelope the intern had handed her. Private and confidential was written in black above a printed address label. Lillian pressed the button for the ground floor and opened the envelope as the elevator descended from the twentieth floor. She pulled out the single sheet of paper and immediately felt the contents of her lunch, mixed with the vodka and club soda, bubble in her stomach. There was the image of Elias Piper, lying in a shallow grave, his legs and wrists bound. His mouth was wide open as though the photographer had caught him in the middle of a scream. It was only when the doors opened on the ground floor that Lillian realized she had been screaming during the whole journey.

22

"It's a shit situation, Anj," said Linh. She pulled out a tin of vodka and tonic from a carrier bag and handed it to Henley. "It's the equivalent of someone giving you a box of matches and a can of petrol and telling you that you can either drink the petrol, or set yourself on fire."

"You're so dramatic." Henley opened the can and took a long sip.

"Am I wrong though?" Linh asked. They were on the roof of the mortuary, leaning against a wall, looking down at the roads crawling with traffic. The sun had begun its descent in the distance.

"No, you're not wrong," Henley replied. "I can't see how I can work on this investigation and be objective."

"We should have gone to the pub instead of sitting on the roof like a couple of sixth formers." Linh opened her can of pornstar martini and took a swig. "What are you going to do?"

"I can either do my job or leave," said Henley. She felt her phone vibrate so she took it out—and felt even worse when she read the text message from Pellacia:

I'm sorry. It really was out of my hands. I would never put you in that position. X

"You're so stubborn that I wouldn't be surprised if you walked out," said Linh.

"Maybe it would be for the best," Henley replied, leaning her forehead against the wall. "I've fucked up, Linh."

"Why? Who was on the phone?" Linh asked with concern. She placed her hand on Henley's back. "Babe, what's going on?"

"I am such a bloody hypocrite and I've been so irresponsible," said Henley, raising her head.

"What's happened?"

"I have a connection to Elias Piper. I spoke with him back in May." Henley took a deep breath. "And I visited Andrew Streeter in prison a few weeks ago."

"What do you…" Linh paused, stepped back, brushed her hair away from her eyes, and chewed her bottom lip. Years of friendship had taught Henley to recognize when Linh was attempting to process the incomprehensible.

"Why the fuck were you visiting a serial killer in prison and meeting with his lawyer before they both ended up on my table?"

Henley winced at the sharpness of Linh's words. She emptied the can of vodka and tonic into her mouth.

"Well?" Linh said impatiently. Henley reached into the plastic bag and took out another can. "Anjelica!"

"I screwed up," Henley said quickly.

"Anjelica," Linh repeated as she stared directly into Henley's eyes. "We talk about everything. I thought we had no secrets between us. Why wouldn't you tell me about this?"

"We don't have any secrets, but what would have been the point?"

"The point is that I could have looked out for you and told you the minute his name popped up in my inbox. I could have prepared you, Anj, for the shock and all the other mental fuckeries that would come from Streeter turning up on my table."

"Linh, you've got to understand—"

"I don't understand," Linh snapped back. "I've supported you through all sorts of shit. You and Pellacia. You and Rob. I don't judge you. I do what friends do. Call you out on your bullshit and support you. All the horrible moments in your life—your mum, your dad and that psycho Olivier—I've been there for you."

"Linh," Henley said more gently. "I didn't want to think about Streeter once I left that prison. But you're right. I should have said something."

"Yeah, you're right. You should have done," Linh replied as her shoulders visibly softened. "Bloody hell, Anj, you really don't make life easy for yourself. You'd better tell me everything."

Henley explained about the email from Piper, her visit to prison, and Streeter's request for her to find his alibi witness. "Do you think I would have seen him if I had the slightest idea of what was going to happen?"

"If you could have predicted this, I would have told you to move to Las Vegas and ask for a three-year residency as a celebrity psychic," Linh said drily, reaching back into her bag for another drink and a packet of chips. "Have you spoken to Simon about this? He's your brother and he was there with you the day you found Melissa."

"Only about the appeal. He's so busy with work, and his wife is about to give birth any minute. I can't add to his stress, but I will tell him."

"I'm going to assume that you haven't told Pellacia either. And the team?"

"What do you think?" Henley said miserably.

"You're going to have to speak to him. All of them, actually," said Linh.

"I know."

"You're probably going to have to speak to the borough commander too."

"Maybe I should ask for a transfer out of the SCU."

"As if Pellacia would ever let you go," Linh said, raising an eyebrow. "Look, stop feeling sorry for yourself. You've been through much worse in the past few years. You can handle some stern words from Pellacia—and if that doesn't work then you can offer him a quickie in the stationery cupboard."

"Linh!" Henley exclaimed, staring at her friend open-mouthed but with a small amount of appreciation for Linh's strange sense of humor.

"Sex is a good tension breaker. Lots of endorphins."

"Oh, for God's sake, woman," Henley said. "I don't know why I tell you anything."

Linh pulled her in for a hug. "Because I'm your best friend. And look on the bright side: at least you're not the one who killed them."

Henley sat at the kitchen table later that evening with her laptop open in front of her. The cup of tea that she had made for herself had long gone cold and she'd only managed to eat half the prawn stir-fry that Rob had made for dinner. She'd left the SCU after speaking with Linh and made it home, much to Rob's surprise, in time for dinner. She'd tried to lose herself in giving Emma her bath and reading her bedtime stories until Emma passed out, as usual, halfway through *Funny Bones.*

"Do you want another one?" said Rob. He stepped into the kitchen from the garden and stood at Henley's side, peering into her cup, "Unless you want something stronger."

"No, the tea's fine," Henley replied as she deleted the last line on the Word document in front of her. She sniffed the air and pulled a face. "You smell of weed."

"Half of the street smells of weed, and I was in the privacy of my garden, not lighting up on the street. What are you working on?" Rob asked. He emptied the contents of Henley's cup into the sink and switched on the kettle.

Henley pushed back her chair, stretched her arms, and then massaged the side of her neck. "I'm thinking of handing in my notice."

She waited to hear celebratory noises from the rear of the kitchen but there was only the sound of the kettle reaching boiling point.

"Did you hear what I said?" Henley said as she twisted around in her chair and faced her husband. "I'm writing my resignation letter."

Rob remained silent as he poured hot water into two mugs. "Resigning from the SCU?" he asked, squeezing out the tea bags. "Or from the police? Because it doesn't mean much if it's just the SCU."

Henley turned back around and looked at the opening sentence of her letter. "From the force," she replied as she deleted the words *Serial Crime Unit* and replaced them with *Metropolitan Police*. "The entire force."

Rob placed the tea on the table and sat down opposite Henley. His pupils were dilated and Henley wondered how much he would be able to absorb of what they said next.

"I don't know what's taken you so long," he said finally, ripping open the packet of chocolate digestives he'd brought over. "You and that job of yours are dragging this family down."

"What do you mean by *dragging this family down*?" Henley asked defensively, closing down her laptop. She much preferred it when Rob drank a couple of beers in the evening and it brought out his docile side. The cannabis removed all the filters in the communication sector of his brain.

"Let's face it, what you do is only a job, it's not really a career, is it? What do you actually gain from it?"

Henley's hackles were up. "I'm a detective inspector of a specialist unit, and if it wasn't for the fact that I was on maternity leave—"

"No, no." Rob paused to swallow. "That's an excuse. You having a baby had nothing to do with your career stalling."

"Why are you being so obnoxious?"

Henley should have known it was too good to last. The last four years of their marriage had been a predictable and miserable cycle of the gentle hum of a harmonious family life followed by mutterings of discontent before reaching a dramatic showdown with accusations of neglect, selfishness, betrayal and threats of separation.

"It makes me wonder why I even agreed to stay at home with our daughter," Rob replied, ignoring the switch in Henley's tone.

"Hold on a second. You offered to stay and work from home and look after our daughter. It's what *you* wanted."

Rob's eyes widened. "What I wanted," he repeated. "At what point did you step in and say, 'Rob, no. I should be at home with our daughter. Let me spend this time, this precious time with her.' I didn't offer, Anjelica. I didn't have a choice."

"You *didn't have a choice*? You're making me sound like a dictator."

"You said it. More dictator than mother. What else was I supposed to think when you kept telling me that you felt stuck, that you were suffocating? You didn't fight to stay home and be a mum."

Henley lowered her head. Every word stung. There was more than a kernel of truth in what Rob was saying. It was bad enough when she questioned her own decision on the occasions Emma ran to Rob instead of her after falling over in the playground. Every word was a bullet piercing her skin.

"You're being cruel," Henley eventually said.

"Not cruel. I'm being honest. This job doesn't do anything for you. All it's brought us is stress and pain."

"You're making it sound as though I actively put myself in danger."

"People do strange things in order to feel validated."

"Fuck off, Rob."

"Oh, come on, Anj. I can't get excited about you *thinking* of resigning. I've been asking you to give up this job for years and you've bitten my head off every time. Something else must have happened to change your mind. Has this got something to do with Pellacia and his new bird?"

"Why on earth would it—Do you know what, forget I said anything," Henley said, pushing her chair back and standing up.

"You've always shut me down whenever I've brought up the possibility of you changing jobs. So what are you really running away from?"

"I'm not running from anything. I don't know… I don't feel that I'm the right person to run this case. In fact, no one in the SCU is the right person."

"And now you're throwing your toys out the pram?"

Henley picked up her laptop and willed herself to calm down. "Wouldn't it make you happy if I was to leave?"

"You don't really care about making me happy, otherwise you would have left years ago. It's not about me. It's never been about me. Sometimes I feel as though you think you're coming home to second best."

"Second best?"

"Yeah. Sometimes it feels like the SCU is your real home, your real family."

"Stop playing the victim, Rob. I wish I'd never said anything. I'm giving serious thought to my future, our future and you're—"

"What about my future? Look how you responded when I

told you I'd been headhunted for the senior business reporter position? I got a better response from the dog."

"Rob, why are you—"

"I've got my interview in Manchester next week and you haven't offered me a single word of support or asked me one single question about it."

"What are you talking about?" said Henley. "We did talk about it, and I do not treat you as though you're second best. You're my family. I can't believe we're even having this conversation."

"You can't believe it because you don't like hearing the truth," Rob said viciously. "What would you say if I said I was thinking about taking the job if they offered it to me?"

"Fucking take it then," Henley shouted, her temper finally breaking.

"Maybe you can take the opportunity to think about what you want out of this marriage while I'm away," Rob said coldly.

"This marriage?" Henley asked, stunned. "How has this conversation gone so far left? Why are you making everything about you, when I was sitting here telling you about a decision that could only benefit us?"

"Why shouldn't I finally make it about me?" asked Rob. "I've bent over backward to accommodate you and protect you."

"How have you protected me?"

"Can I ask you a question?" Rob stood up and pulled out a packet of tobacco from his front pocket. "Have you told *him* about the letters Andrew Streeter sent you?"

Henley reached out her free hand and gripped the chair. She felt a chill run across the back of her neck. "How do you know... have you been going through my things?"

"I'm your husband and, believe it or not, I love you," said Rob, placing a joint between his lips. "And as your husband, I'm entitled to know if there's anything that might put me and my daughter in danger."

"I asked you a question, Have you been going through my things?"

Rob's cheeks reddened. "It wasn't like that."

"What exactly was it? Because there is absolutely nothing in my bag that you could possibly need."

"You left your bag on the bed and I knocked it over by accident."

"Please," Henley said sarcastically, rolling her eyes.

"It's the truth. A letter fell out and I read it. I could tell it wasn't the first letter he'd sent you. I knew that there were more and, as your husband, out of bloody concern for you and our daughter, yes, I went through your things."

Rob stared back at Henley, his expression defiant. Henley searched his face for any signs of the dependable, safe, smart, humorous and tender man she'd fallen in love with.

"What happened to you? When did you turn into this…manipulative, controlling, narcissistic, insensitive—" Henley spat out adjectives, unable to form a complete sentence.

"Have you told Pellacia that you saw Streeter before he died, or is that another secret you're keeping to yourself?" Rob asked, ignoring the fury in Henley's voice.

"Do you know what, Rob?" Henley said, her voice hard. "You make it so easy for me to hate you and go back to him."

Ramouter kneeled on the floor to tie his son's shoelace and craned his neck to check the time on the clock. He tried to ignore the growing sense of panic as he watched the clock hands move closer to 8:20 a.m.

"There you go. You're going to have to learn to do this for yourself, Ethan. Now where's your rucksack?" asked Ramouter, easing himself up.

"In my room," said Ethan, jumping off the edge of the sofa.

"Go and get it. You're going to be late for school. Come on. Quickly."

Ramouter stood in the middle of the room with his hands on his hips as Ethan ran out of the living room. He'd done it all that morning: made Ethan's lunch, woken him up and made sure that he brushed his teeth and washed his face. Then he'd had a quick shower while Ethan ate his breakfast in front of another episode of *Star Wars Rebels*. Michelle's contribution had been to watch Ethan while she nursed a cup of tea and the washing machine entered a spin cycle.

"Miche, it would really help me out if you took Ethan to school this morning. I'm going to be late for the second time this week."

"But you said you didn't start work until nine," Michelle replied, pulling Ethan's empty cereal bowl toward her.

"Technically I don't start until nine, but I've told you before that working at the SCU isn't a normal nine to five. I can't traipse into the office at the stroke of nine o'clock, it will look as if I'm not taking my job seriously. They understood when you and Ethan first arrived that I would have a couple of late starts, but there is no reason why you can't take Ethan to school."

"There's a very good reason. I'm… It's a lot to take in. I forgot my way home when I picked Ethan up last week."

"You didn't forget because of your illness," Ramouter said as he followed Michelle into the kitchen. "You forgot because you've moved to a new area and you're learning your way around. I did the same thing when I arrived. I got lost on my way back from the corner shop and the train station. It happens."

"Maybe in a couple of weeks?" she replied as she placed the bowl in the sink.

"No, Miche. You have to start now," Ramouter replied. He tried to temper his frustration. He placed his hands on her shoulders and gently turned her around to face him. "You're doing well. Really well. You can live a normal life. The doctors said you're responding to the new treatment."

"But for how long, Salim? I could be fine today or for the next year or two, and then the next thing you know, you're having to deal with a woman whose brain can't send the message I need to swallow my food."

"Dad! I'm ready!" Ethan shouted out.

Ramouter dropped his arms and shook his head with resignation. "We take it one day at a time. That's what we've always said. We deal with the here and now, not focus on how things may be in two, three, or ten years' time. Otherwise we'll never enjoy our lives."

"You're right," Michelle said unconvincingly.

"Look, I'll take him to school this morning, but you have to pick him up this afternoon. You can't keep relying on him tagging along with Thea when she picks her kids up."

Michelle bit her lip and turned away. "Fine," she said, turning on the taps and picking up the bottle of dish detergent.

"And you can use the map app on your phone if you're feeling really apprehensive. Or ask our son—he's actually got a really good sense of direction."

"Great. A grown woman relying on her five-year-old child. Fantastic."

"I love you." He felt Michelle stiffen as he kissed the side of her cheek. He tried not to feel despondent when she failed to respond in kind.

Ramouter walked out of the kitchen and joined Ethan in the hallway, where he was doing some kind of dance. "Can I tell you what I learned about whales?" asked Ethan.

"Of course you can, but go and kiss your mum goodbye first," Ramouter said.

He watched Ethan run up to Michelle and kiss her goodbye. He had never expected to feel a creeping sense of doubt when he'd driven down the motorway in the van rental with Ethan asleep in the back and Michelle quietly absorbed in the audiobook that was playing, but as he stepped out of the front door, half listening to his son's excited chatter about whales, he wondered once again if he'd made a big mistake.

★ ★ ★

"Why can't I get rid of the feeling that this is a big, big mistake?" said Eastwood, leaning over the blue barriers in front of the sealed doors that used to be the public entrance to Greenwich police station.

"It is a mistake," Henley replied. "But we've got to get on with it and do our job."

"It's a big job though." Eastwood played with the lid on her coffee cup. "We've never dealt with anything of this magnitude, not even when Rhimes was in charge."

"Yes, we have. How many people did Abigail Burnley kill?"

"But that was one suspect, one investigation. We're dealing with three investigations at the same time, one with multiple murders." Eastwood lowered her voice as a mail courier walked past. "Piper's murder, Streeter's murder—"

"That hasn't been confirmed yet—about Streeter, I mean," Henley replied unconvincingly. "We're waiting for Linh's postmortem report on Streeter, and there's been a delay getting Piper's body to her. Some mix-up with the paperwork which resulted in his body sitting in the morgue at the Royal Free hospital."

"I'm sure there's a very good reason why Streeter's hospital band was stuck under a piece of Piper's thigh. Maybe a pigeon dropped it," Eastwood said, her voice dripping with sarcasm. "Anyway, as I was saying, we've got Piper, Streeter, plus five murders from 1995 and 1996. Seven murder cases in total."

"We'll be fine," Henley said.

"And another thing: there were twelve of us on the Burnley case and we weren't the SCU back then. We were part of Homicide and Major Crimes."

"You don't think we're up to it?" Henley asked wearily.

"Of course we're up to it," Eastwood said. "But just because we can do the job, doesn't mean that we *should* be doing this particular job."

"I know," Henley conceded. "But we've got no choice but to get on with it."

They started making their way back inside the building. "Do you think they're trying to set us up?" Eastwood asked as they walked up the stairs.

Henley raised an eyebrow. "How many specialist units are there in the entire Met who could deal with the 1995 cases? Six units, and I'm not even including the most obvious choice."

"The cold cases unit," Eastwood said. "If they really wanted to farm it out, they could have given it to the National Crime Agency. They're always bleating on about how they're the UK equivalent of the FBI. Yeah, it feels like a setup."

"Eastie, I want you to do me a favor," Henley asked. They had reached the stairwell door that led to the fourth floor and the SCU's office. "I need you to focus specifically on what Rhimes did in 1995. I need you to look at everything he did right, but also focus on any discrepancies, the little things that don't make sense."

"Alongside reinvestigating the original murders, right?"

"No."

"You want me to carry out my own side investigation?" Eastwood queried, a hard look in her eyes.

"You did a secondment with the anti-corruption command," Henley said, sitting down on the top step. "You know what to look for. I'm too close...*was* too close to Rhimes. You won't ignore your gut instinct."

"Neither will you," Eastwood said with stoic determination as she joined her on the step. "You're good like that, you know how to compartmentalize."

"Not this time," Henley said as she shook her head. "I can't trust myself when it comes to Rhimes. I've already screwed up." She paused, and then said quickly, "I visited Streeter in prison a few weeks before he died."

Henley watched Eastwood's face for an expression of surprise or disappointment but there was nothing. Eastwood was taking it all in and considering everything that Henley was saying before she made a judgment. Eventually, she said, "Go on."

"Once you start digging, I want you to look for a name: Kerry Huggins, née Searle."

"Who is she?"

"A friend or an ex of Andrew Streeter. He gave me her details and—"

"Did you go and see her too?"

"Yes. And Elias Piper." Henley held up her hands. "I know how it's starting to look—that I'm more involved in this than I should be."

"It is starting to look that way. Are you going to tell the others? Are you going to tell Pellacia?"

"Yes, and I'll get one of the sergeants from Lewisham police station to take my statement. I don't want any of this coming back to bite us in the ass."

Eastwood simply nodded. "What did Huggins tell you?"

"That she was Streeter's alibi and Rhimes bribed her with two grand to stay quiet."

"He bribed her? No, Rhimes wouldn't..." Eastwood stopped and took a breath. "He...he... I can't." She shook her head angrily, as though she was arguing with herself.

Detective Sergeant Eastwood had little patience for sentimentality and worked on the basis that everyone was guilty until proven innocent, but today she'd allowed herself to drop her emotional guard.

"Do you believe her?" Eastwood asked in a tone that demanded an answer. The same tone that she used when interviewing a suspect.

"I told you, I can't trust myself when it comes to Rhimes," Henley admitted. "I want to believe she's lying but I have doubts. Something inside me says that she's telling the truth, but then I think about us listening to him go on about the dry rub on his ribs when we were at his house for his sixtieth, or him singing the bloody *Peppa Pig* theme tune with Emma. I can't be the one to investigate him."

Eastwood didn't reply as the sound of drilling reverberated around the building and the muted tones of Stanford giving orders to a courier traveled up the staircase from the floor below.

"Fine," said Eastwood, standing up and brushing herself down. "But I'm telling you now that I'm running this side investigation as though I'm the senior investigating officer and I'm going to treat DCSI Harry Rhimes as an alleged bent copper. And if I do find evidence of wrongdoing, boss, then—"

"You won't come to me or Pellacia. You'll go straight to the borough commander."

"That's exactly what I'll do," Eastwood replied. "Make sure you're prepared, because if I discover Rhimes was bent, then that means everything we've done since he became head of the SCU will be questioned. All of it. This could be the end of the SCU."

23

Streeter's corpse showed signs of medical intervention and the incisions caused by Linh's work. His body was covered with bruises and scratches, likely from a needle dragging across his fragile skin. The muscles in his arms and legs had wasted away, following months of lying in a hospital bed. Ramouter shuddered at the sight of him—and then shuddered again as he remembered that the body of Elias Piper lay on the examination table behind him, covered with a sheet.

"No Henley?" Linh asked. There was no hint of her usual dark humor as she switched on the lamp over Streeter's body. Linh in her serious mode scared Ramouter.

He moved to the opposite side of the table and faced her. "She's in a meeting with Pellacia and the borough commander."

"Is this about her little jaunts to see our dead guy here and his girlfriend?"

Ramouter frowned. "Jaunts? What are you talking about?" he asked, confused.

"Ah, forget that I said anything," said Linh quickly.

"How am I supposed to do that?" Ramouter asked.

"Make sure you watch Henley's back," said Linh. "She's not just your boss, she's your partner. Investigating this cold case stinks, and there may be times she'll let her emotions get in the way. Understand? Now, let's talk about Mr. Streeter. You're going to love what I've found out."

"How did Streeter die? Because I can't see any signs of obvious trauma, beyond the usual bruising."

"Sometimes the evidence is below the surface, youngling."

"Still watching Star Wars with the new boyfriend, I see," Ramouter said with a smile.

"I never call him my boyfriend. And he never will be if I have to keep explaining every single thing to him when we're watching the films—'Linh, who's Jango Fett? Why didn't Darth Vader sense Luke as a kid?'—I don't give a monkey's how good he is in bed."

"He's got a point about Vader," Ramouter said.

"Shut it," Linh said. She placed her gloved hands on Streeter's left hip and gently turned him toward her. "Cancer really is a bitch; he only weighed nine and a half stone at the end. Not that it was the cancer that killed him."

"His hospital notes said he was in remission?"

"I spoke to his oncologist, who confirmed it. Right, look here, can you see the bruising on the side of his left thigh?"

The large dark red bruise was the size of Ramouter's fist. "This bruise is a different color than the ones on his arms," he observed.

"The ones on his arms are from Streeter being treated like a pin cushion, with endless blood tests and IV insertions. But the bruise on the left hip is larger, darker and, in my opinion, fresher."

"Are you saying this bruise happened at the time of death?"

"That's exactly what I'm saying. And there's a fracture on the left hip bone. And…" Linh lowered Streeter's hip and picked up his right hand, which hung limply in the wrong direction. "Clean break." She turned away from the body and pointed at the X-ray images on her computer monitor. "One of the side effects of chemotherapy and radiation is that it can reduce calcium levels in the body, which results in bone loss and increases the risk of osteoporosis and fractures."

"So if Streeter fell, he would be more susceptible to broken bones?" Ramouter asked.

"Those breaks, on his hips and wrist, are not in his hospital records," said Linh. "They must have occurred when he died. He was weak. He was found on the floor, right?'"

"Actually, no. The nurse who found him gave a statement saying he was found dead in his bed," Ramouter said.

"If you ask me, that's a lie. To me, that break in the hip is consistent with a fall, and there's nothing in his notes about any breaks or fractures. He would have been in a lot of pain with a break like that."

"Wasn't he on morphine, painkillers?"

"Patience. We'll get on to the toxicology results."

"Let's say he'd fallen, recently," Ramouter said. "Would he have been able to get back into bed?"

"Not with a break like that. And you saw his right wrist. He fell and either put out his hand to break his fall, or he fell in that position, but his bones were weak and they broke. That would have been in his notes if it had happened before he died. It's a new break."

"Why would they cover this up?"

"That's for you to figure out. Now, on to toxicology. Streeter had finished his chemo and radiation treatments three weeks ago, but there are traces of chemo and antibiotics. No morphine, but there was codeine. Not enough to stop him screaming out from pain from a broken hip and wrist. And there's diphacinone in his blood. A lot of diphacinone."

There was a moment of silence while Ramouter stared back at Linh blankly. "What on earth is diphacinone?"

"Rat poison," Linh said simply. Ramouter's face paled. "There were high volumes of rat poison in his blood. More specifically, zinc phosphide and brodifacoum, which is an anticoagulant found in rat poison. The poison was administered intravenously."

"So someone injected it straight into his veins? It wasn't stirred into his mashed potato and gravy?"

"Correct."

"What exactly happened to him?" asked Ramouter.

"Rat poison causes internal bleeding. The zinc phosphide attacks the heart and kidneys. When I opened him up there was a clear buildup of gases in his organs and blood in his urine and rectum. He bled out of his mouth, nose, ears, and eyes. In addition, he vomited, which is why there was hardly anything in his stomach and traces of vomit in his esophagus."

"Bloody hell. How did he end up on the floor?" Ramouter asked.

"That would have been due to the convulsions and seizures. You can see the bruising on his forehead, and there's also some on the back of his head. It would have been chaos in that room," Linh said, covering Streeter's body with a sheet. "Can you imagine? Vomit, shit and blood everywhere."

"But according to the hospital report he was found dead in bed," Ramouter pointed out.

"And he'd been washed and cleaned when I finally got him. Dr. Henry McKay, who I actually know, had recorded Streeter's cause of death as organ failure without actually opening him up."

"Someone at that prison covered it up," said Ramouter. "Streeter was murdered?"

"Yes, and he suffered. A lot."

Henley scanned the faces of Ramouter and Stanford. Eastwood had her back turned. It was only the four of them, and she had finally told them everything about Piper, Streeter and Kerry Huggins. They had listened in silence, astounded and blindsided by what they were hearing.

"Oi, Eastie," gasped Stanford, spinning around and tugging her shirt. "Did you know about this?"

"What is wrong with you?" Eastwood slapped Stanford's hand away. "Yes, I did. But before you get your panties in a twist, she only told me this morning. And the boss and I have talked about it already. She knows how I feel. We don't have to go over it again."

Stanford turned to face Henley, his eyes narrowing. "What about the govnor?"

"That's what the meeting with Pellacia and the borough commander was about." Henley sighed with both relief and guilt. "Full disclosure. I told them everything and, no, they were not happy about it."

"I'm not happy about it either. Why didn't you tell me?"

"Let's be fair," Ramouter said sympathetically. "The boss couldn't have predicted Piper and Streeter would be murdered."

"That's not the point," Stanford insisted. "It's a lot to go through without—Hold on, did you at least tell your husband?"

Henley raised her head and suddenly found herself fascinated by the cracks in the ceiling. She'd tried to apologize to Rob earlier that morning, but it had fallen on deaf ears. "I told Rob," she said. "Let's leave it at that."

"I'm not happy." Stanford folded his arms. "How are we supposed to look out for you if you don't tell us what's going on?"

"Look, I feel bad enough as it is."

"You may feel bad, but that doesn't explain why you didn't tell us. When did Piper first contact you?"

"Bank holiday weekend. I got an email from Piper. You were with me."

"Could be something. Could be nothing. That's what you said." Stanford shook his head in disappointment.

"You've got to understand, I was only a kid when Melissa was killed and for two years of my life I was scared to death. I was not in a good place back then. I didn't want to revisit the past. I've been through enough."

The silence in the room was harsh and numbing.

"I can't take it back," said Henley, her voice breaking. "If you feel—and I would understand completely if this was the case—if you feel that you can no longer work with me, trust—"

"Oh, for Pete's sake. Calm down," Stanford said. He stood up and gave Henley a big hug. "I'll get over it."

"Thank you," Henley said, rubbing away a small tear that had settled in the corner of her eye.

"Are you all right, boss?" Ramouter asked with concern.

"Not really. I feel shitty that I lied."

"You didn't lie," Ramouter said. "At the time, there was no need for us to know. Now there is a need, and we know. But..." he trailed off.

"What is it?" Henley asked.

"The elephant in the room," Ramouter said slowly. "How are you all feeling about Rhimes?"

"Bloody hell. This is turning into therapy hour," said Stanford.

"I'm being serious," Ramouter replied. "I can ask these questions because I didn't know him. I'm not as close to this, to him. I can't imagine that you're not feeling some way about it."

"I do feel a way about it," said Eastwood. "But I'm not going to focus on that right now because I have a job to do."

"Stanford?" asked Ramouter.

"I'm fucking pissed," Stanford said, throwing his hands in the air. "Disappointed, betrayed, let down. Did I say pissed?"

"Aye, you did."

"Do you believe Huggins?" Henley asked. "That Rhimes bribed her?"

"I don't know, but there's no smoke without fire," Stanford

replied. He rubbed his hands across his face. "See? Now I'm angry with myself for even thinking Rhimes might've done it. I can't see him doing it, but then I didn't know him back then, all those years ago."

"People change," Ramouter said.

"Yeah, they do," Henley said. "Or sometimes they're very good at hiding who they really are."

"It's not much of a surprise that Streeter was murdered," Henley said to Ramouter. They were standing in the old canteen on the second floor, watching Stanford and Eastwood unpacking dozens of archive boxes that contained every file related to the original investigations into the 1995 murders.

"Are we sure this is everything?" Eastwood asked, sneezing for the third time as she carefully placed a pile of multicolored, overflowing folders, held together with brittle elastic bands, on the table.

"That's everything they've sent us, so we're going to have to work on the basis that's all there is and fill in any blanks for ourselves," Henley replied. She walked over to a table that was already covered with folders. She ran a finger across one of them, rubbing away some dusty grime from a peeling white label that had *Case File: Stephanie Chalmers. URN: 01IBT04/95* written on it.

"Murdered by poison though," said Ramouter, picking up their conversation.

"Only someone who had access to the prison and access to Streeter could've poisoned him," said Henley.

"But that could have been anybody. He was in an open prison, and it also doesn't fit the MO of The Burier."

"Are you sure it wasn't you, Henley?" Stanford shouted out from the other side of the room. "You walking around with bottles of rat poison in your bag?"

"Shut up, Stanford." Henley opened the file for Chalmers.

"Prisoners may be able to walk in and out of a category D prison as and when they please, but that doesn't mean any old Tom, Dick or Harry can walk in."

"Streeter had been in the hospital wing for six weeks," said Ramouter. "The initial plan was to move him back out into the general population once he'd got signed off by the doctor, but obviously that plan went out the window with the Court of Appeal judgment."

"So, looking at the timelines," said Henley, scanning through the pages of Streeter's postmortem report, "according to Linh, Streeter is murdered on Tuesday morning, the fifteenth, the day after the court's decision. The following night, between 9:30 p.m. and 11:00 p.m., Piper is kidnapped. We're still waiting on time of death for Piper, but the question is why would someone need them both out of the picture?"

"They knew who the real murderer of the 1995 murders was?" Ramouter said cautiously.

Henley nodded. "Yes, more than likely. We're going to have to assume the Court of Appeal was right and Streeter was wrongly convicted. Did Linh give any indication when she'd complete Piper's autopsy?"

"She said she'll have something for us by the end of the day. In the meantime, I'll contact the prison and get a list of staff members on the hospital wing."

"Start with the nurse who said she found Streeter dead in the bed. Find her and bring her in. You've got more than reasonable grounds for her arrest. Making false statements is a good start. I need to go and get ready for this press conference at Lewisham."

Ramouter nodded, turned to walk out, and then stopped. "If Streeter did know who The Burier was and he told Piper, would Piper have been able to disclose anything that Streeter had told him?"

"Not unless Streeter gave him permission to do so. When

I saw Piper, he was working from a paper file, and he made a point of telling me he didn't like the digital case system."

"We'll check if the Streeter case files are in Piper's office," said Ramouter.

"Or possibly at Piper's home," Henley said. "Let's say that Streeter waived legal privilege. Why wasn't the fact Streeter knew the real identity of the killer mentioned in their application to the CCRC?"

"Maybe Streeter suddenly naming people after all this time would have weakened their application." Ramouter shrugged. "Or he might have been protecting whoever it was?"

"Or maybe Streeter really was involved and if he admitted that he knew who the killer was all along, then he'd have had to admit his involvement, and that would've meant never getting out of prison," said Henley.

"Doesn't matter now," said Ramouter. "Streeter is dead, so is his lawyer. And we don't know who else is on the killer's list."

"Nice of you to finally join us," said Linh as her assistant and the junior pathologist, Theresa, walked into the examination room, adjusting her surgical gown.

"Sorry, sorry," Theresa said. "Tube delays. I'm here now." She picked up her camera and adjusted the settings. "Anyway, it's not as if you were alone. You've got the new guy, Ben."

"Ben doesn't laugh at my jokes," Linh replied, pulling back the sheet covering Elias Piper's body.

Theresa took in the lines of bruising on his body, and the coarse thread running across his eyelids and lips. "Shit. Did they really find him in a fridge? We had that woman who was found in a trunk once, but a fridge is a new one."

"Yeah, it's true, but I suspect it wasn't the fridge that killed him." Linh checked the Dictaphone app on her computer was recording, then picked up her scalpel.

"It looks as though the sewing was done postmortem," said Theresa, taking a photograph of Elias's face.

Linh placed the scalpel against the thread that ran through Piper's mouth and sliced it. There was the distinct sound of sharp steel cutting through cotton that had been hardened by blood. She picked up a pair of tweezers, carefully pulled out the thread and placed it into a stainless steel dish. "We'll send these straight to Anthony's forensic team." She pulled the overhead lamp down toward her and picked up a pair of surgical tongs, gently prizing Piper's mouth open. She worked silently as she swabbed the walls of Piper's cheeks.

"There's something here," Linh said, lifting Piper's tongue.

"What is it?" Theresa asked, leaning in closer.

"I'm not sure. It's under the tongue. And I think there's something at the back of his throat too." Linh gripped the bronze object with the tongs and gently pulled. She held it up to the light and then placed it in a separate bowl.

"Is that...is that a £2 coin?" Theresa said, stunned.

"It bloody is," Linh replied. She adjusted the height of the block under Piper's head, repositioned his neck, and inserted the tongs deeper into his mouth. "It's like playing Operation," she said, slowly withdrawing the tongs, trying not to catch whatever was at the end against the roof of the mouth.

"And now a piece of paper?" Theresa asked quizzically.

Keeping the tongs firmly pressed together, Linh carried the folded piece of paper over to a smaller steel table. Picking up another scalpel, she gently pried the folded piece of paper open.

1. Andrew Streeter
2. Elias Piper
3. ?
4. Maybe four

Linh turned the small piece of paper over and checked if there was anything on the other side.

"Theresa," she said quickly. "Take a photo and send it to Detective Inspector Henley immediately."

24

Lillian Klein reached into her bag and her hand brushed against the envelope containing the photograph of Elias Piper. She'd examined the photo carefully when she was in the safety of her own home. There was nothing in the photograph to identify Piper's location or the identity of the photographer. Lillian considered her options. She could pass the photo on to the detectives at the SCU. It wouldn't be the first time that a killer had contacted a journalist, but there was the possibility that the detectives would start asking questions she didn't want to answer. The second option was to do nothing. Lillian took out her phone and scrolled through Twitter while she waited in the queue for her press credentials to be checked. There was a time when the other reporters at these events would gather round her like vultures in a failed effort to uncover her technique and gain access to her sources. Now she was being treated as though she was irrelevant. She looked at Jake, who was hopping from one foot to the other with excitement as the civilian officer ticked his name off the list.

"I can't believe I'm fucking babysitting," Lillian said under her breath as she took a step forward and handed the officer her bag and ID card.

"What was that?" asked Jake, already on the other side of the security desk.

"I was saying you should use the dictation app on your phone," said Lillian, retrieving her belongings and scanning the densely packed rows for a spare couple of seats.

"I plan to, but I still like to write things down and I've got my list of questions ready."

"You need to focus on what comes out of the mouths of those detectives in front of the mics. Base your questions on what they say, not on your preconceptions," Lillian said. She grabbed the strap of Jake's bag and dragged him to two chairs that were currently unoccupied in the second row.

"I know what I'm doing. What was it that Adam said? You're here to assist *me*."

It was all Lillian could do to resist the urge to smack the smirk off Jake's face.

A door opened on the far right and Henley and Pellacia approached the lectern.

"Who's that?" Jake asked, pressing the record button on his phone and placing it on his lap.

Lillian pursed her lips. She cringed as Callum O'Brien, the crime correspondent for the *Evening Standard*, turned around and grinned at her.

"Where did you find this one, Lils? The nursery?" Callum joked. "Actually, I'm surprised to see you here. Not exactly making waves these days. Probably using that dusty old award of yours as a doorstop, eh?"

"Fuck off, Callum," Lillian replied. She turned to Jake. "That's the SIO. Detective Inspector Henley," she reluctantly explained.

"SIO means senior investigating officer," said Callum. "Would you like me to spell that for you?"

"Shut up, Callum," Lillian hissed. She turned her attention to Detective Inspector Henley. She wasn't a nervous teenager anymore. Lillian recalled how she'd stood her ground when she was being cross-examined in the witness box, and how she had described the moment she found her friend's body. Lillian scribbled a question in her notebook.

"Could everyone please take a seat," said Henley. "This press conference is scheduled for twenty minutes only. I have a short statement to make and then I will be taking questions. For those who don't know, my name is Detective Inspector Henley of the Serial Crime Unit and I'm here with DSI Pellacia. Right, three days ago—"

"What are you doing? Sit down!" Lillian hissed as Jake suddenly jumped to his feet. Every journalist turned to look at him quizzically. Lillian crossed her legs and shifted her body away from Jake.

"Why is the Serial Crime Unit dealing with the case of Elias—" Jake began.

"You either didn't hear what I said, or you must be new to how this all works," Henley said loudly, clearly irritated. "Sit down. There will be time for questions at the end."

Jake sat down in embarrassment. "I hope you realize you've blown it," said Lillian, unable to hide the glee from her voice.

The room was pin-drop quiet as every journalist listened to Henley explain that a body had been found in Little Venice, that it had been formally identified as the body of Elias Piper, that this was now a murder investigation, that his family and friends had been informed and that there were no suspects.

As soon as Henley had finished, Callum jumped out of his seat.

"Detective Inspector Henley. You mentioned that the Serial Crime Unit is also investigating the original 1995 murders. Is Piper's murder linked to that case?" Callum shouted over the din of journalists trying to be heard and cameramen taking photos.

"The 1995 cases have been reopened but they are two separate investigations and will be treated as such until we find evidence to suggest otherwise. Next question," said Henley.

"Michela Elroy from Sky News. Are there any updates as to Andrew Streeter's cause of death? I understand his body was transferred from Medway Maritime Hospital to Greenwich Public Mortuary?"

Lillian caught the look that passed between Pellacia and Henley. She couldn't figure out if they were concerned that they'd been caught out about something, or whether it was a silent message between two people who were more than colleagues.

"That's correct," Pellacia said, bringing the microphone closer to his mouth and squinting against the glare of the camera flashes. "His body was transferred to Greenwich Public Mortuary and the postmortem has been completed. The report has been sent to the coroner's office. We can confirm that the senior coroner has ruled that Andrew Streeter died under suspicious circumstances—"

Pellacia's voice was drowned out by the sound of multiple questions being thrown at him.

"Is the SCU investigating Streeter's murder?"

"Is his death linked to the murder of Elias Piper?"

"Can you tell us exactly how Streeter was murdered?"

"Were Piper and Streeter murdered by the same person?"

"Do you have any evidence that the person who murdered Piper and Streeter was also responsible for the 1995 murders?"

"We have no evidence at this time in regard to any of those questions. The SCU will also be investigating Andrew Streeter's murder. There have been no arrests at this time. Enquiries are ongoing," Pellacia replied loudly, and then stepped back from the lectern. Henley stepped forward, taking his place.

Lillian rose to her feet. The photographers were lowering their cameras and the other journalists were closing their notebooks.

Lillian knew all about timing, and she knew this was the perfect opportunity to ask her question.

"We are asking members of the public to come forward with any information that they think may be useful to all three murder investigations. Anyone who provides information will remain anonymous and their information will be taken in the strictest of confidence," said Henley. "I don't want anyone to be put off from talking to us because they're concerned for their safety. The SCU will look after you. That will be—"

"Lillian Klein from the *Chronicle*. Detective Inspector Henley, you were a prosecution witness in the 1995 murders, and you found the body of the first victim, Melissa Gyimah, and identified Andrew Streeter as being present at the scene. Is it appropriate for you to be the senior investigating officer in these investigations? How can you possibly remain impartial when the first murder victim, Melissa Gyimah, according to the evidence which you gave in the trial, was your best friend? Isn't there a conflict?"

Everything and everyone seemed to disappear into the gray walls around Lillian. It was only Henley and her, standing in the eye of the storm. These were the moments she lived for. Knowing that the person in front of her was trapped in a corner. That feeling of power in asking a question that would unleash a flood of trouble.

"It's been a long time, Lillian. For you and for me," said Henley, her voice steady and commanding. No trace of emotion. "Those at New Scotland Yard, people with more authority than DSI Pellacia and me, have concluded that there is no conflict here."

Lillian picked up on Henley's tone immediately. "So it would be correct to say that the SCU didn't agree with New Scotland Yard's decision to allocate these three cases to your unit?" said Lillian. Either unwittingly or purposefully, Henley had given her another angle to her story.

"I'm the senior investigating officer because of my experience as a detective inspector, not because I was a prosecution witness twenty-five years ago."

"Is it correct to assume that the borough commander, Chief Superintendent Geraldine Baker, was not in agreement with the acting deputy commissioner?" Lillian said with a knowing smile.

"You know where to direct any further questions, Lillian," said Henley. "Thank you all again."

They were dismissed.

Lillian tried to hold on to the surge of adrenalin coursing through her body as Henley and Pellacia left the room. The first thing she was going to do when she got home was open that bottle of expensive white wine she'd received for her birthday.

"Why didn't you tell me?" Jake's face was contorted with shame and anger. "You should have told me about the inspector and her history. You're supposed to be assisting me, not hindering me."

Lillian didn't bother to reply. They walked along the hallways of Lewisham police station in silence and eventually stepped out onto the high street. Shouts of overexcited teenagers could be heard over the South London traffic crawling slowly along the main road. A couple were arguing outside the station entrance. Lillian loved this city.

"Listen, Jake," she said, turning to him. "It's one thing to assist you, but I'm not here to hold your bloody hand and do your job for you."

"That should have been my question to ask," Jake said angrily.

"You shot your load too early. You will not survive in this game if you don't learn to think on your feet and be bullish." Lillian laughed. "You already made an idiot of yourself. Take this as a lesson."

"You stood in that press room and sabotaged me."

"Grow up, Jake. You've got two choices: you can go back to

the paper and explain how you showed yourself up as an amateur, or you can go home and forget all about today."

"But this is my story," Jake whined.

Lillian squared up to him, her expression hard. "No. I made it very clear in Adam's office that this is *my* story. It's always been my story. And there's nothing you can do about it." Lillian strode off in the direction of Lewisham train station, leaving a dumbfounded and angry Jake in her wake.

The photograph of Elias Piper was still burning a hole in her bag.

The woman sitting in front of Ramouter had her defenses up. Her arms were firmly crossed, and she had pushed her chair as far back from her desk as possible. Ramouter was sitting on the other side of her desk, claiming space that was clearly hers. The woman pressed her lips together tightly.

"Do I need a lawyer?" she asked. She pushed a long curly strand of black hair back into her bun.

"Why would you think you need a lawyer?" Ramouter asked, turning the pages of his notebook, his pen poised. The first name on his list was the nurse that Henley had wanted him to bring in, Caroline Swann, but so far, his phone calls to her and the knock on her front door had gone unanswered.

The office was generic and small. The furniture was standard beechwood with a dented blue filing cabinet in the corner and a bookcase that was no more than a dumping ground for excess medical supplies, stationery, and half-empty bottles of water. The Venetian blinds were hanging at a lopsided angle across the window. Ramouter looked down at his list again, this time at the third name he'd written down.

"Gabrielle Huston," he said.

"It's *Gabriella* with an *a*," she replied insistently.

"And you're the senior nurse here? You organize the staff,

maintain the schedules and liaise with the hospitals if you have to transfer any prisoners."

"You're making it sound as though I'm just admin. I'm more than that. I'm a professional."

"Of course you are," Ramouter said, forcing a smile on his face. "You understand why I'm here today? Andrew Streeter."

Gabriella's right eyelid twitched rapidly as she nodded. "We did everything right," she said.

"The postmortem results raise more questions than answers," Ramouter said matter-of-factly.

"He was a very ill man. The cancer obviously caused severe damage to his organs. It's such a poisonous disease," said Gabriella without any sense of empathy.

"Interesting choice of words," Ramouter replied. "*Poisonous.*"

"Why is it interesting?"

"Because that's exactly what happened to him. The postmortem revealed that Streeter was poisoned and that the poison entered his system intravenously. That is clear evidence of intent. Clear evidence of murder."

Gabriella opened her mouth and her lips moved silently. Eventually she managed to speak. "Poison?" she asked.

"Rat poison, to be exact," said Ramouter.

"Excuse me?"

"Andrew Streeter was poisoned with liquid rat poison, in the hospital wing of this prison. Now, the chances of him poisoning himself are nonexistent. Someone with access to Streeter and to this wing poisoned him."

"But the only people who had access to him… It's an open prison," Gabriella said quickly.

"How many people work in this hospital wing?"

"We're not a hospital wing. This is a healthcare wing. There's a big difference. We provide primary care, mental health support and palliative care, but we're not a hospital. We send the prisoners to Medway Maritime Hospital or St. Luke's Hospital if they require more intensive treatment."

"You have only six beds here in the hospital wing and only three of those beds were occupied when Andrew Streeter was transferred here eight weeks ago."

"That's correct," said Gabriella. "As I said, we're a health-care wing."

"But you provide twenty-four-hour nursing cover."

"We're a small team," Gabriella said, finally answering Ramouter's question. "There are two general nurses and a mental health and learning disability nurse. And then there's me. I'm in charge."

"But you don't work twenty-four hours?"

"No. Our shifts are 8:30 a.m. to 7:30 p.m. Monday to Friday, and until 5:00 p.m. on the weekend. We have agency nurses to cover the night shifts. They have a habit of coming and going."

Ramouter checked his notes again. There was no mention of anyone covering the night shift. "Who was the nurse on shift the night before Streeter died?" he asked.

"His name was Filip, with an *F*, Szymanski. He's Polish. Well, I say that, but he was like us. He wasn't born there, but his parents were."

"Filip? He's not on my list."

"He left."

"When did he leave?"

Ramouter saw Gabriella's face pale slightly as she made the mental calculation.

"His last shift finished the morning Mr. Streeter died, but he told us he was leaving two weeks before that. He gave us notice. Filip was nice. A professional. Everyone here liked him."

"And this Filip would have given Streeter breakfast and done all the necessary checks in the morning?"

Gabriella nodded. Ramouter knew that look on her face. She was trying to find a way of absolving herself of any mistakes.

"He did everything right. You've seen Mr. Streeter's record, the logbook."

"But Filip wouldn't have been supervised?"

"Why would he? The agency wouldn't have sent anyone who wasn't experienced."

"Did you check his CV or his record with the Nursing and Midwifery Council?"

Gabriella pursed her lips, reaching for the open can of Diet Coke on her desk. She took a sip, leaving some pink lip gloss on the can. "The nursing agency would have done all the checks," she said.

"I'll take that as a no then." Ramouter made a note. "As you relied on the agency, I'm going to assume you didn't check out Caroline Swann's record either? She joined your team seven months ago from the same agency."

"Well…no, no," Gabriella stuttered.

"Right," Ramouter said slowly. "The records show that nurse Caroline Swann was on the morning shift."

"Yes, she found Mr. Streeter when she did her ward checks. She was on her own until I arrived. I usually start my shift at nine thirty, and I don't work on the weekends. But I had a…a personal issue so I didn't come in until eleven that morning."

"She was on her own that whole time?" Ramouter asked with surprise.

"Yes. We didn't have many prisoners in the healthcare wing when Mr. Streeter died. Only two in total."

"Were you aware that Caroline Swann had been before the Nursing and Midwifery Council for a disciplinary hearing and was subject to a twelve-month interim order that was made in February this year?"

"I was aware of the order," Gabriella admitted reluctantly.

"In that case, can you explain why Caroline was alone on her shift when the interim order specifically states that she must not be the nurse in charge of a shift and that she had to be directly supervised by a band six nurse at all times? You're a band six nurse. Where were you on the morning Streeter died?"

The clock on the wall ticked loudly and the printer in the corner of the room spat out the last pages of a report as Ramouter waited for an answer.

"I... I was at a... I said that I had an appointment," Gabriella finally said. "A personal appointment. You've got to understand. This isn't how it looks."

"I'll leave that for you to explain to the Nursing and Midwifery Council," said Ramouter. He opened the plastic wallet on his lap and pulled out copies of the staff logbook. "Let's talk about times," he said, handing a copy to Gabriella.

"The log shows Filip logging out at 8:47 a.m., Caroline logged in at 8:28 a.m.," said Ramouter. "She was on her own for nearly two and a half hours. The alarm that Streeter was dead wasn't raised until 11:16 a.m., over fifteen minutes after you came on shift. The paramedics' witness statement says that Streeter was already stiff when they arrived, which means rigor mortis had set in. This suggests that he would have been poisoned, hemorrhaging, and vomiting on the floor by the time Caroline started her shift, so why didn't she raise the alarm earlier? Why did she cover up Streeter's murder?" Ramouter finished, his voice rising at the end.

There was a moment of tense silence. Gabriella twisted her hands anxiously as a flock of seagulls landed on the grass outside, their load squawks sounding like mourners at a grave.

"She should have raised the alarm immediately. She shouldn't have waited," Gabriella finally said. "I don't understand. Even with her history, it doesn't make sense."

"Where is Nurse Caroline?" asked Ramouter. "I would like to speak to her next."

"But she gave a statement already."

"Where is she?" Ramouter repeated.

"Annual leave. She went on leave two days after Mr. Streeter died."

"Have you spoken to her?"

"Why would I speak to her? She's on leave. Does your boss bother you when you're on holiday?" Gabriella spat back.

"You knew I was coming to see you and you knew Caroline didn't raise the alarm when she should have." Ramouter circled the two names in his notebook and placed an asterisk above each of them. Caroline Swann and Filip Szymanski. "I would be very surprised if you hadn't attempted to contact her."

"We're colleagues, not friends," Gabriella replied with false confidence. She turned her wrist and checked her watch. "Are we done?"

"One more question. You said that both Caroline and Filip came from the same agency?"

"Yes. They're called Hygeia HealthCare. They specialize in providing healthcare to prisons."

"Thanks. We've made a request to the prison to provide us with the CCTV footage from the healthcare wing."

"We didn't do anything wrong," Gabriella said quickly.

"Don't you remember telling me that *you* were in charge?" said Ramouter, gathering up his things. "Andrew Streeter was murdered here while he was under the care of nurses that *you* oversaw. One of those nurses left and hasn't set foot in this place since the day Streeter was found dead, and a second nurse didn't raise the alarm until you arrived on the premises. If you ask me, you've done everything wrong."

Henley could see her resignation letter on the cluttered screen of her laptop as she read through a file containing court transcripts from Streeter's original trial and sentencing. She moved her cursor to the letter and hit delete. Rob hadn't asked her again about the letter and she suspected that he knew what she'd been denying. Her flimsy agreement to resign was because she was scared and looking to save herself, not save her family.

"You look how I feel," Henley said as Ramouter entered the room and flung his jacket on the desk.

"It was a nightmare getting back from the Isle of Sheppey. My train was canceled and then I got on the wrong platform at Victoria, and then… Oh forget it, I need a drink. A large one," said Ramouter as he sat down.

"A massive glass of gin would be nice," said Eastwood. She pulled another antibacterial wipe from the pack and continued to wipe away the dirt from the files from her hands. "I'll even buy the first round if you fancy going to the pub."

"Come on, now Ramouter's back, let's get down to business," Henley said. She pinned copies of the pictures that Theresa had emailed onto the whiteboard. "I know. It's not good, is it?"

"Nope. Not at all," said Stanford.

"First things first. According to Linh and Anthony, who analyzed the swabs, Piper's body had been washed clean," said Henley. "Traces of carbolic soap residue all over Piper's body and under his nails. But his hair had been cleaned with shampoo."

"Similar to the 1995 victims," said Eastwood.

"Exactly. Linh also found traces of dirt in the threads she removed from Piper's mouth and eyes. There was dirt in his esophagus and lungs too." Henley picked up her glass and took a large mouthful, wishing it was vodka and tonic. "There was bruising and internal signs of heavy compression on his chest," she continued. "Piper died from asphyxia. The wound on his leg was postmortem."

"What about the note?" Ramouter asked.

"I'll get on to that," said Henley. "It gets worse, or better, depending on how your detective brain thinks. Yesterday Linh sent the dirt samples that she retrieved from Piper to a soil scientist, Dr. Strickland, together with the forensic reports of the dirt that was retrieved from the 1995 victims."

"I'm telling you, mate, there's an expert for everything these days," said Stanford, shaking his head.

"Stanford, please," Henley said, rising from her desk and rubbing the base of her spine. "Anyway, this soil expert sent Linh a preliminary report. The soil retrieved from Piper is an exact match for the soil that was retrieved from the original victims."

"An exact match?" Eastwood exclaimed.

"Yes, an exact match," said Henley. "I spoke to Dr. Strickland and she explained that the soil that was retrieved from Piper and the 1995 victims is specific to the Folkestone area: silt, clay, cross-bedded sand and marine sediment. But there was also a high quantity of ground rock fragments which she suggested meant that Piper was buried in close proximity to a gravel pit."

"Not *in* a gravel pit?" Ramouter asked skeptically.

Henley shook her head. "No. His body would have been covered in scratches and indentations from the weight of the gravel on his body."

"And Piper's samples match the samples of three of the original victims?" asked Eastwood.

"Yes. Dr. Strickland couldn't say that they were buried in the exact same spot, only that they were in the Folkestone area."

"What about the samples that were taken from Streeter's boots? That was part of the original case, that the samples taken from his boots matched what was found in the 1995 victims' bodies," said Stanford.

"That's where things go off on a tangent," Henley continued. "The forensic report which implicated Streeter was prepared by a Dr. Leslie Fry and in Strickland's words, *he's an absolute fake.*"

"What do you mean, a fake?" asked Ramouter, pulling out his phone and typing.

"He concluded that the samples from Streeter's boots were a match for those retrieved from the 1995 victims, but that would have been impossible," Henley said. "There's no break in the chain of continuity from the samples retrieved from the victims and Streeter's boots, but the results from the comparison and bio-logical and chemical breakdown in the conclusion was wrong."

"Why would he lie? Why would he give a fake conclusion?" Eastwood asked as she turned to her computer and opened up the criminal records files on the police national computer database.

"Not only that," said Ramouter as he handed Henley his phone. "Why is he still listed on the National Centre for Polic-ing Excellence Expert Advisers list?"

"You're joking," Stanford exclaimed.

"And unless there's another Dr. Leslie Fry out there, three weeks ago he was charged with multiple counts of making false statements, misconduct and perjury at Notting Hill police sta-tion," said Eastwood. "He's due to appear at Westminster Mag-istrates' Court next week."

"What would he have gained from lying?" Stanford asked. "It doesn't make sense. Why risk your career?"

"Money," said Ramouter. "That's normally the answer."

"If it's money then the next question is who paid him, but we can ask him that when we question him," said Henley. "What's important is that all the victims from 1995 to 1996, and Piper, were buried in the same place."

"But that would mean Piper was taken from north London to Little Venice and then to somewhere in Folkestone where he was buried alive, then brought back to Little Venice," said Ramouter.

"So, dodgy doctor aside, Piper was buried alive in the same place as the other victims," said Stanford.

"It's either that or the killer carries around a trunkload of dirt like Dracula," said Eastwood. "Sorry, sorry. I couldn't help it," she said when Henley gave her a look.

"If you've all quite finished," Henley said, picking up another printout and pinning it next to the kill list. "Linh also retrieved a coin from Piper's mouth."

"Oh crap," said Stanford. "Exactly like in 1995."

"But unlike 1995, this coin isn't a prototype £2 coin. Linh also retrieved a note from Piper's mouth. As you can see, Streeter's name is first, and then we have Piper."

"What does 'maybe four' mean? Perhaps whoever it is has at least two more victims in mind," said Eastwood. "But the question mark could mean anyone who had an interaction with Streeter, Piper, or The Burier."

Henley connected her laptop to the smartboard. "Speaking of people who had an interaction with The Burier or Streeter, I was reading through the Court of Appeals judgment. Take a look at the board. This is the full forty-two-page judgment that was uploaded to the British and Irish Legal Information Institute. Look at the section that I've highlighted."

11.42. Ms. Johnson QC submits that there was a dangerous circularity in the prosecution's original case which failed to take into account that the investigating officers had failed to disclose that there was evidence of a potential sixth victim who had contacted the Metropolitan Police and Kent Police and alleged that she had been kidnapped and been told that she would be buried alive.

"Buried alive," murmured Ramouter.

Stanford leaned forward and placed his hands in a steeple. "I read the original sentencing remarks and the judge specifically mentioned a kill list. Wouldn't this sixth victim or target be on that list?"

"I would assume so," said Henley. "Look, before you ask, I was only in court for one morning giving evidence. There was no way my parents were going to let me watch every day of that trial."

"We need to find that original kill list," said Eastwood. "It has to be in one of those archive boxes upstairs."

"I bloody hope so. An important part of our investigation is to find evidence of this sixth victim. Sorry, target."

"I'll do it," Stanford volunteered.

Henley nodded her appreciation.

"Bloody miracle that someone managed to escape The Burier. And where's our famous criminal profiler when we need him?" Stanford mused. "Can't he help figure out who we should be looking for?"

"It's not like you to be so eager to get Mark involved," Henley said, smiling for the first time that day.

"This isn't normal, is it? And Dr. Mark Ryan, criminal profiler—"

"Forensic psychologist," Eastwood corrected.

"Whatever," said Stanford. "He ain't normal and this case ain't normal. He's going to love it."

"He's in San Francisco for a conference, but I've emailed him for some referrals if he doesn't have capacity to do a profile," said Henley. "Ramouter, how did you get on with the nurses?"

"That place is a shithole. It's no surprise that HMP Ruxley and the healthcare wing were subject to an inquiry," Ramouter said, his voice weary. "I'm trying to track down the nurses who were on duty the morning Streeter died, but Caroline Swann is not returning my messages and the nursing agency is refusing to give me Filip Szymanski's contact details. They pretty much told me to go and get a court order."

"Then we get a court order. In the meantime, ask Ezra to see what he can find out," said Henley. She looked around at the exhausted faces of her team. "And let's go to the pub. This case isn't going anywhere."

25

Lillian kicked off the duvet which had tangled itself around her ankles. She didn't need to check the time on her alarm clock on her bedside table. It was always the same time every single night: 4:17 a.m. She could try to close her eyes and go back to sleep, but it would simply be a repeat of last night and the 492 nights before that.

She knew exactly when the insomnia had kicked in. It was when her partner, Veronica, announced that she was moving back to Bath and walked out, taking their two children with her. There had been a list of complaints ranging from *You're never home, you're obsessed about your work* and *the kids don't know you*, to the kicker: *No, I haven't met someone else. I don't want to be with you.* Lillian had no reply, except to repeat that she needed to make it again. She needed a good story. She hadn't fought for the twelve years of their relationship and simply made promises to travel to Bath every second weekend and to FaceTime the kids.

The house in Stoke Newington now felt like a tomb. Even the plants were dying—caring for them, and caring for the family, had been Veronica's thing. Lillian walked through the quiet house to the kitchen as the first flashes of morning light began to crack through the sky and brighten the muted darkness of the room. She turned on the kettle and woke up her laptop on the cluttered wooden table. She sat down with her coffee in the mug that her son had bought her for Mother's Day and picked up the tarnished brass key she kept on a ring with several others. Keys she'd kept either in her bag or in the third drawer of her wardrobe ever since the first letter had arrived all those years ago. The letter itself was in a box that Lillian now pulled in front of her.

1 October 1995

Why are you the only one who's noticed me? I read your article in the paper and I think that you're the only one to get me. You haven't called me "sick" or a "monster." You're not treating me like a joke. You're treating me seriously. I am not a joke. I wanted you to know that I couldn't keep them. Returning them back to their families was the right thing to do. Do you know how good it feels to know that someone needs you and wants you to save them? Do you think that they realize that I was saving them from the horrors of this world? Can you tell your readers that the next time you write about me? Can you tell them that I will save them all.

She hadn't thought the letter was real. There was no signature, no name. No indication as to this person's identity. She'd examined the Mount Pleasant and Croydon Mail Centre postmarks on the envelopes but that didn't help her either. Now, she picked up a creased, light blue envelope. The ink that had once been a rich midnight blue had faded with time, but her full name was clearly written in careful and impressive calligraphy. She'd always suspected that the author had used a fountain pen.

17 October 1995

Hello Lillian,

I thought that we could share mementoes. Can you tell your readers that she wanted to come with me? I would never force anyone to do something that they wouldn't want to do.

She should have gone to the police. The second she opened the third envelope and pulled out a charm bracelet that was missing two charms, she should have picked up the phone and dialed 999. Melissa Gyimah's father had broken down in tears when a reporter from a local paper had finally interviewed him about his daughter's disappearance and the lack of media coverage and police action. He'd said that Melissa always wore a silver charm bracelet that was missing the horn of plenty and a diamanté horseshoe. Lillian traced her fingers over the bracelet, nestled in the box among the remaining three letters that the killer, the man she'd anointed "The Burier," had sent her. Each letter sent just after a body was found. Each letter contained an item that The Burier had taken as a trophy. A travel card wallet. Gold earrings. A silver locket. A purple scarf. A watch. Each note including a line of insight that she used in her twelve-month coverage of the original murders. She'd wallowed in the accolades and when her peers, and later interviewers, had asked her how she was able to put herself in the mind of a killer, she told them she'd simply followed her gut and not allowed her ego to get in the way.

The heavy motor of a hovering police helicopter dragged Lillian back from her problematic past and into her even more problematic present. She opened her laptop and clicked on the browser as the soft yellow glow from the helicopter's searchlight cut through the naked window and cast an eerie light over the kitchen table.

"Shit, shit, shit. You fucking cunt," Lillian said out loud to the cold, empty room as the homepage for the *Chronicle* opened up.

ANDREW STREETER CLEARED OF FIVE MURDERS
AFTER 25 YEARS
The Burier Still At Large After Corrupt Police Investigation

A new murder investigation has been launched by the Serial Crime Unit following the violent deaths of high-profile lawyer Elias Piper and his client, Andrew Streeter...

BY JAKE RYLAND
Crime Reporter
@RylandJake

Lillian's name wasn't on the byline. It was her words and her notes, the response to her question that had been incorporated in the piece, but her story had Jake's name written all over it. She had been redacted. Lillian slammed the laptop shut, picked up her mobile phone and made the call.

"I'm assuming you can't sleep," came Veronica's clipped tones.

Lillian bit her bottom lip, listening to Veronica opening the sliding door that led out to her decking. It was almost 5:00 a.m., the time Veronica was usually up to get her meditation and yoga in before she had to wake the children to get ready for school.

"How's Leo and Kayla?" asked Lillian.

"Maybe you could find out yourself if you bothered to come up for your weekends."

"Ronnie, please—"

"What do you want, Lillian?"

"He's back. The Burier."

Lillian heard Veronica take a sharp intake of breath, the sounds of waves breaking against rocks in the distance.

"Jesus Christ, Lils... I don't understand...has he contacted you?"

"No," Lillian said quickly. The helicopter searchlight flooded the kitchen table and illuminated the photograph of Elias Piper lying in his open grave. She'd become immune to the horror and fear in his eyes and was almost enamored with how the flash had picked up the smallest of details. The vein in his temporal lobe as it snaked up its neck and the tautness of the fragile skin around his eyes. She could make out each of the thin lines that broke up the pale pink and white of his dry lips. She wondered how long it had taken him to die.

"I haven't heard anything from him," Lillian continued, turning the photograph over. "That's not why I'm calling. I need some advice."

"I'm not your person for that. Not anymore."

"I don't have anyone else. You can't just dismiss me as though I never mattered to you."

Lillian jumped at the sound of her brass knocker being slammed against the door.

"Doesn't sound like you haven't got anyone else," Veronica said tersely.

"It's probably some drunk," Lillian replied. She pushed back her chair and walked out into the hallway. "Someone stole my story, a rookie who doesn't know his ass from his elbow. His name is Jake Ryland. Go on the paper's website. They've completely erased me," she said.

"So, what do want me to do about it?"

"I need—" Lillian paused. She felt a tremor in her right leg and placed her free hand against the wall to steady herself. A white envelope was on the doormat. Far too early for the postman. Did Piper's murderer know she was an insomniac?

"You need what?" Veronica asked impatiently.

"Advice," Lillian said quietly as her eyes adjusted to the shadowy silhouette of a figure through the frosted glass of her front door. The streetlights made the figure's shoulders appear larger. Lillian wasn't sure if the person had his back to her or was facing the door, waiting to see what she would do next.

"I need to write my story," Lillian whispered. She stood frozen; on the other side of the door, the figure was equally still.

"I can barely hear you," said Veronica.

"My story. I want to write my story, but the paper has muzzled me." The figure shifted suddenly to the left as though he, or she, was trying to see her through the glass. Lillian flattened herself against the wall.

"Why don't you just leave?" Veronica asked. "You should have done it years ago. It's not as if you need the money. Leave. Go freelance. Write your story and sell it to the highest bidder or set up a podcast. To be honest, Lillian, I don't really care. I've got to go. Let me know if you'll be coming for your weekend. You can't keep disappointing the children."

Lillian didn't say a word as the call ended and the figure at the door dissolved back into nothing. She pushed her phone into her dressing gown and hurried to the door, picking up the envelope. She knew who it was from. She knew in her gut. He'd been to her house. Had he been there before? Had she bumped into him on the street when she was leaving for work in the morning? How close had The Burier been? She slowly released the lock. The front door, the hinges stiff as always, resisted slightly as she pulled it open and placed the door on the latch. She stepped out tentatively onto the steps that descended onto the street and looked out. The sky had transitioned to light violet, blue and orange as the sun rose in the distance. There was no one out on the road. Lillian was fully aware that it wouldn't matter if The Burier was lurking nearby—she had no idea what he looked like. She closed the front door, secured all the locks and pushed across the deadlock.

Back in the kitchen, Lillian's heart was racing as she opened the envelope.

Hello Lillian,
Did you like the photo?
I thought that I would forget but muscle memory is a fascinating thing.

It wasn't the words on the single sheet of paper that scared her. It was knowing that The Burier knew where to find her.

He picked up the newspaper from the passenger seat and turned to page seventeen for the fifth time that day. The first twelve pages of the paper were damp—wrinkled and stained brown from the hot coffee with a dash of oat milk that had spilled from his cup. The mechanism in the driver's seat had broken months ago and there'd been no opportunity to ram the seat back and escape the hot liquid as it made its quick descent onto the paper and soaked through the dark blue material of his trousers. He'd thrown the damp newspaper onto the passenger seat, opened the van door and jumped out onto the pavement, surprising a woman who'd been pushing a small purple pram containing a scraggly Cavalier King Charles spaniel, whose head hung limply over the edge of the pram as it released a pathetic growl in his direction.

He'd ignored the disgusted tut from the woman and jogged around to the back of his van, opening the door to pull out a pair of nonauthorized black trousers and quickly changing behind the safety of the van doors. He could feel the anger pulsating in his body, the heat from the anger so intense his pulse pushed against the small muscles around his eye socket.

She'd disappointed him. This wasn't what he wanted. This was not part of the plan. He'd covered every angle, but forgotten that you couldn't predict when a third party would develop fragilities that would interfere with your plans. He walked around the van until he reached the passenger side, pushed his arm through the open window and pulled out the newspaper. The coffee hadn't blurred the print that ran across the pages of *The Chronicle*. He ran his finger over the name on the byline: Jake Ryland.

"Who the hell are you?" he asked quietly. "Where is my Lillian?"

Lillian Klein was the only one who was allowed to tell his story. He'd given her that right more than twenty years ago. Every word she'd written about him, even in the years where they thought that he'd been quiet, he had cultivated. He screwed the paper tightly into a ball. He'd kept all the stories she'd written about him. He could read between the lines and see that Lillian had been celebrating him with every word she'd put to paper. It hadn't even bothered him that she'd named Andrew Streeter as being responsible for the actions that *he* had patiently planned and executed. That was exactly what he'd wanted. To commit the perfect murder, he'd had to make sure that he was in control of every moving piece. He'd been content until Andrew Streeter made moves that he hadn't anticipated. A cancer diagnosis had forced Andrew to take a cold hard look at his mortality, and had ultimately led to the disruption of a plan that he'd perfectly executed.

"Everything all right, mate? You look like you're chewing a bee."

He turned to his right to see his partner, Trevor, waddling toward him, carrying three reels of colored electrical cable in his arms. "Get the doors, will ya?"

"Of course," he replied tersely and dropped the ball of newspaper onto the potholed tarmac. He kicked it under the van and jogged round to open the back doors.

Trevor released the reels from his arms and they dropped with a thud onto the van's metal floor.

He winced as the exhaust pipe briefly scraped against the ground from the increased weight. "That will mess up the suspension," he said, slamming the door shut.

"S'buggered anyway," Trevor replied. He ran the back of his hand across his sweaty brow. "So, you all right?"

"Yeah, yeah. Fine. Got a lot on, plans to make and that."

"Ah, because of the boss's email. I doubt they'll make anyone redundant anytime soon," Trevor said, and slapped him hard on the shoulder in a misplaced gesture of affection and reassurance. "I can see why you're worried with all that time you had off, but you're back now. What are you supposed to do if the doctor signs you off?"

He felt himself wince as Trevor grabbed the back of his neck and squeezed. He hated people touching him. The thought of Trevor's dirty hands on his skin made him sick.

"Yeah, probably worrying over nothing," he replied, getting into the driver's seat and trying to remember how many antibacterial wipes were left in the packet he kept in the compartment in the car door. "But it's nice to have a plan, you know? In case it all goes tits up."

"Have you got one then?" Trevor asked, huffing into the passenger seat as though he'd reached the summit of Mount Everest.

"I'm working on it." He turned on the engine, turned on the indicator and headed south. "Always working on a plan."

Thursday morning, 9:48 a.m., and the ground floor of Bromley Magistrates' Court looked like London Bridge station at rush hour. Every seat in the waiting area opposite the four ground-floor courtrooms was filled with defendants, the expressions on their faces ranging from sheer terror to bored contempt. Henley closed the door of the police liaison officers' office behind her and took in the sight of the defendants who walked around the building with familiarity. She could sense the change in energy as she walked along the corridor, ignoring the looks from the regulars who knew she was police. Their collective hostility was almost feral. As she pushed open the door that led into Courtroom 3, she let out a sigh of relief and welcomed the cool sweep of air in a room that was a temporary refuge. There were only two people in the room. The legal assistant sitting in front of the judge's desk ignored Henley. The court usher was standing to the side, straightening his collection of case management forms and leaflets.

"Can I help you?" he asked, tapping the forms with satisfaction.

"Good morning, I'm Detective Inspector Henley. I'm—"

"Ah, yes, yes. She told me that you would be coming. Follow me."

Henley did as she was told and followed the usher past the spotless glass that separated the public gallery from the body of the courtroom and through a door at the back. The corridor was quiet; their footsteps muted by the blue-gray carpet.

"Right here," he said with a smile, knocking twice on the door. When the door swung open, District Judge Eloise Rhimes stood in the doorway. Her husband, DCSI Rhimes, had always said that he was punching above his weight when Eloise had agreed to date him. She'd only been practicing as a solicitor for two years when she first met him at the front desk of Snow Hill police station and she turned down his requests for a date three times before relenting. They were married for thirty-five years.

Judge Rhimes's sleeveless shift dress showed off toned and tanned arms. The gold band of the watch on her left hand barely concealed the seagull tattoo on her wrist. She looked younger than her sixty-two years of age, but Henley could see the strain her husband's death had taken on her. There was a sadness in her eyes that had deepened the lines on her face.

"Thank you, Cliff." She pushed her red-rimmed designer glasses to the top of her head. "It shouldn't have taken something like this to make you come and see me, Anjelica," she rebuked with a warm smile.

"Don't say it like that." Henley stepped into the room and Eloise pulled her into a hug and kissed her cheek. "You're making me feel bad."

"Good, you should feel bad. I have to keep asking Ezra how you are, and now he's acting like the cat's got his tongue," Eloise replied. "Do you want anything? Tea, coffee, vodka?"

"It's a bit early for vodka, isn't it?"

"Is it? You'd be lining up the shots for me if you saw the day I have ahead of me. How's Emma? It's been ages since I've seen her."

"She's doing good. Getting more talkative by the second."

"She definitely got her tenacity from you and not Rob." Eloise sat down on the small sofa. "You know that all of this is fucked up, right?"

Henley knew better than to be disconcerted by the sudden change of subject. "Just like you to get straight to the point, Eloise."

"I don't know why but they're using my Harry as a scapegoat. He's been dead for less than eighteen months and they're literally pissing over his grave and telling me that it's raining. It's not on, Anjelica."

Henley bit the inside of her cheek and she sat down next to Eloise. She'd known she would have to have this conversation at some point, but still she felt ill-prepared.

"It's not on," Eloise repeated. She was twisting the emerald-set engagement ring on her finger. "I keep expecting him to walk through the door and tell me about his ridiculous retirement plans. Talking about buying a boat, when he got sick on the ferry to France. I know they say it gets easier, but personally I think that's bollocks."

"I'm not sure if it ever gets easier," Henley conceded, thinking back to the first year after her mother's death and the moments when she woke up with a damp pillow, wondering how it was possible to cry in your sleep. She'd accepted her mother's death but that didn't stop her from thinking, for a split second, that it might be her mum when her phone pinged with a text. "You learn…actually, I don't know what happens. You take it one day at a time."

"As I said, bollocks. And it's bollocks that Harry is…*was* corrupt," Eloise said sternly. "He would never break a rule and he would never have done anything to compromise an investigation; especially that investigation."

"I'm sure you know that they've reopened the investigation into the original murders?"

Eloise nodded as she reached for the box of tissues on her desk. "I think Ezra called me about ten minutes after Ian Turner did."

"Who's Ian Turner?"

"Harry's partner back in 1995, until he transferred to CID at West End Central. He must have retired about three years ago." Eloise shifted in her seat so she could look directly at Henley. "I read the Court of Appeal judgment. They named my husband. There hasn't been one day since that judgment came out where I haven't had journalists at my front door, sending me emails, calling the office. The only reason they haven't turned up in the public gallery in my courtroom is because I've been sitting in the youth court for the past week, which thankfully is closed to members of the public."

"I know it can't be easy, any of it."

"He didn't do it, Anjelica. He wasn't that sort of man; he wouldn't have done anything to jeopardize that investigation. You have no idea what it took from him. It changed him. It changed us. Nicholas was just two years old, and he almost died from bacterial meningitis…it was hard."

"I'm sorry," Henley said as she squeezed Eloise's hand. "Rhimes never spoke about the case with me, but I know that it must have affected him."

"He told me that he didn't want to burden you with guilt or make you feel as though he'd taken you on as a charity case."

"He never made me feel that. But I can't lie. He was a pain in the ass sometimes," Henley said with a sad smile, thinking back to the times Rhimes had read her the riot act or challenged her analysis of a case.

"The biggest," Eloise agreed, and she wiped away a tear.

"I do miss him. No matter what…he was a good man. To me. My family. My team." Henley gave her a hug.

Eloise buried her face in Henley's shoulder. Her "Thank you" was muffled. She squeezed Henley tightly before releasing her.

"I'm sorry," Henley repeated, not for Eloise's loss but for the pain that she knew would be inflicted on her because of the investigation.

"I know you're busy, so I won't keep you," Eloise said, all business again. She stood up, opened a cupboard behind her desk, then lifted out a large plastic container. "But can you help me with this before you go? He had all of these in cardboard boxes at the back of the garage, but then there was a flood. I saved what I could."

"What is it?" Henley asked, taking the container.

"Harry's personal files for the original investigation."

"He kept them?" Henley placed the container on Eloise's desk. She could see layers of multicolored folders and a box of cassette tapes through the plastic.

"He was a hoarder, you know that. Here's another one," Eloise picked up a smaller box. "Someone tried to break into our house the day after the judgment, so I moved his important documents here. I doubt that anyone will be breaking into a court building anytime soon."

"Did you call the police about the break-in?"

"You would think that someone trying to break into a judge's house would be a priority," Eloise snorted in disgust. "I waited two days for the police to come round and take my statement and the cctv from the alarm system. I told them that the break-in might have something to do with Harry and his name being out there since the judgment but they were unenthusiastic about that proposition."

"Eloise, promise that you will call me if this happens again. I don't want anything to happen to you."

"Thank you," Eloise hugged Henley. "Now, did you drive?"

"Yeah. I'm in the parking lot."

The phone on Eloise's desk began to ring.

"Good, I'll get one of the security guards to help you," Eloise replied, picking up the handset. "Yes. They're ready? OK. Tell them we'll start in fifteen minutes."

She hung up and looked Henley in the eye. "I know I sound like a delusional wife whose husband has been caught red-handed with the takings of a bank job, but he didn't do this. Harry would never jeopardize a case and I don't..." Eloise paused and brushed away a tear. "You're going to think I'm mad, but I don't believe he killed himself either."

"I don't—"

"He was a lot of things, but he wasn't corrupt, and he wouldn't take his own life. He had plans for his life, for us."

"Eloise... I know that you're—"

"Never, Anjelica," Eloise repeated.

Henley said nothing but she couldn't ignore her gut instinct that Eloise wasn't just a grieving widow in denial.

"I knew my husband as well as you know Rob," said Eloise. "Actually, no—as well as you know Pellacia, and he knows you. So, listen to what I'm telling you. Harry Rhimes did not kill himself."

The smell was familiar. Caroline had picked the scent out herself when she'd finally cashed in her birthday voucher for the luxury spa day she would never normally be able to afford on her meagre nursing salary. The pressure from the thick opaque tights that had been bound tightly around her eyes and the knot that had pressed into the soft piece of flesh between the base of her skull and top of her spine had finally subsided. She tried to move her mouth but only got as far as pushing the tip of her tongue against the rough and tacky duct tape. She couldn't see, but the darkness made the memory of that spa day with her mother shine brighter. She could remember how she'd melted as the heated citrus body scrub was massaged into her back and legs, all the while ignoring her mum's lamentations about how this could have been her life if only she hadn't ended her engagement to that nice (but abusive) architect. Caroline remembered picking out the citrus-scented candle and room diffuser with the leftover credit on her vouchers. It was that same scent that now tickled her nose and made her realize that the man she thought she knew as Filip Szymanski, the man who'd pushed her hard onto the ground and banged her head twice against the fake parquet flooring until she'd lost consciousness, hadn't moved her to another location. She was in her home.

The events of that night were out of order in her mind. Replying to a text message that Filip had sent her. Finding Streeter's dead body. Telling a lie that he'd been awake when she'd taken away his half-eaten breakfast. Emotionally paralyzed with fear and hyperventilating in the toilets as she waited for her boss to tell her "*I know what you've done. The police are on their way.*" Waking up to the smell of cooking oil and eggs, which was strange because she lived alone. The blinds had been closed when she walked into the kitchen on Saturday morning which was odd because she never closed them. Filip sitting at her small dining table with a cup of tea and an empty plate, on his left, flicking through a pile of letters from debt-management companies that she'd made a point of shoving unopened in the junk drawer in her kitchen. She didn't remember screaming, but she could remember the metallic taste of blood as she bit down hard on the supple flesh of the hand over her mouth. She remembered that Filip's voice had changed, losing that playful ripple in his accent that she'd thought came from his upbringing on the northeast coast. There was a harsh frost in his tone that had made her do what she was told: shut up and stop moving.

Now, in the citrus-scented room, Caroline could feel the uneven texture of ancient woodchip wallpaper pressing against the bare skin of her back. She could hear the ticking of the cheap

alarm clock and the muffled sound of children screaming. So
she knew she was in her bedroom, at the front of her house. She
knew it was a weekday and that it was either 10:30 a.m., 1:00 p.m.
or 2:30 p.m., which was when the local primary school children
were usually let loose for their breaks. She heard the click of the
boiler as the hot water tap was turned on. She raised her head at
the sound of fluttering in the loft space above. She felt her blad-
der release the small amount of urine it contained and felt a warm
puddle spread underneath her. She heard someone walking up
the stairs and stepping on the uneven and cracked floorboards
of the third, sixth, eighth and ninth steps. Caroline could hear
her pulse in her ear as the hinges of her bedroom door creaked.
Footsteps made their way toward her, and she pushed herself hard
against the wall. She could hear his knees crack when he bent
down in front of her.

"Where are you going?" His voice sent chills down her spine.

Caroline pushed her heels into the carpet to gain traction,
trying to create as much space between them as possible. Her
cries were muted behind the duct tape.

"You need to calm down," he said and reached behind Caroline's head to untie the blindfold. Dazzled, Caroline bent her
head and squeezed her eyes shut.

"I thought that you liked looking at me," Filip said softly. He
placed his thumb and forefinger on her chin to raise it up. "I
used to see you watching me when you should have been doing
your work, checking on those prisoners. Did you think that I
didn't notice when you used to brush against me *accidentally* in
the break room? Stop panicking. You'll do yourself some damage. Look at me."

Caroline inhaled the scent of woody soap and burnt onions
and garlic as she breathed rapidly through her nose.

"Look. At. Me."

She did as she was told. Her eyes filled with tears—it was
Filip but not quite Filip. His hair was not dark blond but brown

with thin streaks of gray that weaved through thick brown curls. His eyes were gray and not green. He'd shaved his beard. The small scar that cut through his right eyebrow and the trio of small moles on his left cheek were still there. She took in the curves of his ear lobes and several days' worth of stubble on his face. Even though she knew there was no point, she drank it all in. Every line on his face, every place his complexion changed from tanned to pale skin, every chest hair that peeked out from his shirt. Even though she knew she wouldn't live to give her story to the police or identify Filip, she memorized everything.

"I can't leave any loose ends, that's all," he said and pulled Caroline toward him, before forcing her face down on her front. She felt him pulling at the plastic ties on her wrists and feet to make sure that they were secure. Even though her stomach was empty, trickles of bile had traveled up her throat and pooled in her mouth as Filip ran his hand along her spine. His hand stopped at her bra strap—Caroline clenched her body—and then continued to travel to the base of her spine. The pads of his fingers were rough as he ran his hands along her legs. This was all that he did, not that it mattered. It was another small detail she would never tell the police.

The clock continued to tick.

26

Henley turned off the car engine and leaned forward to take in the view of the last house on Cranbrook Road in Deptford. It had taken Melissa Gyimah's parents seven years to finally move from the flat where their life had been violently interrupted by their daughter's murder. Her mother had often said that there was no way that she could have continued living so close to where her child's body had been found. Henley would often see Melissa's dad standing on the balcony that overlooked Deptford Green and the river beyond. She always wondered what he was waiting for, when he knew that his daughter was never coming home.

"Oh my," Tenneh Gyimah placed her hand to her chest, covering up the gold locket and small crucifix that hung from the chain around her neck. "Anjelica. You haven't changed. Older yes, but you haven't changed."

"Definitely older and I'm sure that I've changed," Henley replied, stepping into the narrow hallway. "It's good to see you, Mrs. Gyimah."

"Come on now, after all this time you can call me Tenneh."

"That doesn't feel right," Henley replied. She took in the woman standing in front of her. Grief had aged her. She'd always been the glamorous one when Henley was younger, fashionably dressed and changing her hairstyles fortnightly. Now, her once thick black hair was cut short and every curl was gray. The skin on her face had thickened and the lines that radiated from her eyes were deep set. People who didn't know Tenneh would have called them laughter lines, but Henley knew that it would have been difficult for Tenneh to find anything to laugh about.

"Come on, come through. Are you hungry? I've made jollof rice and beef. I can make a plate for you. Or tea, coffee, a sandwich. Anything?"

"I'll have a small plate of jollof," Henley replied, knowing full well that there was no point in refusing Melissa's mum when she offered to feed you. She smiled sadly to herself, hearing Melissa's voice in her head.

"Mum. We don't need food. Stop embarrassing me. Why can't you cook normal food?"

"And what is normal? Sausage, egg and chips, pizza, frog in the hole?"

"God, Mum. It's toad *in the hole."*

Henley shook the memories from her head and followed Tenneh down the hallway. The house smelled like a home, but even with all the usual artefacts of family life on display—the basket of clothes left on the stairs, the photographs of Tenneh's children and grandchildren on the wall, their paintings and save the date reminders for weddings on the fridge door—there remained a strong sense that something was missing, that there was a hole that would never be filled.

"Sit, sit," Tenneh said, opening the dishwasher and taking out a clean plate and cutlery.

"Do you still run?" Henley asked. She could see leggings and a dripping swimsuit hanging on the washing line, and there was something about Tenneh's slender build and the way she moved around the kitchen that made Henley suspect Tenneh had channeled her grief into exercise. "I remember you running around the green and to Greenwich and back."

"Absolutely," Tenneh noted. "Your mum came with me once and swore that she was never doing it again. But it's the only thing that's kept me sane. And swimming. I go to the swimming pool every Friday in Lewisham. I need it. For my head. Otherwise..." Her voice tailed off as she lifted the lid off the large orange pot on the stove and spooned the jollof rice onto the plate. "I had to make so much because of Nelson—you remember Nelson?"

"Of course," Henley replied, leaving out the fact that she used to fancy the pants off Melissa's older brother when she was a teenager.

"He said that he was coming by after work with the children and the new girlfriend." Tenneh rolled her eyes when she said *girlfriend*.

"You're not eating?" Henley asked as Tenneh placed the overloaded plate in front of her.

"No. No. I'll eat later, once Ekow gets home."

"Where is he? It would have been nice to see Mr. Gyimah."

"He's at work. He's supposed to have retired from the dry cleaner's. I tried to convince him to sell it, but he refuses. Go on. Eat and then we'll talk."

"I never felt satisfied," Tenneh said as she picked up Henley's empty plate, placed it in the sink and returned to the table. "You think that hearing the jury foreman stand up and say the word *guilty* five times would give you some peace, some sense of resolution, but it didn't."

Henley reached out and took hold of Tenneh's hand. "Even when the prosecutor told us later that the man would die in prison. It gave me nothing. The other families, I think...no, I *know* that it gave them no satisfaction. No comfort. He was off the streets, but our children were dead. There is no conviction or life sentence that could make up for the loss of a child. Even if we had the death penalty...no."

"Have you kept in touch with the other families?"

Tenneh shook her head. "Not me. A few of them got together and formed a...a support group. A club. The only bond we share is that our children were murdered. Who wants to be part of a club like that?"

"I wouldn't want to be," Henley admitted.

"It's a horrible club. Every year, I celebrate my other children's birthdays. We get together, sometimes we have a party and we take pictures. Do you know what it's like on Melissa's birthday to look at her picture and know that she will always be fifteen? What's fifteen years, Anjelica? Nothing. She should have been calling you and talking about plans for her fortieth birthday in a year or so. Or sending you videos from whatever country she was visiting. Do you remember that she wanted to travel?"

"I do," Henley smiled. "She told the careers adviser that fifteen was too young to decide on a career for the rest of your life and that she wanted to see the world first."

"It doesn't get easier. No matter what they say. How can it when someone stole your child's life?"

She had known that it would be hard, but Henley hadn't been prepared for the grief that hit her, sitting in the kitchen with her dead friend's mother. Her other cases, even though she'd committed herself a hundred percent, had been "work." But this moment, the butterfly effect of Melissa's murder, wasn't just work. It was her life.

"You know that's why I'm here, to talk to you about the person who stole Melissa's life," Henley said, gently pulling her hand away.

"I...we...saw the news. The press conference outside the court. Everything," Tenneh said softly.

"Did anyone speak to you? Anyone from the CPS, about what Andrew Streeter's conviction being overturned meant?"

Tenneh let out a snort of disgust. "Why would they? It was like it was happening all over again. Melissa going missing. Having to do things for ourselves, begging for the smallest piece of information. Being made to feel as though we were being a nuisance. That Melissa didn't matter."

"Melissa does matter. She's always mattered."

"To you and to us she did. *They* only cared when the others went missing and it became a story. So no, no one told us anything. The first we knew was when a reporter, Lillian Klein, came to see me. She was decent, from the beginning, and she was still nice when she came round the other day."

"Lillian Klein came to see you recently. Here?" Henley asked, slightly taken aback.

"Yes. She always kept in touch. Checking up on me. I even spoke on her podcast. She said that I didn't have to, but she's so nice that I couldn't say no."

"What did you talk about... Actually, back up—when was she here?"

"Yesterday. I came back from a run and there she was at my door."

"So, you weren't expecting her?" Henley asked. "She turned up without calling you first?"

Tenneh nodded. "She came in and had a cup of tea. She brought me that little pot of azaleas over there on the window-sill."

Henley glanced at the small terracotta pot filled with bright pink flowers, nodding at Tenneh to continue.

"She told me how sorry she was that I had to go through it all again," Tenneh said. "A very nice woman. She asked if she could have a quote for her article and I said yes and then she asked if I'd spoken to this Piper man, and I said no."

"OK," Henley said slowly. She wasn't quite convinced by Lillian's display of empathy, although she wasn't sure why.

There was a glint in Tenneh's eye. "Hmm," she said. "You have that same look on your face that Ekow has whenever I mention Lillian's name."

"What look is that?"

"Like he's listening to the crazy right wingers who call up the radio. 'Tenneh,' he says. 'That woman, she looks like *une femme coupable.*'"

Henley had forgotten that Tenneh had lived in Paris for fifteen years before moving to London and was liable to switch to French at any given moment.

"Oh, a guilty woman," Henley said. "Why would he—"

"Exactly, *pour quoi?*"

"Did Lillian tell you that Melissa's case is being reopened?"

"Yes, she did. She texted me on Tuesday."

Henley sat up straighter in her chair. "On Tuesday?" she asked. "This Tuesday gone?"

"Yes."

Tenneh turned and picked up her phone, which had been charging on the counter. She unlocked it and handed it over.

Tuesday 22 June, 23:31

Evening Tenneh. Apologies for texting so late. I'm not sure how to tell you this, but the police will be reopening Melissa's case. I'm so, so sorry. Let me know when you're free and I'll pop in and see you. Lils. xx

She'd hoped that Tenneh had made a mistake, but it was there in front of her, in black and white. The date on the message proved that Lillian had known about the transfer of the 1995 investigation to the SCU hours before Pellacia had called Henley and Ramouter into his office and delivered the news.

"You're in charge of it? Melissa's case?" Tenneh asked quietly. "All of their cases?"

Henley nodded.

"He always said that it wasn't him, you know, that Andrew Streeter," said Tenneh. She picked up a tea towel and started to fold it as if on autopilot. "I watched him. Every day of that trial, I watched him in the dock. He wasn't what I imagined a killer to be. He looked…small. All throughout the trial, he looked… I can't really explain it, but it was as if he was surprised to be sitting there. But the evidence was there, and the jury said that he killed my daughter. All twelve of them said that he was guilty."

"I believe that he was involved somehow, but not in the way they originally thought," said Henley. Her phone began to vibrate in her pocket.

"If it wasn't him, Andrew Streeter, then who was it?"

Henley took a breath and silenced Ramouter's call. "I'm not going to sit here and lie to you. We don't have any suspects and we haven't suddenly found a magic piece of incriminating evidence that identifies someone else. We're starting from scratch, Mrs. Gyimah. From the beginning. We're starting again."

Tenneh was silent for a moment.

"So we're going to have to do this all over again," she said finally, shaking her head with disbelief. "To grieve her and pray for justice all over again."

Eastwood raised her arms above her head and stretched. The tight muscles in her neck and shoulders ignored her silent request to relax a little. Three ibuprofen tablets swallowed with the remainder of the flat Diet Coke on her desk had hardly put a dent in the tension headache that pushed against her temples and made her reach for her sunglasses, even though she was sitting at her desk. It didn't help that the SCU phones had been ringing off the hook since the press conference. She lowered her arms and pushed her chair back, hoping distance would allow her to make sense of the chaos on her desk. She had placed piles of papers from the case files on her desktop and on the floor surrounding her, mirroring exactly what Stanford had done.

"Maybe you wouldn't feel so knackered if you didn't fill your body with additives and sugar." There was more than a trace of misery on Stanford's face as he pushed tofu and steamed vegetables around his bowl.

"Don't take it out on me because your better half has got you eating plants," she replied, reaching across to pull the last jam doughnut out of the bag. She grinned as she took a bite, sugar falling from the doughnut like a small avalanche and blood-red raspberry jam squirting onto her chin. "You know that you're missing all of this artificial goodness."

"Screw it," Stanford picked up his bowl and emptied the bland contents into the waste bin. "What else you got in that bag of junk on your desk?"

"Erm…" she replied, rooting around in the bag. "Scotch egg, roast beef sandwich and some Percy Pigs."

"Jesus Christ. Hand over the sandwich and a couple of Percy Pigs."

"Here you go. You'll feel much better."

"I doubt that there is anything that could make me feel better about this old case," Stanford replied, scooting his chair across the office to take the sandwich from Eastwood's outstretched hand.

Eastwood had learned to read Stanford pretty well over the years. She could see that he was struggling with their task and the fact that they were treating their ex-boss as a suspect. She'd heard him mutter, *For fuck's sake, Rhimes*, more than once. Eastwood wondered if her ability to strip Rhimes of any humanity and see him with only cold objectivity meant there was something wrong with her.

"You have to admit that, even though it's hard, it's kind of fascinating at the same time," she said, brushing sugar off her hands. "Policing hasn't changed that much in the past twenty-five years. It's just that the technology has improved."

"So has there been anything that's jumped out at you?"

"A blue Ford Fiesta," Eastwood said matter-of-factly. "Four witness identified a navy blue Ford Fiesta in the area where the victims were last seen."

"A navy blue Fiesta with a broken number plate at the back," Stanford confirmed. "I spotted that too."

"Right. Partial number plate: B371 5. How old is a B registration car?"

"Why are you asking me?"

"Because you're older than me."

"Bloody cheek. Let me think… My uncle gave me his 1987 Citroën when I was seventeen, in 1994. That was an E reg, so B would have been 1984 or '85."

"So you've got an old clapped-out Fiesta and there's only one note in the file of anyone chasing it up. A DS Ian Turner."

"Turner. Turner," Stanford bit into his sandwich with obvious glee. "He was Rhimes's partner, wasn't he?"

"Wasn't he with you, Henley and Pellacia before I joined the old CID squad?" She picked up a plastic wallet containing a pile of 8x10 photographs. Twenty years of heat and damp had caused the glossy coating on the photographs to become a primer and Eastwood had to pry them apart carefully. She grimaced as a small slither of film pulled away and left a slender streak in the background.

"Nah," Stanford replied, taking another bite. "He wasn't part of CID when I joined. Pellacia might be our best bet. He started working with Rhimes way before I started. There were a couple of old-timers who were part of the unit back in the day, but I don't think any of them had been working with Rhimes in the nineties."

"Here, take a look," said Eastwood as she handed two photographs over to Stanford. "The first one was taken from a CCTV camera thirty minutes before Henley spotted Melissa Gyimah getting into a blue car on Greenwich High Road."

"But from what she said in her witness statement"—the protective tone was hard to miss in Stanford's voice—"Henley wasn't sure about the make and model of the car, but she thought that it might have been a Ford Fiesta."

"*Thought* wouldn't have been good enough for a prosecutor or a jury."

Stanford sighed. "Was this photo ever shown to Henley?" He held the photograph up toward the windows as though he was hoping the sunlight would illuminate the missing piece of evidence. "It's not the best quality."

"It was 1995," Eastwood deadpanned. "That photograph was taken on the junction of McMillan Street and Creek Road, which is 482 meters away from where Melissa Gyimah's body was found."

"Is this the only image of the car?"

"Nope," Eastwood replied, handing over a second photograph. "If you look at the time stamp, that photograph was taken at 4:11 p.m. on the same day at a Jet petrol station on Lewisham High Street, near the railway bridge on the corner of Kings Hall Mews."

Stanford looked at Eastwood blankly.

"It's now a Premier Inn," Eastwood said slowly, with exasperation.

"Oh. I know exactly where it is," Stanford said with a click of the fingers. He shifted in his chair as adrenalin spiked in his body. There was a change of energy in the air. Even if they didn't say it, they both knew it. This was the point where the trajectory of the case changed. "This is from the rear and it's missing half of the license plate, but it's the same car," he said.

"Exactly, and here is the last photograph we've got of the car. If you turn the photograph over, someone helpfully wrote the location of the CCTV camera, the date and time."

Stanford turned the photograph over. "Milbank Road and Horseferry Road junction, third November 1995. Hold on, wasn't that the location of the last sighting of the fourth victim. Penelope Callaghan?"

She nodded. "Callaghan worked part-time at Burger King in Waterloo and had dropped her daughter off at her mother's flat on Herrick Street, which is about half a mile away from the location of this photograph. Two witnesses described a woman, matching Callaghan's description, waiting at a bus stop on Milbank Road but she never got on a bus and she didn't turn up for her shift."

"And it's definitely the same car," said Stanford, handing the photographs back and picking up the remainder of his sandwich. "Problem is, this is only a side profile."

"And it's not the best of images."

"So," Stanford said through a mouthful of emulsified bread, beef and lettuce. "We've got physical evidence of three sightings of the same car, near the location of where either the victim was last seen or lived—"

"Or where the body was found."

Eastwood pushed back her chair as Stanford stood up and threw the now empty sandwich wrapper into the bin. He folded his arms and pursed his lips as he walked away from Eastwood and toward the window.

"What's wrong?" Eastwood asked.

"I'm thinking… I'm just—Tread marks," Stanford said suddenly. He turned away from the window and headed toward his desk. "There's a statement somewhere about tread marks."

"Footprints or vehicle?" Eastwood stood up and followed Stanford to his desk.

He didn't reply, intent on rifling through the archive box on his desk.

"Footprint or vehicle?" she repeated. The muscles in her back tensed even more as he fished through the box.

"Vehicle," he muttered finally. "I've been going through the forensic statements. DNA samples were taking from all the victims and Andrew Streeter."

"But Anthony is rerunning the samples, right?"

"Yeah... Where is it? I know I've seen it. Yes!"

Stanford straightened himself and turned around, clasping two sheets of A4 to his chest. "Samples."

"Yes, you said."

"DNA and soil were retrieved from the victims."

"I know that."

"These are photographs in situ...here's Fallon O'Toole," he placed the first photograph down. Eastwood had seen the photograph before, but she leaned in closer and tried to convince her brain that she was seeing it for the first time. Fallon O'Toole's body had been laid out on the ground in Avery Hills Trails. She'd been wrapped in a white sheet and was wearing a nightdress that Marks and Spencer's had stopped selling three years earlier. She'd been found on Monday, 16 October 1995 at 6:34 a.m. The sun had bounced off the dyed blond streaks in her hair and created a halo effect in the photograph.

"O'Toole was found by a man, Frank Tapper, walking his dog," said Stanford. "In Tapper's statement he said that a car was parked at the end of the trail, but he didn't think anything of it because no vehicles are allowed along that part of the trail—and before you ask, there was no description."

"Give me a sec," Eastwood said, reaching for her phone and tapping furiously. "Avery Hill Trails is 0.3 miles from Bexley Road. The main road."

"That's under 500 meters. The point is that cars can't access the trail. And look to the right of O'Toole," Stanford said. He tapped the photo hard, twice. "There's a clear 'vehicles prohibited' sign on the fence, so explain to me why there are visible tire marks on the trail which stop a few meters from the body."

Eastwood leaned in and placed an index finger next to Stanford's, along the darkened patch of ground with a clear tread mark. "It looks like it rained the night before. There's surface water on the gravel," she said.

"And tread marks from a car tire—but no analysis of the tread marks. No close-up photographs in the files. There was nothing done with this piece of evidence," Stanford said. His neck flushed red with excitement. "A vital piece of evidence and there's not even a yellow marker next to it."

"It doesn't make sense," said Eastwood, taking a step back. "Why wouldn't Rhimes and the rest of the squad chase up the Fiesta? Or get the tire marks analyzed? It was 1995, not 1926. The Forensic Science Service had the capacity to analyze the tread pattern."

"Rhimes was the senior investigating officer, but who was his boss? I can't see anyone with half a brain letting their team get away with this shit."

"James Larsen," Eastwood said.

There was a brief moment of silence that was only interrupted by the sounds of sixties soul music escaping from the open windows of the flats next door.

"James Larsen," Stanford repeated. "Ex-Chief Superintendent James Larsen?"

Eastwood nodded.

"The ex-borough commander James Larsen who jumped ship at the copycat killing conference after he ballsed it up?"

"How many James Larsens do you know, Stanford?" Eastwood snapped.

"He just seems a bit...a bit young. What is he, early sixties?"

"He's fifty-eight."

"Fifty-eight. He would have been—" The doors to the SCU swung open and hit the back wall with a loud bang. Eastwood and Stanford remained silent as Pellacia walked hurriedly through the office, his shoulders hunched almost to his ears and a face flushed red with anger. He walked straight to his room and slammed his own door shut, acknowledging no one.

"Huh," said Stanford and turned back toward Eastward. "Something has definitely happened. Woman problems. He only gets that worked up about Henley."

"He's got a girlfriend now."

"When has that ever meant anything? Anyway, about Larsen. He's fifty-eight. That means he was in his early thirties back in '95."

"I've been doing some research," Eastwood said, not alluding to the fact that her knowledge about Larsen came from her own investigation into Rhimes. She walked the short distance back to her desk and picked up her notepad. "Larsen was one of the youngest police constables at the age of twenty-three and then became one of the youngest inspectors at the age of twenty-seven. He then transferred over to CID at the old Ladywell police station. He was then promoted to detective chief inspector and a year later he became head of the murder squad and Rhimes's boss. He's also got a master's in social policy and passed the fast-track examination and was appointed to chief superintendent."

"When did he leave the murder squad and start running around the halls of New Scotland Yard?" Stanford asked. He picked up a sheet of paper and a pen and started sketching mind maps that only he could understand.

"Not sure, but don't you think it's strange that someone who has a career trajectory as fast and intense as that, who was probably on his way to becoming the commissioner of the Metropolitan Police, would suddenly decide to retire early?"

"And there was no love lost between Rhimes and Larsen."

"None at all," agreed Eastwood.

"So, what are we saying? That Larsen diverted his team's attention away from the Ford Fiesta and whoever was really driving that car, and toward Andrew Streeter?" A smile formed on

Stanford's lips as he foresaw a path that could possibly absolve his old boss of any wrongdoing.

"Andrew Streeter gave evidence and said repeatedly in his first police interview that he was at work when the first two victims were taken and that he was not the one driving the Ford Fiesta. He said he'd never even been in that car."

"But there's nothing in those files to say that they investigated the Fiesta," Stanford said again.

"Streeter also said that he couldn't drive. No license, not even a provisional," said Eastwood.

"So why not look for the driver or the owner of the car, if it wasn't Rhimes calling the shots but his boss?"

"We've got to look more closely at Larsen and why he made it all about Streeter," said Eastwood, closing the file on her desk.

27

"She's not pleased about it," said Jake as he dragged his thumb through the condensation on the side of his pint glass.

"Lillian is never pleased about anything," Adam replied, covering his cheesy chips with vinegar.

"But she handed in her notice. I wasn't expecting that," Jake replied. "She's been at the paper for years."

Adam waited until he was satisfied that the couple who'd walked through the open door weren't anyone that he recognized from the paper. He'd had good reason to text Jake and tell him to meet him at a pub in Shadwell, three DLR stops away from their office. Competition was rife among the *Chronicle*'s staff and there had already been murmurings about Jake being given special treatment due to his uncle being a director of the newspaper's parent company, as well as speculation about Adam's own closeness to the CEO of the paper.

"I didn't think you cared," Adam continued as he carefully selected two chips from the pile in front of him.

Jake took off his signet ring and spun it on the bar. "I don't give a toss about Lillian. I'm only saying she didn't seem the type to throw a fit about not being on a byline."

"She's old-school," said Adam. "She feels as though she owns the story. The fact that she won an award for the original investigation doesn't mean anything. This is your time. You've got to take it."

"I'm more than happy to take it. This story is big and I'm not going to make a name for myself by playing it small but I'm not an idiot. There's stuff that I don't know."

"Like what? You know how to write a story, don't you?"

"Of course I do, but that's the easy bit. Lillian fucking embarrassed me at that press conference because she knows how to navigate the system. She knows how to work the room and who to get information from. She can read people. I need to learn how—"

"You will never learn how to do that," Adam replied with a firm shake of his head. "There are some things that can't be taught and reading people is one of them. That's a natural skill. And there's stuff Lillian knows about this case that you can't find on Google or in the newspaper archives."

"I don't want her around, but I need her if I'm going to claim this story as mine."

"You do realize that this story isn't only about the murder of Elias Piper, don't you, Jake Alexander Sorkin—"

"Don't." Jake grabbed Adam's hand tightly. There was an edge of urgency with every syllable.

"Don't what? Use your real name?" Adam said as he pulled his hand away. "Jake Alexander Sorkin, also known as Jake Ryland," Adam said at the top of his voice, raising his empty pint glass in the barman's direction.

"Stop it," Jake said, lowering his head.

"Stop what? No one here knows who the fuck you are. It doesn't matter if you're calling yourself by your government name or your pseudonym."

"You never know."

"Look, you're working in the newspaper business and one day soon someone is going to work out that your uncle is on the board of directors, and they'll start screaming that you're privileged, entitled, and a nepobaby. All of which is true. Deal with it and move on," said Adam as the barman placed a new pint on the table and he tapped his credit card on the machine. "This story is not just about Piper. Have you done any digging into Streeter's death? Chased up the coroner's report?"

Jake shamelessly shook his head. "No."

"This is why reporters like Lillian will always be miles ahead of you. Get in with the coroner's office. I've got a guy who is more than happy to provide you with information for the right amount of cash. You've got to be ruthless. Lillian may have handed in her notice but that doesn't mean she will leave the story behind. She's dangerous if she's a free agent."

"I get it," Jake said. "So, what else is there? What am I missing?"

"Jesus Christ," Adam replied, rolling his eyes. He took a long sip of his pint. "It's right in front you. It was written all over that Court of Appeal judgment."

"Judgment, what judgment?"

"Did you not read the Court of Appeal judgment that blatantly accused the investigating officers of being corrupt? You really need to catch up."

Jake took out his phone and googled *Andrew Streeter judgment*.

"You're a good writer but you're bloody lazy. You're in love with seeing your name on the byline. The only reason you want Lillian back is because you don't want to get your hands dirty digging for information."

"That's not true."

"Isn't it?" Adam asked as he pushed his stool back and stood up. "Don't forget that Lillian was only twenty-five when she won reporter of the year for her coverage of those murders. She put the work in... Ah, where is it?" he said as he pulled out a packet of cigarettes and placed them on the bar. "I thought I had it."

"What have you lost, your lighter?" said the man who'd been sitting quietly nearby, nursing a pint of London Ale.

"Yeah, I have. You wouldn't have—"

"I stopped a while ago, but I still carry one. Must be a comfort thing." The man reached into his jacket pocket, pulled out a lighter and slid it across the bar. "Keep it," he said.

"Thanks," said Adam as he took the lighter and turned to walk out of the pub. He paused, and looked back at Jake. "Think about what I said. Get your hands dirty."

Jake could feel himself swaying as he waited for the train door to open. He'd left the pub ten minutes before closing, with a faint memory of Adam talking about his wife nagging him about his whereabouts and then jumping into a black cab. The heat from the day had disappeared and Jake felt goose pimples on his chest as the chill evening air cut through the cotton of his shirt. He grabbed onto the strap of his rucksack and walked quickly out of the station, trying to decide whether he would order a kebab or a greasy double quarter pounder once he got home.

Family money, and not his junior journalist salary, had meant that Jake had been able to pay full price for the one-bedroom luxury apartment on the seventeenth floor of a gleaming glass building on the Upper Riverside of the Greenwich Peninsula. The lobby was quiet, and the concierge's desk was empty as Jake made his way to the wall that housed the communal postbox and retrieved his post. He turned around as soft classical music played out from the concealed speakers in the ceiling. Something in his alcohol-marinated brain knew the concierge desk shouldn't be unoccupied, but Jake shoved his post under his armpit and got into the elevator. All he wanted was to get into his apartment, eat his food, change his clothes and get into bed.

Everything felt wrong when he opened the front door. He

couldn't put his finger on it, but something had alerted his sense of flight or fight. It was as though the air had been tampered with. Jake took a step forward but stopped when he heard a sharp whistle as the wind outside performed a cyclonic dance around the building. He felt the wind sweep across his face and gently lift the pages of the open newspaper on the counter. He turned to his right and saw the lights from the buildings outside, but it wasn't those lights that had caught his attention. The sliding door that led to the terrace was open. He was certain he'd locked it before leaving that morning. He should have run when the bright fiery embers of a cigarette end traveled upward, stopped momentarily, and then grew in intensity as the figure on the balcony took a long drag. The muscles in Jake's back tensed as he watched a soft plume of smoke disappear into the night sky.

"Nice place you've got."

Jake squinted into the darkness. He knew this voice.

"How did you get in?" Jake asked as he took a single step back. His rucksack slipped off his shoulder and fell to the ground.

"Does it really matter right now?" the man said as he turned around and flicked his cigarette end over the balcony.

Jake tried to make all the broken pieces of recognition click into place. He couldn't quite place the voice, but he knew that he knew him.

"What do you want?" Jake reached into his jacket pocket, tightly clasping his phone, and tried to remember which of the three buttons on the side of the phone activated the SOS app and would immediately dial 999.

"You stole something from me," the man said, walking into the room. "Actually, you stole something from us." He stepped into the dim light.

"I know you," Jake said. It all clicked into place. "The pub."

There was a brief moment of silence and then Jake turned to run.

"I am not your story," the man said.

And he ran toward Jake.

Jake screamed out as he felt the heavy force of a firm but sharp shoulder barge into him, and he fell hard. He landed on his right side and hot rivets of pain ran across his cheekbone.

"I don't belong to you," the man growled, grabbing the back of Jake's jacket. Jake kicked out as he was dragged across the expensive oak flooring.

"Let go of me!" Jake shouted. He twisted and hooked his arm around the leg of the heavy wooden table, contorting himself into a tight ball.

"You didn't look so fucking tough," the man said. "But you're one of the wiry, muscley types, aren't you?"

Jake screamed out as a steel-capped boot landed in the middle of his back.

"I did not give you permission to write about me." The man kicked Jake again. "Only Lillian is allowed to write about me." He delivered a sharp kick to Jake's ribs.

"Please...stop hurting me," Jake choked out through his tears. He tried to hold on to the table leg but another kick to the side of his head forced him to release his grip.

"Stop hurting me," the man mimicked.

"Don't kill me," Jake begged, pain traveling through every nerve in his body.

"You've only got yourself to blame," the man said as he straddled Jake. He pulled a bottle wrapped in a flannel out of his pocket.

Jake tried to memorize the man's face, but his vision was blurry, and the blood was pulsating violently in his temples. The man removed the cap from the bottle and poured some liquid onto the flannel.

"Take a deep breath," the man said.

"No!" Jake swung an arm out and felt it connect against the man's hand. There was a thud as the man fell back, and the sound of the bottle as it rolled across the floor. Jake felt the man's grip on him loosen, and he turned to his side and began to claw at the floor in the direction of the door.

"You little fucking shit," the man said. He grabbed Jake's legs and turned him onto his back for a second time. "Now. Breathe it in."

Jake tried to move his head, but he was too weak and too damaged. He felt the damp cloth press into his face. Small droplets of liquid coated his nostrils and trickled down the back of his throat. The scent was sweet and reminded him of freshly cut grass after a light rain shower. He held his breath for as long as he could until he couldn't hold it any longer. He breathed in. The man leaned forward and whispered in his ear.

"That's it. Go to sleep."

Jake did as he was told.

28

"Did you listen to that radio clip that I sent you?" Ramouter stopped and waited for Henley to catch up.

"Which one?" she asked, mentally scanning through the memes and podcast links that Ramouter had got into the habit of sending her.

"The one with that woman claiming to be Streeter's sister. Denise Price. She was on LBC insisting that she always knew that her brother was innocent. How she's going to sue the police. According to Joanna, Price has been calling the SCU non-stop demanding to speak to someone in authority."

Henley swallowed the last of her coffee and threw her empty cup into a nearby bin. "Do you think she's someone worth talking to?"

"She could be. Or she could be some random, jumping on the Streeter bandwagon, looking for a quick way to make some cash."

"It wouldn't be the first time a family member suddenly

crawled out of the woodwork. But it can't hurt to see what she has to say."

Ramouter rolled his eyes. "In other words, you want me to speak to her."

"No stone left unturned," said Henley, releasing a yawn. She placed her hand on the broken gate that led to the small garden of Caroline Swann's house, flecks of old white paint sticking to her palm. The rest of the small garden was in sharp contrast to the ramshackle fence—dark pink hydrangeas overspilled from the carefully maintained border on the right, and a multicolored explosion of tulips filled the containers on the right. A window box, planted with pink and white geraniums, sat underneath a large bay window that was concealed by voile curtains with a repeating butterfly pattern.

"Someone loves their flowers," said Ramouter, tapping his foot against a wheelie bin that was completely covered with a daisy-print vinyl sticker.

"Just a bit. Everything that I plant dies a death," Henley replied. She walked up to the window and tried to peer through the butterflies on the curtain.

"See anything?"

"I think I can see the edge of a sofa, but other than that... can't see a thing," Henley replied. She stepped away and ran a finger along the wooden frame. "It looks freshly painted," she said. "Maybe she's doing the place up but hasn't got round to doing the fencing." She nodded toward the broken gate.

Ramouter stepped up to the tasteful blue door, adorned with a gleaming silver Victorian door knocker.

"You can get cheap... That's odd."

"What's odd?" Henley was watching a bright green refuse collection truck that had stopped at the end of the road.

"Take a look," Ramouter said, running his index finger along a rectangular piece of black plastic screwed into the brick wall. "It's a mounting bracket for one of those video recording doorbells. A wireless one. I had to put one in for my mum the last time I was back in Bradford. Haven't you got one?"

"Yeah, but Rob's the gadget freak. Came home one day and there it was." Henley stepped further back and raised her head to look at the two windows on the first floor. "Frosted glass on the right, has to be the bathroom," she said. "Front bedroom window is slightly opened."

"I suppose she could have taken it off to charge it, but it doesn't take that long, maybe a couple of hours. If that's what's happened, it was probably taken off recently," Ramouter said cautiously. He raised the door knocker and banged it twice.

"But you're not convinced?" said Henley, walking back up to the fence. The street was a short one. There were four houses to her left before the street ended and the primary school began. To Henley's right, there were three houses and then the entrance to a small park that led to a sprawling housing estate. As Henley's watch ticked closer to 3:30 p.m., the piercing screech of a speaker experiencing feedback and then the sounds of Beyoncé could be heard from the direction of the park. But it was a poster on a lamppost that caught Henley's attention. A local council notice that they would be trialing waste collection on a Saturday.

"Ramouter. Do me a favor and check the wheelie bins."

"You want me to do what?" Ramouter asked, his right hand resting on the door knocker.

"Check the bins," Henley said again. "Everyone's bins are out on the pavement. Must be collection day. Look, next-door's is almost overflowing. Why isn't Caroline's bin out?"

Ramouter checked. "Both empty," he confirmed.

"Bin collection is weekly; two weeks at a push. Caroline was last seen on Friday, eighteenth June—eight days ago. She should have returned to work two days ago. She hasn't returned my calls. Her parents haven't heard from her and she ain't answering the door. We can enter under section seventeen of PACE. Entering a property to save life or limb."

Ramouter walked back to the front door, bent down and pushed open the letter box and peered through.

"And?" Henley asked. As she took out her phone to make the call for assistance, a woman holding a small child by the hand walked past Caroline's house and pushed open the gate to the house on her right.

"I think I can hear a radio, but other than that, short hall-way, stairs—"

"Excuse me, do you live here?" Henley asked across the low wall that divided the two properties.

"Yes," the woman replied suspiciously, closing her gate firmly and ushering the child toward the front door.

"I'm Detective Inspector Henley. Can I ask you a few questions about your neighbor, Caroline Swann? She's not answering her door."

The woman seemed distracted, searching for her keys in an overcrowded handbag. "She could be asleep. She might be working nights this week…" She looked up suddenly. "You're the police?"

"Yes," Henley said, displaying her warrant card. "Detective Inspector Henley," she repeated. "Does Caroline live here alone, Ms.…?"

"Goodwill. Belinda Goodwill." Henley had her full attention now. "Yes, Caroline has lived alone for about two years now. She moved in with her husband, Billy, when I was pregnant with this one, so about five years ago. Two years ago, she caught Billy in bed with Susan from two doors down. It was awful, absolutely awful, and he chucked it all in poor Caroline's face by moving in with—"

"When did you last see Caroline?"

"Mummy, I'm hungry."

"In a sec, Sienna. I'm talking to the nice lady. Would it have been over a week ago?" Belinda paused, biting her coral-painted lip. "It was half term this week. Well, it was for my kids. They don't go to the school around the corner, which I think is on half term next week and they get two weeks off which is ridiculous. Anyway, we were away."

"So, you think that you last saw Caroline over a week ago?" Henley clarified.

"Must have been. We were in Portugal. Me, Sienna and my son, Hudson, he's twelve, with my sister and her kids. Our mum and dad live out there. The kids love it. We left last Friday, eighteenth June it was, and came back last night. I definitely haven't seen her since we came back. But as I said, sometimes she—" Belinda's eyes widened as though the significance of two detectives standing in her neighbor's front garden had just clicked in her brain. "Has something happened to her?"

"Is she dead?" Sienna suddenly piped up. "My hamster died when we were on holiday at nanna's."

"Sienna-Rose Goodwill," Belinda snapped, pulling her daughter toward her. "I'm so sorry, I need to get her inside."

"That's OK," Henley replied. Sienna wriggled away from her mother and went off to pet a cat that had appeared in her garden.

"Oh my God, I've got a spare key. To Caroline's," Belinda said quickly. "It's indoors. She gave it to me when she changed the locks. I'll get it for you."

Henley entered Caroline's house first, with Ramouter closely behind her. She could feel the sweat in the palms of her hands as the latex gloves cemented themselves to her skin. The tinny sound of a talk radio station came from upstairs, creating the impression there were two people up there having a conversation.

"Look," Ramouter said, closing the front door and pointing to the wire cage letter box attached to the back of the door. It was almost filled to the brim with envelopes and leaflets.

"I'm not liking this at all," said Henley, the stale air tickling her nose. "What do you want to do? Go through the house together or split up?"

"After last time, I'm sticking with you," Ramouter replied. He followed Henley through the ground floor, which had all the signs of someone who had started their day but hadn't returned to finish it. The small living room was cast in muted sepia tones due to the closed window blinds. A mustard-colored blanket was strewn across a two-seater sofa, where an opened magazine was squashed into the corner of the sofa along with the wrapper of a chocolate bar. In the corner, a pile of hardback and paperback books had been stacked haphazardly next to an opened gym bag and a single trainer.

"Not the tidiest," Ramouter mused. The faint light caught a film of dust on a TV screen that was far too big for the small living room.

"Not at all," Henley agreed. She bent to pick up a newspaper from the coffee table. "It's the *Evening Standard*, dated last Friday. The eighteenth."

Ramouter let out a resigned sigh. "That's over a week. How can no one raise the alarm if you've gone quiet for over a week?"

"She was on annual leave," Henley shrugged. "Her parents live in Greece and her husband, sorry ex-husband, is shacked up with the neighbor."

"But she has friends. I can't believe they were all so blasé about not hearing from her." They walked out of the living room and down the short but narrow hallway, past cans of new paint, paintbrushes and a roller kit in a plastic bag.

"There's a receipt," Ramouter said, peering inside the bag. "B&Q on the Old Kent Road, twelfth June."

"Where the hell is she?" Henley asked. She squeezed past Ramouter and stood at the entrance to the kitchen. There was a pile of folded clothes on the table, next to another book, an empty polka-dot mug and a white plate covered with stale breadcrumbs and smears of ketchup dried to concrete-like consistency. The kitchen table carried all the hallmarks of someone having breakfast and then rushing out when they realized they were late for something, but the chair that was lying on its back by the oven door told a different story. A navy blue tote bag with its contents—purse, keys, staff ID card, a tampon, loose change and a small bottle of cheap perfume—spilling out on the floor suggested to Henley that, in Caroline's case, she either ran away from someone or was taken. She took a step into the room but stopped when she heard the familiar sound of her shoe meeting broken glass. She scanned the room again, this time noticing the scattering of broken glass on the floor. Turning to her side, she noticed the door into the kitchen was glazed, and the top pane had broken into pieces while the bottom panel was covered by a large spiderweb crack.

"Look at the back door," Ramouter said, from behind Henley. There was a light breeze outside that moved the door slightly on its hinges. It hadn't been properly closed. "Someone came in through the back—" Ramouter started.

"Obviously surprised—no—*scared* her," Henley continued as they both backed their way carefully into the hallway. "She panics, tries to get away."

"Slams the kitchen door shut." By now, they were both back where they started at the front door, staring at the staircase covered in a blue-striped carpet.

"Either the force of her slamming the door shut breaks the glass, or the intruder broke the glass trying to get to her."

"No visible signs of blood on the floor or"—Henley examined the walls, covered in expensive-looking wallpaper—"on the walls or the door."

"If she didn't run *out* of the house…" said Ramouter.

"Then maybe she ran up," Henley finished. She began to ascend the stairs.

It was the smell that hit them first. The smell of urine and vomit that had soaked into the carpet of the bedroom at the front of the house and had fermented as London sweltered with above normal June temperatures. Again, the room was in muted darkness, with the blinds pulled shut. The double bed had shifted from its original position, leaving behind two circular indentations from the wooden bedposts on the carpet, and the duvets and pillows were entangled on the bed.

"There are scuff marks on the wall," said Ramouter, carefully stepping into the room. He pointed to a streak of gray, with a visible trainer tread, on the lower half of the wall. "God, it stinks in here," he said, doing his best to cover his mouth and nose with his hand.

"Don't move," Henley said sharply. She entered the room but positioned herself against the wardrobe door. "By your feet. Next to the bedside cabinet. It looks like a piece of duct tape."

Ramouter carefully stepped back and crouched down. "It looks used. There's another piece under the bed and…it looks like a couple of cable ties. Bloody hell…smells even worse down—"

Ramouter didn't finish his sentence but began to cough violently and fell forward onto his knees as the combined smell of urine, vomit and human feces caught in the back of his throat. "One of the cable ties is cut in half," he finally said. Henley walked out of the room, unable to handle the overpowering smell. She pulled out her phone to do what she should have done when she first spotted that Caroline's bin was not outside her front garden on the pavement: call for more police officers and the forensics team.

Pellacia leaned back in his chair and released a sigh from the very depths of his guts, which somehow managed to reflect every emotion felt by every single member of the Serial Crime Unit. Despondence, weariness, intrigue, confusion and an overwhelming sense that the investigation had morphed into an unrecognizable beast.

"It's not as bad as it looks," Henley said, in a poor effort to lift the unit's spirits as the sound of an electric drill buzzed in the background. As if to reinforce the point that Henley's proclamation was completely false, a thick dark cloud cloaked the sun.

"It's enough to make me want to transfer to the Outer Hebrides. Did you know that, until a week ago, their last murder case was in 1968? Can you imagine only having to deal with a murder every forty-odd years? Bliss," Stanford said drily.

"You'd be bored out of your mind," Ramouter said, pressing send on a text before turning his phone to silent and placing it face down on his desk. "What would you do all day?"

"Dunno," Stanford said with a shrug. "Judge the village fete, investigate the theft of the parish church collection plate. The point is, I wouldn't be sitting here, trying to make sense of this shit on a Saturday afternoon. Are we even getting paid for all this overtime?"

"All right, enough," said Pellacia. He straightened and ran a hand through hair that seemed to Henley to have sprouted more gray streaks in the past week. "So, where exactly are we and are we sure that this missing nurse—"

"Caroline Swann." Henley tapped a blue marker against the photograph, taken from Caroline's ID card, that was now tacked to the whiteboard.

"Caroline Swann," Pellacia repeated with a trace of empathy. "Are we sure that she's linked to this case, or is she a completely separate investigation that we could palm off to someone else to take the pressure off us a bit?"

"No," Henley said firmly. "I think that would be a big mistake. One that would do us, as a unit, no favors." Pellacia nodded, grudgingly. "So," she continued, "I'm going to split this briefing in two: present day and 1995."

"Like *Back to the Future?*" Stanford quipped. Henley raised an arm and mimed throwing the marker at him.

"Sorry, sorry."

"Present day. Elias Piper was murdered three days after the

Court of Appeal judgment that started this toxic ball rolling. Postmortem result confirmed that he died of asphyxiation after being buried alive."

"Are we looking for someone with surgical experience?" asked Eastwood. "Because of the flesh removed from his leg."

"It's difficult to say. But that leads to another question, when we start looking at potential suspects."

"There can be only one," said Stanford, as the main door opened and Ezra walked into the room carrying a laptop in one hand and a large iridescent green juice in the other. He made a point of not looking at the whiteboard as he made his way to the empty desk next to Eastwood.

"Give me a minute, Stanford, I'll get there," said Henley, pointing at Piper's photograph on the board. "So, Elias Piper here, died from asphyxiation. Buried alive."

"Shit," Ezra murmured as he opened his laptop and swung his chair around so that he was facing the window.

Eastwood raised her hand. "Question," she said. "How did the fridge get there? Both properties had been recently renovated. Wouldn't someone have noticed that monstrosity being wheeled up the garden path?"

"Uniform carried out door-to-door enquiries, but everyone said the same thing. There had been a lot of delivery vans at both properties, which has been confirmed by the video footage, but there was one that stood out. A van arrived at number 135 at 1:42 a.m. on the morning that Piper was found."

"So, we've got footage of someone entering the building?" asked Eastwood.

"No," Henley replied with a slight hint of frustration. She nodded at Ramouter to take over.

"There is no footage of the driver exiting or entering the vehicle," said Ramouter. "The security gate can be entered one of three ways. Entering a code on the keypad next to the gate, the fob, or entering your pin or face ID via an app."

"Don't tell me," said Eastwood.

"Aye. Our driver used either the fob or the app to open the gate and the garage. Once inside the garage, he can access the property through a door that leads straight to the utility room. And—" Ramouter took a breath. "The van. A gray Peugeot Partner but the number plates are registered to a 2014 Suzuki SUV which was stolen three weeks ago in Bury St. Edmunds."

"So now we know how Piper's body was removed from The Burier site and staged in the fridge in Little Venice. And then he accessed the house next door, where we found Andrew Streeter's hospital band and the message on the mirror," Henley concluded.

"Forensics?" Pellacia asked.

"Anthony recovered three separate DNA identifiers from the hospital band," Henley confirmed. "One obviously belongs to Streeter, the second to Piper—cross-contamination—and the third is unknown. A partial fingerprint was also recovered. No matches so far," Henley took a breath and then continued. "There was no other DNA found on Piper's body, but Linh did retrieve soil samples from Piper's lungs and, although the body had been cleaned with bleach, samples were retrieved from the hair on his head and his pubic hair. Our expert has concluded that the soil was from the Folkestone area, and more specifically near a gravel pit," said Henley.

"How many gravel pits are there in the Folkestone area?" asked Stanford.

"Nine," Ramouter said. "Nine working gravel and quarry pits. Our soil expert specifically said that the soil retrieved was coastal, which means we can eliminate three of those quarries."

"Whoever murdered Piper had access to a quarry, and we're concluding they murdered Streeter too. Ramouter, would you like to explain?"

"Streeter was poisoned," Ramouter said, standing up and straightening his shirt. "He was given a fatal dose of rat poison intravenously."

"So, we're definitely looking for someone with medical experience, if not surgical experience?" Pellacia asked.

"To be honest, gov, our killer could easily have watched a couple of YouTube videos about IV bags and administering intravenous infusions. But that does lead us on to the missing nurse. Actually, two missing nurses."

"Hold on, what do you mean *two*?" Eastwood demanded.

"The hospital wing management covered up when Streeter was found and, more importantly, *how* he was found," Henley said. "Their report states that he was found dead in bed, but Linh is of the opinion that Streeter most likely fell out of bed due to convulsions caused by the poison, broke his hip and arm, and then died on the floor. It was Caroline Swann who found Streeter, but there was a second nurse on duty the morning he died."

"Filip Szymanski," said Ramouter, handing Henley an A4 colored photograph. "This was taken from the records of the nursing agency. He'd only been registered for six weeks and started working at the prison almost immediately. According to their records, he's forty-four years old and lived at 94 Vallance House on the Gideon Road estate in Lavender Hill. The only problem with that is that our checks showed no one of that name has ever lived at that address. And the Filip Szymanski that we did find is a sixty-four-year-old truck driver who lives in Wolverhampton and was driving to Munich on June fifteenth."

"And that guy is blatantly wearing a wig," Ezra piped up as he made his way to the smartboard next to Henley and plugged in his laptop. "Lace front, if you must know."

"How on earth do you know about lace wigs?" Stanford queried.

"A lace front, not a lace wig."

"Is there something you want to tell us?"

"I will ignore that," said Ezra. "But if you must know: my sister, innit? She's always switching up her hair. She's got a wicked one that makes her look like Storm from the X-Men. Anyway, look at his forehead. You can see the netting. Your man is not a natural blond. His nose looks funny too. This is what I'm talking about. *Mission Impossible* stuff."

"He's right, you know," Henley said, tracing her finger along Filip's hairline. "If Filip Szymanski isn't who he says he is, then who is he? And where is he?"

"Well, he ain't in Lavender Hill," said Ramouter. "He hasn't been seen since he finished his shift the morning that Streeter died, and he hasn't been in contact with the agency either. The staff nurse suggested Caroline may have had a bit of a thing for Filip but, as far as she's aware, nothing ever came of it."

"So, you're suggesting"—Pellacia cocked his ear as the phone in his office began to ring—"that this geezer calling himself Filip joined the nursing agency and somehow got himself a job at the prison just so he could get access to Streeter. Why?"

"Because Streeter knew who 'Filip Szymanski' really is: the person responsible for the 1995 murders." Henley made air quotes around their suspect's assumed name. "Why else would he want Streeter out of the way?" she went on. "Streeter's appeal case was big. Piper mouthing off in front of any reflective surface. The original investigation being reopened and dumped in our laps. According to Streeter's oncologist, he was in remission. How much longer would it have been before he opened his mouth and told us or someone like Callum O'Brien, who was really responsible for those murders?"

"But why now?" asked Stanford. "That's what's troubling me. Twenty-five years is a long time to keep quiet."

"Exactly." Eastwood picked up the baton of Stanford's questioning as though they were in a relay race. "Streeter is first arrested and bailed in late October 1995. Re-bailed in December and then rearrested and charged in January 1996. Why didn't he talk then? Give Rhimes and his team a name?"

"Streeter said he'd heard that the person he thought it was

might be dead. But to be honest, he didn't sound a hundred percent sure," Henley admitted.

"That's not a good enough answer," said Stanford. "One murder would have been enough for me to start singing like a canary and snitching on anyone that I could think of. But *five*?"

"Don't forget that you've also been accused of burying your victims alive," said Eastwood. "As you said, why not give a name? Bloody hell, give *any* name, anything to get the heat off you. Why wouldn't you do something to save yourself?"

"Scared shitless?" Ezra piped up. "No one wants to be a snitch. Well, not unless you're Stanford." He swirled his straw around his juice.

"You little git. I was hypothesizing." Stanford swung his foot out against the wheels on Ezra's chair.

"The point is," Ezra continued, "Streeter risks informing on someone, and then it turns out that he was wrong. Then what? His name is mud. People suddenly want to take him out. Teach him a lesson. I doubt that he was running around with saints and angels. I doubt—"

"Thinking of changing professions?" Pellacia asked, with a spark of humor in his eyes.

"Good where I am, thanks. Ones and zeros."

"Glad to hear it. But Boy Wonder here does have a point," said Pellacia. "Maybe Streeter was worried about his safety if he named the wrong person."

"Nah," Stanford shook his head. "I don't buy it. Streeter was probably involved in these murders and naming Mr. X would incriminate him. Simple as that."

"Or there is no Mr. X and it was Streeter and only Streeter, and all of this is a wild goose chase," said Eastwood.

"Then why kill him?" Ezra blurted out. "Why poison that poor guy? Man is sitting in prison ready to pack up and go, and the next thing you know: poof. Gone. And there he is plastered on your deathboard."

Pellacia let out a loud frustrated sigh and shot Ezra a warning look. "Once again, he has a point. Why kill Streeter?"

The team dropped into silence, only interrupted by the sound of someone dragging heavy equipment across the cracked tiling in the corridor and the growing sound of rush-hour traffic outside.

"Let's get back on track. Focus on what we're dealing with now, if we believe that there is a Mr. X," said Pellacia.

"You're saying that right now we're looking for a killer who's responsible for all seven murders?" Eastwood asked.

"But we ain't got a clue who he is." Pellacia placed his hands on his head as the phone in his office rang again. After two rings it stopped. "So do we reckon that this Filip has something to do with Caroline Swann's disappearance?"

"No other explanation, far as I can see," said Ramouter. "She was clearly taken from the house. Video doorbell is missing. Obvious signs of a disturbance in the kitchen and then what we found in the upstairs bedroom. Sorry for being blunt, but she literally pissed and shit herself in that bedroom, as well as being sick."

"Fear," Eastwood remarked sadly.

Henley nodded. "Caroline's DNA was also found on the piece of duct tape we found, and the cable ties. But there were also tiny specks of blood that were a match for the DNA found on Streeter's hospital band."

"So, we're possibly looking at our murderer, but we have no idea who he is," Eastwood said, pointing at the photograph of Filip.

"None, at this point. The Missing Persons Unit have already put an appeal out for Caroline. We need to release the photograph of the man calling himself Filip Szymanski ASAP. Ez, do you want to do your bit?" said Henley as she finally sat down, aware that Pellacia hadn't taken his eyes off her.

"*Mission Impossible*," Ezra said with a grin, mirroring his laptop screen on the smartboard. "As Detective Constable Ra-mouter brilliantly explained to you, Caroline Swann's doorbell was missing. More specifically, an Aion video doorbell. One of the new players in the game. A bit cheaper, I wouldn't have it, but you know, each to their own. Anyway, anyone who has one of these doorbells knows that you can access it and control it via an app on your phone."

"Where is Swann's phone?" Pellacia asked.

"No idea," said Henley. "It wasn't in her house. In fact, no electronic devices were found, no laptops, Kindles. Nothing."

"Doesn't matter," said Ezra confidently. "You don't need your phone if you're registered to the Aion storage plan and...look, I don't need to go into the technical details about how I accessed Swann's accounts—"

"He hacked it," said Stanford.

"I'm offended," Ezra retorted. "Anyway, Swann has an ac-count and her videos for the past six months are automatically saved unless she deletes them. So, this is the video taken from her last day at work. Friday, eighteenth of June."

The team watched as a high-quality video recording appeared on the screen and showed the view from the front of Caroline's house. They watched as Caroline came into view, walked down her path, paused briefly to check the hydrangeas, walked out of her gate and then got into a black Volkswagen Passat.

"She has a car?" Henley asked, turning to Ramouter.

"There wasn't a car when we were there. Driveway was empty," said Ramouter. "So, she comes back that night?"

"Next video. Here she is at 7:53 p.m. Next video is her leav-ing again at 8:18 p.m."

"That's the gym bag we saw in the living room," said Ra-mouter. "So, she goes to the gym and comes back at...?"

"Video switches to night mode now, but it's a decent enough camera: 1080p. She's at her door at 10:02 p.m. There's a bunch of other videos while she's at work and at the gym—the camera capturing people taking their kids to and from school, the postman, a couple of delivery men, a jogger running past..." said Ezra.

"No one that looks like Filip?" asked Pellacia.

"Not before she disappears. But here's the last video that was recorded before the camera was removed, at 1:48 a.m. on Saturday morning, nineteenth June."

Henley found herself holding her breath as a figure came into view, the street illuminated by the orange glow of a streetlight somewhere out of shot. The figure was dressed entirely in black, with the hoodie of his jacket pulled over his head. He walked quickly up to the front door, where the microphone picked up his heavy breathing. He kept his head down and the camera went black for a second.

"You never see his face, but he's removing the doorbell," said Ezra. "Look at the next video: it's motion activated, which tells us he's got it in his hand now."

They silently watched the footage of the ground rushing by and then a fence before there was the sound of a gate opening and then a quick flash of a white door before the video ended.

"I think that was the back door to Caroline's house," said Ramouter.

Henley shook her head as she tried to comprehend what she'd just seen and reconcile it with the scene in Caroline's kitchen. "Whoever it was, they entered Caroline's house at two in the morning. Are you trying to tell me that he stayed in her house all night, possibly made himself breakfast, as he waited for Caroline to wake up and find him in her kitchen. He then hid Caroline in her own house and then took her a few days later?"

"Why not take her while she was sleeping?" asked Stanford. "Why go through all that? And how did he get her out of the house?"

"He made his way to the house on foot, and he came from

the left, the direction of the park. He must have taken her in her own car."

"Jesus Christ," Pellacia muttered as his phone in the office rang for a third time. "Let me get that. Henley, you can talk me through the cold case later. And Ramouter? I want a word with you."

Everyone turned and looked at Ramouter, who had visibly paled.

"Calm down, the lot of you," said Pellacia. "Is there anything else before I go, or are we good?"

Henley caught Eastwood's eye, but she was giving nothing away as to where her side investigation was taking her.

"All good, I think," said Eastwood, giving Pellacia a mock salute.

"Fine. Ramouter, I'll grab you when I'm done," said Pellacia, striding to his office. As he brushed past Henley, he subtly touched her elbow.

"I was going to say that we'll call it a night, but let's get hold of the DVLA and pull up the full registration details for Swann's car. Then we can put out a BOLO," said Henley, forcing herself to refocus and take charge of the room.

"Might be a bit late for that," Stanford remarked.

"We don't have much choice. I'm going to get a missing statement out for Crimestoppers and… What road heads to the Folkestone area?"

"Must be the M20," said Eastwood.

"Give me a sec," said Ramouter. "Aye, you're right. From Swann's house in Sidcup, the quickest way would have been the A20 and onto the M20 down to Folkestone."

"I'll get onto National Highways and see what we can do about getting footage from the cameras they've got on the motorway," said Eastwood.

"Thanks." Henley turned to Ezra. "Go home," she said, giving him a quick hug.

"Are you sure?"

"Of course, you've done brilliantly. Honestly, you could give this lot a run for their money."

"Cool, you should go home too." He unplugged his laptop.

"I will," Henley said, turning to face the image of the man who'd pretended to be Filip Szymanski. "I just need to work out if I've seen this man before."

"I know that you don't smoke, but I can offer you a drink," Pellacia handed Ramouter a nonalcoholic beer. "We're still on duty," he said with a grin as Ramouter took the bottle, wiped away the condensation and examined the label.

They were on the top floor of the station, which had once been used as a break room and had access to a large terrace. A cool breeze wrapped around them as they looked down at Greenwich Park stretching out to the horizon.

"I saw the look on your face earlier," said Pellacia, lighting his cigarette and blowing out a plume of smoke. "You haven't done anything wrong."

"Thank God." Ramouter expertly placed the top of the bottle against the wall and pried off the cap. "I was worried for a sec."

"No need. I wanted to check in on you, that's all. Feel free to tell me to mind my own business and piss off, but I was wondering how things are going at home."

"Is this because I've been late a few times?" Ramouter said quickly.

"Yes and no. I don't have an issue with the lateness. I understand that it's going to be difficult to balance everything now that you've got a full house again. And with your wife's condition. I can see you're trying your best."

Ramouter relaxed slightly. "It's not easy," he said.

"It never is. You can have all the plans in place, timetables and a list of emergency contact numbers on the fridge and on paper it seems manageable. But when real life kicks in?" Pellacia inhaled deeply on his cigarette. "It's hard. It's fucking hard and exhausting."

"You sound as though you're talking from experience."

Pellacia looked up with surprise. "Anj—sorry, Henley—didn't tell you? About my mum?"

"No, she hasn't said anything. She doesn't talk about you and—" Ramouter paused, not wanting to cross the line and speak out loud what everyone in the SCU already knew. He had caught subtle signs that had been impossible to ignore.

"Six years," Pellacia said as he flicked his cigarette butt over the balcony. "My mum was diagnosed with dementia six years ago. The crazy thing is that she's seventy-four years old but doesn't look it—she's one of those annoying people who enter marathons for fun. Physically, she can put most thirty-years-olds to shame. But the truth is, she has dementia and she's slipping away from us."

He ran his hand quickly across his eyes. Ramouter said nothing.

"She has good days, really good days, when you think there's nothing wrong with her and maybe the diagnosis was incorrect. But there's less of them now, and the bad days are getting more frequent," said Pellacia. "We're all doing what we can to help. Mum lives with one of my sisters, but it's…well, it's shit."

"I'm sorry. I didn't realize," said Ramouter. "And the boss didn't say a word."

"Henley is good like that. She'll hold your secrets," Pellacia said warmly. "I wanted you to know that I understand, and you're allowed to be pissed off at the situation."

"It's not fair on Michelle—none of this is her fault—but I get so frustrated. And then I feel bad because I know that I'm being selfish when I'm asking her to try to pick up Ethan from school or collect her prescription from the chemist."

"You're not being selfish."

Ramouter bit his lip. "Tell my brain that. The doctors are… I don't know if optimistic is the right word. But it's not over, not yet. Michelle is here now and we can be normal…only, things are not normal."

"I understand what you're saying. You feel bad for wanting to have a life. A good life."

"That's exactly it," said Ramouter. His shoulders visibly lowered and he swallowed the rest of his beer. "And then there's Ethan. He doesn't understand what's wrong with his mum, but he knows something isn't right."

"Don't be so hard on yourself," Pellacia said, patting Ramouter on the back. "One thing about the SCU is that we've got each other's backs. I think you've been here long enough to realize that."

Ramouter turned away and took another swallow of beer in the false hope that the act would stop him from crying. "Thanks, gov," he whispered.

"None needed," Pellacia replied. "We've got you."

29

Ramouter placed his right hand against his front door and closed his eyes as though he was listening to the pulse of his house. He knew what time it was without even checking his watch, because he heard the front door of flat 4 above open, and the opening theme tune of *Match of the Day* blaring out. The tenant emerged, jogged down the stairs and a few seconds later reappeared with a large pizza box in his hands.

"Lost your keys?" he asked as he brushed past Ramouter and took the next flight of stairs, two at a time, without waiting for an answer. Ramouter took a breath, pushed the key into the lock and opened the door. The ground-level flat opened up into a long hallway with Ethan's bedroom, a small box room, on his immediate left and the large double room that he shared with Michelle immediately next door. He kicked off his sneakers and shuffled them to the side before entering his son's room. Ethan hadn't slept with a nightlight since he was two and a half, but he couldn't stand sleeping in silence, which is why small speakers on the windowsill were playing Disney songs at a very low volume. Ramouter kneeled and watched his son; he didn't want to touch him and contaminate him with the dark residue of his day. The hallway light cast a glow across Ethan's face as he slept, highlighting the soft sheen of sweat on his forehead.

"You're late," Michelle hissed as he picked up the comic book that had fallen from Ethan's bed, closed it and placed it on top of the small desk. He turned and faced his wife, who was standing in the doorway. He could see that her fingertips had whitened and the skin had grown taut around her knuckles as she gripped the door frame as if she was using it to absorb all of her anger.

"I'm sorry. I thought I would have been able to get out early. I didn't mean to be late," he whispered, stepping away from Ethan's bed.

"Late is six, maybe seven o'clock," the volume of Michelle's voice grew with each syllable. "Not nearly eleven—"

"Miche, you're going to wake him."

Ramouter could feel the rage emanating from Michelle's body as he joined her in the doorway. She stared back at him and the blue in her eyes became a harsh gray.

"I can't believe you," she said and stormed up the hallway. Ethan stirred in his sleep, raised his head slightly and then fell back onto the pillow as though he'd changed his mind. Ramouter stepped out of the room and closed the door behind him. He could have gone into the bathroom, stripped off his clothes, taken the longest hot shower and then gone to bed. But that would only have resulted in a restless night and waking up to find himself facing a cold front.

"I'm sorry," he said, following Michelle into the kitchen. She tutted and picked up a small sheet covered with stars and planets, placing it over the cage where Ethan's budgie lived. "So, is this how it's going to be? Are you going to ignore me now?"

"It's no different to what you've been doing to me today," Michelle replied. She picked up a half-empty glass of red wine from the counter and made her way into the living area, where she sat on the sofa and pointedly turned on the TV.

"For fuck's sake," Ramouter whispered under his breath, opening the fridge to pull out a beer. It was only when he slammed the door shut that he realized why Michelle was rightfully angry. The usual things were stuck to the fridge with magnets: a newsletter from Ethan's school detailing the term dates, emergency contact numbers, and an appointment reminder for Michelle's MRI scan for 4:25 p.m. that afternoon. Ramouter rested his head against the door and released a low groan.

"Miche, sweetheart, I'm so sorry. I completely forgot about your appointment," he said, when he sat next to Michelle on the sofa. His heart pinched when she got up and moved to the armchair. "Please don't be like that, I'm sorry."

"Sorry. Is that all you have to say? You didn't even call or text me and then, when I called, you ignored me."

"It wasn't like that; I didn't ignore you. We were in the middle of a—"

"It doesn't matter what you were in the middle of, Salim. I'm your priority, and Ethan. You made me come here."

"Hold on, I didn't *make* you come down here. It's what you wanted, Michelle. I gave you the choice. I didn't make the decision for you."

"You're neglecting me. You're neglecting us. I'm starting to think that you preferred it when Ethan and I were up in Bradford and you were down here doing what you like. You probably weren't even working late; you were probably drinking in the pub until kicking-out time."

"Michelle," Ramouter said firmly, struggling to inject calm into his tone. "It's late and we're both tired. I know that you're upset about missing your appointment but—"

"*I* didn't miss it," Michelle interrupted and turned her attention back to the TV.

"You didn't?"

"I went on my own. Ethan went to the cinema with Thea and her kids. I went on my own."

"All the way to the hospital on your own? Guy's Hospital?"

"Yes, I walked to Forest Hill train station and I got a train to London Bridge. Then I did the same coming back."

"On your own?" Ramouter said with disbelief. "You made me feel like shit because I asked you to take Ethan to school, which is around the corner, and there you are traipsing across London?"

Michelle folded her arms and sat back in her chair. There was a clear look of defiance on her face. Her mouth curled in a grimace and her eyes narrowed as though she was processing her next move in a hostile game of chess.

"I didn't have much choice," she finally said. "You abandoned me."

"No, no. I'm not doing this. Don't, don't…sometimes I think you use your diagnosis like a crutch. You say you can't do the simplest of things when you clearly can."

"What the—How could you say that?" Michelle stood up and threw her empty glass onto the armchair. "Not every day is good, Salim."

"But not every day is bad either. I'm doing everything I can to support you, but I don't need to be holding your hand every single bloody day." He shook his head. "Michelle, I am here. I want us here together as a family," he pleaded. "But it's hard. I worry about you every day. I'm not like other people. I can't switch my emotions on and off, and I'm dealing with a lot at work."

"Oh, here we go. Your bloody job. The SCU. Another excuse."

"What are you talking about? I don't use my job as an excuse. I'm trying to explain to you that I'm under a lot of pressure. None of this is easy, but I try my best. I support you, I listen to you and I'm doing all of this because I love you. I spend every free moment googling for new treatments, trying to understand research papers about your condition. I'm trying my—"

"You're hardly trying at all. You keep telling me that I'm normal when I'm not."

"Miche. I'm—"

"Trying to push me out on these strange streets when you know that I'm not ready."

Ramouter placed his hand against his forehead. He felt hot, sick, and that he was losing control. He bit his lip so hard to stop himself from crying that he drew blood. He looked at Michelle. He loved her but he couldn't help feeling as though he'd failed her.

"I'm ill," Michelle shouted. "You're acting as though I've got something straightforward like a broken leg. I have early-onset dementia."

"Early, Michelle!" Ramouter shouted back. "*Early.* You're still here. You're not broken. You can be my wife, Ethan's mum. And you can clearly get yourself to and from a hospital. It makes me wonder how much more can you do."

"Are you seriously suggesting that I'm… I'm taking advantage?" Michelle asked, backing away from Ramouter. "Oh my God, you… I don't believe… Say it. Tell me that I'm taking advantage of my condition, of you. Say it!"

"No, no." Ramouter raised his hands above his head. "I won't let you bait me. I'm going before I say something I'll regret."

"I wouldn't worry about it," Michelle replied bitterly. As she walked out of the room, she let loose her parting shot: "You've already said it."

"I'm not even going to ask," Rob said, leaning over the coffee table and removing the last of his cannabis from the grinder and placing it among the tobacco in the rolling paper.

Henley wearily dumped her bag on the sofa. "Do you have to do that in the house?"

"Would you rather I roll up outside, get myself arrested and then you and Ems can visit me when I'm doing jail time?"

"How much have you smoked?"

"Maybe I should get you an ID card and install an entry key-pad on the front door. You can pretend that this is the SCU. Make you feel more at home."

"Shut the fuck up, Rob," Henley said. "I know I'm late, but you don't have to make such a fucking song and dance about it."

"Oh, so would you prefer it if I sat back like a dutiful little husband and let you walk all over me and our marriage?"

Henley groaned and dropped her head forward, rubbing at her forehead. "You're being ridiculous. I'm going to check on Emma."

"Why would you—Bloody hell, you've actually forgotten, haven't you?" Rob said, leaning back in his chair and laughing. "You don't have to check on Emma because she's at my mum and dad's."

Rob licked the edge of the rolling paper and sealed his joint while she racked her brain to find the conversation where they'd discussed sending Emma to her grandparents. "I didn't forget, I got the days mixed up."

"No, admit it. You forgot, or you weren't that interested in the first place."

"That's not true. I—"

"Isn't it? As always, this is all about you. What about *me*?" Rob stood up, placed the joint behind his left ear and fished inside the pocket of his tracksuit bottoms for his lighter.

Henley turned and walked into the kitchen to check the calendar that was stuck on the fridge with an octopus magnet Emma had chosen. The fact that *Ems at grandparents. Pick up, 11:00 a.m.* was written on today's date in her handwriting made it worse. She ran her fingers across the dates until she stopped on another entry in five days: *Wedding Anniversary. Ems—pri-mary school visit, 11:00 a.m.* She felt as though the small components of her life, things that she should have control of, were slipping through her fingers. Her body tensed as she heard Rob walk into the kitchen.

"I'm not doing this with you tonight," said Henley and began to walk out of the kitchen.

"Typical."

"Actually, no. No." She turned back. "How fucking dare you? You talk about me being selfish, but what about you? What do you actually do to support me?"

"You're not serious? I've been home, doing all the things that you should be doing with me, raising our child *together*, running our house *together*, but you're not interested in that. Do you even remember why Emma's with my parents?"

Rob didn't raise his voice but each one of his words felt like a rusty nail tearing through the skin on her back. Henley kept quiet. She didn't trust herself not to match each one of her words, in reply, with a physical attack.

"My job interview in Manchester is on Tuesday, do you remember that? Not that I would call it an interview, the job offer's already on the table. It's a case of whether I like what I see."

"You never said that the interview was in Manchester," Henley said slowly. "You said the West End. Great Portland Street."

"That was the first…bloody hell, Anj. This is what happens when you're so self-absorbed. You don't bloody listen. My second interview is in Manchester. The job is in Manchester and right now, I'm thinking that I don't even need to bother going up there. I can send them an email and tell them I'm taking the job."

"I'm doing the best I can and you're telling me 'I'm done with you'?"

"Whatever," Rob replied, pushing past Henley and toward the back door.

She waited for a moment, desperate to make him feel as much pain as she was feeling right now. Then the guilt engulfed her like the waves of a tsunami.

"How could I forget my baby?" she whispered, hot tears running down her cheeks.

None of this was what she wanted. She felt leaden as she walked up the staircase. She'd only made it as far as the eighth step when her phone began to ring. It took her a second to remember her phone was in her bag, which she'd thrown onto the sofa. She liked to think that her maternal instinct would have kicked in if her mother-in-law was calling to tell her that something had happened to her daughter, but it was a different form of instinct that compelled her back down the stairs. An instinct that was ingrained in her psyche and more overpowering than the instincts that surfaced when Emma was born. She didn't have to pick up the phone to know that there had been a shift in the case.

Henley picked up the phone and didn't hesitate to press accept when she saw Pellacia's name on the screen. "Stephen," she said.

"What's wrong? Are you OK?" Pellacia asked. She could hear it in his voice—he could sense that there was emotional trauma bubbling inside of her. "Anj," he said again, more softly. She knew in that moment that if things were different, she would have left her house and driven straight to him.

"I'm...sorry. It's...what is it?" Henley asked. She heard the back door close and Rob opening the kitchen cupboards. She stiffened. She felt as though there was a stranger in her own home. "You wouldn't be calling me at 11:40 p.m. if there hadn't been a development," she said authoritatively, in an effort to reestablish some boundaries.

"There's a body," Pellacia replied. "Either your appeal triggered him, or it was part of his plan anyway."

"Where is she?" Henley sat down on the sofa, a wave of nausea sweeping over her. "Where's Caroline?"

"Back on the Isle of Sheppey. Back at the prison."

30

It had started to rain by the time Ramouter jumped into the passenger side of Henley's car a few minutes after midnight and picked up the cup of coffee that she'd bought for him at the twenty-four-hour Costa drive-through. They made a silent agreement not to speak to each other as Henley drove at speed along the A2. She said nothing when Ramouter turned up the volume on the car radio. The rain stopped as they crossed the Kingsferry Bridge, and Henley focused her mind on practical issues. Who found the body? Were there any witnesses? Had the rain washed away any evidence? Who was responsible for dumping the body?

"Is this it?" Ramouter asked, pulling himself up from his slouched position and staring out into the black night. The white crescent of a waning moon had disappeared behind a cloud and only the red and white lights on the sails of the small boats docked in the harbor broke up the stark expanse of nothingness. "It looks different in the dark."

"The prison is coming up on your—"

"Aye, I can see it," Ramouter said. Henley followed the curve of the road, the streetlight flooding the area with an artificial orange glow. She lowered the volume on the radio and turned into the parking lot, where they were met with the sight of three marked police cars belonging to Kent Police and a large white van with Crime Scene Investigation Services written in purple letters on the side. The blackness of night was now broken by the intermittent flashing of blue police lights and the illumination of almost every window in the prison. Henley slowed down as a uniformed officer suddenly appeared in the road with his hand held out. His colleague stood behind him, tying red-and-white-striped police tape around a lamppost. Ramouter wound down his window.

"Oi. No, no. Turn around," the officer said. "You're not allowed to be here. Get lost or—"

"Detective Constable Ramouter." Ramouter held out his warrant card. "Serial Crime Unit, Met Police."

The police officer wordlessly examined Ramouter's warrant card and took a step back. "Why are the Met here? This is a Kent Police job."

Ramouter let out a huff as the car engine ticked over. He leaned back and pointed at Henley. "The boss, Detective Inspector Henley. Talk to her."

"Evening, or technically morning, PC...?" Henley leaned on the armrest and held up her warrant card.

"Regan," he replied.

"First things first, PC Regan, where shall I park up? Secondly, who was the first officer on scene? And thirdly, where's the body?"

"Sorry, ma'am. No one said that you were—"

"Doesn't matter what wasn't said. I need answers to my questions."

"Ma'am, can you park up next to the forensics van? PC Gallagher was the first officer on the scene and one of the prisoners found the body."

★ ★ ★

The wind picked up when they stepped out of the car. Henley was immediately hit with the salty scent of the sea. She would usually find the sound of the waves calming; today it filled her with tension and anxiety.

"You said one of the prisoners found the body." Henley walked up to PC Regan, who was now standing next to the forensic van.

"A Duncan Leavy. One of my colleagues is keeping an eye on him back inside the prison," said Regan.

"Get someone to bring him out here," Henley said. Ramouter handed her a pair of gloves and a blue protective over-suit. "Straight away. I want to hear directly from him—exactly what he saw and what he heard. Are you ready, Ramouter?"

"I am. Looks as though we've got an audience," he said, and nodded toward the prison building, where a small crowd had begun to build.

"Why risk it with an open prison?" Henley asked as they made their way toward the crime scene. "Prisoners literally coming and going when they please. Anyone not meant to be here will stand out. Look at the access road to the prison. I can't see any-one choosing to come up here because they fancy a walk by the seafront. Not when the town center is in the other direction."

"But there's minimal security here. It's not as if it's a Cat A prison like Belmarsh."

"It's not about the minimal security," Henley replied as an-other officer lifted the police tape so she and Ramouter could pass under and make their way to the forensic tent. "It's about making a point. It feels as though he's doing this on purpose. As if he's pissed off and wants to—"

On entering the tent, Ramouter had stopped in his tracks. Henley did the same. She took in the sight of Caroline Swann's body lying naked on top of the same picnic table where she had sat with Andrew Streeter a few weeks ago. A white sheet was underneath the body, the edge touching the ground. Even though Henley knew what to expect, her chest tightened at the sight. The thread that had been sewn through Caroline's lips had caused the now greenish-looking skin around her mouth to become taut. Henley locked eyes with Ramouter, who didn't bother to shift the grimace on his face.

"Her eyelids are almost shredded."

"Look at her hands. Her fingers," Henley pointed. "It looks as if her nails were ripped off. Maybe she was trying to get out of somewhere, or our killer removed them."

"He didn't do that with the original victims," Ramouter reminded her. "Their nails were cut back, right down to the flesh. This feels like it was all done in a hurry. I mean, did our killer intend to leave her exposed like this on the table, or did the sheet come loose?" He stepped closer to the table.

"The 1995 victims were all covered when their bodies were found. It must have come loose," Henley replied.

"And why here?" Ramouter turned his back on the body. "I know she worked here, and Andrew Streeter was imprisoned here, but from Sidcup to the Isle of Sheppey—"

"I can give an estimated time of death of between thirty-six and forty-eight hours ago."

Henley turned abruptly but had to raise her head slightly to meet the eyes of the man who'd appeared behind her. He looked young and had thick, slightly overgrown brown hair that was swept back from his head and prematurely streaked with gray. "Sorry, I shouldn't have ambushed you like that. Dr. Henry McKay. Pathologist for Kent Police," he said, putting his pen behind his ear.

"Detective Inspector Henley, from—"

"Serial Crime Unit. I know, word travels. Also, I know Linh. Dr. Choi."

"Of course you do. So, you said thirty-six to forty-eight hours?" Henley asked.

"Yes. She's already gone way past rigor mortis and her ambient temperature has decreased enough to match the temperature out here, which is already fifty-four degrees. There's obvious trauma to the body, but no external visible causes of death that I can see."

"How soon can you open her up?" Henley asked.

"Unless some great big catastrophe happens in the next few hours, she'll be the first one on my examination table when I officially start later this morning. Unless you want Dr. Choi to perform the autopsy, for continuity with your case."

"No disrespect to you, but my preference would be Dr. Choi."

"No offense taken. In the meantime, take my card. My mobile number is on there, so you don't think that it's some weirdo cold-calling."

"She went missing eight days ago," Ramouter said as Dr. McKay walked away and a group of crime scene investigators made their way toward him. "He kept her for four days at a push and then killed her."

"And she was already dead when we put the appeal out," said Henley. "Maybe that triggered him to leave her here because his face, or some version of his face is out there."

"Are you saying that we forced his hand?"

"Who the hell knows," Henley said as they both walked away from the body.

"I'm wondering if this will all stop with Caroline."

"Hopefully Mark can give us some idea of who we're dealing with." Henley's phone beeped. She read the message and put her phone back in her pocket. "Look. Why don't you head inside the prison and find Duncan Leavy. I'll join you in a bit. Pellacia has turned up."

"The govnor's here?" Ramouter peeled off his protective oversuit. "Not like him to turn up at a crime scene. What's he doing? Checking up on us?"

"It's probably something to do with this technically being a Kent case," said Henley. "Go on. I'll join you in a bit."

★ ★ ★

Henley felt the sharp sea breeze across her face and cold drops of rain on her skin. She pushed her hands deeper into her pockets and lowered her head as she made her way to the back of the parking lot where Pellacia was waiting, away from the activity, with his hands thrust into the pockets of his hoodie. Henley swept her hair back from her eyes as the wind began to whistle.

"What are you doing here?" she called.

"Your voice on the phone... You needed me." His voice was filled with emotion.

Henley stopped dead in her tracks. She closed her eyes and took a breath, trying not to give in to the wave of emotions that she was feeling. But she could sense the walls that she'd built internally breaking down as Pellacia stepped closer toward her.

"I shouldn't need you," she said quietly as he pulled her toward him and held her. They stood like that for a minute, not speaking as the rain began to fall harder. Henley put her arms around Pellacia and pulled him tighter toward her.

"You're not OK," he whispered into her hair.

"It's not what you think. It's not the case. I can handle the case. It's—" Henley pulled away and brushed the tears from her face. "You know who it is."

Pellacia let out a resentful snort and his brow furrowed. He put a hand to Henley's face and then pulled her back toward him. "It doesn't have to be like this."

"Don't say anything," said Henley as she breathed in his warmth. "Let me have this with you for one minute and then—"

She let him kiss her. She knew that it wasn't the right thing, but it was what she needed to keep her grounded in that moment. It was a connection that had been instant and instinctive with Pellacia, whereas with Rob it was something that she had to work on, to learn as though she was reviewing for an exam.

"OK, OK," Henley stepped away and pulled her hood over her head. "I need to do my job."

"I know, it's fine. I just needed…" Pellacia paused and stepped back toward his open car door, picking up his jacket and the lanyard with his warrant card attached. They both stepped back into their roles. "The DCI from the murder team at Sheerness police station is on his way."

"Good. We need someone senior from Kent Police here."

"What about the prison governor, where's she?"

"On her way. No sign of her yet, but she's not my main priority." Henley broke off to send a text to Ramouter letting him know she was on her way to talk to the prisoner. She chastised herself for sacrificing valuable time in the investigation by being selfish and giving in to emotions that she was having difficulty controlling. She silently counted to three and visualized placing her emotions in a box and closing the lid. She needed to focus on the task in hand. To find out if Duncan Leavy had seen The Burier.

Duncan Leavy wouldn't have looked out of place modelling designer menswear on the catwalks of Milan or advertising an overpriced men's cologne on TV. He was tall, with a number-one fade and deep-set hazel brown eyes which at that moment were darting back and forth between Henley in the doorway and Ramouter, who was leaning against a wall next to a half-empty vending machine. The only window in the room looked out onto the parking lot, busy with the comings and goings of police officers and CSIs. Whatever swagger Duncan Leavy might have displayed during the day was all gone now. He bent his head and rubbed his right hand methodically over his scalp.

"Duncan," Henley said, dragging over a chair so she could sit in front of him. "Look up. I'm Detective Inspector Henley."

She wasn't sure if he had begun to cry. He sniffed and slowly raised his head.

"I didn't catch that," Duncan murmured, straightening his shoulders and extending his right hand.

"Detective Inspector Henley. You've already met my colleague, DC Ramouter." Henley shook Duncan's hand, wondering if he wanted the reassuring touch of human contact as opposed to doing what was polite.

"Yeah, I have."

"I'm going to have another officer come in and take your full statement, but I wanted to ask you some questions first, to get an idea as to what exactly happened and what you saw."

Duncan nodded and straightened up again, pulling down on his jacket as though he was preparing for a job interview.

"Where were you coming from?" Henley asked. "I got the call about a body being found at quarter to midnight. I know that it's an open prison, but that seems to be a bit late for you to be out and about."

"I'm not going to lie, it's pretty laid-back here. I've only got a few months left on my sentence and I don't give anyone grief."

"That doesn't mean you can come and go as you please."

"No, it doesn't. The governor has to give you approval, but that ain't difficult."

"So where were you?" asked Henley. She caught the CSI officers working methodically from the corner of her eye.

"Temple. I had a conference with my barrister at 2:00 p.m. at his chambers, Number Two Kings Court Chambers. You can call and check. I've got a confiscation hearing coming up—the government thinks I've got a couple of million stashed away, which I haven't—so he wanted to run through all the questions that'll come up in court. My barrister was stuck in a trial down in Exeter last week, so today was the earliest he could see me. My solicitor was there too—they can both vouch for me."

He was starting to panic, which was never helpful in a key witness. To calm him down and distract him from the gruesome discovery he'd made earlier, she asked: "If you did have a couple of million to stash away, what would you have done with it?"

"I dunno, maybe invest it in a lower league Spanish football club? But I haven't got it. So, pipe dreams."

"Pipe dreams are nice to have. What time did your conference finish?"

"My barrister had a family issue, so we started late—about quarter to three—and we finished after seven. Lots of paperwork, trying to remember what I spent a fiver on three years ago. I left his chambers at ten or quarter past seven and went to Victoria station to get the train back to Sheerness-on-Sea, but it was canceled so I went to the pub, had a couple of pints and a burger and I got the ten past nine train and arrived at quarter to eleven. Then I grabbed a cab up to the prison."

"I know it's an open prison," said Ramouter, "but I didn't think that popping into the pub was part of the deal."

"Of course it isn't," Duncan replied. "I was supposed to go straight to my appointment, come straight back and keep them updated if there were any problems. Which I did. Look, no one would have found out about the pub if I hadn't, well...her..."

Duncan's face contorted with a grimace; he was back in that moment of discovering Caroline's body.

"Hey, Duncan. Did you see anyone when you arrived?" Henley asked loudly to force him out of his dark ruminations.

Duncan shook his head. "No. No one. I didn't see anything and there weren't any guards about. They're pretty lax around here. As long as you come back when you're meant to come back, well they pretty much leave you to it."

"What happened next?"

Duncan took a deep breath and turned to face the window, where a black van with the words "private ambulance" on the side was pulling into the parking lot. He watched in silence as a man jumped out of the van, opened the rear doors and pulled out a trolley.

He shook his head and rubbed his hand over his face, making eye contact with Henley again. "Right," he said, "Right. OK. I wanted a cigarette. I had one left. It had started to rain a bit, but it was only spitting. I went to the back where the seat-ing area is and then I saw her—the nurse. I didn't know what I was looking at, at first. It was as if my brain couldn't connect the dots. I mean, why would there be a naked woman on a picnic table, at a prison?" Duncan turned his entire body and looked at Ramouter. "In what world does that make sense?"

"It doesn't," Ramouter agreed.

"No. It doesn't," said Duncan. He stood up and walked away from the sofa, his back to the window. "Makes no sense. So, I walked up to the table and then...saw her face."

Duncan paused. His face was pale, and he put his hand to his stomach. He tried to swallow but instead let out a strangulated dry heave. "I think I'm going to—"

Henley didn't wait for him to finish. She leaped up and grabbed the stainless steel bin and pushed it toward him. She turned her head while Duncan vomited three pints of beer and a quarter-pounder into the bin.

"I'm sorry. I'm so sorry," he said when he was done. He looked into the bin and winced. "Give me a sec," he said, as he disappeared into a side door with the bin. There was the sound of a flushing toilet and then a tap running.

"Sorry," he said again, reentering the waiting area, the spotlight bouncing off the droplets of water on his chin. "It was her face..."

"You don't have to apologize," said Henley. "So, you didn't notice anything, hear anything?"

"I was thinking about it when I was in the toilet. I came outside, took out a cigarette and was having trouble with my lighter... I remember smelling cigarette smoke but that couldn't have been right because I hadn't sparked up yet. And then I thought that I heard someone behind me, like someone walking on gravel, but then I noticed the body. When I realized what I'd found, I ran in and hit the fire alarm because I didn't know what else to do."

"What did you do after you hit the alarm?"

"I went back outside. To the table. I suppose I wanted to check that I wasn't imagining things. I was only there for a few…oh, oh, a car!" Duncan said brightly. "I heard a car."

"Are you sure?" asked Henley.

"Definitely. It sounded like the gears had got stuck because I heard the clutch grinding."

"But you didn't see a car?"

"No."

"What about the direction, could you tell where the car was?"

"It wasn't in the parking lot. When I think about it, it must have been behind me. Behind the trees. There's an access road they use for deliveries and stuff."

"But you didn't see anything?"

Duncan shook his head and whispered. "Only her. Only her."

"What do you reckon?" Ramouter asked Henley after the uniformed officer arrived and took Duncan away.

"I'm wondering if he, The Burier, actually left," said Henley. "All Duncan said was that he heard a car and that the gears were stuck. He never said that he heard the car driving away."

"Do you think the killer stayed? That he watched?"

"It's not beyond the realms of possibility, is it?" Henley had a flash of memory from the day that she found Melissa and saw Streeter sitting on the wall and a van driving away, before she ran home to tell her mum to call the police.

"We need to check if there are cameras on that access road at the rear of the prison," said Ramouter.

"You get a move on with that," Henley replied, wondering how long The Burier had waited and whether she'd ever have the opportunity to face him in an interview room and ask him *why*.

"So, what are we thinking? That he stayed and waited for someone to discover the nurse?" Ramouter asked. They were standing on the decking that led out to the crime scene, watching the CSI officers carefully examining the area where Duncan said he smelled smoke and heard someone walking on gravel.

"That sycamore tree is big enough to conceal someone," Henley noted.

A CSI investigator placed two yellow markers on the ground and a few seconds later the area lit up with the flash of their camera.

"There isn't much light here, is there?" Ramouter looked around. "A couple of lamps in the parking lot. I checked about the cameras—there's one monitoring the delivery area, but no vehicles were seen approaching or leaving the site by that road."

"Perhaps Duncan made a mistake," Henley said. She sounded unconvinced.

"I don't think he did. I suppose it wouldn't have been that difficult to drive up here without anyone noticing. The prisoners aren't housed on this side of the building..." Ramouter looked doubtful suddenly. "Oh, I don't know. It may be an open prison, but it's still a prison."

"He knows how the prison works—Filip, or whatever his real name is. The timings of the guards' checks, their patrols. Otherwise, what was he going to do, wait here all night until he got his cheap thrill of seeing someone finding Caroline?"

"Looks as if they've got something," Ramouter said as the CSI officer stepped carefully around the area that he'd been photographing and approached them.

"Detective Inspector Henley?" the CSI officer asked, pushing the hood of her oversuit back to reveal a ruffled mess of ginger hair that had been scraped back into a ponytail.

"That's me."

"I'm Kate. And I've got prints. Here, take a look."

Henley leaned forward as Kate took the camera from around her neck and pointed the screen in Henley's direction. Among the trodden-down leaves and mud was a full footprint and, on the next screen, half a print.

"Usually, I'm not overjoyed to see a crime scene that has had the benefit of a passing rain shower, but it's a good thing it did in this case. The ground was damp enough for an impression to be left behind."

"Our witness said he could smell smoke," said Ramouter.

"Bingo!" said Kate, and flicked to the next screen. "Picked up a couple of cigarette butts a foot away from the tree. And a used tissue."

"Seems a bit—" Ramouter bit his lip as he searched for the right word. "Reckless. Assuming that these belong to Filip. Could easily have been one of the prisoners."

"Maybe," Henley replied as Kate walked away. "Ready to go?"

"Aye. Think I've had enough of the seaside." Ramouter stretched his arms and yawned.

"I'll get you home and see you in about"—Henley glanced at her watch—"four hours."

"Might as well sleep at the SCU."

Henley could tell from the look on his face that Ramouter wasn't joking. She was about to ask if he was OK when she felt Pellacia by her side.

"What is it?"

"Nothing to worry about. They're doing us a favor," said Pellacia, rubbing at his eyes. "We ain't got the manpower to have half of us out here all day tomorrow, so the DCI is going to help us and have some of his officers take statements from Leavy and anyone else who was about last night. They'll send them down to the SCU soon as they're done."

"I'm more than happy to pay the favor back one day," said Henley as Ramouter let out another yawn. "Right, let me get this one home, before he drops at my feet." She handed Ramouter the car keys.

"See you in a sec. Night or morning, gov." Ramouter walked toward the car, his shoulders drooping.

Henley felt a wash of calm as she felt Pellacia's fingers gently intertwine with hers.

"Are you OK?" he asked.

"Better than I was. Must be something wrong with me if coming out to a crime scene like this is the best thing for me mentally," Henley replied, caressing Pellacia's index finger with her thumb before she pulled her hand away.

"There's nothing wrong with you, Anj. What are you doing once you've dropped Ramouter home?"

"Home." Henley shook her head as she turned and walked toward her car. "Shower, sleep and then back at the SCU."

"Early?" Pellacia asked.

Henley held on to the top of the car door and absorbed the question. She watched Pellacia's face. She knew what he was asking. Would she be there once the cleaners left at 6:00 a.m., or leave him waiting like a fool?

"Early," Henley replied.

31

Ramouter had slept uncomfortably on the sofa. He released a low groan as the tiny sinews of muscle and ligaments that had twisted and tightened began to unwind. He hadn't even showered after Henley had driven him home. He'd walked into his flat as dawn was breaking. He felt like an intruder as he closed the front door. The music that Ethan had fallen asleep to had stopped hours ago. He'd barely glanced at his bedroom door before heading straight to the sofa for some sleep.

He heard a door opening. He knew it was Michelle. He could hear the rubber soles of slippers slapping against the stripped oak floors as she left their bedroom. They had joked about her heavy-footedness when they'd first started living together. That felt like a lifetime ago now.

"It's ten past six," Michelle said, entering the living room. She walked past Ramouter and opened the curtains. There was no bright summer light—just a heavy gray sky. "Where did you go?"

"I had work, Miche," said Ramouter. He pulled the throw

over his legs, suddenly self-conscious of his semi-nakedness. "The woman who was missing. The nurse, I told you—"

"Caroline Swann. I remember," Michelle snapped, then left the room.

"For fuck's sake." Ramouter stood up and stretched his neck to the left and right. He bent down and picked up his dirty clothes as the sound of the kettle reaching boiling point sang out. If he went to the kitchen and tried to talk to her, it would probably end in another argument. The second option was to say nothing, but then she would think he was punishing her for her diagnosis and for her presence in their home. Either way, he couldn't win.

"I'm taking Ethan to football practice," Michelle said as Ramouter walked into the kitchen almost twenty minutes later, fresh out of the shower. Her back was turned as she took a cereal bowl decorated with planets out of the cupboard and placed it on the table next to a box of Cocoa Puffs. Ramouter could feel her hostility like a storm disrupting a calm sea.

"We can both take him to practice," Ramouter said. "I've got to go back to the SCU, but I can—"

"No. I'll take him. You've made it clear that my…condition is not that much of a problem. That I'm overreacting and that I should carry on as though there's nothing wrong with me." Michelle opened the fridge, took out a bottle of milk, and slammed it shut again.

"I never once said that you were overreacting. I would never say that, Miche," Ramouter replied as calmly as he could, placing his hand on her shoulder.

"You might as well have done," she said, shrugging away from him. "This is not an act. None of this is an act. Do you think I want this for myself? To be losing my mind at the age of thirty-six? Do you have any idea what it's like to wake up scared, Salim?"

"I know exactly what it's like to wake up scared. I have no

idea what the day is going to bring, whether today is going to be the day that you slip further away from me and from Ethan."

"It's not the same thing."

"Of course it's not the same, and it will never be the same, but that doesn't mean your condition doesn't affect me, Michelle. It doesn't mean that I don't have my own fears."

Ramouter sighed heavily with exhaustion and frustration as Michelle's mouth twisted in annoyance.

"It's not the same thing," she repeated slowly and deliberately. The alarm on Ramouter's phone began to beep. "You made me feel guilty. As if I was…was milking my condition," she said.

"I have never said that—"

"You didn't have to say it!"

"I never thought it either," Ramouter said, his voice rising. "Look, I'm so sorry that I hurt you. I'm your husband and I meant it when I said 'in sickness and in health.' They weren't empty words. I'm doing the best I can."

Michelle didn't say anything. The ticking of the kitchen clock seemed impossibly loud in the silence. It took both of them a moment to realize that Ethan had walked into the kitchen, un-noticed, Superman action figure in his hand.

"You woke me up," Ethan said, rubbing at the sleep in his eyes.

"I'm sorry, sweetie," Michelle said, the steel in her voice gone. She brushed past Ramouter and picked up Ethan. "Ooh, let me get my big boy ready for football."

"Daddy, are you coming to football too?" Ethan asked from over his mum's shoulder.

"No, he's not. It's just me and you," said Michelle as she kissed the top of Ethan's head and walked out of the kitchen.

Ramouter felt his legs go weak, and he grabbed the back of a kitchen chair. He didn't want to become a cliché—the detective who prioritized his job over his family. Losing his family would mean he had failed, but he could feel it happening. He was losing them. Ramouter closed his eyes as the sound of Michelle and Ethan laughing traveled through the flat. Instead of their laughter filling him with light, it only filled him with darkness.

Henley shook out the rain from her umbrella and pushed open the door that led into the old canteen of Greenwich police station. She could remember when the Serial Crime Unit first moved into the station and the building had hummed with energy as suspects screamed in their cells in the custody suite on the ground floor, irate locals registered their complaints at the front desk, and police vans exited the parking lot at speed. Officers ending their night shifts would line up for their full English breakfasts in this canteen. Henley could swear that, sometimes, she could see the ghosts of the once-active police station.

"Why are you sitting here in the dark?" Henley said as she ran her fingers across the light switch and the fluorescent tubes came to life.

"Give it a second," came Pellacia's voice from the back of the room.

"Oh crap," Henley said as the lights began to flicker and then died. "It's amazing this building is still standing." She walked toward Pellacia, who was sitting on the worn sofa, and sat next to him.

"Some things are built to last," Pellacia replied. "Here, I got you a large tea. One sugar, semi-skimmed. English breakfast. Be careful, I swear they boil the water with a nuclear fusion reactor or something."

Henley took a sip and shook her head as the hot tea burned the tip of her tongue. "Jesus Christ."

"Told you." Pellacia took hold of her hand. Henley didn't resist as he pulled her toward him, and her head was resting against his chest. "What's going on?"

"Everything," Henley replied, curling her legs up under her and wrapping her arms around Pellacia. "It's a lot."

"Rob?"

"I don't want to talk about him," Henley said as her shoulders tightened with tension. "I don't want to talk about my marriage. I want..." Henley let her voice trail off as she sat up and placed her hand on Pellacia's face. "I didn't come here for sex."

"I wasn't thinking that," Pellacia said. "You're not just someone that I screw, you know? I knew you needed me. Not as a friend, but not as a lover either. Fuck, whatever the in-between of whatever this is, is. You're worth more to me than a quick shag on a dusty sofa."

"Thanks," was all Henley could manage through the thick emotion.

"I'll happily pay out for the Travelodge on Blackheath Road, though."

"Look at you, last of the big spenders," Henley said with a laugh. Pellacia began to gently rub at the small knots in her neck.

"All right, I suppose I could splash out on a supreme room at the Novotel down the road," he said quietly.

Henley felt the familiar warmth of longing and belonging course through her body, a combination of emotions that she'd never felt with Rob. "It's all a mess, Stephen," she said.

The rest of her words were lost as Pellacia leaned in and kissed her. Henley allowed herself to be lost for that moment, giving in to the familiarity and memories of what she and Pellacia had once been, before they'd both let fear and insecurity creep in.

"I can always tell when you need me," Pellacia said when they pulled apart.

"I know you can; it works both ways. But we've both got commitments," said Henley, taking Pellacia's hand.

"I don't have commitments."

"Really?" Henley raised an eyebrow. "What's Laura Halifax then?"

"Are you asking as a friend or as something else?"

"I'm not jealous, if that's what you're thinking. I'm…we're not sitting here as two single people."

Pellacia let out a small groan. "I don't want to talk about her. Me and her… Laura. It's…let me have this moment with you right now, OK? Let me be here for you at least until the clock strikes nine."

"Let's say eight. Ramouter might be here way before nine," said Henley. "Come to think of it, Eastwood and Stanford will probably rock up early too. This investigation, I can't get a handle on it," Henley admitted.

"Which part? Rhimes, or finding the person really responsible for the murders?"

"It's all one and the same thing: Rhimes, the case… And I feel guilty. I can't sit here and pretend that I don't feel like I'm being disloyal to Rhimes."

"I know what you mean," said Pellacia, twisting his hands. "I feel as though I need to protect him, his family, and his legacy, but then I've got to remind myself that I'm in charge and it's not all about Rhimes. I've got to protect my team."

"It's a lot of pressure," she said, gently prizing his hands apart. "For all of us. Jo and Ezra must be affected by this too."

"Of course they are," Pellacia replied. "In all the years I've known Jo, I've never seen her shaken. But even she's beating herself up over this one. Questioning if she's missed something. She prides herself on knowing where all the bodies are buried, and knowing when to warn us that the shit is about to hit the fan."

Henley suddenly felt overwhelmed. "Maybe Rhimes took advantage of us and was playing us all along."

"Stop it," Pellacia said unconvincingly. "We're heading down a slippery slope if we keep thinking like this."

"Can you stop? I used to be really proud of myself for being able to compartmentalize, but it's not that easy anymore. I have to keep telling myself not to think about Rhimes the man. To

keep thinking of him as a suspect. Someone unreliable. Untrust-
worthy. If I start to think about him on an emotional level—"

"Then none of us can do our jobs, and we need to do our
jobs. We need to get this one right. Uncover the truth, no matter what." Pellacia sighed. "For fuck's sake. He made me into
the detective I am. One of the reasons I said yes to running the
SCU was because I didn't want to let Rhimes down. I know
it's stupid, but I feel as though I *have* let him down, because I
didn't see that he wasn't OK."

"No one knew he was going to kill himself," said Henley,
"But I know what you mean."

"Is that why you've given the nasty job of investigating
Rhimes to Eastie?" Pellacia said with a knowing smile.

"You know?"

"Of course. I know you, remember. I would have done the
same thing."

"Delegation. That was always Rhimes's thing," said Henley.

"Exactly," Pellacia said. His phone rang and he looked at the
screen before sending the call to voicemail. "And yes, in case
you were wondering, that was her."

"I wasn't asking," Henley said.

Pellacia quickly typed a six-word text and hit send. "So, what
can't you get a handle on?"

"I can't work out the 'why' of the original victims. There is
absolutely nothing that links them. Not a mutual friend or a random interaction. The only thing they share is how they died and
whoever killed them. I even went round to my parents' house
and dug out my old diaries from the attic, wanting to see if I
mentioned something, anything, that didn't make sense at the
time. Or something Melissa might have said to me before she
died. But there was nothing, I was whining about my mum not
letting me have a boyfriend, and sneaking out to all-dayers in
Burgess Park with Melissa."

"You'll go mad if you keep looking for ways to blame your teenage self."

"I know. I know," Henley replied. She checked the time and saw it was twenty past seven. "It's really odd though. The 1995 victims meant absolutely nothing to each other, but with Elias Piper, Caroline Swann and Andrew Streeter, it's the opposite."

Pellacia frowned. "Piper and Streeter appeared on his kill list, and they're obviously linked, so they clearly meant something to The Burier, but Swann wasn't on that list and her only association with Streeter was as his nurse. Number three on the list was a question mark."

"Well he didn't kill her for no reason. This time around his kill list is made up of people who did something that posed a threat to him, or were a risk because they could identify him. And then we've got this unknown sixth victim who may have escaped in 1995."

"It all comes back to Streeter," Pellacia said thoughtfully. "I know he said he wasn't responsible for the killings, but he's the common denominator. He's the—"

"He's the bridge. The link."

"We need to figure out who exactly he was linked to. It won't be random. It will be someone close to him."

"I need to speak to his sister," Henley said. "She's come out of the woodwork screaming that she wants reparations. She's told the press more than once how close they were before Rhimes stole him from their family."

"It can't be you," said Pellacia. "You're part of the problem. You gave evidence in court against Streeter. She'll clam up and I'll put money on her running off to the IPOC with some ridiculous allegation."

"Ramouter can do it then," said Henley. "I'll brief him when he gets in."

"You said Ramouter would probably be here by eight. How long have I got you for?" Pellacia asked.

"You've got about forty minutes," Henley replied, reaching for Pellacia. "Forty minutes for us to just be."

"This is nice, isn't it?" said Stanford, sitting down on the bench. "Almost feels civilized."

"Civilized?" Eastwood said, piercing the plastic cap of her Coke with a straw. "We're sitting in the middle of the park, eating McDonald's like a bunch of sixth formers on a Sunday afternoon, instead of having a roast dinner at home. Civilized we are not."

"God, you're miserable," Stanford said, pulling the gherkins from his burger.

"I think it's quite nice to feel normal for a change," Ramouter replied. He swirled his fries around the tub of curry sauce.

"How are things at home?" asked Stanford, serious suddenly, concern in his eyes.

Ramouter let out a sardonic laugh. "What do you think? It's not great at the moment. I don't think I've spent more than ninety minutes with Ethan and Michelle all weekend. This is two Sundays in a row now that I haven't been with my family."

"This case is all-consuming. But you know how the SCU works. Weeks and months of craziness and then a lull," said Eastwood. "Stanford will tell you, it takes a while for your other half to get used to it."

"I don't think Glen is used to it even now," said Stanford. "He tolerates it, but Eastie's right. There will be a point when we're done with this case."

"What if it's never done, though? Rhimes probably thought this case was over when Streeter was convicted," said Ramouter. "What if this case is the one that hangs around our necks like a bloody albatross for the next twenty-odd years?"

"Jesus Christ! I know life is a bit tough at the moment, but it's not like you to be this miserable. Hurry up and eat your chicken burger, you might feel better," Stanford replied.

"All you can do is take it one day at a time," said Eastwood. "Maybe it would help if Michelle had a chat with Glen."

"Maybe. But Glen isn't living with early-onset dementia," said Ramouter. "It puts a different spin on things."

Eastwood's phone ringing interrupted the conversation.

"Who is it?" Stanford asked.

"Looks like DC Caningly has finally returned my call," Eastwood said, scrambling to her feet. "She was part of Rhimes's squad back in 1995. I'll be back. Hello?"

"Hello? Is that DS Eastwood?"

"Yes, it is."

"Great. This is DS—sorry, not DS. Old habits die hard. It's Penny Caningly. I'm sorry it's taken me so long to call you back. I hope I haven't interrupted your lunch."

"No. It's absolutely fine. I'm really glad you got back to me. You're a hard person to track down."

"That's on purpose. I wanted to get as far away from London as possible once I jacked in the job. We're in Truro. So, what do you need to know? I know what it's like to be on a big investigation. Can't be hanging around exchanging pleasantries."

Eastwood appreciated Caningly's no-nonsense attitude. "The original Streeter investigation. You were part of Rhimes's team?" Eastwood asked. "From the beginning?"

"Yes. I transferred to CID about five months before the Gyimah murder case was allocated to us."

"How involved were you?"

"This was the mid-nineties. Female police officers were wearing skirts on duty and were called WPCs. They treated me like shit. Sexism was rife and as far as my boss, Larsen, was concerned, the best place for me was behind a desk, dealing with every crackpot phone call, logging witness statements and putting up with him touching my ass. I wish I had been out there on the streets, but I wasn't. Glorified admin and not a detective."

"I'm sorry that you had—"

"Don't be," Penny said. "That's how it was and now I'm out. So, what about the investigation?"

"I'm trying to find out if you ever had any dealings with, or did any of those crackpot phone calls come from, anyone saying that they'd escaped from The Burier?"

Penny laughed. "Every other day there was someone saying that they were The Burier or had met him. Most of it was a load of rubbish." She paused. "But there was one girl who I thought was legit because of what she said."

"What did she say?"

"First, she said she'd been kidnapped, and I remember thinking she was another wind-up merchant wasting my time. Then she called again and said that whoever took her said that he was going to bury her alive. Well, that woke me up, because—"

"The information about the victims being buried alive wasn't released to the public until after Fallon O'Toole's body was found," Eastwood concluded.

"Exactly. Anyway, I tried to convince her to come to the station, but she refused. She kept saying that she wasn't safe in London."

"Did she give any other information?"

"No, that was it. Insisted that she wanted to talk to the detective she'd seen on the telly."

"Who was that. Larsen?"

"God no! That man was only interested in having a camera in his face once he had a result. He made sure that our inspector, DI Vikram, was the face on the news. That way, if the case went tits up, well, he wouldn't be the one being spat at in the street."

"So did Vikram meet her?"

"No. Vikram refused. He said that meeting random nut jobs was below his paygrade and told me to deal with it. So, I spoke to Larsen, and I offered to meet the girl but he shut me down. Told me to stay in my lane."

"What an idiot."

"You're being polite. He was a bastard. I do remember one thing, though. Her phone number. It was a landline: 0171 area code, which I remember thinking was odd."

"Why was that odd?" Eastwood asked, watching Ramouter and Stanford making their way toward her.

"Back in 1995 there were two telephone codes for London: 0181 was outer London and 0171 was inner London."

"Why would this girl say she wasn't safe in London but give you an inner London number?"

"Exactly. I remember saying that to Vikram."

"What happened next?" Eastwood asked.

"I don't know. As I said, I don't know if Larsen or anyone else in the team met her, and I didn't hear from her again. Sorry, I'm going to have to go. I've got to feed these kids. Is there anything else?"

"One more thing. Do you have the girl's name?"

A chill ran through Eastwood's body as she heard Penny take a deep breath. All she needed was a name.

"No," Penny said regretfully. "I'm not saying that she didn't tell me, I just can't remember."

32

Sharp gravel and stones pierced Jake's feet, his begging pleas muffled against the tape on his mouth. Stripped down to his pants, the English Channel's icy wind slapped his skin. He recognized the early-morning signs: eerie silence, occasional seagull cries, and distant car engines. The misty dawn hadn't fully arrived yet, but the horizon was obscured by mounds of dirt and gravel. Everything was a blur. He'd woken up in an unfamiliar room. He remembered fighting back, kicking out despite his bound feet, his desperate promise to pay if they would let him go. He stopped as glass cut deep into his right sole, the pain intense. His salty tears were dissolving the tape's glue, and saliva dribbled from his mouth.

"Please, don't," Jake pleaded weakly, warm urine streaming down his leg. A knife's point pricked his neck, arm, and back.

"Don't turn around. Keep walking."

Jake was motionless for a second as he considered the man's accent and the precision of his speech. It was distinctly South

London but not full East End cockney nor the clipped tones of the West London elite.

"Walk!"

The knife pierced the skin on his back, and Jake obeyed, tears and pain blinding him. If he ever recounted what happened next, he'd say it happened fast. The push was sharp and quick, making him tumble into a grave. His wrists were tightly bound, unable to break the fall. His legs buckled, then he fell onto his side. Grains of dirt landed on his face as he glanced up. There was a dull thud as someone jumped in the hole next to him, grazing his leg. He was pushed onto his back as the tape was ripped from his mouth, taking skin and beard hairs. The man blocked the growing light as Jake screamed, trying to raise himself up, but he was shoved back into the earth. He smelled his fear, wetting himself again, and then the stench of his own excrement. The first shovelful of dirt, gravel and sand fell heavily onto his chest, the second his face, coating his mouth and hitting the back of his throat. He tried to turn, to fight it, but the weight crushed him, stealing his breath.

Jake never felt the moment the oxygen ran out.

When he buried Melissa Gyimah, he debated how long to wait. An hour? Two? Three? Ultimately, he started digging her up after two hours and six minutes. He needed to return her home, all the while thrilled by the death he had orchestrated. It aroused him, seeing her lifeless form in the dirt—more than being with men or women ever did. Melissa had laughed at his inability to get an erection when she'd unzipped his trousers at the river. But it was only when he saw the bodies of his victims that he was able to perform.

Now he knew suffocation took three to five minutes. He pulled Jake out of his grave after thirty-five. Dragging the heavy weight and wrapping him in a sheet turned him on.

He couldn't wait to get Jake home.

33

―――――――――

"Right, that wraps things up," Adam said. "The main story is the reinvestigation of the 1995 murders and the new spate of recent murders," he said. "We're thinking of expanding our news coverage to our weekly podcast. I've spoken to Jake about it and he's on board to host it. Lillian, I'm sure that you'll provide Jake with research. We might as well reduce your duties now, considering you're leaving the paper shortly."

Lillian opened her mouth to protest and then thought better of it. "I'm not leaving. Obviously, the news hasn't made its way down from HR, but I've decided to stay on."

"Stay…what—" Adam stopped when he realized that the crime team hadn't moved from their seats, and were watching the drama unfold. "OK, everyone. Out you go, this meeting is done."

Lillian remained seated as the others filed out hesitantly, their journalist instincts smelling the scent of a new story.

"That was very unprofessional of you, Lillian, declaring that in front of everyone." Adam tried to regain the upper hand. "It doesn't make you look that reliable, does it? Throwing a fit because your name is accidentally left off the byline, saying you're leaving, then changing your mind. Not exactly a good look when the company is restructuring and they're asking me for recommendations."

"I spoke to the editor-in-chief last night and he understands that sometimes emotions can get in the way when you're passionate about a story."

"You called the editor-in-chief on a Sunday?" Adam sneered. "I forgot you two were close. Well, that's what I heard. I suppose talent will only get you so far."

"Talking about reliability, where's your golden boy this morning?" Lillian said brightly, pushing the flames of anger away.

"I was going to ask you," Adam replied. "You're supervising him. I don't want you working this story without him."

"I can't work the story with a ghost. I don't know where he is."

"You haven't heard from Jake this morning?" Adam asked, frowning. "He's usually one of the first ones in."

"No, I haven't," said Lillian.

"Doesn't matter." Adam waved a hand dismissively. "You can catch up with him later about the podcast."

"The podcast isn't going to work," said Lillian. "It would have worked six months ago when it was a dead case, but this case has been resurrected and it's alive and kicking."

"It's a cold case," Adam said stubbornly.

"No, it's not," Lillian said sternly. "You may be comfortable with the possibility of being charged with interfering with the course of justice and jeopardizing a live investigation by talking about it on a podcast, but I'd rather not see the inside of a police station, thank you very much."

"I'll talk to legal," said Adam. "Make a third-party disclosure application to the high court if I have to."

"I doubt you'll get far with that," Lillian replied.

"Where are we with the story?" Adam asked, ignoring Lillian's comment. "As Jake's not here, you can update me."

"I doubt he's holed up somewhere working on the story. He was supposed to file his story, an update on the investigation, on Friday but he hasn't. I checked. There's nothing from him in the Dropbox folder that we share," said Lillian. She cleared her throat. "But there have been more developments in the Caroline Swann investigation."

"Who's Caroline Swann?"

"Bloody hell," said Lillian, not bothering to hide the fact that she was rolling her eyes, but she somehow stopped herself from saying, *This is what happens when you work with fucking amateurs.* She opened the file in front of her and took out two sheets of paper. She didn't care if she was mocked for her habits; she was old school and she liked feeling the paper between her fingers.

"Caroline Swann was a nurse who worked at the prison where Andrew Streeter was murdered. And before you say anything, I have it verified that the coroner's report will confirm that Streeter was poisoned. Swann went missing the week that Streeter was killed, and on Saturday night her body was found on the Isle of Sheppey."

"The Isle of Sheppey?" Adam asked, confused. "How is that, or Swann, linked to the investigation?"

"It's where Streeter's prison is located, and Caroline Swann worked there," Lillian said sarcastically. "According to my source, Caroline was found in a similar condition to the 1995 victims. Naked, wrapped in a sheet, eyes and mouth sewn shut. May have been dead for thirty-six to forty-eight hours before she was found. Her body is being transported to Greenwich mortuary."

"Who is this source? You've got an in with the police? The mortuary?"

"You know better than to ask that." Lillian smiled sweetly.

"Have you shared this with Jake? A bit childish to hold back on sources—"

"I've told you before. This is my story," she said, placing the sheets of paper in front of Adam. "I've done the work on my own. I've tracked down the sources and I've used *my* resources, *my* talents and experience to turn what would've been mediocre filler written by a junior journalist who's only here because of who he shares his DNA with into a front-page story. You want Jake to write the story, but he has no idea how to *work* the story."

Adam remained silent as he picked up the pages.

"You're new to this business and I understand that you're trying to make a name for yourself, but removing my name from the byline and actively encouraging nepotism—"

"Nepotism?" Adam said. "What are you—"

"I know who Jake Ryland is," Lillian said with a smile. "I'm a reporter, not some clueless intern kissing your ass, so let's leave it at that."

"This isn't commentary," Adam said, looking over the pages again. "You're carrying out your own investigation."

"I'm going where the story takes me. I sat through every single day of that original court case, and I've gone through the application that was sent to the CCRC."

"How did you get hold of the application? That's not a matter of public record."

"I know how to do my job. The story doesn't belong to the paper; it belongs to me. I could walk out of here and get a cab to Clerkenwell and give this story to the *Guardian*. Actually, *The Times* offices are closer. I can be in London Bridge in fifteen minutes."

"Fine. Fine," Adam said. "But you don't give the orders here. I'm the boss. You're going to work the daily story with Jake, once he turns up. And you will share a byline. But the bigger story, this side investigation of yours…well, it's yours. We can upload it tonight and update the print edition. Happy?"

Lillian sat back at her desk and looked around the newsroom. Was she happy? Absolutely. She'd tried to take the high road, but she'd needed a sharp reminder that that wasn't how the business worked. The euphoria quickly dissipated as she thought about how she'd spent her weekend. She'd spent Friday night in a hotel in Kensington before returning home and waiting for a locksmith to change her locks and install an overpriced alarm system. She'd barely slept and was surviving on coffee, cigarettes, and the knowledge that she had illegal pepper spray in her bag. She shook her head and forced herself to focus on work. She woke up her computer and checked the clock on her desk. It was almost quarter past ten and Jake's desk was empty.

"Here."

Lillian jumped as Omid from the marketing department dropped a small pile of envelopes onto her desk.

"New mail boy. Keeps mixing up the mail. Like it's that hard. I would have sent one of the interns down, but I needed to get my steps in."

"It's mail person," Lillian replied, trying to sound normal while her heart hammered in her chest.

"Call HR and complain that I'm a wokeist."

"That's not even a word," Lillian said to Omid's already retreating back.

She flicked through the mail and stopped when she saw the A5 black padded envelope. There was nothing distinct about the address label. It was a generic label that had been printed by someone with access to a thermal label printer. With equal parts excitement and trepidation, Lillian ripped the envelope open and pushed her fingers inside, but she couldn't feel anything. She turned it upside down and shook it until an object fell out, bounced off her desk, and rolled onto the floor.

"No," Lillian gasped.

She pushed her chair back and got down on her knees to look at the item that had rolled under her desk. It was a ring. Lillian picked it up and sat back on her chair. She turned toward the window and held the signet ring to the light. The excitement disappeared, leaving only fear when she saw the small diamond in the middle of the letter *S*.

"Jake," Lillian whispered.

Desperate now, she pushed her hand back inside the envelope and pulled out a note.

Dear Lillian,
You should be pleased I made things right.
   Smile.

Lillian's hands shook as she shoved the note back into the envelope. She looked across the office at Jake's empty desk. The Burier had Jake. The signet ring was proof of that. Lillian felt sick. She didn't like Jake but that didn't mean she wanted him dead. He certainly didn't deserve whatever The Burier was doing to him.

"Come on, girl, get it together," Lillian whispered to herself. She opened the contacts app on her phone and pressed call on the SCU's direct number. Her heart skipped several beats as she listened to the ringing tone. She hung up, panicked, the moment someone answered. Telling the SCU that The Burier had sent her Jake's ring would leave her exposed, and she would be forced to answer more questions: *Why did The Burier choose you? How long have you been in communication with The Burier? Is this the first time he's sent you an item belonging to a victim? How close are you to The Burier?*

Lillian grabbed the ring, letter, and phone, and threw them into her bag. She opened the lower drawer of her desk and took out a cheap phone that contained an unregistered SIM card. Lillian's plan was simple: jump on the DLR, get off at Tower Gateway, make one anonymous call to the SCU and throw her burner phone into the river. The plan was simple but Lillian was not at ease. Her body shuddered with fear as she walked out of the office. How close was The Burier? Was he waiting for her? Would he let her live if he found out?

Stanford shielded his eyes from the sun and called out, "Ian Brandon Turner?"

Eastwood scanned her surroundings. Ardgowan Road in Catford was no different to the streets that ran parallel to it. Almost identical terraced Victorian houses set back from the pavement, bordered either side of the road with gardens that had been transformed into driveways or had been left in their protected states with low brick walls or hedges.

"The only people who call me by my full name are my dad and the Old Bill. My dad died six years ago, so I'm going to assume you're Old Bill." The disembodied voice came from within the depths of a cascade of luminescent green leaves from the overgrown wisteria plant, which engulfed the side of the house. Only muscular and hairy calves were visible on the ladder.

"Detective Sergeants Stanford and Eastwood from the Serial Crime Unit. We're investigating, er, reinvestigating one of your old cases," said Stanford as a large clump of leaves and purple flowers landed at the bottom of the ladder.

"This stuff is a bloody monster," Ian replied. More leaves and flowers fell, and the ladder wobbled precariously. "The wife said it would look pretty in the spring, but it's a pain in my ass."

"We need to have a word," Eastwood said, holding the ladder steady. "We'd rather talk to you with your feet on the ground."

"Then you're going to have to wait," said Ian as another clump of foliage narrowly missed Eastwood's head.

"Looks much better," said Stanford. "Now if you don't mind, would you please get down? We need to talk about our old boss, DCSI Rhimes."

"And Larsen," Eastwood added.

"Larsen," Ian repeated with contempt. The resentful sigh that followed was audible even above the heavy bassline of Kendrick Lamar's "Humble" coming from the open windows of a passing car. "Should have been him who gassed himself in a fucking garage," he added, finally descending the ladder.

Ian opened the fridge door, pulled out a bottle of beer and held it out. "Probably too early for you, right?"

"It's five o'clock somewhere," Stanford replied, ignoring Eastwood's look and taking the bottle.

"What about you?" Ian asked Eastwood.

"Water will do."

Ian handed Eastwood a bottle of water and gave Stanford a bottle opener. Stanford studied the man in front of him. Ian looked younger than his sixty-three years. His face was heavily tanned, and deep lines were visible around his green eyes. His dark blond hair was graying, but it was still thick. His neck and shoulders were broad, and he looked like a man who took care of himself. Ian returned Stanford's stare without saying a word.

Stanford broke first, his curiosity getting the better of him. "Were you at his funeral?"

"Of course I was at his funeral," Ian said. He indicated for them to follow him into the conservatory. "There were a lot of people there. I would have been a pallbearer, but I'd had an operation on my shoulder the month before."

"When did you last see him?" Eastwood asked, settling herself into a chair. "Before he..."

Ian took a sip of his beer. "Seven or eight months before he... before he died. Mate of ours was getting married. It was the stag weekend. Golfing trip in Gran Canaria." Ian stared out the window. "He never seemed the type, you know? To take his own life, I mean."

The three of them sat in silence for a while, each lost in their own memories of Rhimes.

"Did he talk to you about anything that was going on with him at that time?" asked Eastwood eventually.

"You're asking me? I thought you were a close team. As far I could work out, he practically adopted that computer whiz-kid lad."

"Ezra. His name is Ezra," said Stanford. He glanced over at Eastwood. "And we are a close team."

Ian sighed. "I know. Sorry. I could see that at the funeral, and the way Rhimes used to talk about you all."

Eastwood tried to steer the conversation back to the reason they were there. She didn't want this to get too personal. "What about text messages or phone calls before he died?" Eastwood asked.

Ian straightened up, a sign he understood what Eastwood was trying to do. "If you're asking if Rhimes and I spoke about the corruption allegations before he died, then the answer is yes. You don't work with someone for over fifteen years on the sort of cases that we worked on and not have each other's backs."

"What did he say about the allegations?" asked Stanford.

"That someone was trying to frame him. And before you ask, I didn't ask him if he had proof. Didn't have to. He was one of the good ones. Not that the Court of Appeal judgment made any effort to point that out. Pretty much stuck a scarlet letter on his grave. Plenty of us weren't so good, but he was."

The sound of a lawnmower drifted through the open conservatory doors. Ian and Stanford drank their beers. Eastwood wondered if Ian included himself in that group of "not so good."

"Andrew Streeter," Eastwood said. "We've been going through the case files, and we have questions."

Ian placed his empty bottle on the table and clasped his hands. "There's always questions."

"We've listened to all the tape-recorded interviews you had with Streeter," said Stanford. "Five interviews in total. He was interviewed three times without a brief and then with a lawyer in the last two interviews."

"That's right." Ian looked thoughtful for a moment. "The

cases that matter, they stick with you. You never forget. I can remember the smell of the ink that they used to take the fingerprints, and I can remember what Streeter was wearing when we first interviewed him. Dirty white Armani T-shirt. I remember looking at the collar and thinking, it's a knockoff. Probably got it for a fiver down Walthamstow market. Black jeans and old Avia sneakers."

"From the get-go, Streeter denied everything. In every interview, he denied it all," said Stanford.

"He admitted meeting Fallon O'Toole though. At the Ship pub in Bermondsey, near the river. Witnesses saw them together, including her friends," said Ian.

"But he was never seen with the other victims: Chalmers, Callaghan, Alves," Eastwood countered.

"But he was at the scene when your Henley found Gyimah's body," Ian replied.

"And he gave an explanation for that," said Eastwood, taking out her notebook and flicking through the pages. "He said he was killing time because he'd arrived for his interview at the Convoy early."

"That's what he said," said Ian.

"Why were you all so hot for him?" asked Stanford. "With the exception of meeting O'Toole in the pub and him being in the area when Gyimah's body was found, you didn't have much evidence."

"Streeter was known."

"Having previous for handling stolen goods is a long way from murder."

"There were also a couple of indecent assault allegations back when he was seventeen. Granted, he was found not guilty in the youth court but—what would they call it now…?—reprehensible behavior counts when you're looking at bad character."

"But there was no evidence Streeter was the one who sexually assaulted the victims. Where were the forensics?" said Eastwood. "And unless you're about to tell me differently, Streeter was straight, and the fifth victim, Tiago Alves, was a man. There was no forensic evidence until Alves's body was found, and then the next thing you know there's evidence flying all over the place."

"Are you suggesting we planted evidence? Because if those are the next words out your mouth, then you have the choice of walking out by yourselves or me throwing you out," Ian said angrily.

"That's not what we're suggesting," Stanford said calmly.

"I'm suggesting it," said Eastwood. She sat back, making it clear she wasn't going anywhere. "But not planted by you."

"And not Rhimes either," said Ian, his voice firm.

"What about Larsen? He was your SIO."

Eastwood and Stanford saw it at the same time. The flash of anger, resentment, and disgust on Ian's face at the mention of Larsen's name.

"Did he ask you to focus on Streeter? To build the investigation around him?" Stanford asked.

"Not in the beginning. We had three suspects."

"Tony Harris, Clinton Fennelson and—" Stanford raised his head as Ian finished the list for him.

"Russell Leary was the third one. He was Fallon O'Toole's ex-boyfriend and he also worked with Streeter at a construction site in Bellingham. He was a nasty piece of work; I quite fancied him for the murders. He had previous for a nasty kidnapping back in '92 and served six months for ABH on O'Toole. But he had an alibi."

"What was his alibi?"

"On remand in Scotland when Gyimah and Chalmers went missing and shacked up with another bird in Ilford when O'Toole was last seen in the pub with Streeter."

"But he worked with Streeter on the construction site?" Eastwood asked, looking over at Stanford. "That wasn't mentioned in the case files."

"Maybe it went missing," said Ian. "Not that it mattered. Larsen wasn't keen on it."

"And what did Larsen want?"

"To go after Streeter." Ian stood up, cracked his neck and sat back down. "It was as if he needed it to be him."

"Is that why you didn't follow up the Ford Fiesta lead?" asked Stanford.

"That's not true. We did follow the Ford Fiesta angle. That car was mentioned by three witnesses. Gyimah was seen on CCTV getting into a car that may have been a Fiesta, and then other witnesses mentioned it in line with the last-known sightings of Chalmers and Alves."

"So, what happened? Streeter couldn't drive. As far as we can tell, he didn't even have a provisional license. Two people could be seen getting in that Fiesta."

Ian shook his head. "You're not getting it. Larsen became fixated on Streeter once he was in the picture. That's all he wanted us to focus on. Larsen said just because Streeter didn't have a license, didn't mean he didn't know *how* to drive. Then, when Alves's DNA was found in the white van, it all fell into place. I'm not saying that Streeter wasn't involved somehow, but it... it never felt right. And then the Renault Trafic van turned up with hairs from three of the victims. Streeter's prints were on the steering wheel and there was soil in the driver's footwell which matched the soil that was found on Streeter's boots."

"But didn't that seem a bit too neat for you?" asked Eastwood. "For months there are hardly any forensics linking Streeter to the victims, and then it all comes together once Alves is found."

"Of course it was too neat. Streeter's prints weren't even on the steering wheel itself. They were on a steering wheel cover so, nah, not convinced. But how could you argue with DNA and forensics? And you definitely couldn't argue with Larsen."

"You could argue it, if someone planted it," Eastwood pointed out.

"That's what Rhimes said," Ian said. "Look, if you're asking me if someone was digging around, manipulating the evidence, then my answer is yes. Was that person Rhimes? Fuck no. He wasn't a saint, but he wasn't corrupt."

"What about Larsen?" Stanford asked. "Any chance he was corrupt?"

"Three months after the investigation is closed and Streeter is convicted, Larsen is promoted to Special Branch. Fast-forward twenty years and he's the fucking borough commander and he's pissed off that Rhimes has been granted the Serial Crime Unit. That's also the same time when the rumours about our esteemed forensic expert, Dr. Fry, start circulating."

"We need to find who owned that Ford Fiesta," Eastwood said to Stanford.

"And Georgina Bridges," Ian said.

Stanford frowned. "Who's Georgina Bridges?"

"We were trying to track her down. She'd made a report about being kidnapped. She called the incident room, and I think she spoke to Larsen, if I remember correctly, but he dismissed her. Wrote her off as a crank."

"Hold on," said Eastwood. "I spoke to an ex-colleague of yours—DS Caningly."

"Ah, Penny," said Ian. "Good detective, that one."

"She told me she remembered speaking to a woman who claimed to be a victim of The Burier and that she passed her details to Larsen. Could this be the same person, this Georgina Bridges?"

Ian shrugged. "It could be, but it also could have been someone taking the piss. You know what it's like. A million and one hoax calls from a bunch of sickos looking for their fifteen minutes of fame."

"Then why was Rhimes trying to track her down after Larsen had written her off?" Stanford asked.

"He found bits of her witness statement in Larsen's bin. Don't ask me why he was looking in there in the first place, but Bridges claimed that whoever took her didn't touch her. But he did promise to bury her alive."

34

Caroline Swann's mouth and eyes remained sewn shut when Henley and Ramouter entered the examination room fifteen minutes earlier. It wasn't lost on Henley that we enter this world unmarked, but our bodies tell a story through scars, tattoos, and piercings by the time we depart. As Henley examined Caroline Swann's body, she noticed flattened red scars beneath her breasts, and wondered what Caroline's story had been. Linh, standing nearby, looked exhausted but concentrated.

Linh explained, "I didn't finish here until late last night. I was late getting in—accident on the South Circular. Then I had a murder-suicide case to wrap up, a family of three. So, Ms. Swann is unopened and waiting, I'm afraid."

"That's OK," Henley replied. Ramouter was in his usual spot, leaning against the counter but close to the door. "Is there any preliminary information you can share before you begin?"

Linh managed to find some resolve from somewhere and inject it into her voice. "Caroline Swann had been dead for about thirty-six to forty-eight hours by the time she was found. Recent breast augmentation surgery left horizontal scars on her breasts. There are small laparoscopy procedure scars on her abdomen— you can see the scarring. No other injuries on her torso, that I can see. I've put a request in for her medical records. There were cable ties in her bedroom?" she asked.

"They were on the bed. Forensics has them," Ramouter confirmed.

Linh examined Caroline's swollen wrists. There were deep ligature marks indented on her skin. She moved her finger along the bruising. "These ties were tight, causing reduced blood circulation and skin damage. There are signs she tried to get out of them, but all she ended up doing was tightening them. Same with her ankles. She's also missing some fingernails. They don't appear to have been ripped out by force, so that could be from her clawing to escape."

"Can we retrieve DNA from her?" Henley asked. "Our killer used bleach to clean the bodies. He did it with all the 1995 victims, though not with Piper. But I can smell it on Swann."

"I've collected samples from her hair and what's left of her nails. He did a thorough job of cleaning her, but bleach won't get rid of everything. I found dirt in her pubic hair, anus, and between her toes. But look at her back..."

Linh lifted Caroline's body and Henley and Ramouter both leaned forward. There were small red marks visible—some resembled large pinpricks, while others were superficial cuts.

"It appears someone poked her back with a sharply pointed knife. The wounds aren't deep, but there would have been some bleeding. There are eighteen of them. There was a lot of dirt recovered from the back of her scalp. She may have tried to escape, and rubbed against the dirt."

"Trying to get out of the grave," Ramouter murmured. "Why kill Caroline Swann, though?"

"She saw him," Henley said. "She could identify him."

"But Filip isn't really Filip," Ramouter said, frowning. "Any description she could have given would've been useless, and she couldn't link him to the 1995 murders."

"We'll have to ask him when we catch him." Henley's face was set, determinedly.

Linh nodded. "No point wallowing in hopelessness."

"I hope no one ever hires you as a motivational speaker," Henley replied, smiling.

"If telling it like it is is motivational then sign me up. Right, let's proceed."

Linh's joviality dissipated and was replaced with a steely concentration. She gently placed a finger against Caroline's lips and cut through the coarse black thread. The sound of steel cutting through the stiffened thread made Henley tense.

"It's better stitching than Piper, more precise, as if he took his time with Caroline. It appears to be one continuous thread, without any breakage," Linh remarked as she picked up a pair of tweezers and delicately pulled the thread through Caroline's lifeless flesh. "I wonder what type of needle he used. The puncture wounds aren't very wide, suggesting a thin needle, yet this thread is quite thick."

"You would only take your time if you cared," Henley mused.

"Hmm," Linh murmured as she gently pried open Caroline's mouth and shone her flashlight inside. "I see soil in the back of her throat, on the roof of her mouth, and in her teeth. If I lift her tongue, I can see it," she said as she reached for the tweezers and carefully inserted them into Caroline's mouth. Henley moved closer to the body as Linh retrieved a coin and placed it in a metal dish. Henley winced, and Ramouter turned away when Linh tilted Caroline's head back and inserted the tweezers deep into her throat.

"Come on," Linh said as she carefully maneuvered the tweezers. "This one is much deeper than the one I removed from Piper's throat," she explained. "And here we go." Linh extracted a small piece of paper and placed it in a bowl.

Both Henley and Ramouter inched closer as Linh delicately unfolded the small piece of paper, treating it as if it were a piece of delicate origami art. Henley silently prayed that Caroline Swann's name was the last entry on The Burier's kill list.

"Is it the same coin?" Stanford asked, pulling the chair from under his desk and placing it next to Eastwood.

"No, it's not. The coin found in Piper's mouth was minted in 2014, clearly different from the coins found in the mouths of the 1995 victims," Henley explained, displaying a photograph of the coin on the smart screen. "The 1995 victims had £2 coins, which we know were prototypes. According to the Royal Mint, they officially started minting £2 coins in 1997, and they weren't introduced into public circulation until 1998."

"Where are those coins now?" Pellacia asked, flicking through a printout.

"No idea," Eastwood replied. "They weren't in the exhibits box removed from archives, but there's no record of their destruction. Most likely, they were lost in that ridiculous excuse for a police archive."

"What about the witness statements?"

"There are over thirty thousand witness statements." Eastwood leaned forward in her chair and unwrapped a Twix. "We're going through them, but from the court transcripts, no one gave live evidence about the coins. It was a section nine statement from the coin-making plant, stating they weren't aware that the prototypes left their premises, and they were conducting their own investigation."

"But wasn't Streeter's DNA found on the coin from Alves's mouth?" Stanford asked.

"That's what the DNA report from the dodgy forensic scientist concluded," Ramouter added. "The investigating team probably thought there was no point investigating further when they found Streeter's DNA on one coin."

"On one coin?" Pellacia said in disbelief. "I'll visit the archives this afternoon. I can't believe they've vanished."

"You're actually leaving the office and risking getting your shirt dirty?" Eastwood teased. "Gov…unbelievable."

Pellacia rolled his eyes at Eastwood in mock exasperation before saying, "You said Piper's coin was different from Swann's?"

"This is the coin found in Swann's mouth," Henley said, displaying the next photograph.

"Does it say…1996, and is that a football?" Stanford asked. Henley zoomed in on the image.

"It's a commemorative £2 coin for the 1996 European Championships," Ramouter explained. "There were over five million nickel brass versions, but, if I'm not mistaken, if it's verified as a 22ct Gold Proof coin, there were only two thousand made."

"What's it worth?" Stanford asked.

"The gold one, about a grand, but they go for more on eBay."

"Our killer, Filip, or Mr. Nobody, whatever you want to call him, is clearly making a statement, telling us he's back. Why else would he use a coin from 1996?" Henley pondered.

"He's a conniving and smug little shit," Stanford said. "1996 was the year Streeter was convicted for The Burier's crimes. This is probably his way of gloating: 'You didn't get me in 1996, and you won't get me now.'"

"Doesn't bring us any closer to identifying him, though," Eastwood noted.

"No, it doesn't, but I refuse to believe there's nothing in the original case files about those coins," Henley said.

"What's our brilliant criminal profiler, Dr. Mark Ryan, saying about this?" Stanford asked cynically. "Is he stumped?"

"No, he isn't. He's at a conference in San Francisco, but he emailed this morning and plans to FaceTime me later. He knows how much you miss him."

"Shut up."

"Here's the kill list," Henley said, scrolling to a photograph of the piece of paper retrieved from Caroline's throat.

1. Andrew Streeter
2. Elias Piper
3. Caroline Swann
4. J
5.   Maybe four

"Who the hell is *J*?" Stanford asked.

"If I knew that, I wouldn't be standing here," Henley retorted.

"What about our missing sixth victim? Any progress on identifying her?" Pellacia asked.

Stanford cleared his throat. "We spoke to Rhimes's former partner, Ian Turner, this morning. He recalls Rhimes trying to track down a Georgina Bridges."

"Bridges?" Henley said as she retrieved her file containing notes from Rhimes's personal files that Eloise had given her. "That name was written in one of Rhimes's old notebooks. Here it is: *G. Bridges. Caningly dealing. Low. Possible/Unreliable?* That's what he wrote. I couldn't read the rest due to water damage."

"According to Turner, this Bridges woman initially spoke to Larsen. If Turner's right, she gave a statement, and—"

"If she gave a statement, where is it?" Pellacia interrupted.

"Hold on, gov," Stanford replied. "According to Turner, and I understand this is all hearsay, Rhimes found the statement torn to shreds in Larsen's trash."

"Did he take the statement out of the bin?" Pellacia asked.

"Gov, my name ain't Marty McFly and I haven't got a time machine," Stanford retorted.

"Watch it," Pellacia warned.

"Georgina Bridges is real," Eastwood interjected quickly, handing Pellacia, Ramouter, and Henley two sheets of paper. "This is the criminal record of Georgina Alice Bridges. No aliases. Date of birth: sixteenth March 1975. There's not much. Just a caution for possession of class B in April 1994 and a conviction for possession with intent to supply class B in March 1995."

"No wonder Rhimes noted 'unreliable' next to her name. She would have been twenty-one when the first victim was taken," Henley pointed out. "Have you checked her last known address?"

Eastwood nodded. "Yes, we have, and it's an address on the old Aylesbury estate in Elephant and Castle, which we know was—"

"Demolished in 2009," Pellacia sighed.

"Exactly. Her record shows that she received an eighteen-month conditional discharge from Bow Street Magistrates Court for supply in '95 and then she vanished."

"'Vanished'?" Ramouter asked.

"No sign of her on the police national computer after March 1995, and no record of a driver's license or a passport either. There could be a million reasons why her criminal record is clean after March 1995. Either she stayed out of trouble or her arrests were deleted because no further action was taken," Eastwood explained. "I've asked Ezra to see what he can find."

"That's something," Henley said as she erased the question mark under *victim 6—1995* on the whiteboard and replaced it with *Georgina Bridges—tbc.*

"Did Turner say anything else?" Henley asked.

"He believes that Larsen may have set up Rhimes," Stanford said, his anger flaring up suddenly. "I'm trying to take it all with a pinch of salt, stay impartial and all that shit, but let's look at the facts. Larsen destroyed crucial witness evidence, ignored the Fiesta's evidence…"

"And he was hell-bent on pinning the entire case on Streeter, even when there was no forensic evidence," Eastwood added.

"Why would Larsen set up Rhimes? Why jeopardize such a massive case?" Henley wondered aloud, her anger growing.

"Because he's a cunt," Stanford said bluntly, "and he clearly hated Rhimes."

"I knew it," Pellacia said, banging his fist on the desk. "It never felt right, Rhimes being bent. No way."

"I don't understand why Larsen would risk it," said Henley. "It's absolute lunacy to think that Larsen would be prepared to leave a serial killer on the street because he hated Rhimes."

"It wasn't only Rhimes that he hated," said Stanford. "Larsen must have had some warped reason to want to put Streeter away for life."

"I should be relieved but I'm not. I'm angry," Eastwood said, looking pointedly at Henley, signaling that she could be winding up her investigation into Rhimes. "As far as I'm concerned, Larsen is just as responsible for those deaths, including Rhimes, as The Burier."

"It didn't have to be five," Henley murmured, gazing at the whiteboard and the 1995 timeline and photographs of the five victims. "Georgina Bridges was in contact with Larsen and perhaps Rhimes as early as October 1995, before Penelope Callaghan went missing. Her body was discovered in mid-November. It didn't have to be five. Callaghan's daughter wouldn't have grown up without her mother and Tiago Alves would still be alive."

The room fell into silence as everyone digested the latest revelations.

"There's something I can't quite figure out," Eastwood said. "Why did Rhimes go along with it, making Streeter the sole suspect?"

"It had to be the DNA," Henley replied. "Rhimes was a science man. He would have followed the science, not Larsen."

"So, what's next?" Pellacia asked. "Eastie's going through the old files, I'm headed to the archives. Ramouter, I want you to pay Andrew Streeter's sister a visit."

Ramouter groaned. "That woman is strange. Did you hear her on the radio this morning?"

"I did, and she's obviously seeking her fifteen minutes of fame. But there's a chance she'll speak with you," Henley said. "I'll even drop you off."

"What about Swann?" Pellacia asked. "She needs to be formally identified. Sooner is better than later."

"Her parents should be arriving this evening, but she's had extensive cosmetic surgery, including dental work. Ramouter has already requested her dental records, so worst case, we'll ID Swann that way if her parents are delayed. In the meantime, I'll release a statement confirming the discovery of a woman's body."

"What about the missing journalist, Jake Ryland?" asked Ramouter.

"Are we taking that seriously?" Eastwood asked. "It was an anonymous call to the SCU. It could be a wild goose chase."

"We are not taking any chances," Henley said sharply. "Bridges was initially written off as a crank call and look at where we are now. Jake Ryland has written about The Burier for the *Chronicle* and according to the anonymous caller, he hasn't been seen since Friday. I'd rather follow this through and discover that he's been at home suffering from the biggest hangover as opposed to ignoring it and later receiving a call that Ryland's body has been found in a shallow grave."

"Can't argue with that," Eastwood conceded.

"What about Larsen?" Pellacia asked. "It's time someone spoke to him. He fucked with the original case, and he has a history with that unreliable expert witness, Dr. Leslie Fry. He's not part of the police force anymore. He's not protected."

"What are you saying? That I bring him in?" Henley asked. Stanford let out a low whistle.

"Not Larsen, not yet. We need more before we show up at

his doorstep. But we can bring in the doctor. He's already dis-
credited, so he shouldn't be too surprised to get a call from us."

"What do you expect him to tell us?" Ramouter asked.

"Simple. Whether it was Rhimes or Larsen who instructed
him to falsify the DNA results."

35

Henley turned off the ignition, listening to the engine winding down. Gray clouds had lifted fifteen minutes ago, but raindrops teased her windshield as sun and blue skies emerged. The earthy, musky scent of rain-soaked soil wafted in. Henley checked her phone. No calls or texts from Rob, despite her earlier message asking him to let her know when he arrived in Manchester. She couldn't even feel angry at him anymore. She felt no guilt about spending time with Pellacia; in fact, Henley wondered what her therapist would say if she explained that being with Pellacia didn't feel like a betrayal, but being with Rob did. Her phone rang, the caller ID showing it was a FaceTime from her mother-in-law.

"That was quick," Natasha said. "You usually don't pick up right away unless it's work."

"You're looking after my daughter, so I'm not going to keep you hanging," Henley replied, wiping away a trickle of sweat from her forehead.

"Are you OK? You look tired. Maybe you're overdoing it."

Henley fought back sudden tears, seeing Natasha's genuine concern.

"I won't pretend to understand what your job is like," Natasha continued, "but I know it's not easy. Kids, work, marriage…" Natasha's voice trailed off as she became aware of Henley's stricken expression. She changed the subject. "Anyway, I was calling to update you on Emma."

"Is she OK?" Henley asked, trying to swallow down the familiar burning of tears welling up.

"She's fine. We went shopping today," Natasha continued, rattling off more details about the day her daughter had had without Henley.

Henley fixed a smile on her face, masking her inner turmoil. Her daughter's face filled the screen, and she couldn't help but feel like she was fucking everything up.

Henley stood on Stockwell Park Road, double-checking the address she'd copied into her phone. Dr. Leslie Fry did live in this short block of identical flats, and not in one of the impressive Georgian terraces further down the road. She knocked on flat number 5's lime-green door, noticing the plants and cluttered windowsill. A person seemed to move inside. Henley knocked again and then crouched down and pushed open the letter box.

"Dr. Leslie Fry, Detective Inspector Henley from the Serial Crime Unit. I need to speak with you urgently." She could hear a kettle boiling and the distant sound of a news anchor's voice. "I'm going to push my warrant card through your letter box and then I expect you to open the door. I would prefer to have this conversation inside. Or I can arrest you for perjury and obstructing the course of justice, and take you down to the station instead."

The door opened, revealing Dr. Fry's mismatched attire. He was tall, with thick white hair, and wore a crisp white shirt, tracksuit bottoms, and a pair of black flip-flops. He ushered Henley inside and she stepped into the narrow corridor.

"I was going to make a cup of tea. Would you like one?"

"Why not? One sugar."

"I used to live better," he said, placing two mugs on the table. There were plastic bags filled with clothes, overflowing bin bags and boxes of files and books everywhere. "I used to live in Maida Vale," he continued, "but my wife kicked me out. To be honest, I think she's been looking for a reason to get rid of me for years but now that I've brought her stellar reputation into disrepute…well, here I am."

Henley sipped her tea and got straight to the point. She didn't have time for this pity party.

"We know you tampered with DNA results from 1995. Why did you do it?"

Dr. Fry watched her silently. "I adjusted the findings to fit the hypothesis," he finally admitted.

"The point is you lied. You attributed the results to Andrew Streeter. Someone paid you, right? Someone from the original investigation? The detectives or the prosecution?"

"Not the prosecution."

"I'm not going to spend hours going around the houses with you. I've got a missing journalist who may be the next victim of The Burier, so I'm going to give you three names and you're going to tell me which one paid you." Henley waited for Fry to nod. She held up three fingers. "Rhimes. Larsen. Turner. Which one?"

Henley waited for Fry to answer. He remained silent.

"Who was it?" Henley asked with more force.

Dr. Fry took a deep breath and ran his hand over his forehead.

He looked like he was going to be sick. Henley could barely hear him when he eventually spoke.

"You're going to have to speak up," she snapped.

"Larsen," Dr. Fry repeated. "It was Larsen."

Henley watched Eastwood spin in her chair before facing her. "Did you hear what I said?"

"I heard it, gov," Eastwood replied, still rotating. "But I'm not done investigating Rhimes's corruption allegations, and—"

"It doesn't put Rhimes in the clear," Henley interrupted, "But you can't deny it changes things."

"With all due respect, I can." Eastwood reached for chips but opted for a banana and ginger nut biscuits instead. "Rhimes did some shady stuff, things that weren't exactly aboveboard. It could've led to disciplinary action, but not gross misconduct, at least not twenty-five years ago."

"What did he do?"

"He conducted interviews that breached the codes of practice. He threatened Streeter's sister for not revealing his whereabouts. But Ramouter says to take her words with a kilo of salt. Where Rhimes went wrong was not taking over the Melissa Gyimah case from Deptford CID."

Henley felt sick, realizing Rhimes had downgraded Melissa's case. He'd relegated it.

"I found PC Kelly, who took your statement back then," Eastwood continued. "He said his DCI made three transfer requests for the case to go to Larsen's squad, but they were refused, even when her rucksack with blood was found. Rhimes said it was still a missing person's case at that point. Portland said that he escalated it to his boss who spoke to Larsen, who again refused."

Henley knew that Deptford CID wouldn't have made the transfer request without good reason. Was it ego or narcissism that had caused Rhimes to reject the transfer request? Maybe

Rhimes could have prevented two decades of pain for the other victims' families if he'd taken Melissa's case.

"When did the murder squad take on Melissa's case?" Henley asked.

"Two weeks after Stephanie Chalmers' body was found," Stanford explained. "DNA found matched the DNA found on Gyimah's body, but the DNA didn't belong to Streeter. The first DNA report concluded that the DNA retrieved was of poor quality, so it wasn't enough to obtain a DNA profile. We then get a second report, after Streeter's name is brought into the picture, and lo and behold, Dr. Leslie Fry produces a report saying that the DNA is a partial match for Streeter."

"Fry admitted to falsifying the report," Henley noted on the whiteboard. "And Anthony confirmed: retesting Melissa's rucksack and the sheet Penelope Callaghan was wrapped in produced matching DNA profiles, distinct from Streeter's, but consistent with the DNA on cable ties found in Swann's bedroom and Streeter's hospital band."

"What about Streeter's DNA on Alves's body? Hair and blood, right?" Ramouter asked, turning to his computer. "But no skin—which is odd, given Streeter had seborrheic dermatitis."

"What's that?" Stanford asked.

"It's like severe dandruff, affecting areas with oil glands, similar to psoriasis and eczema," Ramouter explained. "Forensics should've found more than a few hairs and a tiny blood spot if Streeter had been anywhere near Gyimah and Chalmers' bodies."

"But can we completely dismiss Streeter's involvement in Alves?" Stanford questioned. "He knew Alves, they were seen together, and Streeter's loon sister claims she saw Alves near her brother's flat."

"But look at the forensic evidence," Henley said. "Just a few of Alves's hairs on Streeter's headboard in his bedroom, and that's it."

"Are you suggesting someone planted Alves's hair in Streeter's flat?" Eastwood's face paled.

"Let's look at it logically." Henley shifted her attention as Pellacia entered with Ezra. Between them, they carried a large green container. They looked disheveled. "Eighteenth October 1995, Streeter is arrested after a witness called Crimestoppers and said that they saw Streeter with victim three, Fallon O'Toole," she continued. "Rhimes is the arresting officer. SOCO search Streeter's flat, no evidence is recovered. Streeter is released and bailed to return to Ladywell police station on the twenty-ninth December 1995. Streeter attends his BTR date. Rhimes books him and interviews Streeter about the murder of Penelope Callaghan. Streeter denies knowing Callaghan and denies murder. There is no forensic evidence linking him to any of the victims. Unknown to Rhimes, Tiago Alves was already missing. A second search is conducted at Streeter's home. SOCO is there, and the evidence recovered confirmed that only Streeter's family and a few unidentified individuals had been in his flat. The garden was searched, and Rhimes's notes clearly state there are no signs that the earth had been disturbed. Streeter is bailed for a second time. Fourth January 1996 and Alves's body is found. Streeter is arrested at an address in Stepney and another search is conducted at his home address in Bellingham."

"Where was Rhimes for that one?" Stanford asked.

"At the hospital with his wife," Eastwood replied. "Their son was ill with bacterial meningitis. He's not there for the arrest; Larsen conducted it."

"Hold on a minute," Stanford interrupted. "At this point, in January 1996, there's still no direct or circumstantial evidence that implicates Streeter in the murders of Gyimah, Chalmers, O'Toole and Callaghan or in Alves's disappearance."

"But they've got Streeter's association with Alves and that's enough to bring him in," Eastwood explained. "Larsen's arrest notes state that nine officers, including himself, attended the

Stepney address. They force entry, Streeter does a runner but he doesn't get very far and is arrested. Now, this is where things get strange. Five hours before the arrest, a neighbor called 999, says someone is trying to break into Streeter's flat in Bellingham. Local uniform go to the address, and the only person there is Larsen and he says that he's there to arrest Streeter."

"Why is that strange?" Stanford asked.

"Larsen has no backup. He's on his own," Henley retorted. "When have you ever known an officer to go against protocol and arrest a dangerous suspect, on their own?"

"And five hours later Larsen takes an entire team to Stepney to arrest Streeter," Stanford laughed and shook his head disbelievingly.

"Are you seriously suggesting Larsen planted evidence?" Pellacia said, as he and Ezra placed the box on a table.

"It's the only thing that makes sense," Eastwood asserted. "Search one and two, no evidence is recovered. Third search, after Larsen attends the address alone, and bingo: we've got Alves's DNA everywhere, along with soil from Streeter's garden in Alves's hair."

"But the soil in his lungs doesn't match," Henley added. "Why did Larsen have such a hard-on for Streeter? There was forensic evidence and a complete, not partial, DNA match of a third party."

"Maybe Larsen thought having someone was better than no one," Pellacia mused.

"According to Rhimes's notes, he thought Streeter was involved somehow but that he wasn't the—"

"What the fuck?" Ramouter exclaimed, looking at his computer screen. "Henley!" he called urgently, rising and then hesitating, unsure of his next move. "Boss," Ramouter beckoned, tapping his computer screen. "You need to see this."

"What is it?" Henley said. She, Stanford, and Eastwood hurried to Ramouter's desk.

Silence enveloped the room as everyone absorbed the grim sight. Jake Ryland's terror-filled image filled the screen. His mouth was covered with silver tape, reflecting the flash's light. His bloodshot eyes were wide open in fear, surrounded by stretched, tear-glistened skin on his face, marked by the strain of fear. There were no clues to his whereabouts.

"There's another one," Ramouter stated flatly, clicking the mouse.

"Jesus Christ," Stanford muttered.

Henley bit her lip while mentally cataloguing the horrific scene. The early-morning light cast an eerie glow on Jake's face and upper chest, the only visible parts of his body from a disturbed grave. Soil spilled from his mouth, and a visible cut ran from his left collarbone to the armpit crease.

Finally breaking the silence, Henley asked, "Who's the sender?" Her desk phone started ringing. "Jo, can you get that, please?"

"You didn't have to ask," Joanna replied as Henley's phone silenced.

"161096 burier," Ramouter said with a shake of his head. "How recent is this? Ryland has been missing for what, four days? Where the hell is he?"

"161096. It's the date Streeter was sentenced," Eastwood realized. "Sixteenth October, 1996. The question is, why did he choose to contact Ramouter?"

"I have no bloody idea," Ramouter admitted as Henley's phone rang again. "But there's more. He's cc'd someone in the email. Lillian T. Klein. Who the hell is Lillian Klein?"

"She's a journalist at the *Chronicle* newspaper."

"He hasn't used her work address. This is a personal account."

"How on earth would—" Henley began.

"She's on the phone," Joanna interrupted. "Pick up, Henley. Lillian Klein wants to talk to you."

"He's sent another message," Ramouter said.

Tuesday 29 June at 15:58
From: 161096 burier
To: Salim Ramouter, Met Police, Serial Crime Unit
CC: Lillian T. Klein
Subject: Your To Late

It didn't have to be this way. Let sleeping dogs lie, allow them to do their work in piece. You didn't do your job, Lils, so I had to fix things, to show you. There's still one more dog to put down. I didn't know this dog was lose.

36

"An email?" Dr. Mark Ryan's voice echoed from Henley's computer speakers.

"Yes, and can you please turn on your camera?" Henley sighed as she reopened the email from Ramouter.

"Oops, sorry. The Wi-Fi is shit over here. Did you send me the email?"

"About five minutes ago. Look, let me share my screen. Can you see it now?"

"Yeah," Mark replied slowly, adjusting his glasses. Henley watched as he silently mouthed the words on the email. "Spelling and grammar aren't the best. He misspelled 'you're,' 'loose,' and 'peace.' Obviously, he wrote 'to' instead of 'too.'"

"What does that tell you about him?"

"To be fair, many people mix up 'to' and 'too,' but 'your' 'and 'lose' could suggest someone with no more than secondary school education or poor spelling skills. He's definitely egotistical. Look at his email handle and name."

"The Burier is what the press called him—or rather, what

Lillian Klein named him. We've never referred to him by that nickname."

"But he's embraced it now. He's owning it. And from this email, he's determined to continue his... 'work.'"

"He hasn't communicated with the police or the press before," Henley noted.

"But he communicated with this Lillian woman. Notice what he called her," Mark pointed out. "Lils. He's comfortable and familiar with her. He's telling her that she didn't do her job, and he's expressing disapproval."

"Do you think they know each other? Have a relationship? She's been writing about him and the murders since 1995."

"Whether it's a relationship in his mind or in reality, I can't say. But this email supports my profile theory on him."

"Tell me," Henley said, uncapping her pen.

"When Elias Piper and Andrew Streeter were murdered, the first question was, where had The Burier been for the past twenty-five years? There are three options. One, he got married, had a family, and lived a stable life until Streeter's appeal triggered him. Two, he aged out."

"Aged out? Is there a retirement age for serial killers?"

Mark smiled, but his expression was serious. "Serial killers are rarely over fifty. The Yorkshire Ripper, Peter Sutcliffe, started killing in his late twenties, Dennis Nilsen in his thirties, and Jeffrey Dahmer was eighteen when he killed his first victim."

"Eighteen?" Henley exclaimed.

"I don't think there's an acceptable age to start a killing spree. But in general, people don't usually hit their late fifties or sixties and suddenly decide to start killing instead of buying a Porsche or Bugatti."

"What about that doctor, Harold Shipman? He killed two hundred and fifty people and he was in his sixties."

"No, he was only fifty-two when arrested. He likely started

killing as early as 1975, when he was around twenty-nine or thirty."

"So, it's a young person's game?"

Mark nodded. "Seems that way. There's a theory that Shipman faked the will of one of his last victims because he planned to take the money and retire at the age of fifty-five. So you can argue that serial killers *do* age out and retire."

"You said three options?"

"I did. The third is that he was in prison. But his fingerprints and saliva would have been taken when he was arrested, which means he'd be on the DNA database."

"Anthony and his team ran samples from the victims, old and new, but found nothing. No matches on Interpol's DNA database either."

"Then you're left with two options: either he's in the UK and Streeter's actions and appeal triggered him, or he moved to another country and never stopped killing."

Henley closed her eyes for a moment. "Do you really think he could have killed somewhere else?"

"It's a possibility, but his specific modus operandi, burying victims alive, exhuming their bodies, sewing their eyes and mouths shut, and the coin ritual, would have alerted the police in that country. We also have the kill list."

"What about the coins in the victims' mouths? The 1995 victims had £2 prototype coins, and one of the new victims had a 1996 Euro football commemorative coin. Stanford thinks it's The Burier's way of gloating."

Mark smiled and cleaned his glasses. "I'll make a criminal profiler out of him yet."

"He won't like that."

"He's not wrong. I'd interpret it as gloating, a sign of one-upmanship. But as for the symbolic meaning of the coins, it's Charon's obol."

"Charon's obol? What's that?"

"It's a term for placing a coin in the mouth. Did you ever study Greek mythology?"

"Does watching *Jason and the Argonauts* count?"

"Absolutely. Charon was Erebus and Nyx's son, ferrying souls of the dead over the Rivers Styx and Acheron, and they paid with a coin in their mouth. Others say the coin symbolizes regret, an apology."

"An apology?" Henley raised an eyebrow. "Are you saying The Burier feels sorry for his actions? That's ridiculous."

"It's a possibility. The coin in the mouth signifies regret. Sewing the victims' eyes and mouths shut, he doesn't want to be seen or criticized. He digs them up because he feels ashamed, and returning them is his twisted way of apologizing."

Henley absorbed the idea that The Burier might be taking responsibility for his actions or seeking redemption. "Or he's just a sick fuck."

"More likely that he's a sick fuck who likes Greek myths."

"So, who am I looking for?"

"A contemporary of Andrew Streeter, a white male now in his late forties or early fifties, who began killing in his early twenties or even younger. Someone who kills for lust, even though sexual activity, except for Tiago Alves, occurred postmortem, a necrophiliac."

"It's bloody disgusting," Henley shuddered, trying not to dwell on the horrors her best friend had endured.

"Looking at the email, despite poor spelling and grammar, I don't think he's of average intelligence. Serial killers, especially white males, tend to target victims of the same race. It makes me suspect that both Melissa Gyimah and Tiago Alves knew him and had some kind of relationship. Their profile doesn't fit."

"She was fifteen," Henley said, suppressing her emotions. "If it doesn't fit, could The Burier not be a white male?"

"Anything's possible," Mark replied softly. "But I think it's unlikely. Henley, are you OK?"

Henley nodded, grateful for the brief interruption of laughter coming from the engineers somewhere in the building.

"I know she was your friend, and this case… Personally, I'm not sure why you're on it."

"Thank you, Mark."

"I didn't mean to—Sorry, that came out wrong."

"A million psychotherapists couldn't help me with this one." Henley saw Ramouter had sent her a message. "I'm trying to make sense of a lot of things in my life right now, but it's not about me. I have to go. Ramouter's at Lewisham station with Lillian Klein."

"And I've got to get ready for this seminar. But don't forget to ask Lillian Klein what The Burier has on her."

Lewisham High Street bustled with buses and cars, flouting the speed limit as they traversed the A20. Market stall vendors shouted about kilos of grapes at half the supermarket price and four plantains for £1.50. The energy was palpable as shoppers bartered down the price of a suitcase, college kids screamed excitedly at their friends, and local drug dealers unsuccessfully tried to blend in near Lewisham shopping center, one phone to their ear and another burner in their hand. Henley always felt Lewisham was a cacophony of voices, languages, accents and dialects, competing with police and ambulance sirens.

"We were about to enter the Limehouse tunnel when she insisted on her lawyer," Ramouter said, passing Henley her bag of satsumas while biting into his beef patty. "She must have her lawyer on speed dial."

"Why do you think she lawyered up?" Henley asked as she took her change, the energy of the streets noticeably dipping as they headed toward Lewisham police station. "It's a voluntary interview. There's obviously more to this than a simple email cc."

"She didn't reveal much during the car ride," Ramouter said, tossing his greasy bag into a bin. "Odd for a journalist emailed by a serial killer who's been in hibernation for twenty-five years."

"He emailed you too," Henley noted, sitting on a silver bench near the front of the station as she handed Ramouter a satsuma. "Mark thinks he probably picked your name at random. Which is good—better to be a random choice rather than a serial killer's intentional focus."

"Ah, I feel so wanted," Ramouter said wearily, sitting down on the bench and stretching his legs.

Henley hesitated, then asked, "So, how are things at home, Salim?"

Ramouter adjusted his posture on the bench and leaned forward, his focus on peeling the satsuma. "I didn't think it was going to be easy, even though we had a life in Bradford together. I knew it would be a big adjustment—not for Ethan; he's fine, happy as Larry. But I knew Michelle would have to adjust."

"Is she struggling?" Henley asked.

"She was, but the new medication she's on, along with cognitive behavioral therapy and her new consultant, is helping. I know the medication isn't a cure, but it's slowing down the progression of the dementia. It's working. I can see that, and Michelle knows that, but it's like she panicked and started accusing me of not supporting her, not being there for her."

Henley nodded thoughtfully. "It's the job, not you. Michelle needs stability right now, and we find stability in routine. There's no routine to your job. Our contracts may say office hours 8:30 a.m. to 6:00 p.m., unless we're on a shift pattern, but you and I both know that's…well, bollocks."

"Aye, it is bollocks."

"You had a routine for three weeks when Michelle and Ethan moved down here. You took time off, and you were with your family. Then you're back at work. You're now a detective constable in the underfunded Serial Crime Unit in southeast London, not a trainee in Bradford. Reality kicks in—"

"And reality is a bitch."

"Absolutely. No one likes reality."

"I'm doing the best I can, but I want Michelle to help herself too, while she can. But that makes me sound like a coldhearted bastard. All I'm doing is trying to help her."

Henley gently placed her hand on Ramouter's back, feeling his muscles tense and then relax as he fought back tears. "I'm not going to pretend that I have any idea how life is for you," Henley said softly, "but you're not a coldhearted bastard, Salim."

Ramouter sniffed and nodded.

"It's going to take a bit of time, OK?"

"Aye, OK," Ramouter replied as he straightened up. "Life, eh?"

"Yep, life," said Henley as she pushed the rest of her satsuma into her mouth.

"Boss, across the road," said Ramouter, standing up quickly. "They've come out of Boots, walking toward the NatWest bank. That's her, Lillian Klein, the brunette wearing jeans and the green blazer."

"I can see her," said Henley as she observed Lillian and another woman waiting for the traffic lights to turn red. "I'm going to hazard a guess and say that must be her lawyer with her, the black woman in the suit holding the coffee cup."

"It has to be," said Ramouter. "They're talking to each other."

"That's our cue to go then," said Henley. "Let's see what Ms. Klein has to say for herself."

"This is a voluntary interview, right?" asked Wendy Reeves, handing Henley her business card.

"As I and my colleague, DC Ramouter, both explained to Ms. Klein," said Henley as she tucked the card into her notebook, "this is a voluntary interview. She's not under arrest, and she does not have to give her consent, but she's here, and you're here."

"Yes, we are. So shall we get on?"

"Of course. Once DC Ramouter has completed the paper-work, we'll be good to go," Henley replied, silently urging Ramouter to take his time. She carefully observed every detail of Lillian Klein's appearance as Ramouter, perhaps sensing her thoughts, diligently completed the paperwork and entered the relevant information on the recording system. Lillian looked ex-hausted, her makeup struggling to hide the signs. Henley jotted one word in her notepad: *stressed*.

"Sorry about that. This machine is a bit temperamental," Ra-mouter said brightly. "Ready now."

"Great," Henley replied. "As your solicitor has probably al-ready explained, Lillian, this interview is voluntary and you're not under arrest, so you're free to leave at any time. You have the right to inform someone you're here and to have legal ad-vice, which you've taken. However, I'm required by law to cau-tion you. Do you understand?"

"Yes, I do," Lillian said, clasping her hands on the table.

"Good. You don't have to say anything, but it may harm your defense if you don't mention something now that you rely on in court. Anything you say may be used as evidence. Is that clear?"

"Yes, it is," Lillian replied, perhaps a bit too brightly.

"In that case, I'll get straight to the point. Can you tell me why the serial killer who has adopted the name 'The Burier' emailed you?"

Lillian's neck flushed red despite the cold air in the room as she clasped and unclasped her hands. "I have no idea who he is, you have to believe that. I really don't."

"That wasn't the question I asked," said Henley. "Why did he email you?"

Lillian produced a plastic wallet from her bag, sliding it across the table. "I started reporting on the original investigation when Stephanie Chalmers went missing in September 1995. I sug-gested there were similarities between her case and the murder investigation of Melissa Gyimah. I worked that out before the police."

"Good for you," Henley replied, then instantly regretted it.

"He first communicated with me after the third victim went missing, Fallon O'Toole," Lillian said as she handed over a small blue envelope. "It was sent to the *Chronicle*'s office, which was on Bouverie Street, off Fleet Street back then."

"You never told the police about this letter?" Henley asked, examining the letter.

Lillian looked away and gave a single-word answer, "No."

"*Dear Lillian*," Henley read aloud. "*I wanted to say thanks for the things you said about me in the paper. How did you know what the police didn't? Fallon is OK. I'm being kind. I'm sending you a present. Yours. Question mark.*" Henley checked the back of the letter and then handed it to Ramouter. "The letter is dated twelfth October 1995 and Fallon was reported missing on the ninth and the first appeal went out on—"

"Almost immediately—on the eleventh. I covered the press conference," Lillian replied.

"And you received this letter, when exactly?"

"Sunday morning. The thirteenth. I'd been in and out of the office all weekend. I can't remember the exact time, but it was in the early evening and the letter was there on my desk."

"There's no stamp," said Ramouter. "How did it get to you?"

"I can only assume that someone left it at the reception desk for me. It wasn't unusual. It happened—and still happens—all the time. Readers send you letters. Sometimes the letters are complaints about whatever article you've written, sometimes there are threats."

"This isn't a complaint or a threat," Henley said, her voice trembling. "This is someone writing to you and telling you that they have Fallon O'Toole."

"I thought it was a hoax," Lillian said defensively. "I'm sure that you've experienced the same thing. Randoms contacting you and telling you that they're Peter Olivier, the Jigsaw Killer."

Both Henley and Ramouter tensed in their seats as Lillian sullenly sat back.

Henley couldn't hide her frustration. "The letter mentioned a gift."

"I didn't know what the letter was talking about until I started receiving other things," Lillian explained, pulling out a yellow travel card pass holder, a silver charm bracelet with only three charms, and a pair of gold creole-style hoop earrings from her bag. Ramouter examined the items, and Henley's stomach churned as she noticed the items' significance.

"I received the silver bracelet first. I didn't know the significance until the police provided further information about what Melissa may have been wearing. The earrings belonged to Stephanie Chalmers. They were the same earrings she was wearing in the photo used for her appeal. I didn't receive those until a week before Penelope Callaghan's body was found in November 1995."

Henley couldn't contain her anger. "And let me get this a hundred percent straight, for the record: you didn't disclose any of this to the investigating officers?"

"You don't understand," Lillian said with pursed lips. "I didn't know what the significance of these items was, not at first. The silver bracelet was sent to my home address, and I didn't open it for weeks because my flatmate at the time had picked it up with her post."

"These items were sent to your home address?" Henley asked incredulously.

"Yes, I know that this won't make sense."

"Well, make it make sense," Henley demanded, her panic growing as Ramouter opened the travel card holder, revealing Melissa's smiling photo. Henley knew exactly what lipstick was on Melissa's lips—a brown Mac lipstick that she'd stolen from her sister's collection. Melissa had stuffed her school tie into her blazer pocket, unbuttoned the top three buttons of her shirt and applied her lipstick a few minutes before she took that photo.

"He improved my stories, made them richer," Lillian murmured softly. "He gave me insights into his mind."

"That's a poor excuse for breaking the law," Henley retorted as Ramouter placed the items into separate evidence bags.

"What are you doing?" Lillian protested. "Those things belong to me."

"How many times did The Burier contact you?" Henley pressed on, ignoring Lillian's protests.

"Back then?" Lillian sought clarification.

"Yes," Henley confirmed.

"He sent me a letter after Tiago Alves's body was found," Lillian explained. She handed over a stained, wrinkled white envelope, which Henley passed to Ramouter as though avoiding contamination. "Someone had dropped tea or coffee on my desk. The letter is a bit smudged, but it's readable."

"Fifth January 1996," Ramouter read aloud. "*Happy New Year, Lils. How was yours? I had company. He's usually more fun than this. I read your stories in the paper to him. What do you think of the police? Running around like headless chickens. Don't spend it all at once.* What did he mean by 'don't spend it all at once'?"

"He sent me a two-pound coin," Lillian revealed. "I don't have it with me here; I couldn't find it when I looked. The police never disclosed that the victims' eyes and mouths had been sewn shut and that a coin was found in their mouths. I only found that out during the trial, and then I realized that the coin he sent me was a prototype of the new £2 coin."

"But again, Lillian, you didn't say anything," Henley said in frustration. "What the hell is wrong with you?"

"You don't understand. You have no idea what it was like for me back then," Lillian defended herself. "I was twenty-two years old when I first started out. You wouldn't believe how hard I had to work to get onto the crime beat in the first place. My editors wanted to dump me on the showbiz desk, writing stupid puff pieces about whatever girl-band member was dating a footballer or covering pointless film premieres of another model turned actor who couldn't even finish a Mr. Men book. I wanted real stories, and I had insight. I had—"

"You're talking absolute shit," Henley interrupted.

"Detective Inspector, I really don't think it's appropriate for you to speak to my client in that manner. She's come here voluntarily to assist you," Wendy interjected.

"Feel free to make a complaint to the IPOC if you feel that hard done by," Henley retorted, nudging Ramouter discreetly.

"Tiago Alves was the last victim," Ramouter stated. "He went missing on the twenty-ninth of December 1995. Is that who the letter was referring to when he wrote, 'I had company. I read your stories in the paper to him'?"

"It had to be. I received the letter in the post; you can see the postmark: SE16. That's the area where Tiago Alves lived. That was the last I heard from... The Burier."

"No letters, no gifts?" Ramouter asked.

"Nothing. Andrew Streeter was arrested for a second time, and he was charged with the murders. I assumed that...well, The Burier was Streeter, and he couldn't communicate with me anymore. He couldn't brag about what he'd been doing because he'd been caught," Lillian explained.

"He didn't communicate with you again?" Henley pressed.

Lillian shook her head.

"You need to speak. This interview is being tape-recorded, you need to speak."

"Sorry, sorry," Lillian stammered. "No, I didn't hear anything from him. Nothing for twenty-five years."

"Did you ever try to see him in prison?" Henley asked.

"You're a journalist. This, as you keep telling us, was your story. You never saw Streeter in prison or made any attempts to communicate with him in twenty-five years?"

"I did in the beginning. I can't tell you how many times, but I tried a couple of times after he was sentenced and again when I wrote the book and when I did the podcast, but he never replied."

"Not once?" Henley asked in disbelief. "The man who had been writing to you, calling you Lils, made no attempt to communicate and basically ghosted you. Is that what you're telling me?"

"Yes. There was nothing from him."

"And you didn't find that strange?"

"I… I didn't think… I got on with my life," Lillian admitted quietly.

"Right. No guilt, just happily getting on with your life, picking up your awards. When you think about it, you could have been instrumental in helping the police catch the real person responsible, and Andrew Streeter wouldn't have had twenty-five years of his life stolen from him. You gave up your morals, principles, and ethics for what, a story?"

Silence filled the room, only interrupted by the muted sounds of activity outside. The red light on the smoke alarm overhead blinked methodically. Henley seethed with anger, her body tensed, and her nerves felt like they'd been set on fire. She didn't need to ask Ramouter to turn his head; she knew the signs of his rising temper. He fidgeted, leaning one way and then the other as if a stone were pressing into his back. He intermittently rubbed the back of his right earlobe and crossed and uncrossed his feet under the table. Henley noticed he hadn't stopped rubbing his right earlobe for the past twenty seconds.

"The Burier," Ramouter said coldly. "The real killer. Do you know who he is?"

Lillian picked up a water bottle in front of her, unscrewed the cap, and took a shaky drink, buying herself time.

"I have no idea," she finally answered. "I'm a journalist. I've been through all my notes, read those letters again, and the best I can come up with is that Andrew Streeter knew him. But that's all I know."

"Did he ever call you?" Ramouter asked. "I know this was back in the mid-nineties, and not everyone was walking around with mobile phones—"

"There were mobile phones in the mid-nineties. I think I had a Motorola Flare."

"Never heard of it," Ramouter snapped. "So did he ever call you, either at home, at the office, or on your Motorola Flare?"

"No. I never spoke to him. There were no calls. But I did think that The Burier had some kind of relationship with the last victim, Tiago Alves, because of what he wrote in his letter. *He's usually more fun than this.* Doesn't that suggest there's something between them, a relationship of some kind?"

Ramouter leaned back, chin in hand. "Have you ever met him?"

"No, of course not," Lillian exclaimed. "I would have…no, no. Never met him."

"But he knew where you lived and worked," Henley pointed out. Something had been niggling at her for a while.

"Obviously, yes."

"Let's jump forward to earlier today," Henley said as she placed the email and photographs of Jake in front of Lillian. "You were cc'd on an email that was sent to yourself and DC Ramouter. That is your colleague, Jake Ryland."

"Yes, that's him. Have you found him yet?"

"No, but that's not how The Burier works. He exhumes and then dumps them. From this photograph, I'm expecting Jake Ryland to appear within the next twenty-four hours. But he wasn't the first victim after the twenty-five year hiatus, was he? That was Elias Piper."

Henley noticed a flicker in Lillian's eyes as she shifted defensively. There was something she hadn't told Wendy. Something Lillian had been keeping to herself.

"What are you hiding, Lilian? How many letters and trophies did The Burier send you?" Henley asked.

"I'm…there's nothing else," Lillian replied as she tilted her head and her complexion paled.

"You're lying to me."

"I promise you that I'm not."

"The Burier communicated with you about each and every one of his original victims from 1995 to 1996. And then, twenty-five years later, he emails you—not your work email, but your personal email—about Jake Ryland. I'm finding it very difficult to believe that this is the first email or communication that you've received from The Burier in the last few weeks. So tell me, have you received any gifts lately?"

Silence hung in the room heavy as concrete as everyone waited for Lillian to respond. She didn't need to speak; her admission was evident on her face. Wendy turned a page in her blue counsel's notebook, poised to make the inevitable intervention.

"Lillian Klein," Henley said calmly. "You're under arrest for perverting the course of justice, assisting an offender." She paused. "Ramouter, do you think we can arrest her for conspiracy to murder?"

Ramouter adjusted in his seat. "I think that might be pushing it a bit."

"You're probably right," Henley conceded as she jotted the time in her notebook. "I'll start again. Lillian Klein, you're under arrest for perverting the course of justice and assisting an offender. You do not have to say anything, but it may harm your defense if you fail to mention when questioned something that you later rely on in court. Anything that you do say may be given in evidence. Do you understand?"

"Shit, shit!" Wendy jumped out of her chair, pushed herself against the black rubber strip on the wall, and activated the alarm as Lillian responded by vomiting on the floor.

37

"Do you really think it was wise to release Lillian Klein?" Stanford asked, glancing at his smartwatch for the fourth time in fifteen minutes. "The woman is a blatant liar."

"I'm aware she's a liar, but she's also strategic," Henley replied, hoisting herself up onto the low wall outside the station. "She mentioned The Burier sent her gifts but only disclosed personal items from three victims. What about the others? I can't believe he'd communicate with her about these new victims but not send her anything."

"But the search of her house hasn't produced anything," Stanford pointed out.

"No, it hasn't," Henley acknowledged. "And the *Chronicle*'s lawyers are currently objecting to our warrant application to search her desk at the newspaper's offices."

"She probably wouldn't be stupid enough to leave evidence in her office desk," Stanford commented. They both heard a piercing alarm followed by an abrupt stop.

"Sorry," an engineer on the station steps apologized. "Just

doing the last alarm checks. We'll be out of your hair in an hour."

"About bloody time," Stanford grumbled. "Feels like they've been here forever. Supposed to finish last Tuesday, and it's Wednesday now."

"It's all for your safety, you miserable git," Henley retorted, playfully squeezing his shoulder.

"It's giving us a false sense of security, in my opinion," Stanford insisted. "They make it seem like they're invested in the SCU, and then they sell the building to some developer, and I end up in Ilford police station."

"Ilford doesn't even have a police station," Henley corrected him.

"You know what I mean," Stanford replied. "So, where is she now, our lying journalist?"

"I have officers keeping an eye on her. Barker somehow got a couple of DCs from Walworth," Henley informed him. "She went home last night after being released, then to a local Sainsbury's around 9:00 p.m., bought wine, and had a pizza delivery. She also went for a run around 6:30 a.m."

"Did she meet anyone during that run?" Stanford asked.

"No idea, our officers couldn't follow her," Henley replied. "Now, what's bothering you so much? You've been checking your watch every five minutes, and it's making me anxious."

Stanford raised his head and emitted a low groan. "It's this adoption thing. I made the mistake of suggesting to Glen that maybe we should take a break. The whole process, the meetings, assessments, even social services demanding copies of documents they already had from three months ago. Then they match us with a child and you think it's finally happening. But something always comes up—some random family member comes forward claiming they want the child. All sorts of chaos. Glen's worn out, I'm worn out."

"And it's incredibly stressful."

"That's a fucking understatement," Stanford replied, leaning forward while Henley rubbed his back. "I got home last night and Glen laid into me. I completely forgot about a meeting with the new social worker. I was supposed to leave early, but this case… We had a massive argument. He accused me of not being committed, of not wanting a family with him. I told him he was being overdramatic and selfish."

"Oh, Paul," Henley sympathized.

"There was more said. I might have accused him of being controlling; I can't quite remember. You know the saying 'never go to bed angry'? Well, he went to bed angry, in the spare room. He was still pissed this morning, and I walked out."

"And I assume he's not responding to your texts?"

"He's fucking sulking," Stanford replied bitterly. "And don't you dare defend him. He was out of line."

Henley sighed, hopped off the wall, and stood in front of Stanford. "Look at me and be honest. Do you genuinely want a child, a real family beyond you, Glen, and the cat?"

"Of course I do. How could you even ask that? You know how much I adore kids. Hell, I'm waiting for the day you finally keel over so my godfather duties can kick in, and I can have Emma."

"Piss off," Henley said, playfully punching Stanford in the chest.

"Oi, be careful," Stanford teased as he lost his balance and gripped the wall. "I always knew you had the potential to kill someone."

"Sorry, but I had to ask. I wouldn't be a good friend if I nodded and agreed without questioning anything."

"I know, I know, and I'll say it again: I do want a family with Glen. I want kids, maybe more than one. I knew it would be challenging, but I didn't expect it to be this tough."

"Would you like a hug?" Henley offered.

Stanford looked left and right. "Nah. I can't ruin my reputation by bawling on the street."

"You don't have a reputation," Henley quipped.

"What about you? How are things at home?"

Henley chose to remain nonchalant and not tell Stanford that Rob had been offered a new job in Manchester and that he'd canceled dinner plans to celebrate their wedding anniversary.

"Same ol', same ol'," Henley said. Spotting Ezra's approach, she shifted the conversation. "Hey, can you smell smoke?"

Stanford confirmed, "Yeah, I can. Can't see anything though."

"I'm going to put a tag on you," said Ezra as he made his way toward Henley and Stanford. "You had me looking all over the building for you like a—"

"Don't finish that sentence," Henley warned.

"You really know how to take the fun out of things," said Ezra. "Anyway, I'm going to the kebab shop."

"Ooh, can you get me a chicken shish kebab, chips and a Sprite?" Stanford handed Ezra twenty pounds.

"Cool. Do you want anything, boss?"

"Lamb donor, salad, no onions, chips and a full-fat Coke," said Henley as the sound of sirens filled the air, and a fire engine sped past. "So, other than taking our lunch orders, any other updates?"

"I've done some digging on the photos and emails Ramouter and Klein received. Give me ten minutes."

"What have you found?" Henley asked, curious.

"Ten minutes," Ezra said with a smug grin. He held up his hands, flashed his fingers twice, turned and jogged away.

"It smells like my flat on a Saturday morning in here," Eastwood commented, scrunching her face as she sat at her desk with a pasta salad.

"I did offer to get you something," Ezra replied as he wiped his hands with a wet napkin. "You must be ill or something; you never say no to a kebab. Anyway, let me show you."

Henley and the rest of the team swiveled their chairs to face the smart screen.

"I'll start with the email that Ramouter and Lillian Klein received," said Ezra as he displayed the email on the screen. "Pretty standard stuff. The Burier created a Google email account with all fake info, named himself 'Guess Who,' used Streeter's sentencing date as his birthdate, created a password, and voila, he has an email. But, you know, people are stupid. I've got the IP address. The internet provider is Pan Media, but whoever handles their online security is, well, let's say he's good. So, I'm doing my best to, you know, break through." Ezra switched the screen to Lillian Klein's inbox.

"Did Klein give us access to her emails or phone?" Pellacia asked.

"We've got her phone, but she refused to hand over her account details and passcode," Ramouter replied between bites of kebab.

"Boss, I honestly don't understand why you bother asking these questions," Ezra chimed in, rolling his eyes. Pellacia simply shrugged. "The point is, the email The Burier sent to Klein and Ramouter wasn't his first. He sent three emails."

"We need to bring her back in," Henley declared. "I'll have the officers watching her arrest her."

"Finally," Ezra said loudly, "about those photos they received. They were cropped, but I managed to revert them."

Henley stood up, and the screen displayed a photograph of Jake Ryland, partially exposed in the grave. However, the grave appeared smaller now and seemed to be in the middle of a construction site. A shovel was visible on the left, and mounds of dirt and gravel resembled miniature mountains.

"It could be a builder's yard or maybe a terribly neglected garden," Eastwood suggested hesitantly.

"It doesn't offer a complete panoramic view, but here's the thing," Ezra explained. "This photo was taken with a phone camera, and most phones these days have really good location settings. Specifically, it's an older model iPhone, and I've managed to pinpoint a location. Well, not down to a specific address, but I can give you the general area."

"Where is it?" Pellacia asked.

"It's in a place called Sandgate, near Folkestone. There's a marina nearby, if that helps."

"Boss, didn't the soil expert suggest somewhere coastal?" Ramouter remembered.

"Yeah, she did," Henley confirmed. "Ez, are you sure you can't narrow it down more than just Sandgate geographically?"

"If it were one of those newer phones, I could pinpoint an actual street," Ezra said regretfully. "With this, all I can tell you is that this geezer was buried somewhere in Sandgate, but I'll keep digging, no pun intended."

"Thanks, Ezra," Henley said as her phone began to ring. "Hello, yes, this is DI Henley. OK. Right, right. Where was the body found? Nunhead. We're on our way."

"Is it Jake Ryland?" Pellacia asked as Henley hung up the phone.

"A body matching Jake Ryland's description has been found on a building site in Nunhead," said Henley, grabbing her bag.

"What about his face?"

"What do you think?" Henley replied, and both she and Ramouter left the SCU.

The fire brigade had extinguished the fire over twelve hours ago, but the lingering stench of smoke, burnt rubber, and gasoline hung in the air. The traffic slowed near the blackened, twisted car wreckage as curious onlookers snapped photos. Red-and-white warning tape encircled lampposts and railings spared from the fire's fury. Three firefighters waited in the fire en-

gine across the road while the fire investigators examined the
scorched site. Absent were ambulance service personnel, as there
was no life to save, only a corpse to retrieve.

"It's kind of perfect, isn't it?" Ramouter commented as they
observed the site from across the street.

"What do you mean?" Henley asked, inhaling the toxic air
reluctantly.

"I mean, The Burier placed the body in the middle of an abandoned building site that had been closed for eighteen months.
There was no guarantee anyone would've found the body, if he
hadn't started the fire."

"But look around," Henley pointed out. They crossed the
road and walked toward the scene. "He'd be incredibly exposed
here. Shops on one side, houses on the other, and a busy street
right opposite. There's a primary school nearby, and we're on a
bus route. It's too risky. And remember what time the fire was
reported: 6:04 a.m."

"Maybe he enjoys the challenge," Ramouter mused. "Think
about it, he's been taking more risks with every crime scene."

"Why change things now? Why dump the body here and
then set a car on fire? Why all the drama and desperate need
for attention?" Henley wondered.

Ramouter shrugged as they approached the burnt remains of
the wooden hoarding.

"I can't see any CCTV cameras on the street," Henley said,
looking upward and scanning the opposite side of the road.

"We're on a bus route," said Ramouter, handing Henley a
forensic oversuit. "We can check with the bus company and see
what buses came past around the time the fire was set."

"Are you ready?" Henley asked, noticing Ramouter's hesitation near the site entrance.

"I don't think I'll ever be ready for a crime scene with a dead
body in the middle, no matter how many times I have to do
this," Ramouter admitted.

"How high do you think this hoarding is?" Henley asked, examining the tall barrier.

"Close to three meters," Ramouter estimated. "And with anti-climb paint and those rotating spikes, climbing over is impossible."

"So how did The Burier get in? The security company claimed no alarms were activated until the car exploded."

"Remember the CCTV footage at Jake's apartment the night he disappeared?" Ramouter recalled. "The Burier entered without any difficulty, no alarms triggered. He had access, likely a key."

For the first time in months, the Evelina Road development site was bustling with activity as Anthony's forensic team combed the area. The unfinished luxury flats and commercial units stood silent, wrapped in tattered plastic, supported by scaffolding. Pallets of bricks leaned against a roofless Portakabin. Puddles and a trail of footprints led to Jake's body.

"He's been dead for at least forty-eight hours," Linh reported, examining the body. Henley and Ramouter made their way carefully around the yellow exhibit markers on the ground.

Jake was on his back, his arms were spread out by his side. Animal teeth marks could be seen on his discolored and bloating flesh. The skin on his face was particularly swollen around the areas where his eyes and mouth had been sewn shut.

"It's Wednesday. Forty-eight hours would mean he was killed sometime on Monday morning which ties in with the metadata that Ezra retrieved from the photos that Ramouter received," Henley noted.

"The Burier didn't keep him for long," mused Ramouter as he surveyed the site. "He went missing on Friday night, and Monday morning, he's in the ground."

"But how long has he been here, waiting for someone to find him?" asked Henley.

"If it helps, I don't believe he's been out here overnight," chimed in Linh, making a final note on her tablet. "If it were longer, we'd see more decomposition and foxes or other scavengers would've had a field day during the night."

"Hold on. Are you suggesting that The Burier dumped Jake's body yesterday, not necessarily in the middle of the night, and then waited until this morning to set the car on fire?" questioned Ramouter.

"But where did he wait?" Henley mused, stepping further away from the body and scanning the surroundings. "Did he hang around on the street or was he waiting in the car?"

"Or did he never leave?" Ramouter added cautiously. "Didn't Dr. Ryan mention that most arsonists like to stick around and watch the firefighters deal with the fire they created? Look at the number of people out there watching. What if The Burier is in the crowd, watching us?"

Henley couldn't make out the expressions on the faces of the distant onlookers, the crowd made up of people of different ethnicities and ages.

"I'm going to head out," Linh said, stepping away from Jake's body and removing her mask. She raised her head to take a breath but quickly closed her mouth, realizing the air was toxic. "I'll let you know once he's at my place."

"Linh," Henley called after her as she noticed Linh wasn't her usual self, full of enthusiasm and inappropriate quips. Henley walked with her toward the exit. "Are you OK?"

"You know I don't usually let things get to me," Linh began. "Other than the usual office politics and bureaucratic nonsense, I don't let the mechanics of this job affect me. I mean, I wouldn't last two minutes if I couldn't shut myself down and get on with finding out how the people who end up on my examination table died. But I don't know...two fourteen-year-old boys were brought in last night, dead because of some stupid viral social media prank. And then this guy—he looks so young, Anj. He was probably making plans for his future, just like those two kids

I have to cut open in a couple of hours. But someone treated him…treated him as though he was disposable, as if his life had no value."

"You're allowed—" Henley began, searching for the right words to comfort her friend. "You're allowed to feel something sometimes, Linh. You're allowed to have a moment. I think I've been guilty of taking it for granted that this stuff doesn't bother you, like it's your superpower?"

"Superpower? Living with the dead?" Linh made a face, and the returning sunlight revealed a subtle spark in her eyes. "I'd rather shoot bolts of lightning from my hands, thank you very much."

"I don't know how you do it."

"I don't know how you do it either," Linh admitted. "To me, coming to a crime scene is the easy part. The hard bit is dealing with the families. All that emotion, all that hurt and those questions." Linh shivered. "I don't think my heart could take it."

"What exactly is he playing at?" Stanford questioned, pacing back and forth from his desk to the window. "Elias Piper, Andrew Streeter, Caroline Swann, and now this poor guy, Jake Ryland. Why him?"

"That's a good question," Eastwood replied. "As far as I can tell, Ryland has no connection to the other three victims. The only thing we've got on him is that he works with Lillian Klein at the *Chronicle*."

"All the others had some interaction or relationship with Streeter," Henley noted, turning away from the whiteboard, where photographs of Jake Ryland's body now joined the grim collection of victims of The Burier. "But the question is, why Jake and not Lillian Klein? She's the one who's been writing about him for years, following his every move until he went quiet."

"But she didn't write about him when he came back," Eastwood pointed out, typing away at her keyboard. The ancient printer in the corner roared to life. "You mentioned she was present at the first press conference when Elias Piper's body was found and we officially took on the case, right?"

"Exactly," Henley confirmed as Eastwood retrieved her printed document.

"So why wasn't she the one to write the first article about The Burier if she's been covering him from day one?" Eastwood said as she handed Henley the document. "Jake's name appears on the byline for the first and second articles about The Burier, with no mention of Lillian. Her name only shows up in the subsequent articles after Jake went missing."

"Do you think Lillian somehow influenced The Burier to target Jake because he stole her story?" asked Henley.

"Or The Burier went after Jake because he was pissed that Lillian hadn't penned the first two stories about him," Eastwood proposed.

"He's territorial about Lillian," Henley concluded as she handed the document back to Eastwood.

"Do you think she's in danger?" Stanford asked.

Henley shook her head. "If The Burier believed Lillian was a threat, she'd have been a victim long ago. Now she's just a means to keep him in the public eye."

"He's doing an excellent job of that on his own, without making friends with a bloody journalist."

"So, what's next?" Stanford wondered.

"We need to track down this Georgina Bridges," Henley announced, glancing at the door where Pellacia had just entered, a grim expression on his face.

"Good luck with that," said Stanford. "We've scoured the case files, DVLA database and checked with the Home Office—nothing. Ezra even tried, but there are too many Georgina Bridges out there, and most don't fit the age range."

"What about HMRC?" Eastwood asked. "Everyone receives

a National Insurance number four months before they turn sixteen and you're stuck with that for life. You can't change it, you can't work legitimately without it and HMRC don't give you a new one even if you've forgotten it."

"HMRC confirmed that a national insurance number has never been allocated to Georgina Bridges," Stanford explained wearily. "Georgina Bridges could be a made-up name and a made-up story. Just another crank looking for attention."

"But what if she isn't?" Pellacia asked, taking off his jacket and sitting down at Henley's desk. "What if we've approached this case all wrong? Maybe he's trying to find out where Georgina Bridges is."

Henley turned and faced the whiteboard head on. "But what's the likelihood of this Georgina Bridges suddenly emerging and telling everyone who The Burier is after all this time?"

"You could have said the same about Streeter—twenty-five years in prison, keeping his mouth shut. But things have changed now," said Pellacia. "She might not be safe."

"You think all this is The Burier's way of trying to track down one person?" Eastwood asked incredulously, gesturing at the whiteboard.

"Maybe," Pellacia replied, looking increasingly grave. "What if he's manipulating us to do his dirty work for him?"

38

Ramouter immediately regretted accepting tea when he noticed faint traces of lipstick on the side of the mug, resting on a table that seemed untouched by disinfectant or furniture polish. Denise Price's house was an abyss of clutter. A smoke alarm, whose battery seemed to be on its last legs, emitted an incessant beep. Denise herself appeared as neglected as her home. The once-plush rose faux velvet three-piece sofa had sunken over time and was now coated in a layer of cat hairs. The patterned wallpaper, torn in places, was a sickly yellow hue from cigarette smoke. Denise sat across from Ramouter, tugging at her overstretched brown T-shirt. Her hair was haphazardly piled on top of her head in a messy bun, and her makeup seemed to belong to another era, twenty years outdated. Ramouter wondered if Denise could even see him through her thick eyelashes, which grazed her glasses every time she blinked, leaving smudges of brown mascara on the lenses.

"My brother's been dead two weeks, and you're showing up

now," Denise said, grabbing a cigarette box. "Murdered in his sickbed."

"I'm truly sorry for your loss," Ramouter said, discreetly moving his tea behind flowers.

"Are you? Are you really?" Denise asked, opening and closing a matchbox. "My brother, dead, poisoned like vermin."

"You never visited him in prison, not once," Ramouter said calmly. "Not even when he was sick with cancer."

"I had my reasons," Denise replied, sipping her tea loudly.

"Care to share those reasons?"

"Visiting a serial killer in prison? No thanks," Denise scoffed. "It was bloody embarrassing. It would've condoned his actions. We weren't that close anyway."

"You're his half sister," Ramouter noted.

"Same dad, different mothers," Denise said bitterly. "Dad had kids everywhere, maybe more ready to crawl out the woodwork."

"Why now?" Ramouter asked. "It's only since the Court of Appeal decision and his death that you've been making noise about a miscarriage of justice."

"How is wanting justice for my brother making noise?" Denise said, eyeing the TV.

"I heard you were trying to sell your story to the papers."

"I was, and then I realized the real money is in documentaries or one of those podcasts. People love stories like this, an innocent man locked away for life while the real killer is out there. I can tell the world how you only wanted to talk to me once you realized you fucked up."

Ramouter said carefully, "I'm not from the original investigation, but we're trying our best to find his murderer."

"Will I get paid for helping?" Denise asked, her eyes lighting up.

"It's not about payment," Ramouter replied.

"That's why you lot struggle," Denise scoffed. "Expecting people to risk their lives for nothing."

"Are you at risk?" Ramouter asked, looking for a clean spot on the table for his notebook.

"Of course not," Denise hesitated, her uncertainty evident.

"Let's get started," Ramouter said, giving up on the table and resting the notebook on his knee. "Tell me about your brother and the people he was hanging around with at the time of the murders."

"I told you, we weren't that close," said Denise, striking a match and lighting her cigarette.

"You didn't spend any time together growing up?"

"Well, yeah, I used to see him every weekend and summer holidays when I would stay with our dad at his house in Rotherhithe."

"As I understand it, your brother was living there from 1993 until his arrest."

"Yeah, he and my dad worked at a printing press in Wapping back then," Denise remembered. "Andrew really liked it there."

"And you were fourteen in '93?"

"Yeah," Denise said. "Mum lived in Bermondsey, down the Blue."

"What's the blue?" Ramouter asked.

"You're not from round here, are you? It's around Blue Anchor Lane in Bermondsey, we call it the Blue," Denise explained.

"So, what can you tell me about who Andrew was hanging around with back then?"

Denise took a hard drag of her cigarette and blew the smoke toward Ramouter. "I'm not being funny, but I didn't keep a logbook of Andy's mates."

Ramouter coughed as the smoke caught in his throat. "How about the victims?"

"I never saw any of those girls," Denise replied quickly.

"What about the male victim, Tiago Alves?"

"Oh, I saw him."

"I thought you said you didn't keep a logbook of your brothers' mates?"

"I said I saw him. I didn't say he was Andy's mate. We've got another brother called Fergus who was living with my dad for a while. Fergus was a cokehead. That's where I first saw Tiago. Selling Fergus his drugs."

"Tiago was a drug dealer?" Ramouter clarified.

"Yeah, a rubbish one," Denise said as she brushed away the ash from her cigarette. "He was always getting caught by the police."

"Where's your brother Fergus now?"

"He sorted himself out, got a decent job, got married to a geezer. Did not see that coming. They've got a couple of kids and pissed off to Canada."

"Did you ever talk to Tiago?"

"Tiago never used to talk to me. I was the annoying little sister."

Ramouter jotted down "drug dealer" next to Tiago Alves's name. "You must remember a few more of Andrew's mates."

Denise leaned back and scratched her head. "There were a couple of others," she said. "Jerry Tucker. He and Andy used to play pool together, and another guy called Declan used to hang around, but I think Declan was more Tiago's mate than Andy's."

"The case files said that Tiago worked on a fruit and veg stall in East End Market."

"Yeah, right," Denise said with a snort. "His mum owned the stall, and he used to help out, but he was a proper thief. If it wasn't nailed down, he would steal it. That's how Andrew ended up caught up in all of their shit that summer, and Dad had to kick him out for a bit."

"What shit are you talking about?" Ramouter asked, intrigued.

"The dodgy coin business," Denise said in a hushed tone. "Our dad worked with Declan's dad, Archie, in the printing press. Archie was dodgy as fuck, and he did a bunch of robberies, and got Andrew involved."

"What type of robberies?"

"Cash-in-transit. I don't know why Andy got involved; he wasn't like that. Anyway, he got involved. I remember that one day Andy gave me a bunch of £1 coins and some of those coins you get for a special occasion. I tried to spend the £1 coins in Woolworths, and they said they were fake. I was so—"

"Hold on, Andrew gave you fake coins. Do you know where they came from?"

"He didn't tell me, but it must have been from a robbery because the next thing I knew, it was all kicking off at Dad's, and the police arrested Andy, Declan, Tiago, and Declan's dad, Archie, for robbery."

Ramouter bit the inside of his cheek as he skimmed through the notes about Tiago Alves and the connections he had with Andrew Streeter. There were no notes about a robbery arrest in the mid-nineties.

"You didn't know," Denise observed with surprising insight. "You don't know about everything that happened."

"No," Ramouter conceded.

"Andrew was an informant," Denise said with disdain, flicking the stub of her cigarette with disappointment. "And where we're from, being a snitch is one step away from being a pedophile. I knew Declan, his dad, Tiago, and Andrew were involved in the cash-in-transit jobs. They would rob the vans when they were parked up. Archie was the driver, and Declan and Andrew would jump out and rob the vans. They would rock up in a little Fiesta, and Tiago would be on a motorbike. One job too many because the police were onto them. They chased Andrew back to my dad's and literally, and I mean literally, caught him washing the money in the sink trying to get the blue dye off it."

"So, he was arrested?"

"I'll never forget it. It was a Thursday; I turned up after school and the Old Bill was everywhere. Andrew was arrested, and somehow, don't ask me how, he was let out on bail. Two days after that, on a Sunday afternoon, this policeman turns up. He was quite good-looking and young. I didn't think he was a copper at first."

"When exactly was this?" asked Ramouter.

"Back end of '93, maybe the summer. I can't remember exactly. Larsen his name was, and he literally dragged Andrew out of the house."

"Larsen," Ramouter said, his voice rising slightly, feeling a familiar sense of discomfort creeping across the back of his neck.

"Larsen, the prick, dragged my brother out into his car and—"

"Can we go back to the robberies for a minute? You mentioned Declan's dad Archie drove a Fiesta. Can you remember the color?"

"Blue. Not dark blue, but not bright blue either, and it was old. Declan and Andy picked me up at school in it a few times."

"And this car definitely belonged to Declan or his dad?" When Denise nodded, Ramouter continued, "What was Declan's last name?"

"Weathers," Denise said quickly. "I've got a head for these things. Long story short, this Larsen copper convinced Andrew to go QE, that's—"

"Queen's Evidence," Ramouter cut in. "So, Andrew agreed to give evidence against Declan and Archie for the robbery case."

"Snitch. That's what he agreed to do," Denise replied. "Inform on everyone, and they would drop the charges against Andrew to something minor. But the day of the trial, Andrew bottled it, refused to give any evidence, and the main case collapsed. I think they could only do Archie for handling stolen goods and possession of the dodgy coins in the end, and Tiago and Declan got away with it."

"And your brother," Ramouter paused as he flipped back

through his notes to find Streeter's list of previous convictions. "He got six months for—"

"Handling stolen goods. I think he spent a couple of months in Brixton prison, and then he was out. Got given a hero's welcome in the pub by my dad because it turned out that his son wasn't a snitch after all."

"So, Declan Weathers." Ramouter circled the name with his pen. "What happened to him? Did he keep in touch with your brother after the…the court case?"

"I think so. My brother wasn't like me," Denise said disappointedly. "He was easily led, know what I mean? The only time he ever showed any backbone was when he refused to give evidence in court. But the last I heard, Declan died. Got run over in north London."

"Where was Tiago Alves in all of this?"

Denise shrugged. "No idea. He's Portuguese, so the rumor was that his family shipped him back home, but then he came back. Idiot. He should have stayed in the Algarve. He would probably be alive. Right, is there anything else? Because I've got to get to work in a bit," Denise said, picking up Ramouter's mug of untouched tea and standing.

"Just one more question. Despite what you said earlier, you seem to have known your brother's friends quite well. Does the name Georgina Bridges mean anything to you?" asked Ramouter, standing up too.

"Georgina…oh, do you mean Georgie? I don't know if her last name was Bridges, but Declan had a friend, or maybe it was Tiago. I was never sure if she was his girlfriend or not, but she looked the type who would give it up to anybody, if you get what I mean. I think my brother had a thing for her. She came round to my dad's a couple of times."

"Can you remember how old she was?"

"Everyone looked like a grown-up to me back then, but she was probably about twenty."

"And can you remember the last time you saw or spoke to her?"

There was a look of intense concentration on Denise's face. "It was sometime in the Christmas holidays because I wasn't at school. Right after that black girl disappeared."

●

39

Pellacia reread Ramouter's message for the third time, now on his way to James Larsen's home, uninvited. A round-robin email from Ramouter confirmed a history between James Larsen and Andrew Streeter dating back over a year before Melissa Gyimah's disappearance. Parking in front of Larsen's impressive Tudor house in Chigwell, Pellacia glanced at a two-year-old red Land Rover in the driveway. Despite Larsen's almost–£94,000 salary before early retirement, Pellacia had his doubts whether he could afford this kind of lifestyle.

Pellacia rang Larsen's doorbell. A moment later he heard a dog's aggressive barking. Turning around, Pellacia saw Larsen clutching his dog's lead in the driveway.

"You looked like a double-glazing salesman from where I stand," Larsen said, approaching Pellacia, a green shopping bag in one hand and the dog's lead in the other.

"I doubt double-glazing salesmen do cold calls these days." Pellacia restrained himself from addressing Larsen as "sir."

"Why are you here, Pellacia?" Larsen asked, glancing at the street.

"It's just me," Pellacia replied. "No sting operation or reporters hiding in the hedges, if that's your concern."

"Why would I worry about reporters?" Larsen's voice hinted at uncertainty.

"I'd worry about more than reporters if I were you," Pellacia said, patting Larsen's dog. "He's quite a softy, really."

"What do you want, Pellacia?"

"Maybe we can discuss it inside."

"I'd rather you not be in my house," Larsen said stiffly, walking past Pellacia and unlocking his front door.

"Fine by me," Pellacia said, leaning against the doorway. "I don't give a shit where we talk. I want answers about Streeter. Why were you hell-bent on pinning the murders on him when you knew he didn't do it? You knew you didn't have the evidence, so you fabricated it."

"What are you talking about?" Larsen said. "I know it's hard to accept that Rhimes wasn't a saint, but you heard what the court—"

Pellacia grabbed Larsen by his collar and pushed him against the door frame.

"Get the hell off me," Larsen cried, grabbing at Pellacia's hands.

"Dr. Leslie Fry already confessed that you paid him to falsify DNA results to frame Streeter," Pellacia said calmly, making Larsen pale. "We also know Streeter was your informant until he screwed up your cash-in-transit robbery case."

"You have no fucking idea... Let go of me!"

Pellacia twisted Larsen's shirt tighter. "You knew Streeter was associated with The Burier."

"He *was* The Burier!" Larsen exclaimed.

"Bullshit," Pellacia retorted, pushing Larsen harder against the door. "You seized the chance to frame him for murder after he messed up your case." He let go suddenly, and Larsen fell to the floor. "You're a liar and a bent copper. We've got you. I know you think that retiring early means you won't get done for corruption and misconduct, but you're wrong."

"I did my job," Larsen said, gasping for air. "I wasn't bent and didn't pay anyone to mess around with the DNA results. I don't care what that fucker Fry told you."

"What about Georgina Bridges? She approached you, and you dismissed her."

"She had nothing worthwhile to say," Larsen claimed. "You can dig all you want, try to resurrect old ghosts, but the Court of Appeal and CCRC were after your beloved Rhimes."

"Fuck you," Pellacia snapped and started to walk away.

"Rhimes was a piece of shit, and you knew it," Larsen said, regaining confidence and following Pellacia. "The only officer they pointed fingers at was Rhimes. And he was seen by a jailer threatening Streeter when he was sentenced," Larsen said, finding his stride. "He paid Bridges two grand, not me."

Pellacia stopped dead in his tracks, recalling what Henley had told him after her confession about Kerry Huggins.

"Two grand," Pellacia said, turning to face Larsen, who now looked fearful. A silver Audi R8 pulled slowly into the driveway. "There was no mention of a bribe in the CCRC application or in the court hearing."

"My wife is here," Larsen said, panicked now.

"The only way you'd know it was a two-grand bribe is if you were the one who offered it," Pellacia deduced.

"You don't know what you're talking about," Larsen said, now afraid.

"You bribed Streeter's alibi witness," Pellacia said, the pieces falling into place and catching Larsen in a lie.

"Oh, for God's sake, Streeter's alibi witness was Georgi—"

"Can you help with the bags, love?" Larsen's wife asked. She frowned. "Is everything OK?"

"Everything is fine, Mary," Larsen assured as he swiftly distanced himself from Pellacia and approached the woman in her late fifties. She was wearing a vibrant yellow shift dress and designer sneakers, clutching a shopping bag on the verge of overflowing.

"Michaela mentioned she'd be coming down later with the baby, so I thought I'd grab some bits for dinner," Mary said. "Who's your friend?"

"Not a friend, Mrs. Larsen," Pellacia responded cheerfully, masking the forced politeness with a warm smile. "But there were times when it did feel like I lost one. Your husband used to be my boss. He always insisted I should drop by if I were in the area, so here I am."

"How lovely," Mary replied, clearly appreciative and relieved. "I initially mistook you for that dreadful reporter who's been hounding James. A dreadful little man called Callum."

"Callum O'Brien," Pellacia confirmed. "Yes, he can be quite a nuisance, especially when he believes he's on to a story. Like a dog with a bone. If you'd like, I can speak with him and ask him to leave my old govnor alone. What do you reckon, sir?"

"No need, really," Larsen responded tersely.

"Oh, it won't be a problem, sir," Pellacia insisted, his gaze fixed intently on Larsen until Larsen had no choice but to look away. "I'll have a strong word with Callum O'Brien, and I'll instruct my team to handle Georgina Bridges."

Pellacia flashed another smile, observing the internal struggle playing out on Larsen's face, all while Mary watched the two men with curiosity.

"Who's Georgina Bridges?" Mary blurted out, unable to tolerate the tense silence and mounting anticipation.

"Someone the govnor used to work with," Pellacia explained. "Although I suspect she may have changed her name. Isn't that right, sir?"

"So, we've received word from the fire investigator," Stanford began as he reached for a tube of Pringles on Eastwood's desk. "Remember, this is only the preliminary report. The fire was deliberately started, though we didn't need confirmation on that. However, they managed to recover the chassis number."

"How on earth did they manage that?" Ramouter asked, tearing his eyes away from his computer screen. "The car looked like it had been charred beyond recognition. I would have thought the fire would have obliterated the chassis number."

"Not in this case," Stanford explained. "The number had been laser-etched onto the engine. And here's the kicker—the chassis number matched a car registered to Caroline Swann." Stanford distributed copies of the email from the fire investigator and DVLA records for Caroline Swann's car.

"We're talking about an eight-year-old Volkswagen Passat Estate, previously owned by two others before Swann's ex-husband passed it on to her after their breakup."

"I'm chasing CCTV footage from the surrounding borough councils, National Highways, and TfL," Eastwood chimed in as she activated the smartboard, displaying a series of CCTV images. "The first sighting we have of the car is at the Lordship Lane junction in Dulwich at 5:23 a.m. yesterday, which aligns with Linh's observation that Ryland's body was left out for no more than twenty-four hours."

"Do we know which direction the Passat came from?" Henley asked as she approached the smartboard. The pavements were deserted, with only the glow of a stuck-on-red traffic light and lampposts for illumination. Although the number plate was visible, the rain made it impossible to see through the windscreen and identify the driver.

"The car turned right onto East Dulwich Road, so it could have come from East Dulwich or Herne Hill," Eastwood answered, hitting play on the next image. "Cameras tracked it down to Evelina Road, where the driver adhered to speed limits and obeyed traffic signals. The next image is from a passing P12 bus, capturing the car parking in front of the building site at 5:29 a.m. We can only partially see the number plate, but it's definitely Caroline's car."

Henley grimaced as the almost-blurred image of the car in front of the building site appeared on the screen.

"But we hit the jackpot, thanks to uniformed officers conducting door-to-door interviews across the road," Eastwood continued, displaying another image on the smartboard. "Directly opposite the building site is a block of flats. Six tenants in the block have kitchen window cameras that face Evelina Road. A few months ago, a burglar attempted to break into one of the flats. Here's footage of our guy getting out of the car."

Henley held her breath as Caroline's car appeared on screen, parking haphazardly in front of the chained gate. A man dressed entirely in black, wearing a black hat, exited the car. "Look across the road," Henley muttered to herself as the man moved around to the trunk, scanned left and right, and then turned his back to the camera.

"Is that a suitcase?" Stanford asked, incredulous, as they watched the man wrestle a large black case from the trunk.

"How tall was Jake Ryland?" Ramouter asked, pulling up the postmortem report on his computer while they continued to watch the man wheel the case to the front of the car. "He was five eleven. So he managed to squeeze a nearly six-foot-tall man into that suitcase," Ramouter confirmed as the man disappeared into the building site.

"He reemerged twenty-eight minutes later and turned right, indicating he was headed toward either New Cross or Peckham," Eastwood added.

"That's yesterday morning," Henley noted. "What about this morning when the fire brigade was called?"

"Give me a sec," Eastwood said with a wry smile. "There's more. The 999 call for the fire brigade came in at 6:04 a.m. Here's footage from the same camera across the road."

"He's holding a gas can," Stanford observed as the CCTV

footage played out. A man dressed in black, head lowered, hurried to the front passenger side of Caroline's car. The hazard lights flashed, the alarm activated, and the man opened the door. Seconds later, he dashed across the road toward East Dulwich Road. Orange flames appeared in the rear windscreen of the car, and a minute later, they broke through the glass as the fire raged.

"It may seem like midday, but it was early morning, right at the start of rush hour," Ramouter said, shaking his head.

"Do we know where he went?" Henley asked, glancing to the door as Pellacia entered the room, jacket in hand and sweating.

"Nope," Eastwood replied, shutting down her screen, and the smartboard went dark. "As I said, I'm awaiting more footage, but I wouldn't be surprised if we have a clear face shot, especially if he's on foot."

"But the bottom line is, we're no closer to identifying him," Henley concluded, turning to face Pellacia, who leaned on a chair, trying to catch his breath. "What's wrong with you?" she asked.

"The bloody elevator is out," Pellacia replied as he gulped for air. "Don't know why those engineers needed to… Never mind. I saw Larsen," he added.

"What did he have to say?" Stanford asked sternly.

"Enough to implicate himself," Pellacia replied. The room fell silent, everyone listening intently as he gave a blow-by-blow account of his encounter with Larsen.

"So, indirectly, he's admitting he bribed Kerry Huggins, who may be Georgina Bridges?" Ramouter asked.

"No one knew how much the bribe was except us," said Henley. "Huggins mentioned a two-grand cash bribe specifically, but she also claimed the person who bribed her was Rhimes." She sent a quick email to Ezra. "I didn't show her a photo of Rhimes though."

"That's what we need to do next," said Pellacia. "First, we need to find out if Kerry Huggins and Georgina Bridges are the same person. Then we get her to identify the person who gave her the money. And then persuade the National Crime Agency to consider witness protection."

"Will they agree to it? Right now, it's all speculation and conspiracy," Stanford said doubtfully.

"A few months ago, it would have sounded like a conspiracy theory if someone had said Streeter was innocent and the real culprit was still out there." Pellacia thumped the desk. "But look where we are now. I'll make them listen."

"I've already asked Ezra to dig deeper into Huggins—I'll get him to check out the Georgina angle too," Henley said. "Meanwhile, Eastwood and Stanford, you two go visit her. Even if we can't confirm she's Georgina Bridges, we can at least get a visual ID of the man who paid her. Show her photos of Larsen and Rhimes from the nineties."

"What will you be doing?" Pellacia asked.

"I'll follow up on Streeter's connection to Tiago Alves," Ramouter said. "It appears Alves was into drug supply. Odd that it wasn't in the original case files. Rhimes's team might have known."

"To be fair, Alves's criminal record wouldn't have made much difference to the overall investigation, and it certainly wouldn't have aided Streeter's defense," Henley remarked, gesturing to Ramouter to continue.

"The last entry on Alves's record was a bail notice to return to Snow Hill police station. Georgina Bridges didn't have any bail to return dates on her record but that doesn't mean she wasn't under investigation at the time," Ramouter explained.

"Bridges and Alves were running drugs together," Eastwood added.

"It appears so," Ramouter confirmed.

"Huggins told me that she used to be involved in drug-running back in the nineties," Henley said with regret. "I had her. I had her all along."

"Don't do that to yourself," Pellacia reassured her, gently placing his hand on Henley's arm.

"There's something else we need to follow up on," said Ramouter, grabbing his notebook from his desk. "Denise Price provided me with the names of a father and son who were her brother's co-defendants in the cash-in-transit robberies case: Declan and Archie Weathers. Price believes Declan Weathers died in a traffic accident, but I've got an address for his father, Archie, in Kingston. I asked Ezra to see what he could find out about Archie and get this: Archie's wife and Declan's mother, Florence, was murdered in 1986."

"Do we know the cause of death?" Pellacia asked.

"Her body was discovered in a shallow grave at Mudchute Farm," Ramouter replied, "and the cause of death was asphyxiation."

40

"Badge to the camera," the disembodied voice from the inter-com demanded as Henley and Ramouter stood outside a new block of flats.

Ramouter held up his badge to the camera, and Henley fol-lowed suit. "Now, Mr. Weathers, we'd appreciate it if you'd let us in."

"It's Archie," he replied. The door unlocked with a click. "The door's on the latch. I'll be in the living room."

Ramouter muttered, "Charming," as they entered, climbed one flight of stairs, and made their way to the last flat at the end of the landing.

"Mr. Weathers, Archie, this is DI Henley. I'm coming in," Henley announced, cautiously pushing the door open to check for any surprises.

"Interesting," Ramouter said as they saw the wheelchair in the hallway. The flat smelled of fresh paint and new carpet. They walked past the bathroom and saw the silver grab bars next to the toilet.

"I was supposed to have a ground-floor flat, but the council messed up," Archie explained when they entered the living room. "You're pretty for a copper."

"Thank you," Ramouter replied, remaining standing.

"Poor you, Detective Inspector Henley, stuck with a joker," Archie remarked, moving his crutches. Archie wore a white vest and burgundy tracksuit bottoms, the right leg cut off halfway, revealing what remained of his leg. Aside from that, he seemed in good health, absent-mindedly touching a patch of sunburn on his arm.

"They amputated my leg just below the knee," Archie explained. "Diabetes. I stepped on a piece of glass, cut my foot, and four months later, they took it off. I find it's best to get the story out when meeting someone new."

"Thanks," Henley replied, unsure of the appropriate response. She sat down next to Ramouter on a loveseat beside Archie. "I briefly explained our reason for wanting to see you in the message."

Archie nodded, picking up a mug of tea from the side table. "I was at the doctor's for a checkup, so I couldn't answer. Honestly, I doubt I can tell you more than you already know."

"Mr. Weathers," Ramouter began.

"I told you, it's Archie. No need for formalities."

"Aye, I'll remember that. Earlier today, I spoke with Denise Price."

Archie sipped his tea, staring blankly.

"Denise is Andrew Streeter's half sister."

"Ah, I see. Don't think I ever met that one."

"But you did work with Streeter's father at the Wapping printing press?"

"That was donkey's years ago and, to be fair, Gordon—that's Andrew's dad—had kids all over the gaff. None of them were murderers like his Andrew, though, far as I know."

"But you did commit robberies with Andrew."

"If you've done your homework, you'd know I was only found guilty of handling. Don't know nothing about any robberies."

"Robberies that your son, Declan, committed," Ramouter clarified.

"What do you want me to say about that?" Archie replied, lowering his head. "I made some mistakes as a dad."

"We're reinvestigating the 1995 murders Streeter was convicted of, which the Court of Appeal later overturned," said Ramouter. "Firstly, where's your son, Declan?"

"Declan?" Archie said. "He's..." He placed his mug on the table, ran his hand over his brow, and bit his lip. "I thought you lot did your research," he said, his voice cracking.

"What do you mean?" Henley asked, her attention briefly shifting to the photographs on the windowsill.

"My Declan...it doesn't get any easier," Archie said, rolling up his trouser leg. "He passed away in 1998. Hit-and-run in Tufnell Park, coming home from a club."

"I'm so sorry," Henley sympathized. "That must have been tough, especially after your wife's loss. Was Declan your only son?"

"Yeah, Declan is my only child. So, what do you want to know about him?"

"You said 'is my child,'" Henley pointed out. "I suppose it's hard to talk about someone you loved in the past tense, no matter how long they've been gone."

Archie didn't reply but offered a weak smile.

"I'm sorry for your loss, Archie," Ramouter said. He followed Henley's gaze to the photographs and then back to Archie. "Now, a couple of questions. Did your son ever own a blue Ford Fiesta back in the nineties?"

"A blue Ford Fiesta," Archie said, scratching the back of his head. "Dec had a lot of cars. He'd buy them, fix them up, and sell them. But yes, he did have a blue Fiesta. I think he got it from a mechanic in Willesden Green."

"Did he let anyone else drive it, like Streeter or a girlfriend, Georgina Bridges?"

"Are you mad?" Archie laughed. "Let me tell you one thing: Dec wouldn't let anyone touch his car, not even me. Andrew couldn't drive anyhow, so he was the one who'd grab the—"

Archie stopped abruptly, catching himself, and took a sip of tea to halt his confession.

"How close were Declan and Streeter?" Ramouter asked.

"I don't know. I didn't get involved in my son's business."

"But you got him involved in your criminal activities," Henley interjected, standing and moving toward the window. "What about his girlfriend, Georgina Bridges?" she asked, holding up a photograph of a boy and girl who appeared to be six or seven years old. "Grandad?" Henley read the inscription on a birthday card from Najat and Mason. "Is this for you?"

"What? Nah," Archie quickly denied. "I haven't got any grandkids, not that I know of. A mate left it behind when he visited the other day. You were asking me about some girl?"

"Yes, Georgina Bridges?"

"I didn't know any Georgina, but Dec always had girls hanging around him. Young man sowing his oats and all that," Archie explained.

"What about your wife? Do you have any idea who killed her?" Ramouter asked.

"No, no," Archie replied softly, taking a tissue from his pocket. Henley and Ramouter watched as he wiped his eyes. "They thought I did it at first because we had an argument once. Our nosy neighbor called the police, claiming I was hitting her because they saw her with a bruise on her face."

"Did you hit her?" Henley asked. "An earlier police report suggested there were bruises on your wife's face and hands."

"Never. I'd never lay a hand on a woman," Archie said vehemently.

"What about your son?" Ramouter asked cautiously, noticing Henley's skeptical expression.

Archie's eyes darted between Henley and Ramouter, then to a photograph on the wall of a younger Archie in a wedding suit, holding the hands of a woman in a lavish wedding dress. "It was an accident," Archie finally admitted. "Declan...he was a bit...it was an accident."

"The bruise or..." Ramouter couldn't hide the shock in his voice. "Or the murder of your—"

"No, no," Archie cut in loudly, adjusting his crutches. "I meant the bruise. I don't know who killed my Flo."

Henley went to open a window to let in some fresh air. "Can I ask you about the counterfeit coins you were convicted of handling?"

"For crying out loud," Archie exclaimed, pushing himself up. "Why are you dredging up the past? Why bring up stuff from decades ago?"

"Because it's relevant," Henley explained. "Andrew Streeter is dead, and the person responsible for his murder, and the original—"

"It wasn't my son. Dec didn't do it," Archie asserted firmly, his anger causing him to grow unsteady on his one leg as he reached for his crutches.

"I didn't say he did," Henley clarified. "Why? Did you suspect he did?"

"Don't be bloody ridiculous," Archie retorted. "Dec isn't a monster. You lot screwed up twenty-five years ago, and now you're accusing people—"

"We haven't accused anyone," Henley interrupted. "We came here for information and clarification."

"No one wants to upset you," Ramouter added. "You've been through a lot, and it seems like you're still going through a lot."

"My wife is dead—murdered. And then to have to face..." Archie turned away, heading to the kitchen area again, where he picked up a large plastic pill pack from the counter and poured himself a glass of water.

"We checked your record, and in addition to your conviction for handling stolen goods, you also have a conviction for making counterfeit coins," Ramouter continued. "We want to know if you passed them on to Streeter or your son, and if you ever had prototypes for a £2 coin."

Archie took his time to swallow the water, thinking through his response. "Yes, I did have prototypes for a £2 coin," he finally admitted. "No, I won't tell you how I got them. No, I didn't give my son or Andy the counterfeit coins or the prototypes. Declan took them."

"Were you making the coins for yourself?"

"No. Those coins were made to order, if you want to put it that way. I was paid fifteen grand to make £150,000 worth of £1 coins and two hundred grand's worth of fivers and twenties. I didn't realize I was about £200 short on the coins until I did a final check before handing the cash over. Turned out to be a mistake because I handed it to one of your lot."

"One of *our* lot?" Henley questioned. She could feel herself growing agitated, and the room was getting warmer.

"That's right," Archie replied. "A copper, innit. A bent one, at that. Turns out the Flying Squad was on to us. The entire thing was a sting. I didn't give a shit that Declan had taken some of the fake money once I got the handcuffs on me."

"All right, let's take this slowly," Henley said, opening the window further. "And don't be shady with your answers."

"OK," Archie adjusted himself in his chair, clasping his hands as if gearing up for a quiz show. "Shoot," he invited.

"In the summer of 1993, you, your son Declan, Tiago Alves, and Andrew Streeter were arrested for a series of cash-in-transit robberies. Is that correct?" Henley asked.

"That's right," Archie confirmed.

"Six months later, the case went to trial. Streeter was supposed to go Queen's Evidence, but he didn't, and the trial fell apart."

"Exactly. Tiago and Declan got away clean, but they had evidence to charge me and Andrew with handling stolen goods. We both got six months in prison."

"But you didn't stay clean?" Henley probed.

"A man's got to eat," Archie replied with a grin.

"And you were offered a counterfeiting job?" Henley continued.

"Yes. Not the first time, mind you. I'd done jobs for this bent copper before. I'd make counterfeit cash for him, hand it over, and he'd pay me and agree to look the other way when I was involved in other things."

"So, did this copper agree to look the other way for the cash-in-transit robberies?"

Archie laughed. "Well, he couldn't do that. The cash-in-transit jobs were his cases. I should've known better. Realized he'd want to settle the score in some way."

"And you believe he got back at you through this order for £150,000 worth of fake coins and £200,000 in notes?" Henley asked.

"Exactly," Archie confirmed.

Henley's heart raced as she asked the next question, "Archie, who was this bent copper?"

"Back then, he was DI James Larsen," Archie said venomously. "The same asshole who tried to set me up for the cash-in-transit jobs."

"Let me clarify," said Ramouter, sensing Henley's relief. "Larsen was the senior investigating officer for the cash-in-transit robberies, and you also supplied him with fake coins when you came out of prison, and this wasn't the first time?"

"As I said, bent as fuck," Archie declared. "Counterfeiting was my thing—passports, driving licenses, cash. I supplied it all to him. And one thing about me is that I'm not a snitch. Larsen knew he was safe."

"Until now," Henley concluded.

"I don't give a shit now," Archie said, his anger palpable. "Remember when I told you I got fifteen grand for that counterfeit job? Well, I kept the money in a safe in my bedroom. There was at least thirty grand and change in that safe. I was there when they searched my gaff, and I saw that Larsen geezer take my fucking money."

41

"There's no sign of him," Ezra reported as he opened the office windows.

"What do you mean, no sign of him?" Henley asked.

Ezra pulled his keyboard closer and displayed information on the big screen. "Look up here. This is his birth certificate. Declan Weathers, no middle name, born at Chelsea and West-minster Hospital on thirtieth June 1974. Parents are Archibald Clayton Weathers and Florence Mabel Weathers, née Gift. His National Insurance number was issued in 1990, but there haven't been any tax or National Insurance payments since 1998."

"But that doesn't prove anything," Henley pointed out. "He could have been working off the books or using someone else's National Insurance number."

"Fair enough. The point is, there's no record of Declan Weath-ers being deceased," Ezra explained. "I checked the death cer-tificate register from 1995 to today, and he's not on it. So either his dad is lying or his son died in another country."

"No, no," Henley said, shaking her head. "Archie Weathers

specifically said his son was killed in a hit-and-run in Tufnell Park in '98. Are you sure you—"

"Boss," Ezra interrupted, his expression serious. "Of course I'm sure."

"I'm sorry," Henley replied. "I should never have doubted you."

"Now you're being snarky," Ezra said with a grin as he reached for a bowl of pick 'n' mix. "So, as far as I can tell," he continued through a mouthful of raspberry bonbons, "your boy Declan isn't dead, but your girl Georgina Bridges, on the other hand..."

Henley put a hand to her stomach, a heavy stone dropping into the pit. "She's not...she's not dead, is she?"

"Nah, mate, she's alive and kicking," Ezra replied as he handed her the pick 'n' mix bowl. "I'm sending a copy to your printer upstairs, but look at the monitor."

Henley unwrapped a lemon sherbet and studied the screen.

THE UK DEED POLL OFFICE LONDON
THIS CHANGE OF NAME DEED *made by me the undersigned Georgina Alice Bridges of Hull now or lately known as Kerry Louise Searle, British citizen.*

WITNESSES AND IT IS HEREBY DECLARED as follows:

1. I absolutely and entirely renounce, relinquish and abandon the use of my said former name of Georgina Alice Bridges and assume, adopt and determine to take and use from the date hereof the name of Kerry Louise Searle in substitution for my former name of Georgina Alice Bridges.

2. I shall at all times hereafter in all records, deeds, documents and other writings and in all actions and proceedings as well as in all dealings and transactions and on all occasions whatsoever use and subscribe the said name of Kerry Louise SEARLE as my name in substitution for my former name of Georgina Bridges.

"What year is this dated?" Henley asked.

"Twenty-fourth of September 1996," Ezra answered. "I then found a marriage certificate. She married this guy, Tobias Blake Huggins in June 2004, and they've got two kids. Six months ago their divorce was finalized. She never changed her surname on her driving license. Probably didn't want to pay the fee. But that's not all. I also found her fingerprints, both as Georgina and Kerry. She visited the prison four months ago. You know they scan your fingerprints when you visit, right?"

"Wait, she visited Streeter before he was transferred to HMP Ruxley?" Henley asked.

"Yep, she visited him twice," Ezra confirmed.

"But she never visited him at Ruxley?" Henley asked.

"Not that I can tell," Ezra said. "But here's the kicker—her criminal record under Georgina Bridges is quite extensive. I've got a scan of her fingerprints from when she was arrested and booked in at Snow Hill police station back in September 1995. Maybe your experts can compare them."

"Have I ever told you that you're brilliant?" Henley said as she took the printouts of the fingerprints. "I don't know what I'm going to do to thank you, get you a pay rise or something."

"Well, you might want to double it, boss," Ezra quipped as he followed Henley to the door. "Because you know what else I found out?"

"What?" Henley asked.

"Archie Weathers has a gravel pit registered in his name down in Folkestone."

"Are you OK?" Pellacia asked as Henley leaned back, frustrated.

"This case... I absolutely hate this case," Henley vented. "There wasn't one morning I didn't wake up thinking today will be the day we find out Rhimes is dirty and that he lied to me, and betrayed us all."

"I kept telling myself to take it one day at a time, assess the evidence, and not dwell on the time Rhimes came to my flat and drank whisky with me the day before your wedding," Pellacia shared.

"Is that why he was hungover?"

Pellacia grinned. "I wasn't at my best, and he was there for me."

"I knew it, Stephen. Every fiber of my being told me Rhimes wasn't corrupt."

"I can't wait to go back to New Scotland Yard and see the looks on their faces when I tell them the truth about their golden boy, Larsen," Pellacia declared.

"And that they owe Rhimes's family an apology," Henley said, tilting her head back and cracking her neck.

"You never answered my question. Are you OK?" Pellacia asked, his concern evident.

"I'm fine," Henley replied, looking up at Pellacia, who still wore a concerned expression. "Honestly, I'm OK. It's...all the lies. Don't get me wrong, I can understand Georgina Bridges or whatever she wants to call herself, the reason why she changed her name and took on a new identity, if what she's saying is true."

"That she escaped from The Burier?" Pellacia confirmed.

"And if she thought that he was dead, then there was nothing stopping her from living her life, but Archie is the one that I can't get my head around. Why would he lie about his son?"

"To protect him. That's the one and only reason."

"I knew that something wasn't right," Henley admitted. A sharp knock on Pellacia's door interrupted their conversation. The door swung open and Stanford walked in. "I thought that it was a slip of the tongue when he kept referring to his son in the present tense, but it would make sense if he knew that his son was alive and kicking. And the photos on the windowsill of the kids and a birthday card to grandad. He tried to fob it off, but... I should have listened to my gut."

"So where is this Archie Weathers now?" Pellacia asked. Stanford continued to hover.

"No idea," Henley replied, as Stanford poked her shoulder. "He wasn't in when a couple of officers from Kingston police station went round just now. They're going to keep doing random checks until he turns up. What is it, Stanford?"

"We've got a photo. I think we've got our first clear picture of The Burier."

Eastwood downed the remainder of her coffee as she approached the smartboard. Henley sympathized with the exhaustion on Eastwood's face and the redness in her eyes from scrutinizing hours of CCTV footage.

"This is the image taken from the P12 bus on the morning Ryland's body was found," Eastwood explained, pointing at the screen. "The council offices came through, and I traced the man who set fire to the car. He cuts through a housing estate and makes his way to St. Mary's Road, showing that he knows the area well. Then he boards the seventy-eight bus, where we get this image."

The screenshot displayed a slim, white man on the top deck of the bus, his right hand gripping the support rail and his left resting on a seat. His hat was missing, revealing salt-and-pepper hair.

"I had the image enhanced," Eastwood continued, displaying another image. This time, the man's distinct features became more visible, showcasing a long nose, a small scar that cut through his right eyebrow, and a trio of small moles on his cheek.

"It's a good image," Ramouter commented. "A very good image. Someone is bound to recognize him."

"You're right, it's a good image, but take a look at what the enhancement revealed," Eastwood said, zooming in on the man's chest. "He's unzipped his jacket, and you can see the start of a logo in red on his shirt. If you look closely, you can see it's a padlock inside a shield, with the letters H.U.D."

"Wait, this guy is going around setting fire to cars in his work uniform?" Stanford exclaimed. "Some people. Were you able to identify the company?"

"Hudson Securities," Eastwood answered. "Their head office is in Nine Elms, and they install security systems for construction companies in residential properties."

"That would explain how he gained access to Ryland's apartment block and possibly Caroline Swann's house without setting off alarms," Pellacia remarked.

"That's not all. They also have a contract with the Metropolitan Police to install and update alarm systems in their police stations, including this one," Eastwood added.

Henley, for the first time in a while, was left speechless. Her mind raced with thoughts of the possible implications.

"But it hasn't been Hudson Securities working here; it was Firebird Securities, and they have a phoenix logo," Ramouter pointed out.

"Hudson Securities use subcontractors for some jobs, and Firebird Securities is one of them," Eastwood explained. "Look, I know what you're thinking, that The Burier may have been wandering around this building and had access to sensitive information."

"Fucking hell!" Stanford said. "Are you seriously telling me he could have been here, walking our corridors, going through our desks, standing in front of our whiteboard, laughing at us, while we ran around trying to catch the psychotic bastard?"

"Let's all calm down for a minute," Pellacia suggested, stepping into the center of the room. "I believe the likelihood of this guy walking around here is low for three reasons. Firstly, he's wearing the uniform of Hudson Securities. Secondly, none of you have recognized him from the still image. Does he look familiar?"

The team responded with a unanimous "No" and shaking heads.

"Thirdly," Pellacia continued, "if this is the same person, he was pretending to be a nurse named Filip at HMP Ruxley long before we were given a sniff of this case."

"That doesn't make me feel any more comfortable," Henley admitted. "The possibility he could have had access to this building and sensitive information is mind-blowing."

"I understand, but for now, I agree with the govnor," Eastwood said. "I've tried contacting Hudson Securities, but this late, all I get is an automated voicemail service for security breaches or to leave a message for reception."

"Our priority is to circulate this image," Pellacia said. "Someone out there knows who this man is. Secondly, let's get an update on Kerry Huggins."

"Nowhere," Ramouter replied, rising from his seat. "The phone number she had is disconnected. I went to her house earlier, but she wasn't there."

"What about the spa where she works?" Henley asked, her phone ringing. "Do we need to be worried?"

"I'm reluctant to say that we shouldn't worry," Ramouter answered. "But I called her spa, and the manager told me that Kerry worked from home yesterday, doing admin, and that she'd mentioned going to see her ex-husband and kids. I've been trying to reach her ex-husband, but I'm hitting a wall."

"We're all going to hit the wall at this rate," said Pellacia. "I'm going to speak to the press office and get this image out there and then I'm going to see Barker and give her the full lowdown on Rhimes and that conniving shit Larsen."

"Victory for Rhimes," said Stanford. "Larsen is going to pay for everything he did."

"Would be nice to get a public confession from him," said Ramouter. "Fully absolve Rhimes."

"I doubt that's going to happen," said Pellacia. He looked around at his exhausted team. "I suggest we call it a night and, unless something happens, we pick this up first thing in the morning."

"Kerry is out there, which means she's at risk. We may have absolved Rhimes, but this isn't over," said Henley, rubbing the knot of tension in her neck. "The last thing I'm going to do is rest."

"We might all struggle to sleep tonight," Stanford remarked.

"Better sleep with one eye open," Eastwood said. "I doubt anyone will be getting much rest tonight."

42

Henley lay in her bed, alone, with her daughter Emma sleeping beside her. The absence of Rob, snoring away in the spare bedroom, left her feeling strangely uncomfortable. It had been nearly 1:00 a.m. when she'd unlocked the front door, and it took until 1:38 a.m. for her to finally pull the duvet over herself. She'd hardly managed a couple of hours of sleep, and now she was here, in bed, waiting for the birds to start their morning chorus. Henley edged closer to her daughter, her eyelids heavy as the night sky slowly gave way to dawn.

Five minutes later, her phone interrupted the quiet. Henley sat up abruptly, reaching for her phone on the bedside table as Emma stirred. Pellacia's name lit up the screen, causing Henley's heart to race. She pressed accept and whispered into the phone, "One second," before slipping out of bed and tiptoeing out of the bedroom and downstairs.

"What's going on?" Henley asked as she settled on the bottom step.

"I'm sorry to be calling you so early," said Pellacia. "But we've had a break, and we've also got a problem."

"What is it?"

"We've had three people call in with a name for the man on the bus. Two of the callers work at Hudson Securities and have identified him as Scott Beckett, and the third caller was Denise Price."

"Denise Price, that's Andrew Streeter's half sister."

"Exactly, and she swears blind that the man in the photo is Declan Weathers."

"Shit," Henley muttered, hearing a car door slam and an engine start. "We're going to have to ask Hudson Securities to provide us with contact details, but if he's working and paying PAYE and tax then—"

"I'm one step ahead and have already woken Ezra up—and he made it crystal-clear that he was not happy about it," said Pellacia.

"So, what's the problem?" Henley asked, moving into the kitchen and grabbing some dry clothes from the tumble dryer. "You said that we had a problem."

"We think that The Burier might have Kerry Huggins."

Lillian Klein sat in the vulnerable witness room at Greenwich police station, her fingers absently stirring her coffee cup. The room was on the ground floor, three levels down from the SCU.

"You're not arresting me this time," Lillian remarked as Henley and Ramouter entered the room.

"Technically, you're on bail, and until you tell us something that we don't like or basically incriminates you, then no, we're not going to arrest you," said Ramouter, his Yorkshire accent sounding more pronounced as fatigue and irritation crept in. "And don't get it twisted, just because you're in a room that was used for poor kids scared out of their wits and women who had to sit and talk about the man who raped them doesn't mean that you're vulnerable. As far as I'm concerned, you're complicit."

"I'm not looking for special treatment," Lillian almost pleaded. "I can't have another death on my conscience. It's not always about the story."

"Oh, now you've come to that sudden realization," said Henley as she settled on the old sofa next to Ramouter.

"There's nothing that you can say that will make me feel more guilt than I already do," said Lillian, placing her cup on the ground and opening her tote bag.

"Forgive me if I'm finding it a bit difficult to believe you," Henley retorted as Lillian produced an envelope.

"He was in my house. I don't know how he got in without triggering the alarms, but he was in my house," Lillian revealed, her voice cracking. "I couldn't sleep. I've had trouble sleeping for a while, but it's been worse this week."

"Guilt will do that," Ramouter observed, and Henley gave him a nudge with her knee.

"I woke up after 3:00 a.m., and I felt... I just knew. It was as if the air was different. The house didn't feel right," said Lillian.

Henley didn't respond, though she understood what Lillian meant.

"I found this on my kitchen table," Lillian said, handing over a white A5 envelope with her name handwritten on it. "He came into my house," she repeated. "It wasn't the first time."

"What do you mean it wasn't the first time?"

Lillian's eyes darted between Ramouter and Henley, trying to gauge who would be more receptive to her confession. Her gaze settled on the floor.

"I lied when you interviewed me the first time," she admitted.

"Go on," Henley prompted coldly.

"The Burier... He first got back in contact with me after Elias Piper disappeared. He sent me this." Lillian reached into her bag and pulled out the photograph of Elias Piper screaming in his grave, placing it on the table. "There's more. He came to my house, left a note, and then he sent me this."

Lillian placed a gold signet ring with the letter S next to the photo. "It belonged to Jake," she whispered.

"You had all this," Henley said through gritted teeth as Ramouter placed the items into evidence bags. "You knew before we did that he had Piper and Jake—your own colleague—and you did…you did bloody nothing."

"I didn't do nothing," Lillian protested. "I called the police about Jake. I called."

"There was an anonymous call," said Ramouter. "That was you?"

Lillian nodded.

"Well done, you," Henley said sarcastically, giving Lillian a slow clap. "Nice to see that your conscience kicked in. You're unbelievable."

"I'm sorry."

"Don't apologize to me. Apologize to Piper's family, and Jake's. Apologize to your kids. They're the ones who are going to suffer when they find out that their mother is—"

"Boss," Ramouter interrupted calmly as Lillian reached into her bag again, tears streaming down her face, and handed another envelope to Henley.

Henley felt her back stiffen as she lifted the broken seal of the envelope and emptied it into her lap. A diamond tennis bracelet fell out first, followed by a glossy 7x5 photograph.

"No note?" Henley asked as she carefully picked up the edge of the photograph and turned it over.

"No. No note. Only the bracelet and the photograph," said Lillian, curiosity in her voice despite her tears. "Who is she?"

"Shit, that's Kerry Huggins," said Ramouter as Henley held the photograph in the air. Kerry Huggins lay on her kitchen floor, eyes wide open, mouth covered with duct tape, and wrists and ankles bound with cable ties. She seemed to have accepted that no one would save her.

"Who's Kerry Huggins?" Lillian asked.

"Or Georgina Bridges, as she was originally," Henley replied, scanning the photograph for any hints of date or time. If it had been more than forty-eight hours, she knew Kerry's chances of survival were slim. She would be dead the next time she saw her.

"I've never heard of her," said Lillian, her head tilted as she watched Henley. "But you're aware of her. You don't even seem that surprised to see her. It's as if you were expecting it."

"Lillian, you're not here in your professional capacity as a reporter. You're here because the truth is that you're a dishonest hack and a lying cow who, for some inexplicable reason, was chosen by The Burier to be his mouthpiece," Henley snapped. "Don't, for one second, think that your actions don't have something to do with this woman being a target."

Lillian said nothing, slipping effortlessly into her role as a reporter, letting the insults and frustration wash over her.

"Have you ever come across the name Georgina Bridges since you started covering this case back in 1995?" Ramouter asked, trying to ease the tension between Henley and Lillian.

"First time I'm hearing of her," Lillian replied as she picked up her coffee and bag, stood up, and headed for the door. "Why her? What is she to The Burier?"

Henley carefully placed the photograph and bracelet back into the envelope and handed it to Ramouter. "Make sure you show up on your bail date," she said. "And I would recommend that you bring your lawyer with you."

"Everyone, this is where we are," Henley began as the team settled at their desks. "Kerry Huggins was last seen by her husband, or ex-husband, at 7:45 p.m. on Tuesday night when she left his house in Wandsworth."

"Where are her children?" Stanford asked.

"With the husband," Henley confirmed. "According to him, the children were supposed to return home with her, but she insisted they stay. He said he received a text from her new number at 8:30 p.m. confirming that she arrived home, but she was supposed to FaceTime the children to say goodnight, and she never did. We've been calling her phone, but it just keeps ringing, not even going to voicemail. Officers from Wimbledon police station attempted a welfare check at Kerry's home but there was no answer. She's been missing for nearly thirty-eight hours now."

"And what about the guy on the bus?" Eastwood asked.

"He's been positively identified as Scott Beckett, but Denise Price also identified him as Declan Weathers," said Ramouter. "Hudson Securities sent over his employment details this morning. Apparently, he's been working with them for seventeen years. Ezra had already pulled up his personal details by the time we all arrived here this morning. Scott Beckett or Declan Weathers has been married to Gwendoline Marshall for the past eight years, but it seems they've been together for much longer, according to their council tax records. Two kids, a dog, a mortgage, a car on HP, and credit card debt. They've been living a normal, everyday life."

"A period of stability," Stanford noted. "Isn't that what Mark said was the reason for The Burier being quiet all these years? You can't get more stable than a wife and two kids."

"He's fitting the profile," said Ramouter. "Anyway, I went to his property with officers and TSG from Walworth Road this morning at six."

"And let me guess," said Eastwood, "no sign of him?"

"Exactly. If you ask me, his wife is absolutely clueless. She has no idea about her husband's other life, but I'm prepared to be proved wrong," said Ramouter. "Long story short, they finished searching the house about an hour ago, and nothing has come up yet."

"When was he last seen by his wife?" Eastwood asked.

"Five thirty yesterday. She's not working at the moment, recovering from a knee operation," Ramouter replied. "She said Scott had to go back to work because there had been a mix-up with the schedule. She didn't think much of it because it happens all the time. That was the last time she saw or heard from her husband. She said he left in his van."

"We've got an attention drawn out on both Beckett's van and Kerry Huggins' BMW, which isn't at her property," Henley added. "In my opinion, when it comes to the wife, she's either extremely clueless, as Ramouter said, and her husband has completely deceived her, or she's very smart and has kept her head in the sand all these years."

"So, what's next?" Stanford asked. "We can't just sit here, twiddling our thumbs, waiting for something to happen."

Henley placed her hands on her hips and turned to the whiteboard covered with crime scene photos and images of The Burier's victims. She tried to ignore the growing sense of fear and nausea, realizing there was space for another victim's photograph on the board.

"We need to figure out where Beckett might have taken Huggins," Henley said as she turned to face the team. "We have two areas of interest: the gravel pit owned by Archie Weathers—"

"But, boss, the soil expert said it was unlikely The Burier was burying his victims in a gravel pit. Nearby, maybe, but not in it," Ramouter interjected.

"I know, but we're grasping at straws here, and that's the best lead we've got," Henley admitted. "We've also got the fact that Piper's location was first pinned down in the Sandgate area. Folkestone isn't a big town, but it's still a lot of ground to cover, and we would literally be looking for a needle in a haystack."

"I suppose I'll get on the phone to National Highways—they monitor the major roads to Folkestone." Eastwood sighed, rolling her eyes. "They're going to love me."

Henley didn't get a chance to respond before Pellacia burst out of his office.

"British Transport Police just phoned," Pellacia announced. "They picked up Archie Weathers fifteen minutes ago at Waterloo station."

Archie sat at the Formica table in interview room 4 at Charing Cross police station, tracing his fingers along the grimy beige walls perilously close to the alarm strip. "What exactly am I supposed to have done?" he asked. "I'm on the train, minding my own business, and the next thing I know, I'm being hauled in. It's nearly ten o'clock. I've got medication to take."

Henley responded as Ramouter activated the recording system. "The nurse has checked you, and she's given you what you need, so stop complaining," she said. "You've been fully cautioned and informed of your right to legal representation."

"I don't want it, and I don't need it," Archie stubbornly declared, picking up the white Styrofoam cup filled with weak tea.

"Fine," Henley said wearily. "Archibald Weathers, you've—"

"It's Archie," he interrupted.

"Stop interrupting me. You've been arrested for perverting the course of justice."

"And how exactly did I do that?"

"By lying about your son, Declan Weathers."

"My son is dead."

"Is he?" Henley asked skeptically. "Prove it."

Archie placed his cup down, looking to Ramouter for support as he did. "Nothing can be more traumatic than losing a child," Ramouter gently interjected. "I think that I would remember every second of the day that I learned that my child was killed until the day they put me in the grave. What time did Declan die?"

"I'm not sure of the exact time. I only found out when the hospital called me," Archie said, lowering his head.

"And what hospital was that?" asked Ramouter.

"Chelsea and Westminster Hospital."

"No, that's the hospital where he was born," Henley corrected sharply. "Which hospital was your son taken to?"

"I told you, he was taken to Chelsea and Westminster."

"Do you know what, Archie?" said Henley, leaning across the table. "I was always told that the best lies to tell were the ones that sounded like the truth. Keep it simple and get your story straight."

"I told you. It was Chelsea and Westminster," Archie said shakily.

"So, he's knocked over on Tufnell Park Road in north London and taken to a hospital seven miles away in southwest London. Try again."

"I...maybe it was a different hospital."

"OK. In that case, who registered his death? It wasn't his mum, because she died in 1986," Henley said coldly. "So, it must have been you? That would have been a hard day for you?"

"It was. It was terrible," Archie replied unconvincingly.

"Which registry office did you go to?" asked Ramouter.

"I can't... I can't remember. It was a long time ago," said Archie, pushing his empty cup away.

"The reason that you can't remember is because it never happened," Henley stated. "Look, Archie, it's ten o'clock. I'm knackered, and I know that DC Ramouter is tired. And looking at the state of you, well, you've probably had enough too. So, we're going to stop beating around the bush and playing these stupid games. Where is your son?"

Archie pursed his thin lips, and his hands began to shake. "It's not what you think."

"If I'm honest, I don't know what to think," said Henley. "The only thing running through my brain is how could a father defend his son, knowing that he was a killer."

"I'm not defending him—how could I ever defend that? But

he's my boy," Archie shouted, sweeping his hand across the table in anger, sending Henley's papers flying across the room.

Henley sighed and got up from her seat to retrieve her papers. "Ramouter," she said.

"Let's start from the beginning," Ramouter said, grabbing his pen. "What name is your son, Declan Weathers, using now? Because we can find no trace of him since 1998, which led us to believe you when you originally said that he was dead, but there's no record of your son being involved in a car accident and admitted to any hospital in the London area, and most importantly, there's no death certificate."

"You've got to understand, I thought that it was for the best," said Archie. "I only wanted to protect my boy. He made a mistake, that's all."

"You think that murdering five innocent—" Henley stopped herself. "Sorry. That was—"

"Name?" Ramouter asked sternly.

Archie swallowed hard and looked between Henley and Ramouter. "Scott. Scott Beckett. It's not on his birth certificate because we—Flo, my wife—she didn't like it, but Scott is his middle name and—"

"And Beckett?" Henley said, managing to regain a sense of calmness.

"My mum's maiden name," Archie said. "You've got to believe me that I didn't know, I didn't know that he'd taken those girls, not until I...not until...sorry, sorry. I can't do it."

"Not until what, Archie?"

Archie leaned to the side and scratched his leg. "He kept their clothes. I found their clothes in the back of his car, the Ford Fiesta. And a rucksack. I opened the rucksack, and it was full of schoolbooks, a pink woolly hat, a girl's PE panties and netball skirt. And then I found the bus pass in the front pocket, and I saw her picture. It was the same picture that was all over the news—of the little black girl who'd gone missing, and they found her body by the river."

"Melissa Gyimah," Henley said quietly, almost to herself. "Did you confront your son, Declan?"

"Are you mad? Confront him?" Archie exclaimed. "You don't understand, Declan wasn't…isn't…normal. He was… He scared me. I couldn't confront him. Besides, he would only come up with some lie if I asked him."

"Why did he scare you?" asked Ramouter. "He's your son, as you keep on saying. Tell me about your son and your wife. Tell me about their relationship."

"I can't."

"Archie. Talk to me," Henley demanded.

"It wasn't good," Archie whispered. "She didn't…it was as if she knew that something wasn't right with him, and she…she rejected him. She wasn't a mother, not really. It's like she just tolerated him. She wouldn't play with him or read to him when he was a kid, and when they accused him of touching that girl—"

"What girl?"

"He was twelve years old, and she said that Declan tried to…" Archie covered his face with his hands, struggling to continue. "Touch her, you know, touch her down there when she didn't want him to and tried to strangle her."

"What happened, were the police involved?" asked Ramouter.

Archie shook his head. "It was different back then. The school said that it was kids messing about, experimenting, and the girl transferred to another school, but Flo, my wife… It was like she went off Declan. Disowned him. Said that he was a sociopath. How could she say that about our boy? Our twelve-year-old boy. It was like she gave up."

Tears fell down Archie's face as he twisted the gold wedding band on his finger.

"You've never taken it off after all these years?" asked Henley.

Archie shook his head and then wiped his face with the back of his hand.

"Do you know who killed your wife, Archie?" Ramouter asked as he turned to Henley, a mix of question and surprise in his eyes.

"I can't say it. Don't make me say it," said Archie as he continued to cry harder.

"Your son would have been twelve years old when his mother, your wife, was murdered," said Ramouter. "The age of criminal responsibility is ten years old. Was he ever questioned?"

"They found his DNA on her, but they dismissed it because he was her son and he was a kid. No one would think that a kid could do that to their own mother." Archie spoke as though there was no one else in the room. "They'd argued that day, they always argued. She wanted him out of the house, but I'm not sure what happened. All I know is that I came home from the printing press at about 4:00 a.m. and she was there on the sofa, dead. And Declan was sitting on the floor, holding on to the cushion. He was staring at her, like he was in a trance. She was so stiff, so cold."

"What did you do, Archie?" Henley asked, even though she had a very good idea already.

"Took her upstairs, out of the way, and the next night I took her out to the farm. Mudchute Farm. She used to like it there," said Archie quietly.

"And what happened to Declan?" asked Ramouter.

"I took him to my dad's place. I didn't want anyone to be... it was better that way."

"But he murdered his mother," Ramouter said.

"It was an accident," Archie said meekly.

"Is that what you tell yourself in order to sleep at night?" asked Henley.

"I don't sleep."

Henley closed her eyes briefly as she imagined shutting her personal feelings in the box as she tried to comprehend the actions of a fearful and grieving man.

"When's the last time you saw your son Declan?" Henley asked.

"I'm telling the God's honest truth," said Archie, his wet eyes sparkling with certainty. "I haven't seen my boy since Christmas 1998. That's the last time I saw him in the flesh. He just left, walked out on Christmas night and I haven't seen him since—but he would call, every few months. Always sent me a postcard on his mother's birthday. Told me that he'd changed his name."

"So, he kept in touch?" asked Henley.

"He does. Three times a year. Christmas, my birthday, and his mother's."

"And do you contact him?"

Archie shook his head. "I don't know where he lives or have a number."

"But he has a family, your son. The photos of the kids in your flat."

"My grandkids," Archie said sadly. "I've never met them, but he sends me pictures."

"Why would two little kids send a birthday card to a man they've never met and write *Happy birthday, Grandad* in the card?" Ramouter asked.

"You're protecting him, aren't you?" said Henley. "You have a relationship with your son and your grandchildren. You know exactly where your son is. You know how to contact him."

"I won't do it. I won't give him up," Archie said stubbornly, hot tears streaming down his face. "I won't do it. He's my boy."

"Fine, fine," Henley said as she rubbed her forehead. "Ramouter, show him the Land Registry documents."

"Aye," Ramouter said as he pulled out a sheaf of documents from his folder and placed them page by page in front of Archie. "I want you to take a look at these documents."

"What are they?" Archie asked, not looking at the documents. "My eyesight isn't great, and I haven't got my reading glasses."

"These are documents from the Land Registry confirming that you are the owner of Copper Still Gravel Company in Folkestone."

"A gravel pit?" Archie grabbed a page from the table and held it to his face. "A gravel pit. I don't own a...why the hell would I own a gravel pit? This must be a mistake."

"No mistake. The title deeds were registered in your name back in 2016. That's your name and your address," said Ramouter.

"No way. Look at me. I'm missing a leg. What on earth would I be doing with a gravel pit? This is...this is fraud or something."

"Take a look at the forms. Isn't that your signature?"

"I can't really tell, I need my glasses—not that it matters, because I don't own a bloody gravel pit. I don't know how much those things cost, but if I had any spare cash, I wouldn't be dumping it in some godforsaken gravel pit in... Where did you say it was again?"

"Folkestone," said Henley as she tried to stifle a yawn.

"Folkestone!" Archie exclaimed. "Let me tell you something for starters: that place is a shithole. I hated it growing up and there's no way in hell that I would buy anything there. And secondly, I haven't been back there since my dad died in 1997."

"Hold on," said Henley. She straightened up, took a sip of the tepid water from her bottle, and Ramouter slid over his notebook and tapped a pen on his page. "You said that after your wife died you sent your son to your dad's place. Where was that?"

"Sandgate, in Folkestone," said Archie as he scratched the top of his head. "That's where my dad lived. He paid five grand for that house back in the late fifties. You can see the sea, if you like that sort of thing."

"And you sent Declan there?" Henley asked again, just to make sure she was hearing things correctly.

"Yeah, he liked it there," said Archie.

"And what happened to your dad's house after he died back in 1997?"

"He left it to Declan which pissed my sister off. She tried to contest it but it's a bit pointless fighting a will unless you've got the cash," said Archie. "Declan said that he was going to do it up and sell it."

"And did he, did he sell it?" asked Ramouter.

"I'm not—" Archie paused as he looked down at his hands and pulled at a hangnail. "He said he was going to, but I'm not actually sure."

"Oh, don't give me that," Henley said furiously. "Your son, your *sociopathic* son—as his own mother rightly called him—is an abductor. A serial rapist. A serial killer."

Archie's face twisted in pain as though each accusation Henley made had twisted around his intestines like barbed wire.

"Your son has a kill list." Henley took the photocopies of the original 1995 list and the small pieces of paper that had been removed from the mouths of Piper and Swann, and spread them out across the table. "Look," she said as Archie turned his face away. "There are nine names on those lists, and I do not want Kerry Huggins to be the tenth."

"Where is he, Archie?" Ramouter asked sharply. "Where is Declan?"

Archie groaned as though he'd been punched in the stomach and was winded. "The address is forty-eight Birchmount Road," he finally said. "Sandgate. I've got a spare key. It's in my flat."

"Suspend the interview, DC Ramouter," said Henley.

"Don't hurt him," Archie pleaded. "Promise that you won't hurt my boy."

"I was told by my boss DCSI Rhimes not to make promises

that I can't keep," Henley said once Ramouter confirmed they were no longer recording. "But he meant making promises to the victim's families. As far as I'm concerned, you're not a victim. You're an enabler, and I promise you that your son will suffer."

43

The house that belonged to Archie Weather's father stood as the fifth-to-last house along Birchmount Road. The sun shone brightly, nearly bleaching the sky white. To Henley's left lay an overgrown green mound that sloped toward an extensive, empty stretch of land, while to her right, a row of white-bricked houses faced the sea, their roofs barely visible from this vantage point.

Ramouter, who had been mostly silent during the journey, suddenly sat up and lowered his window. "What's the plan?" he asked, letting in the refreshing sea breeze.

"Local police have blocked the end of the road," replied Henley. "They've been monitoring the house, and Beckett's van is in the driveway. Put your vest on," she said urgently.

"Don't worry, I wasn't going to get out of the car without doing that," Ramouter reassured her, grabbing two stab vests from the back seat.

"No one has left the house, but the officer watching from the beach reported some activity. Lights flickering, someone seen through the windows."

"It has to be Beckett. The property is registered in his original name of Declan Weathers, and unless he's renting it privately, he hasn't been renting it out," said Ramouter.

The police radio crackled to life: "Detective Inspector Henley, this is DS Colbert. We're pulling up onto Birchmount Road now. You'll see us in your rearview mirror as soon as you turn the next corner. The dog support unit is five minutes away."

"I can see you," Henley responded, noticing the black Volvo in her rearview mirror. She flashed her lights. "I'm parking outside the neighboring house. Can you confirm your officers' positions?"

"The paramedics are behind me, and we've got a marked van that should be coming up on your right. Officers are marking the rear wall bordering Beckett's property and the ones stationed along the beachfront."

"Thank you," Henley acknowledged before parking the car on a patch of green that doubled as a pedestrian footway on the narrow coastal road. "We're getting out now."

Henley and Ramouter swung open the gate and proceeded across the trodden ground toward the house. Henley realized upon approaching that it was a bungalow, nestled on a relatively small piece of land. Beckett's navy van occupied the driveway, and to the left lay another path leading to the back of the house. Beckett's closest neighbor was a hundred meters away at least.

"Ready?" Henley asked Ramouter, making sure their stab vests were secure.

"Don't worry. No one's getting to me," Ramouter grinned. Two officers appeared behind him, slightly to his left, one carrying a battering ram in case Beckett resisted opening the door.

"Good," Henley replied, gripping the brass knocker and delivering a hard bang on the solid wooden door. She couldn't detect any sound of movement inside the house. She lifted the knocker for another try when the sound of a deadbolt unlocking and a lock clicking open reached her ears. The door swung open.

"What is—?" Beckett's words caught in his throat as he locked eyes with Henley and Ramouter.

"Scott Beckett, also known as Declan Weathers," Henley announced as Beckett glanced over her shoulder. "I'm Detective Inspector—"

The door slammed shut with such force that Henley had to step back. "He's running!" she heard Ramouter shout into his radio as an officer behind her forced the door open again, almost tearing it from its hinges. Inside, there were sounds of crashing and shouting. Henley and Ramouter sprinted into the house.

In the living room, Beckett had thrown an officer hard against a wooden cabinet, and the officer cried out in pain, doubling up as he hit the sharp cabinet edge with his back. Beckett stood there for a brief moment, staring fixedly at Henley, his eyes filled with malevolence. The injured officer screamed in agony when Beckett kicked him in the ribs. Beckett roared and pulled the mahogany cabinet down, causing china plates and dusty crystal to fall and shatter on the hardwood floor. Henley ignored the glass shards that pierced her cheek, but Ramouter scrambled over the fallen cabinet, and Henley dragged the injured officer to safety, helping him sit up.

"Are you…?" Henley began.

The injured officer nodded, muttering through gritted teeth, "Go, get him."

The bungalow was a maze of rooms, but Henley was certain Beckett would head toward the seafront. She and Ramouter dashed down a corridor, reaching the kitchen where the back door stood wide open. A gust of wind blew dirt into Henley's eyes as Ramouter sprinted ahead. She watched as Ramouter extended his baton as Beckett grabbed a shovel, raising it overhead and swinging it. Ramouter sidestepped swiftly, striking Beckett's back with his baton.

Henley pulled out her Taser gun and fired. Beckett screamed

as he fell. Henley released the Taser, and Ramouter approached Beckett, who was removing the dart prongs embedded in his arm.

"Shit," Henley muttered as Beckett scrambled to his feet, rushing toward the broken gate. She drew her baton, extending it, but before she could strike an officer ran past her, tackling Beckett to the ground, yelling, "We've got him! We've got him! He ain't going anywhere."

A uniformed officer forced Beckett to stand against the wall while Ramouter secured the handcuffs. Henley knew Beckett was the man from the bus; she didn't need more proof. She noticed dust and dirt on his boots and trousers, calloused palms, and dirt under his fingernails. At a towering six feet four inches, he was a daunting figure. Beckett's eyes, a soulless, steely gray, sent shivers down her spine.

"Where is she?" Henley demanded, fighting the urge to knock Beckett down. "Where is Kerry Huggins?"

"Kerry," Beckett said bitterly, spitting out a piece of broken tooth and bloody, frothy saliva. "It's Georgina. My Georgie."

"I'm not going to ask you again, Declan or whatever your name is," Henley warned. "Where is she?"

"She's everywhere and nowhere," Beckett replied, nodding toward Ramouter. "I had to work quicker this time."

Ramouter turned around the backyard, which was surrounded by a tall wooden fence with a gate leading to the sea. "She's in the ground?" he asked.

"Probably still warm," Beckett grinned.

"I need the search dog and more officers in the backyard now, and the paramedics," Henley ordered. "Where exactly did you bury her, Declan?"

"Find her," Beckett simply said, spitting out more blood. "You came this far."

"Are you seriously not going to tell me where she is?" Henley asked, maintaining a surprising calm.

"You're wasting time," Beckett retorted. "It only takes three to five minutes for someone to suffocate. How much time has passed since you first knocked on my door?"

Henley pressed the button on her radio. "Look for disturbed ground," she said into the device. "Both front and back of the house."

"It all looks disturbed," Ramouter noted as they ventured deeper into the garden, leaving Beckett with two officers. Ramouter was right; patches of grass, weeds, and scattered gardening tools surrounded various points of the yard. Garden upkeep clearly hadn't been on Beckett's mind. Henley trod carefully; Kerry might already be beneath her feet. The only sounds were the crashing waves and seagulls' cries overhead as they searched for any recently disturbed earth.

"How deep is she, Beckett?" Henley shouted from her end of the garden as an officer entered the garden with his search dog.

Beckett didn't reply, slowly turning his back to face the wall.

"Hey, hey! I think it's here," PC Keating called out, dropping to his knees and grabbing a nearby shovel as the dog handler raced over with his dog. The dog barked enthusiastically as she pushed her nose against the dirt, sniffing intensely as her breathing became more rapid.

"This has to be her," the dog handler said as he gently pulled the dog back and gave her a treat.

"Be careful," Henley warned as she and Ramouter hurried over to the spot. They both stopped in their tracks when they saw the rectangular mound of earth, darker and richer in color than the surrounding ground, with blades of grass and weeds intertwined within the gravel, mud, and sand. Henley used her radio to call in the paramedics as Ramouter grabbed another shovel and began digging.

"Careful," Henley said as she moved around the shorter side of the grave, uncertain whether she stood near Kerry's feet or head.

"Stop!" Ramouter shouted as Keating's shovel exposed a glimpse of pink material. Ramouter knelt and brushed away the dirt, revealing the cut flesh underneath the material, slowly turning crimson as blood started to seep.

"Shit," Ramouter uttered, frantically digging with his hands. "Her blood is flowing. She's alive."

Henley and Keating fell to their knees on either side of the grave, digging at the dirt with their hands. Two paramedics rushed over.

"It's her leg," Ramouter announced, climbing out of the grave. Henley felt her heart race as Kerry's face was quickly exposed. She scrambled to her feet as Keating and Ramouter pulled Kerry out of the grave, her wrists and ankles bound.

"She's not breathing, she's not breathing," Ramouter shouted, making room for the paramedics.

"There's no pulse," said the first paramedic, placing a stethoscope on Kerry's chest. He cut through Kerry's shirt with a pair of scissors and began to perform CPR.

The second paramedic opened Kerry's mouth and began scooping out dirt, while the first paramedic turned on the defibrillator and placed the two electrical panels on Kerry's chest.

"Clear!" shouted the first paramedic as the electrical current surged through Kerry's body, jerking her upward.

"Come on, Kerry," Ramouter said as the first paramedic shook his head.

The paramedic watched the monitor silently for a few seconds, and it beeped, signaling a pulse. Kerry suddenly opened her eyes and began to cough violently. She turned to her side and vomited, bringing up clumps of bile-covered dirt.

"We've got you, Kerry," Henley said as Kerry started to cry and shake uncontrollably. She tried to speak, but tears and the urge to vomit held her words back.

"Kerry, I need you to calm down, sweetheart," one of the paramedics said. "I'm going to put this oxygen mask on your face. Breathe deeply; we need to get some oxygen into your lungs, OK?"

Kerry nodded weakly as the mask was placed over her face.

"I'll get the stretcher; we're taking her straight to Royal Victoria Hospital," said one paramedic. "She's very lucky."

"I'm not sure if she is," Henley whispered as she watched Kerry struggling to catch her breath.

44

Scott Beckett, also known as Declan Weathers, sat beside his solicitor, Bill Fellows, at the table. Henley and Ramouter sat across from him. Henley hadn't spoken a word yet, and Ramouter handled the paperwork. Henley repeated a mantra in her head: *Do your job.*

"Things have changed since I was last in a police interview room," Beckett remarked, absent-mindedly tearing strips off an information leaflet about his rights and entitlements. "Back then, it was cassette tapes. If I recall correctly, I was interviewed at Rotherhithe police station. It's shut down now. I think it's a building site. I might have put her there."

"Mr. Beckett, the interview hasn't begun yet, and I must remind you of the advice I gave you," his solicitor chimed in, pen at the ready.

"I know, but I've changed my mind about that advice," Beckett replied, finishing the shredding and stacking the strips in a small pile.

"I'm going to start the interview now," Ramouter said.

"Detective Inspector Henley will introduce herself and issue the caution."

"Fine," Beckett agreed, smiling as Henley performed the introductions and caution.

"I remember you," Beckett said, after the introduction and caution were complete. "I wasn't sure at first, but then it clicked when you were trying to get me to tell you where I'd buried Kerry."

"So, you admit that you abducted and attempted to kill her," Henley stated.

"Of course I admit it. You found her at my house, and you had my picture from the bus. That was my mistake. I'd been very good at not making mistakes. But getting on the bus wearing my work top was a big mistake."

Henley glanced across the table at Beckett's solicitor, who managed to maintain an impassive demeanor while fervently scribbling notes.

"I'll remind you once more of the legal advice I gave you during our consultation: 'No comment,'" Mr. Fellows interjected.

Beckett's voice remained firm as he replied, "I heard you, and as I've already told you, I changed my mind." He turned his gaze back to Henley. "It clicked this morning. You were Melissa's friend."

"Yes, I was," Henley responded calmly.

"I'm not sure if you should be interviewing me." Beckett looked to Ramouter. "What do you think, DC Ramouter?"

"I think you need a reminder that you're here to answer our questions," Ramouter retorted.

Henley pressed on, asking, "You kidnapped and murdered Jake Ryland?"

"Is that a question or a statement?" Beckett challenged.

"It's a question, and you know it."

"He would have been fine if he hadn't got too big for his

boots. He needed to earn my story, and he hadn't earned it," Beckett asserted.

"You're talking about Lillian Klein's name not being on the byline?" Henley asked.

"He was too big for his bloody boots, and he needed to learn that you have to earn my respect, and he didn't have the right," Beckett replied.

"What about the others? Did they not earn your respect? Caroline Swann, Elias Piper," Henley probed.

"They did not. It was their decision to get involved, and there are consequences when you choose to interfere."

"But those people hadn't done anything to you. You created this fantasy in your head," Henley countered.

"They were putting everything that I'd worked for at risk," Beckett insisted. "I'd worked hard on myself. I was…normal. I've got my wife, my kids. I changed my name and my life. I was one of those people they talk about in the news. I turned my life around."

"And Andrew Streeter was about to jeopardize that when he decided to go to the Criminal Cases Review Commission?" Ramouter questioned.

"This is all down to him. He'd kept his mouth shut for twenty-five years. He was doing his time," Beckett replied.

"Your time," Henley pointed out.

"His time," Beckett corrected slowly. "And then he decided to ruin my life."

"He had no idea that you were alive," Henley argued.

"He was going to name me," Beckett claimed.

"He was going to name Declan Weathers, not Scott Beckett," Ramouter noted. "It's possible no one would have made the link."

"You're fooling yourself. It didn't take you lot long to figure it out," Beckett retorted.

"Regardless, you didn't have to kill Andrew Streeter," Ramouter asserted.

"I had to, and I did," Beckett stated.

Henley redirected the conversation. "Let's go back to 1995. Five innocent people were murdered from August 1995 to January 1996. Did you abduct and murder your friend, Tiago Alves?"

"Yes," Beckett replied flatly.

"Did you abduct and kill Penelope Callaghan?" Henley continued.

"Yes," Beckett repeated.

Henley marked the names on her list. "Did you abduct and kill Fallon O'Toole, Stephanie Chalmers, and Melissa Gyimah?"

"Yes, yes, and yes," Beckett admitted, folding his arms and glancing at his solicitor's notes.

"Did you abduct Georgina Bridges, now known as Kerry Huggins, between June and December 1995?" Henley asked.

Beckett nodded. "It was October 1995."

"Let's talk about her. How did you know Georgina?" Henley asked.

"Drugs," Beckett replied with a sly grin. "She sold drugs with Tiago."

"To be clear, that's Tiago Alves?" Henley clarified.

"Who else would it be? Of course it was Tiago," Beckett affirmed. "I'd known Tiago since we were kids. He was a bit thick, easily led. Suggestible is what the psychologists would call it. He was dealing drugs, ecstasy, cocaine, special k. I was never into drugs. It's a mug's game."

"Did Tiago deal drugs with Georgina?" Henley asked.

"Yeah, that's how they met. Running drugs for the same dealer," Beckett explained.

"And how did you meet her?" Henley probed.

"At a party at Andrew's dad's house. Well, his dad wasn't in, and it wasn't Andrew who threw the party—it was his brother, Fergus. I met Georgina there, my Georgie. I wanted her. She was…" Beckett's eyes glazed over as he reminisced, "She was everything."

"And did she want you?" Henley asked.

"She would have done. She needed time, that's all. To get to know me," Beckett claimed.

"But she didn't want you, did she? She wanted Andrew. In fact, they were in a relationship," Henley pointed out.

"Did you see him?" Beckett leaned forward, staring intently. "I saw him the day he died. Obviously, he was sick, weak, but back then, in the nineties, he was even more pathetic. Worthless. All she needed was time with me. She would see."

"And you thought you would make her see by kidnapping her and then killing her like the others?" Henley accused.

"It didn't have to be that way," Beckett shouted, standing up and slamming his hands on the table. He lowered his head, his shoulders rising and falling as though recovering from a race. "All I needed was time. Time for them to get to know me, and then everything would have been all right."

Henley clenched her fists under the table as Ramouter let out a frustrated sigh.

"Two at a time. That's where I went wrong. I couldn't keep them both safe," Beckett admitted.

"Hold on," Ramouter interjected. "Are you saying you kidnapped those girls, tied them up, and…" He paused, visibly struggling with the words. "Are you saying you did all that to keep them safe?"

"They were safe. I gave them water. Fed them. I looked after them," Beckett claimed.

"You raped them," Ramouter stated firmly. "You took them, abused them, violently. You made them suffer. Don't for one second think that you were ever looking after them. Every second they spent with you was pain."

"They weren't in pain," Beckett protested.

"You tortured them and then you made exhibits out of them. A macabre display to satisfy your ego," Henley accused.

"Macabre? I'm not a monster," Beckett retorted.

"That's exactly what you are, a—" Henley choked on the word, picking up her water and taking a sip. "You're a monster. Only a monster would bury his victims alive, dig them up, place a coin in their mouths, and then sew their mouths and eyes shut."

"You're being a bit dramatic. It was kindness," Beckett remarked, peeling off a bandage from his wrist. "I was being kind. I gave them back to their families. I took them home."

"What about the coins?" Henley asked, refusing to let him justify his brutality further. "Why place the coins in their mouths?"

"In all honesty," Beckett admitted lazily, "it was something I read in a book that my mum gave me. The only thing that she gave me."

"Your mother, Florence Weathers," Henley said. "Let's talk about her. After all, it started with her, didn't it."

"Are you trying to psychoanalyze me?" Beckett retorted.

"Wouldn't dream of it," Henley replied.

"We're here to talk about everyone who was on my kill list. Not my mother." Beckett sat up straighter in his chair, adjusting his police-issue white tracksuit.

"Your mother's murder is technically unsolved. For over thirty years, your mum's case has been sitting in an archive box. As I understand it, they arrested your dad for murder, but he had an airtight alibi," Henley stated. "But you. No one looked at you."

"Why would they? I was twelve. A boy who had lost his mother."

"And who had also attempted to rape a twelve-year-old girl only a few months earlier," Henley pointed out.

"That was a lie. It was two kids messing about. Experimenting. A big overreaction."

"Your mother knew exactly what you were," Henley concluded.

"I can't imagine how that felt," Ramouter added, opening a folder and showing a photograph of Florence Weathers' body in the mud. Beckett showed no emotion as the photo fell to the table. "Knowing that the woman who gave birth to you didn't want you."

Beckett snorted. "She's dead. No evidence that I was the one who squeezed the life out of her. Let's go back to my kill list."

"Fine," Ramouter agreed, taking notes. "Did you ever look for Georgina after she escaped?"

"Of course I did," Beckett said, visibly brightening up. "I drove all over Sandgate that day. Even went to the police. Told them that I was really worried about my friend, that she was high on drugs and kept screaming about being kidnapped. Told them poor Georgie had," Beckett tapped his temple, "problems."

"And?" Henley pressed.

"Nothing. Not a sight of her. I came back to London, asked around. No one had seen her," Beckett continued.

"Did you speak to Streeter and Tiago Alves about her?" Henley interjected.

"Andy said he hadn't heard from her."

"Did you believe him?" Henley asked.

"I did, actually. Anyway, time went on. The police weren't knocking at my door accusing me of kidnapping, so I got on with my life. And then I met Penelope," Beckett recalled.

"But you didn't stop there. You killed Tiago," Ramouter said. "Why?"

"Because he could have given Georgina back to me, but he didn't," Beckett replied, anger simmering. "He was on bail for supplying drugs—and guess who'd been arrested for dealing with him."

"Georgina Bridges," Ramouter answered with resignation.

"Bingo," Beckett said, pointing his finger like a gun. "They were on bail for months. I think that they got arrested late summer, a month before I took Georgina. Tiago had been banging on and on about going back to the station, scared shitless about getting charged, going to prison. On and on he went, and then at Christmas we're having a drink and he tells me the case got dropped. *Georgie told me we'd get off, and we did*, he said. Obviously, my ears pricked up. *Georgie*, I said. *Our Georgie. You spoke to her?* All this time, Tiago had been in contact with Georgie. I'm not saying that he knew where she was hiding out, but he knew how to get hold of her."

"And that upset you?" Henley asked.

"Of course it fucking upset me. After everything that Tiago and I had been through? A little bit of loyalty wouldn't have gone amiss," Beckett grumbled.

"So, what did you do?" Henley asked, a chill running down her spine.

"I took him on a ride. It was those funny days between Christmas and New Year. I picked him up in my car, took him back to my grandad's house, and...you know. I showed him what I did to people who lied to me. He stopped me from having what was mine," Beckett explained.

Henley clenched her jaw. "Georgina Bridges wasn't yours. She didn't belong to you. None of them did. Their lives were not for you to take."

Beckett yawned and leaned back in his seat.

"Did Tiago know what you'd done? To Georgina? To the others?" Ramouter asked, adjusting his posture.

"He said that Georgie hadn't told him anything, but how could I believe him?" Beckett replied. "He lied to me."

"Oh, now you've got a moral compass," Ramouter remarked. "What about Streeter? Did he ever give you any indication that he knew?"

"Not at first, not until the night I met Fallon at the Ship pub," Beckett continued.

"Fallon O'Toole. Andrew Streeter was seen with her at that pub," Henley noted.

"We'd gone there for a drink. I was feeling a bit sad about Melissa; her face was all over the news, and Stephanie's. *Call Crimestoppers. Help us find this murderer*," Beckett mocked.

Ramouter shifted in his seat. "So, what happened next?"

"It was a nice night; everyone was getting along. I could tell that Fallon liked me," Beckett recalled, his eyes narrowing. "Kept giving me the look, touching my arm, offered to...you know." Beckett leaned back and tapped his groin. "Then I heard Andy telling her that he didn't want her to get hurt. That he would call her a cab. She wasn't having any of it, thank God. But I kept it in my arsenal."

"What do you mean?" Henley asked. "What did you do?"

"My civic duty," Beckett replied casually. "I called Crimestoppers when they put out the appeal for information about Fallon O'Toole. I provided a full description of the man I saw her with: Andrew Streeter. Funny coincidence, it was the same detective, Larsen, who had gone after us for the cash-in-transit jobs the previous year back. So I gave him a call—anonymously, of course. I told him I'd seen poor Andy with a woman who looked like Fallon O'Toole, getting into a van."

"But that was a lie," Henley pointed out.

Beckett shrugged, unfazed. "Neither here nor there."

Henley crossed her arms, studying Beckett. He sat there, recounting his story as if explaining a minor inconvenience. Henley couldn't detect any hint of conscience, no remorse for the pain he had caused.

"Why Melissa? Why her?" Henley finally asked.

Beckett's eyes glistened with a strange intensity. "I was wondering when you were going to ask. Why not Melissa? She was nice, funny. Andrew met her. He was with me the day I picked her up from school, and the day I returned her. He didn't know that, though. He had no clue what was in the back of the van when I dropped him off that day. Melissa needed to give me a chance. I know I was a few years older than her–"

"A few years? She was fifteen years old. A child."

"You seem a bit upset. Why is that? Is it jealousy. Did you want me to pick you?"

"You took advantage of her."

"You are jealous," Beckett smirked. "Age is relative when you have a genuine connection with someone. When they make you feel things. You must know what it's like to just click with someone. I liked Melissa. I really liked her. She didn't want me, though."

"You murdered her because she rejected you," Henley said, fighting to keep her voice steady.

"Don't oversimplify it," Beckett replied.

"You murdered them all because your feelings were hurt," Henley stated firmly.

"Now you're mocking me," Beckett retorted. "But I didn't murder Kerry—sorry, Georgina. Because, as you know, she got away. She got away from me twice. Now, I can see that long list of questions in front of you, so let's press on. Ask me anything."

45

"I'm sure his plan is to run a defense of diminished responsibility," Ramouter said as he punched the security panel code, opening the doors to the Serial Crime Unit.

"On the grounds that he couldn't cope with rejection," Henley replied with contempt as she pushed the door open. "I seriously doubt that a jury would acquit him on that basis."

"Stranger things have happened," Ramouter remarked. "But at least we've got the right person behind bars."

"He would have been behind bars earlier if it wasn't for Larsen," Henley said bitterly. She watched as Stanford removed the crime scene photos from the whiteboard.

"Tea or coffee?" Ramouter offered. "And there are some cakes here if you want one."

"Tea," Henley replied as she approached Eastwood's desk.

"Have you heard the news?" Eastwood asked, swiveling her seat around and handing Henley a copy of the *Evening Standard*. "The IPOC is launching an official investigation into James Larsen after this article appeared in the early edition. Page eight."

A cesspool of serious corruption by a high-ranking officer at New Scotland Yard

By Callum O'Brien

Evidence has been uncovered that reveals ex-borough commander, James Larsen, engaged in a targeted campaign of corruption that resulted in the wrongful arrest and conviction of Andrew Streeter, who was found guilty in October 1996 of five counts of murder.

"It's going to be bad for him," Eastwood commented. "He's looking at prosecution, prison."

"I don't really care; he deserves everything he's got coming to him," Henley said. "There's no mention of Rhimes."

"It's a good thing. I'm going to put my report together and hand it over to the IPOC. They'll probably want us all to give evidence at some point."

"I'll do anything if it means clearing Rhimes's name," Henley said, returning the newspaper. "Thanks, Eastie. You did everything the right way. No compromises."

"I did my job, boss. Isn't that what Rhimes always told us? Just do the job," Eastwood replied as Stanford and Ezra entered the room.

"So, is that it?" Joanna asked as she handed Henley a cup of tea. "This entire mess, this nightmare, is over?"

Henley felt empathy for Joanna, hearing the vulnerability in her voice. Joanna had taken on the role of a strong matriarch, trying to hold the SCU together. Henley glanced at her team's faces—Ramouter, Stanford, Eastwood, Ezra and Joanna. Relief was written across their expressions. Now wasn't the time to share Eloise Rhimes's doubts about her husband's death. How she didn't believe that her husband had killed himself.

"I miss him," Ezra said, breaking Henley's train of thought. "I miss his moaning, his unhealthy diet and having to explain to him how the cloud works fifty times."

"And making really bad tea," said Stanford. "God, it was terrible. Tasted like dishwater."

"Remember the time when he broke the coffee machine?" said Eastwood, sniffing and wiping her eyes quickly before turning back to her computer. "Useless man," she said.

"Completely useless," said Joanna. "But he was a good one."

The tension knotted Henley's neck as she knocked on Pellacia's office door.

"Come in," he called. "One sec," he mouthed to Henley when she entered and sat down. "Yeah, no problem," Pellacia spoke into the phone. "The detective inspector is with me right now. Have the press officer meet us here at five. We should have the CPS decision for Beckett, aka Weathers, by then."

"Another press conference," Henley sighed as Pellacia hung up.

"You know we have to," Pellacia replied, rising from his chair and moving to the front of his desk. "The CPS are recommending that we charge Lillian Klein with five counts of obstructing the course of justice."

"No surprise there," Henley commented, finally ceasing her neck-rubbing. "Have you heard about the inquiry?"

"Barker called me about it while you were interviewing Beckett. It won't be easy, but it will be worth it. Larsen deserves everything he gets," Pellacia said with a smile.

"Stephen," Henley said slowly. "Did you speak to Callum? Are you his source?"

"No comment," Pellacia replied, the smile still on his face.

"Jesus Christ," Henley muttered, rubbing her neck again. "Don't make it a habit."

"Any updates on Kerry Huggins?" Pellacia asked.

"They had to sedate her; she was hysterical when they placed her in the ambulance. They're going to keep her in for a couple of days. She was buried alive—how the hell do you get over something like that?"

"I can't even... I can't imagine," Pellacia said.

"We'll have to talk to her and get a full statement, but, I don't know, I kind of don't want her to be forced to relive it all, do you know what I mean?"

"I do, but what about you? You've been hiding it, but this case—"

"I'm OK," Henley assured him. "I'm still here. And I'm going to see Melissa's parents and tell them exactly what's happened."

"I think I should come with you. To see all the families. They deserve that," Pellacia said. "But are you sure you're OK?"

"Honestly, all of this has made me look at what I want for my life," Henley said as she pushed her chair back and stood up. "I've got to make some changes. I can't keep living like this— and I don't mean work. I need the SCU."

"Not here. Let's walk," Pellacia suggested.

"How long are we going to keep doing this?" Pellacia asked as they sat on a bench in a small grassy area across from the station. "We can't go on like this. It's not healthy."

Henley leaned back, letting the sun warm her face. "I know we can't," she said eventually. "It's painful, unfair, selfish. It's so many things, but most importantly, it's not right."

"Of course it's not right," Pellacia agreed. "But I'm not going to pretend that I don't feel anything for you. My feelings have never changed. They won't."

"It's not that straightforward," Henley said. "I didn't marry Rob because I had nothing to do one Saturday. I... I loved him."

"I know that, but you don't need Rob," Pellacia said firmly. "You need me."

Henley studied Pellacia's determined, protective, and loving face.

"You've got commitments," she said.

"Not anymore," Pellacia declared. "I'm not going anywhere."

"I know you're not, and I know that I have to make changes, but this is a big decision."

"What's so big about it? You just…leave."

"It's not only about my marriage," Henley explained, gazing up at the fourth floor of Greenwich police station where her team was hard at work. "Leaving Rob and being with you would mean having to leave my team, and I don't think that Rob will let me walk out of our marriage with Emma. He will fight me for her. This isn't a decision that I can make on a whim."

Pellacia remained silent for a while, absorbing Henley's words. "I'm not going anywhere," he repeated.

"I know, but I have to close one chapter before I think about the next. Let's focus on the families of the 1995 case. They're the ones who need closure. They need to know that we did our jobs."

46

"She's in the garden," Kerry's ex-husband, Tobias, informed Henley. "She spends a lot of time out there, as if she's trying to breathe in all the air she can."

"Did you know?" Henley asked, observing the lone figure of Kerry Huggins in the garden.

Tobias shook his head as he sat down. "I knew she'd had some trouble with the police when she was younger, but she never told me about knowing Streeter or what Declan Weathers did to her. If I'd known, maybe—"

"There's nothing you could have done to change anything," Henley reassured him. "Believe me, that's a game of *what if?* And there are no winners."

"I can't handle the quiet," Kerry admitted, lowering the radio's volume. "Usually, I'm telling the kids to keep it down, but now..."

"Let them be," Henley advised. "We have to find a way to move forward."

"I should have told you," Kerry said, regret in her eyes. "Told you from the beginning about Andrew, about Declan. I should have told you that Andrew was desperate for my help. Maybe this wouldn't have happened if I'd been braver."

"You saw Andrew before he died?"

"I used to write to him. I told him that I'd changed my name, that I had a family. That I was safe," Kerry inhaled painfully and wiped away tears. "I'd never visited him in prison until he contacted me last September and told me that he had cancer. I felt that I owed him. We'd been friends and I didn't want him to feel that he was alone or to die alone. I saw him last September and again in the New Year and that's when he asked me. To speak to his lawyer. To tell the truth about Declan and what he did to me but I couldn't. All these years being someone else and protecting myself. I couldn't do it."

"What happened, Kerry?" Henley asked gently.

"Two weeks ago, or back in 1995?" Kerry shivered, even in the summer heat.

"In 1995."

"I never trusted Declan," Kerry confessed. "There was something about him—the way he looked at you, as if he was undressing you. I'd heard things too, about how he treated his girlfriends. I saw him at a party with that girl, Stephanie Chalmers. The way he spoke to her, like she was nothing, grabbing her arm, hurting her. I saw him outside with her. They were arguing, and she was crying. He put his hands around her throat. I told him to leave her alone—and do you know what he told me? That she liked it, and I could join them."

"Did you tell anyone what you saw?" Henley asked.

Kerry shook her head. "I went back inside the party. Got high. I was pathetic. I should've done something. But a week later, in September, Tiago and I got arrested, and all I could think about was the drugs charges we were facing. I was living in Harlesden while I was on bail, but I used to visit Andrew at his dad's.

One night when I was there, I got upset about something and stormed out. I was walking to the bus stop in the rain and Declan pulled up and offered me a lift. That's how he got me. We drove for about five minutes, and then he pulled up outside a scrapyard, and he…raped me in the car."

"Oh my God," Henley said as tears streamed down Kerry's face. Henley clasped both of Kerry's hands, squeezing them reassuringly. "I'm so sorry."

"I blamed myself for years," Kerry continued. "I should've listened to Andrew. I should have called the police when Stephanie Chalmers was found dead. I blamed myself for wearing a cropped top, blamed myself for smiling at Declan. I told myself all sorts of rubbish."

"I don't have to tell you that you shouldn't blame yourself. You are not responsible. None of this is on you. Do you understand? There's only one person responsible for the years and years of hurt."

"I know. I always thought that evil was a myth, but Declan is evil. A monster."

"But you escaped. You got out. You're here," Henley said, getting up and hugging Kerry. She could feel the tremors in the woman's arms, the fear, the vivid memory of what had happened.

"I didn't do enough," Kerry sobbed. "I should've tried harder to tell the police about what happened. I should've gone back to the police, gone to the papers. I should've done more. I shouldn't have run. I should have done more to help that other girl, Fallon. I can still hear her screaming. Begging."

"Kerry, you need to understand that this was not your fault. Mistakes were made, but those mistakes were not yours, do you understand?" Henley said firmly.

"I do, but I can't stop myself from thinking it."

"You said you ran. Where did you go?"

Kerry wiped her nose. "Bolton. I went to stay with my cousin for a couple of weeks. Then I came back to London and stayed with my gran in Stepney, kept my head down."

"Why did you come back?"

"I was still on bail for supplying drugs with Tiago. I was hoping they were going to drop the case, but I couldn't risk not showing up at Snow Hill police station on the bail to return date. So I came back, and then I ended up staying because my gran got sick. I wanted to leave, was desperate to leave, but my gran needed me. It would have been cruel to leave her over Christmas."

"Who knew you were in Stepney?"

"Only Andrew. I didn't tell Tiago, and he didn't ask. That was in December 1995. Then, a few days after Christmas, Tiago went missing, and I just knew it had something to do with Declan. That's when Andrew came to stay with me at my gran's. When Tiago's body was found, Andrew and I both knew it was Declan. Andrew wanted to protect me."

"Did Andrew know what Declan had done to you?"

"Yes," Kerry said softly. "That's why he stayed. He was scared shitless, but he looked out for me. I should've done the same for him, but instead, I ran. Back to Bolton, Hull and then Rotterdam. I didn't come back. I didn't help him."

Henley couldn't find the words as Kerry leaned into her and started crying again. Henley knew the pain and guilt survivors carried.

"Do you need me to do anything?" Kerry asked, pulling away from Henley.

"We don't need anything from you, not yet," Henley replied gently. "Take your time, rest, be with your family, and make sure you talk to someone. And please, don't blame yourself. There's only one person to blame."

"I hope someone kills Declan in prison," Kerry said as she stood up, picking up her radio. "I know I shouldn't think that, but I want him to suffer every single day. I want him to feel pain. Don't you want that? He hurt you too. He hurt so many of us."

Henley closed the gate and walked back to the car. For the first time since she had found Melissa's body on the riverbank, she didn't feel guilty. She was no longer carrying the weight of blaming herself for twenty-five years. But she wasn't entirely at peace. There were questions to be answered, a chapter not yet closed. She crossed the road, entered Wandsworth Common, and called Ezra.

"Yo, what's up, boss?" Ezra greeted her cheerfully. "Are you making it back for lunch? Eastie is offering to treat us with her own money—clearly suffering from a bump on the head."

"I should be back in an hour, but Ezra, I need you to do something for me."

"What is it?"

Henley took a breath, shielding her eyes from the sun. "This is between you and me. You do not discuss this with anyone else in the SCU. Do you understand? No one."

"I understand," Ezra replied, his tone serious now.

"I need you to find everything you can on the investigation into Rhimes's death. Coroner's report, original investigation report, everything and anything."

Henley listened to the silence before Ezra spoke again. "Rhimes. Our Rhimes."

"Yes. It might lead to nothing, but there's a possibility it could lead to something."

"How far do you want me to go?"

"As far as you can."

★ ★ ★ ★ ★

ACKNOWLEDGEMENTS

Endless thanks to my family and friends. Your love and support is priceless. A special thank you to my cousin Charlene who would always send me photos of herself pointing at my book on supermarket shelves and always told me how proud she was of me. She would be screaming with laughter to see her special mention in the acknowledgment. I miss you dearly my bright shining star. Thank you for being unapologetically you.

How could I not thank the readers? I enjoy seeing your reactions and reading your emails and DM's. Your enthusiasm is a joy and makes all the hard work worthwhile.

You never write a book alone. Writing a book is truly a team effort. As always, thank you, Oli Munson and the AM Heath Team. Thank you to my editor Manpreet Grewal, the HQ team and John Glynn, and his team, at Hanover Square Press in the US.